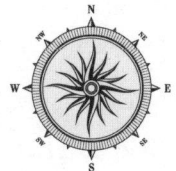

It is a warm midsummer evening in the city of London in the year 1836. Caroline hears her father whistle outside the house in Chelsea where she is employed. She lays down the book she is reading and, wrapping a light shawl about her, she takes the stairs up to the street. He is standing by the wrought-iron fence, his manner agitated, skin ashen in the streetlight.

'Papa, what has happened?'

His eyes will not meet hers. She reaches for his hand to console him and is stung by something. She gasps and sees that her palm has been cut. She seizes his sleeve and withdraws a short knife he is concealing. It is smeared with blood but it is not from the small wound on her hand.

'What have you done, Papa?' she asks. 'Are you hurt?'

'There is nothing that can hurt me now,' he replies, as if it is a diagnosis.

And then he is gone, walking away from her. She hurries to keep up with him, but sees that it is fruitless. He is in the other world he inhabits, where nothing is familiar, sometimes not even her.

The knife is still in her hand. It gives her an ill feeling. What has it done? She wants it gone where it cannot hurt him or anybody else. She walks the short distance to the Thames and flings it into the languid black waters.

The next day the story is everywhere. A woman has been murdered on the Battersea Bridge. There are witnesses. A manhunt is underway for the well-known Frenchman Jacques-Louis Colbert, apothecary and chemist. Four days later he presents himself at the police station in Chelsea and admits his guilt. He is imprisoned awaiting trial at the Old Bailey. He refuses all visitors.

In the crowded courtroom, the judge sentences him to death by hanging. Jacques-Louis does not raise his head to look at Caroline, or her sister Augusta weeping beside her, before he is borne away by guards. Awaiting the noose at Millbank Prison, he is deemed insane. He is transferred to Bethlehem asylum for appraisal; the Crown averse to the hanging of madmen.

He is insane, Caroline thinks, and it is the first time she has allowed it. He had held her, nurtured her, imagined a bigger world for her. She had failed to understand that he had become dangerous not only to himself but to other people. How had she let it happen? How is she to find any peace knowing he has done this thing?

Through the year that follows, she is a wintering tree unable to respond to spring. She cannot grow new leaves, nor feel the sun or breeze. There is an immense solitude at the heart of her life. There will be no future for her in medicine. No father to assess a suitor and deem him sufficient. He has made their family name infamous. The stain will never leave them.

A GREAT ACT OF LOVE

A GREAT ACT OF LOVE

HEATHER ROSE

JOHN MURRAY

First published in Great Britain in 2026 by John Murray (Publishers)

1

This project has been assisted by the Australian Government through Creative Australia, its principal arts investment and advisory body.

This is a work of fiction based on several real events. Dates and place names have been changed and stories woven together to create this novel. While much has been imagined, and all characters are completely fictitious, some are inspired by historical figures and continue to have their real names.

A CIP catalogue record for this title is available from the British Library

Hardback ISBN 9781399823821
Trade Paperback ISBN 9781399823838
ebook ISBN 9781399823852

Maps by Guy Holt

Typeset in Garamond Premier Pro

Printed and bound in Great Britain by Clays Ltd, Elcograf S.p.A.

John Murray policy is to use papers that are natural, renewable and recyclable products and made from wood grown in sustainable forests. The logging and manufacturing processes are expected to conform to the environmental regulations of the country of origin.

Carmelite House
50 Victoria Embankment
London EC4Y 0DZ

www.johnmurraypress.co.uk

John Murray Press, part of Hodder & Stoughton Limited
An Hachette UK company

The authorised representative in the EEA is Hachette Ireland, 8 Castlecourt Centre, Dublin 15, D15 XTP3, Ireland (email: info@hbgi.ie)

For Evan

Happiness is the settling of the soul into its most
appropriate spot.

Aristotle

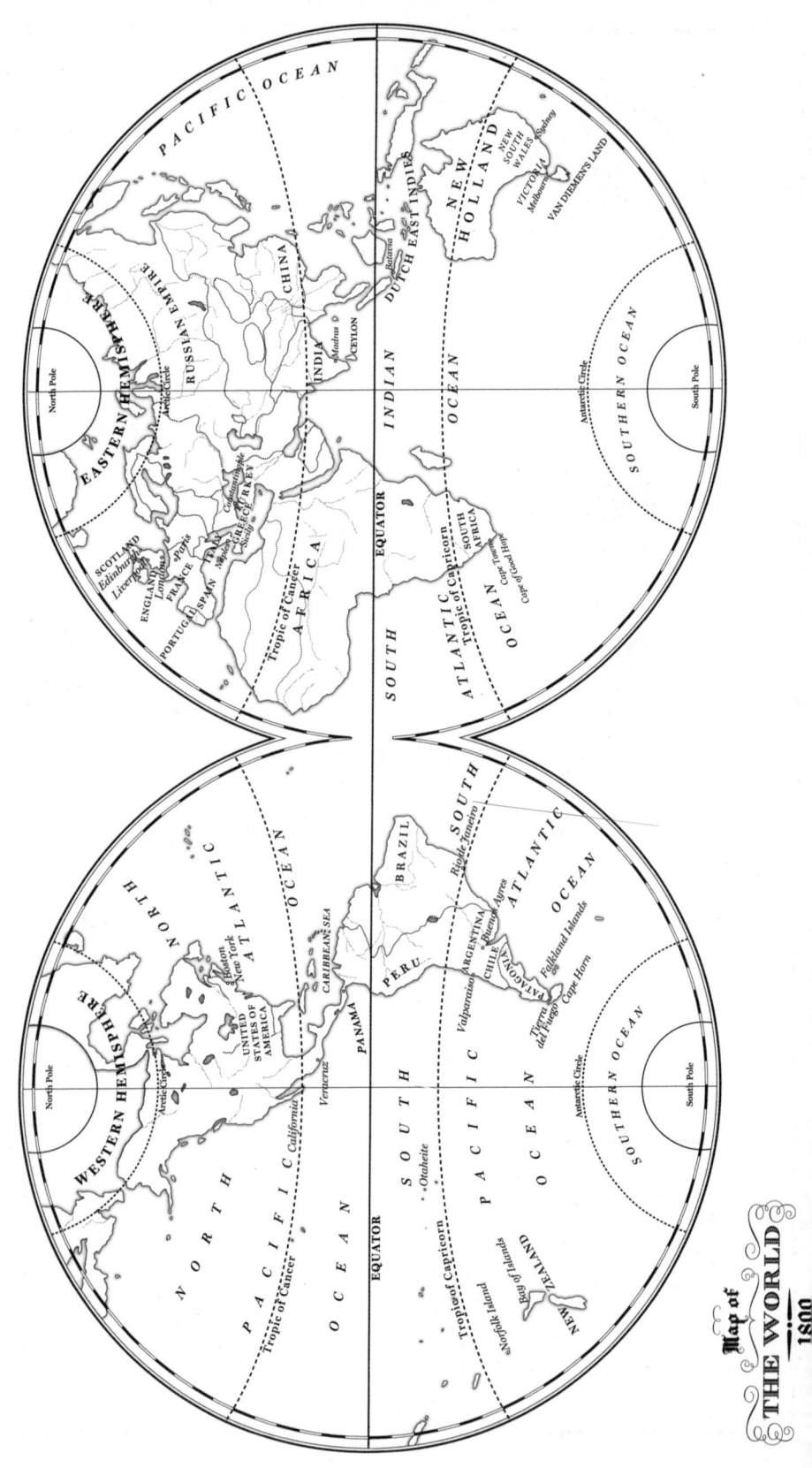

Map of
THE WORLD
1800

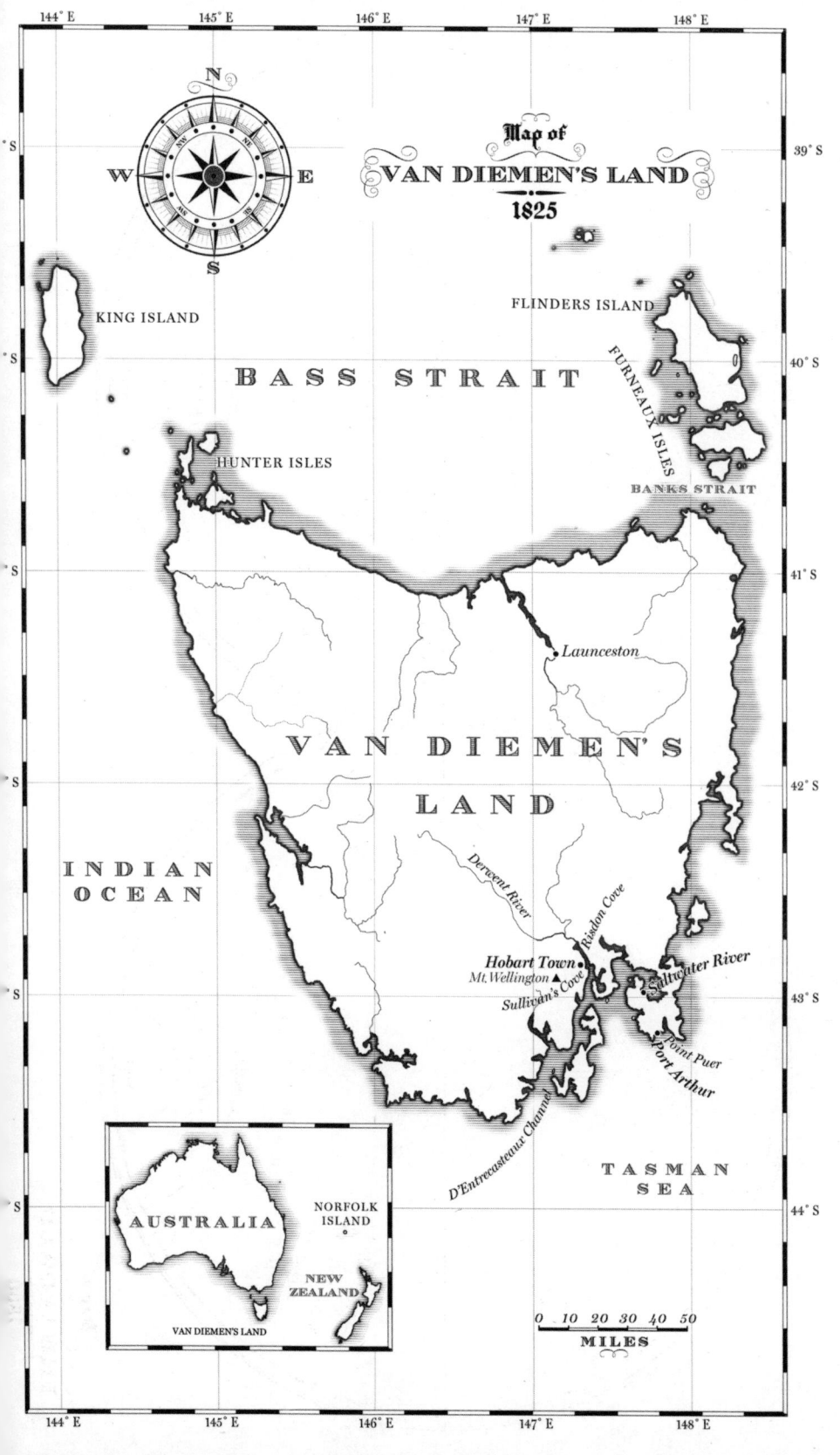

N
NW NE
W E
SW SE
S

Map of
VAN DIEMEN'S LAND
1825

39° S

KING ISLAND

FLINDERS ISLAND

FURNEAUX ISLES

40° S

BASS STRAIT

HUNTER ISLES

BANKS STRAIT

41° S

Launceston

VAN DIEMEN'S

LAND

42° S

Derwent River

**INDIAN
OCEAN**

Risdon Cove

Hobart Town •
Mt. Wellington ▲
Sullivan's Cove

Saltwater River

43° S

Point Puer
Port Arthur

D'Entrecasteaux Channel

**TASMAN
SEA**

44° S

AUSTRALIA

NORFOLK
ISLAND
○

NEW
ZEALAND

VAN DIEMEN'S LAND

0 10 20 30 40 50
MILES

144° E   145° E   146° E   147° E   148° E

Based on several true stories.

Thanks to the human heart by which we live,
Thanks to its tenderness, joys and fears,
To me the meanest flower that blows can give
Thoughts that do often lie too deep for tears.

William Wordsworth

When a letter arrives from the asylum, it is the first word she's had from him since that full moon night.

Ma chère Caroline,

I feel as if I have been away on a long voyage and I am only now returning. The land I left is greatly changed. I am not sure where I have been but I know I have done terrible things. The pain of this is indescribable.

I do not ask for your forgiveness. If you harbour any vestige of affection for me, I beg you to do away with it. Forget me, my beloved daughter, and encourage your sister to do the same. Read the words that follow and know them not as exculpation but as both a reckoning and a warning to you both.

She wore a blue bonnet and a dress of light blue muslin. We stopped at a pub where we liked to have a gin and cloves, which she favoured.

The lanterns were lit as we strolled across the bridge. She was gazing at a group of men gathered about a fire, their fishing boats pulled up on the shore of the Thames. A barge was gliding upriver in the moonlight. I took the knife from my pocket.

I might have held her in my arms and kissed her, for she was dear to me, as you know. But instead, when I embraced her, I sank the knife into the sweet part of her neck, above the collarbone. It was an easy thing, the blade very sharp, the skin very soft, the vein at the ready. She gasped, cried out, and I withdrew the knife. Instead of guiding her to help, I stepped away and left her there.

When I awoke days later, in some dank place upriver, I knew then what had been done. I knew that within me there was another self who departed from reality and returned days later uncertain, ravaged. I had tried to walk my loathing for him out of myself. I had tried to draw him close that I might know him better, but he was not to be befriended.

You are familiar with that man.

I was insensible, insane. I had intended the knife for myself.

She had made a fool of me. Any man would have done the same.

But I cannot excuse myself with such inventions or explanations. The truth is, I had imagined myself in love. Worse than that, I had imagined that I was loved. When it proved to be untrue, and I found I had been blind and deluded, I took her life.

May you and your sister never again know such a man as I.

From he who was once privileged to call himself your loving father,

Jacques-Louis Auguste Henri Colbert

· *1* ·

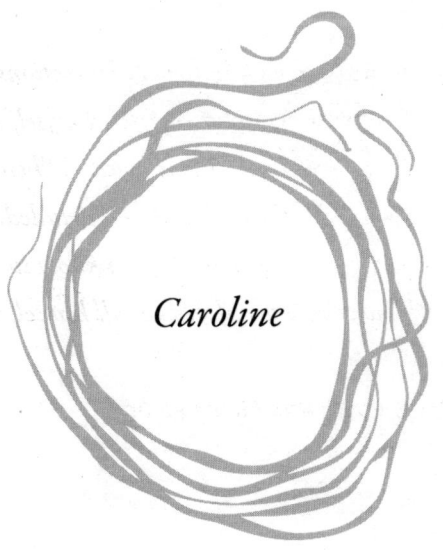

Caroline

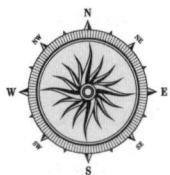

Caroline examines a map. The eastern and western spheres of the world resemble two orbs of an amulet. She sees, to the far left, *Great Britain*. How unlikely that it is so small. France dominates it. All of Europe dominates it. She thinks of her father saying, 'The British are never to be underestimated. Look what they have done with so little.'

She sees *North America* and, passing over the words *Hudson Bay*, her hand moves down to *Florida*, *Gulf of Mexico* and *Caribbean Sea*. How easy it is to travel on a map. *Amazonia*, *Brazil* and *South Atlantic Ocean*.

Alert to the danger of approaching footsteps, her gaze lingers on a finger of land as far south as that continent stretches. She has heard stories of the Straits of Magellan and Cape Horn. Tales of men shipwrecked and rescued after months of living on seabirds. Men who drew sticks to see who would be eaten next. She considers the notion of eating a friend. Perhaps it would be easier than eating a stranger.

She moves her hand back to *Europe*, across *Arabia*, *Hindoostan* and the great landmass of *Asia* until it rests on the autumn leaf of *New Holland*. It is almost as big as Europe, but without cities or history. She wonders what it smells of there. Prisoners, she imagines.

And there she finds it, at the edge of the Western Hemisphere, a black mark at the 30th latitude smaller than a flea. *Norfolk Island*. The dream returns. Her father caught in a shaft of sand. The walls are collapsing and he is reaching up, calling her name.

Tante Henriette is at the doorway indicating they must depart. She is sporting a neat black beard, cravat and frock coat, and carrying a satchel. Caroline quickly rolls up the map and slides it into a long leather cylinder beside the desk. She swings it over her shoulder. Her aunt raises an eyebrow but says nothing. Downstairs the party is continuing in the ballroom. Music, dancing, conversation, all receding as they stroll past unnoticed. They meet no one as they step from a side door into Belgravia, and they are away.

Back at Tante Henriette's apartment, they shed their wigs and shoes, frock coats, braces, collars and cufflinks. They peel away beard and moustache. They brush out their hair and pin it up, then button and lace their dresses.

Caroline makes *chocolat chaud* in two silver cups and carries them on a tray into the sitting room. As she sits she sighs deeply, her body settling after the evening's activities. Tante Henriette places a polished wooden box on the low table. It is finely carved with a budding vine of gold entwined around a pattern of squares. Caroline opens it to reveal ebony and ivory pieces laid on green velvet. The horses look as if they are rearing in the wind. The robes of the clergymen each bear a tiny crucifix.

'Beautiful,' she whispers, examining the pieces. 'From tonight?'

'*Bien sûr*,' says Tante Henriette and begins to set up the game. Despite making London her home for many years, Henriette prefers her native tongue. Caroline has moved between French and English all her life.

They each lead with a pawn, then Tante Henriette brings out her bishop. As Caroline weighs her next move, she describes the dream of her father being swallowed by sand, his hand reaching out to her.

'You have had such a dream before?' her aunt asks.

'Several times now,' says Caroline. 'The same dream. The sand. His face.'

'The map? Did you think it could lead you to him?'

Caroline says nothing.

'Sometimes,' says Henriette, 'I see him in the fields walking between the vines. A boy again. Strange, *non*? Though it is best not to think of him; what good can it do?'

Caroline moves her knight, and her aunt responds by moving another pawn. Caroline loves the loyalty of the smallest pieces. They could easily be disregarded in the face of more powerful players. Yet they remain obstinate and steadfast in a battle waged to defend an ideal.

She says, 'There are offers of passage for unmarried women to New South Wales and Van Diemen's Land.'

Her aunt arches an eyebrow. 'You are not still considering that?'

'I am,' says Caroline.

'But why?' asks Tante Henriette. 'He will never be released—and even if he was, he will not be the man you remember.'

'It is nothing to do with *him*,' says Caroline, progressing her attack on the board, keenly aware of her aunt's greater skill.

'Then why would a young woman of your talents take herself to such a place? Hardly to raise sheep, I think.'

Caroline does not want to admit to the fear that has shadowed her of late. The cry of 'Police!' at a most unexpected or inconvenient moment.

'Of course,' continues her aunt, 'someone of military rank may offer his hand. Perhaps he is blind in one eye from a wound he took for England as a young man. It oozes and smells. He has the gout, too . . . and four or five very ugly children in need of a new mother . . .' She takes Caroline's knight.

Caroline admonishes herself for her lapse in attention. She stares at her pieces. But her mind is thinking of the map. *Atlantic Ocean, Indian Ocean, Pacific Ocean.*

'You could come with me,' Caroline says.

'And be without my ladies to take me on their tours of Europe?' replies Henriette. 'Without the shops and cafes and theatres of London and Paris that bring me so much pleasure? I have no wish to see these fingers dirtied by potatoes.'

'We have enough, though, don't you think?'

'A sweet notion, but if we are to forgo our ways, *enough* must last us a very long time.'

'Still . . .' Caroline says.

'This wriggling worm of loyalty, it is making you restless.'

Caroline does not reply.

'I assure you, dear Caroline, there is no debt you must repay,' says Henriette, her voice kinder now. 'The past is not something that can be left behind, but nor is it wise to carry it ever upon your shoulders.'

For some time there is only the drinking of *chocolat* and the quiet movement of pieces.

'I could advertise,' Caroline says at last. 'Young woman of disreputable family seeks rich husband for colonial adventure.'

'Young woman of unique talents seeks a man unworthy of her character,' says Tante Henriette. 'And you must remember to beware the strong man offering you his hand, Caroline. Your father was one of those . . .'

Caroline sees she is entangled in a series of strategies her aunt has employed and feels momentary dread. She moves her queen out of danger, only to realise that she should have moved her king.

Henriette says, 'If you go, you must invent a new story.'

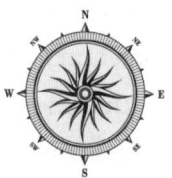

Caroline meets Captain Willem de Hoog in his offices near the Hudson River. His ship, the *Alliance*, a brigantine of one hundred and twelve feet, is soon to depart for South America and the Pacific island of Otaheite. De Hoog is a Dutchman with a bald pate and narrow silver eyes. He was a merchant in China and California before embroiling himself in the commerce of New York. In this city of wealth, filth and relentless industry, there are many people whose knowledge of the world surprises him, yet the young woman seated before him is particularly intriguing.

Caroline is wearing a dress of black silk, a black bonnet and a silver cross about her neck. Although she has found New York intoxicating, and learned to be at ease with her new identity, she has remained vigilant. London is but a few weeks across the ocean and there are frequent arrivals.

'I have the means to make a modest investment in the journey, if your ship were to continue on from Otaheite to Van Diemen's

Land,' she says. 'I believe you have some experience in acquiring a suitable cargo of goods, Captain de Hoog?'

Captain de Hoog regards her, and she is a pleasure to regard with her youthful prettiness: the dark curls and attentive gaze; the dimple he glimpses in her left cheek. How had she acquired her head for business? The black man standing guard outside his office also intrigues him. Servant or slave, he cannot be sure, but he is well dressed and clearly a formidable protector of the petite Mrs Douglas.

'Does Mrs Douglas have any hesitation in investing in sugar and rum? Coffee? Salt?'

She does not. But she would require a comfortable cabin. The most spacious he can make available. She will also require a servant, a maid.

'And your manservant?' he asks.

'Jefferson will remain here,' she says.

'I see,' says Captain de Hoog. 'Well, it may not be what you are used to, but there is a capable lad.'

'A maid would be preferable.'

'The boy will do. You will not be displeased. He has been under my instruction for three years and more.'

The captain's weathered head sits on a long narrow neck, a neck that Caroline finds improbable on one who spends so much time at sea. Where are his tattoos? she wonders. Did he have a rose or a trident upon a forearm? An anchor on his shoulder? Or was he the sort with a naked Aphrodite rising from her shell above his buttocks? What words would he utter, what god might he pray to, what woman does he imagine when the seas threaten to break his ship in two?

'We do not like to stretch our luck on a voyage more than necessary,' the captain adds.

Caroline pauses, almost willing to let this pass, but cannot. 'I suspect, Captain de Hoog, the success of the voyage relies on whether a captain has the skill to bring his ship to harbour without incident rather than the surfeit, or absence, of women aboard.'

The captain offers a wry smile. 'There you have it, Mrs Douglas. The superstitions of a sea dog. I could beg your forgiveness, although it would hurt me a little to do so, for in my experience superstition is often grounded in fact—aboard a ship, at least.'

Caroline raises her eyebrow, waiting for an example, but he offers none. Instead he says, 'If the boy does not do all your ladyship requires, he knows the punishment.'

The evening before their departure, Caroline alights from a carriage wrapped in a long fur coat and hat. The *Alliance* is at anchor amongst trading ships, military vessels and ferries. A carpet is quickly laid to assist her crossing the deck.

Jefferson carries the trunks, and together they see them safely stowed in the hold before he transfers the remaining luggage, containing her personal items, to her cabin. Jefferson's assistance in navigating this maritime city of men, ships and cargo has been invaluable. As has his companionship in the sprawling house in Harlem where they have both been employed by the eccentric and adventurous Audubon family this past year. She farewells him, squeezing into his hand a gift, a set of cufflinks with ruby studs, a relic of her life with Tante Henriette. It is a poignant moment, for they are sure they will never see one another again.

After he departs, Caroline removes her furs and tidies her hair. The cabin is not large but it is well appointed. The linens are fresh, the wash jug filled and the brass lamps polished, all with particular care. The ship itself has an odour of brine and fish, a smell she understands she must befriend. The captain has invited her to dine with him in his private quarters along with two fellow passengers on their way to Brazil. She has insisted that he refrain from disclosing her intention to travel beyond Otaheite to Van Diemen's Land, and her financial interest in the voyage.

Señor Clementi bows when they are introduced and kisses Caroline's hand. He wears lace cuffs and several turquoise rings. His necktie is a turquoise amulet on a length of dark leather. He has the lined, lean face of an aristocrat. The scent of aniseed drifts about him, and Caroline suspects it is in his hair oil.

'How fortunate to find ourselves with your companionship, Señora Douglas,' he says. 'I am told by the captain that you are in mourning, but beauty must always be noted. I offer my condolences. I know well the pain of the grieving heart. I lost my wife some years ago.'

Despite the man's charm, Caroline senses in him a reptilian coldness. His son José is stooped in gait with soft jowls and a stutter that prevents him from speaking easily. His father ignores him.

Over a joint of pork, the captain tells Caroline that Señor Clementi and José are bird collectors. Clementi tells her that in Brazil he has collected more than three hundred and eighty species of toucan, macaw, ibis, parakeet, parrot, manakin, curassow, aracari, vulture and rhea. Some three thousand birds in total. Caroline almost speaks of Monsieur Audubon, her recent employer in New York, and his extraordinary illustrated book, *Birds of America*. But she bites back her words and asks instead, 'And what do you intend to do with all these birds, Señor Clementi? Are they in an immense aviary?'

José shakes his head in an almost indiscernible gesture but he does not look up.

Clementi smiles and says, 'I doubt you have heard of the Teotihuacanos of New Spain, Señora Douglas? They sacrificed young men to encircle their kings when they died. The birds in my collection are at my home in Madrid, arranged by species, size and colour in many drawers and glass cabinets. When I am at last laid to rest, they will surround me in a design of ancient significance.'

The following day José's two sisters and their children board the ship. They are returning to their estates in Brazil. Twelve Jesuit priests are the last to board, standing at the railing as the ship departs, black-robed and silent, as if the voyage is to be one of biblical significance.

Caroline is twenty-three. Her mother lies in a grave in Chelsea, reunited with baby Isobel who had been lost to a fever at age two. Her sister Augusta lies beside them, taken only the winter before last. Each loss evokes unfathomably painful recollections. Their bones have been left behind. Frost and falling leaves, new grass and sunshine, wind and cloud shadows will be their only visitors now.

It is more than eighty years after the birth of Mozart. More than fifty years since America absolved itself of all allegiance to the British Crown. Soon someone will write that '. . . *it was the epoch of belief, it was the epoch of incredulity, it was the season of Light, it was the season of Darkness, it was the spring of hope, it was the winter of despair, we had everything before us, we had nothing before us, we were all going direct to Heaven, we were all going direct the other way . . .*'

Time curves and bends like a prism through which one may observe a lunar eclipse or calculate the mathematics of an unfolding rose. But what of time and the chalice of the human heart? Surveying the receding city, it is not a biblical story that comes to mind for Caroline, but Scheherazade. A woman who must summon a new story every day in order to live.

Caroline will tell the story of how she came to Tasmania, when it was still called Van Diemen's Land, many times. She will cast her inventions into the future. Those who carry them on will call it history, but she will call it her life.

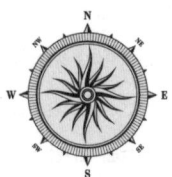

The cabin boy's name is Quill, he tells her, and his movements are quick, as if he is ready for flight at any moment. When he brings her breakfast, she gives him a cloth for his face and makes him scrub his hands. She inspects his head and discovers the anticipated lice in the brown tumble of hair. She requests and receives from him a kettle of hot water, a bottle of oil and a blade. On deck she cuts his hair, and then she shaves his head. He complies, ignoring the cries and jests from the crew as they witness this transformation. Afterwards, he startles at his reflection in her mirror. She insists he go wash his body and return in fresh clothes.

'You do have fresh clothes, Quill?' she asks.

The boy nods.

When he reappears, she says, 'Now you may bring food and tend to my cabin. But I will inspect your hands and face each day, and I will expect you to be clean.'

•

As the ship turns south, the sky is heavy with clouds. A piercing wind whips the sea, rain thrums the decks and the coastline evaporates. For two days Caroline steels herself for each dreadful pitch of the ship. She drifts and dreams, gritting her teeth against the rising tide of her stomach, determined not to vomit. Quill carries her slops bucket, replenishes her water jug and refills the oil in her lamp. He lays a cool damp cloth upon her brow. She listens to the sea running along the hull beside her bunk and imagines her mother's fingers running through her hair.

'Ah, Mousie, you're a brave lass,' she hears her mother say.

She hears her father murmuring, *'With sloping masts and dipping prow . . . and southward aye we fled . . .'* and feels for a moment his presence.

'Papa,' she whispers.

When she wakes on the third morning, the nausea has passed. Quill brings her broth and a small loaf of bread which she devours, suddenly ravenous. She leaves her cabin, reeling with the movement of the ship. On deck she finds a malachite sea, marked at the highest tips with white froth as the waves crest and the ship succumbs, falling and climbing, an undulating seascape. Above them, an army of clouds is moving north.

Gulls accompany the ship, broad in wing and graceful in flight, and she thinks briefly of the Spaniard Clementi, but he is nowhere to be seen. Fish jump in schools, fluid as mercury, bright as quicksilver, rising above the waves then diving as one.

She observes the horizon, a curve of faded light that conveys what had only been agreed when first Copernicus and then Galileo focused their attention on the heavens: the world is a mighty sphere. The earth is not flat and the oceans do not come to an end with sea monsters and a crescendo of waterfall. Yet what folly it seems to trust to canvas and timber, halyards and sheets, iron and brass. To rely on a compass and a sextant to traverse this blue invitation, calculating their position by invisible magnetic forces and a canopy of stars.

She hears her father say, 'Your future is a catapult you must launch into the sky.'

She hears her mother say, 'You'd be a fool not to try.'

She stares into the sea and knows she is a thing of little account who would hardly be missed if she tumbled into the Atlantic Ocean. She wonders how Tante Henriette fares. But she puts this thought aside, disturbed for a moment by a parting vision of her aunt.

She reflects on the investment she has made in the cargo housed below, and what she might acquire with the proceeds of this venture. There is no retreating now. The sails crack, the rigging whistles, the wind burns chill on her cheeks, and her body learns to gimbal with the ship's momentum.

At some point Quill comes with a blanket and she wraps it around herself. The captain shouts his orders, the crew respond. Day five passes, day seven, day fifteen, and still they travel south.

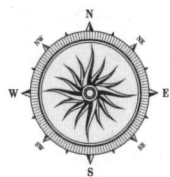

Her preference is to be on deck, facing the sombre sea and the keening wind. She is rocked and knocked, buffeted and blown, cradled and lulled. A book of verse allows Caroline the guise of distraction while she observes the sailors' rituals, the inclinations of her fellow passengers and the hierarchy of the men.

The Spanish sisters, Clementi's daughters, approach her and attempt to engage her in conversation, inviting Caroline to join them below for cards. They quickly realise she is not to be persuaded. One surreptitiously offers her a bottle of Aromes de Montserrat saying that she, too, was widowed young—but she remarried, and look at her now, with three children and another on the way. Caroline thanks her, refusing the bottle gently, saying she finds solace only in her Bible. After this exchange, they offer her the hushed deference only the devout can summon. Her black-garbed demeanour also earns her a muted respect amongst the crew.

Early in the voyage she seeks communion from the most senior of the Jesuits. She takes confession, offering her narrative into the ears of the good servant of the Lord, doing exactly as Tante Henriette had instructed: replacing the past with invention. She receives God's grace and is forgiven for her sins. On Sundays, the captain leads a service which all attend, crew and passengers alike. Caroline considers one of de Hoog's greatest achievements is to keep these services brief.

At first, when Señor Clementi notices her on deck, he comes quickly to her side, taking her elbow with some pretended concern or affection. One morning he tells her that she is too beautiful to be a widow for long. He offers her a book. She finds it is an account of the tribes of Amazonia with illustrations of children and adults, their heads and necks wreathed in feathers and bones, their eyes staring back at her with curious detachment.

'You have seen these people?' she asks.

'Trade has made me a rich man,' he says. 'I am willing to go to places other men are not.'

'They have a dignity,' she says, of the people in the drawings.

'They are all dead,' he says, 'so their dignity was of little use.'

She realises he was expecting her to laugh.

'Señor Clementi,' she says, 'forgive me this abruptness, but I intend to use this voyage to grieve my husband. I wish to surrender conversation and companionship for prayerfulness and contemplation. I am sure a man of your sensitivities can understand that.'

After this, he too leaves her alone.

In her quarters she boils water from a barrel, plucking out dead mice, squeezing the water out of their soft bodies and stowing them in a jar until she can toss them overboard later. She kills the cockroaches that are also making their way south.

She reads the many books she has brought, eats the bland and limited fare of meat, biscuits and porridge. Most of the fresh vegetables have been consumed by now. She rations her stores of marmalade and tea, preserved lemons, pickles, sugar, hard cheese, dried fruit and cacao. She washes her smalls and hangs them to dry on a line she has fixed in her cabin.

If a storm is brewing, rats run across her feet in the companionway. After a battle of gale and ocean has been won, the wind in retreat, the sea subdued, she descends into the hold. When she is certain she is quite alone, except for the cats that lurk below decks seeking mice, she hangs a lamp and unlocks the wooden chests. She touches linens and silver, china and jewellery, boxes of herbs, powders, seeds and vials, all that has survived yet another drowning.

She meets Señor Clementi's daughters in the passageways with their children. She has an urge to reach out and touch a small arm, to offer a riddle or a game that might light up those young faces, but she resists. Sometimes the children's cries wake her in the night.

On occasion the captain orders her to return to her cabin. Sailors are clambering up masts, crawling along the crossbeams, roping in sails. A bellowing fury descends upon them seeking to whip away anything unfixed. Ocean washes over the railings and sweeps across the deck. During such events, the timbers in her cabin are prone to leakage and she sleeps in damp bedding until she and Quill can carry up the straw mattress, linens and blankets to dry on deck. Together they bail out her room. The restoration of the ship after such events occurs as a ritual of reprieve and increases her respect for captain and crew.

Another visitation of lightning and thunder has them in its grip. She has invited Quill to stay in her cabin until the worst has passed. She considers the boy and their circumstances, the two of them far from home.

HEATHER ROSE

'A person without family is a person in darkness,' the boy says, the longest sentence he has uttered in her presence since they set sail. She is stirred by his prescience. His eyes are golden in the lamplight. A faded scar the shape of a crescent moon marks his left cheekbone. Had it been caused by an accident or a fist?

'We are all capable of darkness, Quill,' she says. 'Sometimes it is because we have a family rather than because we do not.'

The boy looks hard at her and she adds, 'But we must remember to urge towards the light. Sometimes it is a daily struggle, the hardest thing we do.'

He blinks, his lashes shadowing his cheeks. They are both gripping timber, she the edge of the cot upon which she sleeps, he the table fixed to the wall.

'Why are you on this ship, Quill?' she asks.

'Given to the captain to settle a debt,' he replies perfunctorily.

'Your father's debt?' she asks.

'Yes.'

'And where was your home?'

He shrugs as if he has no recollection. She cannot place his accent. A hint of Irish, perhaps. Cork, Cardiff, Boston, New York? Or some other place where gambling men give up their sons?

'And what of your mother? Does she await your return?'

The boy gives a shake of his head but says nothing.

They are nearing the equator. The breeze has steadied and the bilges are pungent. The moon is a swelling ripeness amidst unfamiliar constellations, a blazing omnium gatherum that leaves her awestruck night after night. The air has warmed and softened. By day the sea is peacock blue. She exchanges her garments of wool and fur for the discreet pleasure of light black muslin. When the ship

24

crosses the equator, muskets are fired into the air. The captain is given a dousing, and several officers, too. There is a general mood of merriment amongst the passengers and crew.

Some evenings as she lingers on deck, unwilling to go below, she sees columns of light that appear to plummet to the sea floor. Other times she is enthralled by a swathe of vibrant green phosphorescence that trails the ship. On the upper topsail yard, sailors sing a shanty in Gaelic and others from the Caribbean sing in a language Caroline has never heard, their music hypnotising and bittersweet.

She invites Quill to listen to a poem. Afterwards, she hears him repeating it softly to himself as he sets her cabin to rights.

'Continuous as the stars that shine
And twinkle in the milky way.
They stretched in never-ending line
Along the margin of a bay . . .'

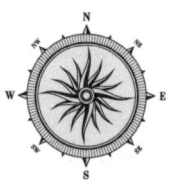

'I could write a letter for you, to your family,' Caroline offers.

Men are mending sails, the blacksmith is taking measurements for some part of the rigging that has broken away. The sea is a slow rolling swell, the breeze a steady sou'easterly. The Spanish women's maids have hung out washing to dry. The sailors make fun of the undergarments pinned to the makeshift line, until the Jesuits walk the deck and silence descends. Even the children, playing hide-and-seek amongst the barrels and rowboats, quell their cries and begin to whisper to one another when the priests are present. Caroline wonders what Quill makes of children his age playing while he is part of the crew. He appears to take little interest in them, as if they are other than him.

'We could tell them you are doing well. That you have become quite the sailor.'

He shakes his head. 'Father said not to look back.'

'I know what it is to have your life determined by your father,' says Caroline.

The hair on Quill's head has grown back, a chestnut fur she keeps trimmed. She wants to run her hand through it as it stands to attention, but she does not.

'Shall I read to you?' she asks.

He shrugs.

She opens a small volume and finds a page.

'And now the STORM-BLAST came, and he
Was tyrannous and strong:
He struck with his o'ertaking wings,
And chased us south along.

With sloping masts and dipping prow,
As who pursued with yell and blow
Still treads the shadow of his foe,
And forward bends his head,
The ship drove fast, loud roared the blast,
And southwards aye we fled.'

'A ship,' he says.

'You can learn the words, Quill. And write words of your own, if you are able to read and write. It will make you more useful, more valuable, than someone who can only fetch and carry.'

He says nothing.

'Learning will free you from all manner of smallness. And in time, it might be used to gain you something of great importance.'

'They call you "the Widow",' Quill says.

'My husband died.'

'How?'

'He drowned.'

'In a storm?'

'He fell into the most enormous waterfall you have ever seen.'

'Did someone push him?'

'No . . . Perhaps.'

'Nobody wants to die,' he says.

'I'm not sure about that,' says Caroline.

She could record in her journal the hard bread with barely an ounce of butter in a week, the daily measure of lime juice in water that tastes of the pungent barrel from which it was drawn, the precariousness of the weather, the unceasing movement of the ship and the strange thoughts and dreams she is having. She could write of Captain de Hoog, who is both respected and feared by his crew. He takes the whip to those who have broken some sailor's code or disregarded his authority. She watches a flogging and walks away. The broken skin could use some salve but she does not offer it. She could describe sailors who seem born to this life, and those who appear to have abandoned all feeling, but she does not. The blank pages of the journal seem to require a different kind of honesty from her and she doesn't want to explore what that honesty might reveal.

Instead, she slices the pages away from the binding. On each one she writes a word— *apple, mouse, cat, rat, ship, rope*— and with varying success draws each item.

Quill identifies the objects and she has him practise writing each word in chalk on a tray that makes a useful surface. She encourages him to sound out the words and then think of another that might be like it. *Sail, pail, tail, hail, sea, pea* and also *tree* and *bee* . . . these she writes and he copies.

When he is writing well enough, she offers him one of her unused journals. She invites him to inscribe his name below the words she has written: *This book belongs to . . .*

Quill, he writes carefully.

'My name has a porthole at the front,' he says.

'Yes,' says Caroline. 'Or an eyeglass to see the world.'

Quill's hand becomes steadier. Each letter of the alphabet takes on a personality that is his alone. He draws numbers. He counts the headsails and staysails, the clews, buntlines and leechlines, the hens, ducks, cows, sheep and goats in the hold. He counts, too, the sacks of grain and tobacco, the boxes and bags of provisions, the barrels of water, beer and rum. He draws an iron shackle, a cup, the anchor line, the bowsprit, the sails filled, flying fish skipping across a dappled sea. He runs out of numbers when trying to count the porpoises accompanying them as they move down the coast.

The afternoon before they are to make landfall, Caroline meets Señor Clementi in the passageway. She suspects he has been waiting for her to descend.

'Señora Douglas, all this time and we have barely spoken. Must you travel on quite so soon? I have a plantation beyond the city where the orange groves are very beautiful. It would be my pleasure to host you there.'

He pauses. 'If you are running from something, Señora Douglas,' Señor Clementi continues, 'I would be happy to shelter you. I am a powerful man. You would wish for nothing.'

'Perhaps I would wish for my freedom, Señor Clementi.'

'Ah,' he says, 'but would you? A woman of spirit is always looking for her match. I find that most compelling.'

He is very close now. He strokes her cheek. An incident in London comes back to her with ferocious clarity.

'Señor Clementi,' she says, 'your proximity gives me the sensation of being traversed by cockroaches. Move away, or I will scream.'

At that moment, Quill's head appears in the open hatch above. 'Señor Clementi,' he says, 'there is a condor.'

Señor Clementi moves back and is gone. Caroline leans against the wall, chagrined and weary. A small hand takes hers and she realises it is Quill's. He has dropped through the hatch to stand beside her.

'There is a condor?' she asks, calming her breath.

'No,' he says. 'Just a cockroach.'

The following morning, six miles off the shore of Rio de Janeiro, they are surrounded by fishing birds, the sky filling with dark wings and soaring cries. Clementi has José shoot at them. Many fall into the sea but one falls to the deck and is claimed.

Mountain peaks lie ahead and islands rise high and green within the harbour. The heat and clamour of the jungle envelops Caroline, the noise of insects, the scent of flowers. As the ship docks, she feels the city quivering with voices, people, music and lights. She is unexpectedly awash with loneliness, an emotion that has hitherto been kept at bay. There is no one awaiting her arrival. Yet this voyage had called her. How often she had taken the map from London out of its leather cylinder and traced her fingers across it. To round Cape Horn. To sail the Southern Ocean. She wants to be able to say to herself, 'I saw that. I was there.' But perhaps more than that she wants to know herself capable of this.

Clementi and his son depart the ship along with his daughters and their entourage of children and servants. The senior Jesuit and five other priests disembark. One of the remaining priests offers his services for the ongoing voyage, but Caroline makes no commitment. She has established her disguise. Perhaps there is no need for further pretence.

•

For the weeks the *Alliance* must reprovision, she takes rooms in a guesthouse Captain de Hoog has recommended. It is high above the city, overlooking the harbour with a view to the Corcovado mountain. Quill accompanies her.

In the Botanic Gardens, she is mesmerised by a boulevard of royal palm trees, their trunks patterned with quivering butterflies. The proliferation of flowering plants amazes her, as does the exquisite fragrance of the orchidae. She and Quill sit by the fountain and let the spray settle on their faces. The air vibrates with the wings of insects, the cry of birds, the call of monkeys. They eat *pão de queijo* bought from street sellers and drink passionfruit juice. They devour bananas and oranges. Caroline acquires camphor leaves, cinnamon bark, cloves and three different kinds of pepper for her supplies.

When night falls, the boy is awed by the singing of frogs in the gardens, fireflies in the hedges, the haunting cries from the nearby hills. She tells him stories of jaguars, alligators and parasitic plants. He is startled by the jumping spiders and avoids the long yellow webs that span the pathways. He gently touches lizards on the walls and uses a stick to investigate nests of mud in high corners, running inside when wasps chase him away. He is fascinated by the tiny wings of hummingbirds.

'There are so many things I do not know,' he says.

They see Latin ladies in their finery and Catholic priests and merchants, all carried in palanquins by slaves like Egyptian queens and pharaohs. There are barefoot slaves shouldering goods for their mistresses and masters, driving carriages and pushing carts laden with sacks and boxes. One day they pass a cathedral and, just beyond, see a group of slaves being herded into a wagon. The men, women and children are scarred and mutilated. Missing ears, missing fingers, missing eyes. All of them in tattered clothes, two of the children white.

'What happened to them?' Quill asks, but Caroline is at a loss to explain to a boy whose own life has been purchased.

'It is the way it is,' she says. 'I have learned that no amount of wishing for life to be another way will make a feather of difference.'

She might have told him that, even if you once had a title, a grand house on the rue Saint-Honoré in Paris with carriages and many servants, and an estate with ten thousand vines, when the houses are gone, the fields and the servants, and all the money, then the laws that have defined your world, that might offer you restitution or protection, also disappear. There is no point in outrage or petitions. No point in fighting at all.

'This is something we share, Quill,' she says. 'We both know how easily everything is lost—which makes each day worthy of appreciation.'

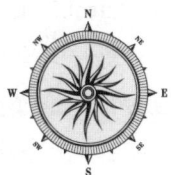

Returning to the ship, Caroline moves into a large cabin below the poop deck where the senior Jesuit had resided. The movement of the ship is easier here, and from the portholes she can while away time watching the wake of the ship and all the wide sea. It gives her a new appreciation of the distance she is placing between herself and the past.

Nearing the port of Buenos Ayres the ship is beset by thousands of black beetles that cling to the rigging and rise in clouds. When the ship is at last at anchor in the harbour, two more of the Jesuits disembark. Tobacco is added to the cargo, another investment Caroline has made. Two Quakers come aboard, a husband and wife who have lived in Argentina for five years.

'They have waited three months to find a ship,' says de Hoog. 'They will come first to Van Diemen's Land and then on to Sydney where I understand they have family.'

'Perhaps they will pray for us as we round the Cape,' Caroline says.

'Especially now we have again added to the number of women aboard,' says de Hoog, with a brief smile.

Caroline offers him a wry look in return.

'I have heard men pray in many languages in those waters,' de Hoog adds. 'Even the most ardent of non-believers.'

'And women?'

'If they were all as fearless as you, Mrs Douglas, perhaps there would be no need of prayer.'

Caroline knows she must endure at least one meal with the new passengers. They are dressed in their muted grey Quaker garb and speak of the school they established in the city. Later in the evening, once brandy has been offered by de Hoog, but refused by his new guests as they had also refused the wine, the Quakers talk of an expedition on which they witnessed the wild Indians being shot en masse.

'The children, some just a year or two old, were shackled and taken for slaves,' says the husband. 'It is an old war and many of the Indians are tamed now. By nature they are a gentle people in my observation.'

'The coffee farmers use slaves, too, but they are all blacks from the African coast,' says the wife. 'In the morning, we could hear them across the valley, singing their hymns. I do not think I will ever forget it.'

'If one can blind oneself to the suffering and brutality,' says the husband, 'it is an idyllic way for some to live. It has made many families immensely rich.'

I have invested in slavery, Caroline reflects. The coffee in the hold, the tobacco, the sugar. Perhaps even the muslin of my dress.

'Nothing is achieved without sacrifice,' she hears Tante Henriette say. 'Sometimes the sacrifice is other people.'

•

Near the Falkland Islands large seabirds attack the rigging, hungry for the leather. Many are shot and some are taken to be cooked. Flocks of turkey buzzards pass over the ship, too. More than one hundred and fifty-six, according to Quill's count. Several are brought down. They have an oily meat that Caroline finds delicious.

Through a hailstorm, Caroline glimpses the impenetrable black cliffs of Patagonia, the bare land rising up and away into towering embankments of thunderous clouds. Hundreds of seals and thousands of penguins play in the ship's wake. The sea becomes increasingly turbulent, the barometer dropping along with the temperature.

In Tierra del Fuego she sees snow-capped mountains. Condors soar and she marvels at the spread of their wings, their floating grace. One of these is also brought down with a shot from one of the officers, but it is unable to be retrieved. Whales that might swamp the deck pass nearby, the noise of their breath searing the air, their spumes of water rising into the sky.

She is glad of her furs again as she grips the railing, her body moving with the ship's heavy dance. She lets it come, lets the blast of ice burn her eyelids, pushes her face into the fury of it. The cold seeps through her woollen stockings into her legs, into her fingers, making her cheeks sting and her teeth ache. The mountains are shrouded by fog and rain.

'Best to get below, Mrs Douglas,' de Hoog says.

Quill is at her side, his eyes alive, though he says nothing. She retreats with him to her cabin, hail rattling on the deck above.

The weather becomes violent, the waves terrifying. Icebergs are sighted, green and gigantic, that might split a ship in two. Caroline and Quill curl in blankets in her cot, holding one another as the *Alliance* is assailed by wounding seas and rampaging winds.

Fear serves no useful purpose, Caroline tells herself. No useful purpose.

'You do not need to be scared,' Quill tells her. 'She is a good ship.'

Day after day it continues. Caroline recounts for Quill the story of Odysseus and his long voyage home after the Trojan War. When there is light, she tries to read to him from the illustrated edition of *The Arabian Nights* she has kept from childhood.

At last they are beyond the Cape, beyond the Straits of Magellan, through the East and West Furies. The sailors take respite. Beards are shaved, uniforms are restored.

Courage is a form of excitement, Caroline thinks, emerging from her cabin to billowing spray. Despite the weeks of tempest, still the *Alliance* holds them. Or is it the sea that holds them?

Quill is at his favourite pursuit; he has climbed to the fore upper topsail set.

'I'll flay him when he comes down,' says the captain, looking up.

'You will not,' says Caroline.

'And why would that be, Mrs Douglas?' he asks.

'Because, while he may be counted as a member of this crew, until I take leave of your ship any flaying falls to me.' She surveys her black gloved fingers, as if imagining a whip resting across them.

'There will be other days,' says the captain.

'Of boys climbing the rigging, I am sure,' Caroline replies. 'For the flaying of them, too, I assume.'

'He's a good lad,' the captain says.

'He is. Do you know why he is called Quill?' she asks.

He shrugs. 'The only name I was given.'

'Was it a game of cards? A wager?'

'No business of yours,' the captain says.

'Perhaps he is writing his own life,' she says.

'Rain coming,' he replies, as if she had not noticed the squall approaching.

She looks up and sees Quill descending the mast with the ease of a cat. She knows she will miss this uncommon life of sea and sky when it is at an end.

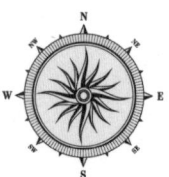

They make repairs and reprovision in the port town of Valparaíso before heading west into the Pacific Ocean.

The trade winds are a relief after the low grey skies and irascible seas of South America. Still, it is a long passage, punctuated by turtle soup and Quill's increasing facility for reading and writing. Otaheite is but a week away when the Quaker wife knocks on Caroline's cabin door.

'Will you come?' she asks. 'My husband has taken ill.'

For days the man has been afflicted with headaches and nausea. Now he is becoming more agitated and will take no fluids. The ship's surgeon diagnoses malaria, acquired in the jungles of South America, but he does not have the fever dreams Caroline knows are common to that disease. The surgeon wishes to bleed the man, but the wife won't allow it. She says to Caroline that it will only weaken him, and the rum he is offered by the surgeon is merely poison.

'Can you help?' she asks. 'I had a sense that you would know what to do.'

Caroline does not wish to draw attention to her stock of medicines, nor her knowledge, the thing she has been good at, the future her father had envisioned for her. But when she finds the puncture wound on the man's leg healed over, red and hardened, she knows she cannot abandon the woman.

'He was bitten?' she asks.

'A dog, in Valparaíso,' says the wife. 'I treated it with a powder. You do not think . . . ?'

'Rabies,' says Caroline, nodding. 'Or hydrophobia, as some call it. I am so sorry.'

The woman retreats into an anguished silence. The man is strapped down. Caroline descends below to fetch the ointment of *Datura metel* and *Piper nigrum* from India which she had packed in one of her trunks. She rubs it into the wound and drops laudanum tincture into the man's mouth. He has moments of lucidity followed by increasing periods of violence. It is a death of ferocity and desperation.

The captain and first mate bring a sailcloth to wrap his body. On deck it rests on a pallet set across barrels. A sunrise of crimson and saffron spears a sombre mass of tropical cloud. Prayers are spoken and a hymn sung before the body is slid from the pallet into the sea.

The following morning the black volcanic peaks of Otaheite loom on the horizon.

Crossing the reef and entering a small harbour, the breeze carries an exotic fragrance. The ship is quickly surrounded by canoes. Native peoples, laughing and calling, urge them to inspect a selection of shells and carved items. Captain de Hoog will not let them aboard, telling Caroline they would take anything that caught their eye.

The last of the Jesuits are rowed ashore in a longboat. Caroline and Quill are also ferried to the brilliant white-sand beach. Caroline had invited the Quaker widow to join them but she had declined with a brief shake of her head.

Caroline and Quill delight in milk of the cocoa-nut, a baked fish wrapped in palm leaves and the delicious fruit of the pine-apple. The smiling faces of the local people enchant her. She observes the churches and warehouses, the white colonial houses of French and English design amidst the luxuriant vegetation of this rustic and beautiful place.

Children surround Quill as if his arrival has been anticipated and invite him to join them. At first he is reluctant to engage, but Caroline encourages him. 'I will be very comfortable here in the shade. Now, go!'

Soon he is running on the sand as the children throw a ball, leaping and falling in a skirmish of elbows and knees. When he stands again, the ball in his hand, she sees him laugh for the first time.

Christmas comes and goes before the *Alliance* is readied for departure. Caroline gives Quill a pink conch shell sold to her by one of the natives. She shows him how to put it to his ear so he can hear the sea.

'I have given you nothing,' he says.

'You have helped me to avoid invitations to join the ladies of the London Missionary Society for tea, and kept me company through some very hot and dull church services,' says Caroline. 'More importantly, you have given me your smile every day. Those are gifts of great value.'

Later that evening, after they have eaten in the guesthouse where they are residing for the sojourn, he presents her with a jar of frangipani which scents her bedroom.

•

The Quaker's death, and his wife's mourning as they sail on, turn Caroline's thoughts to her father's illness. The long disappearances when his brain tormented him, and the times when he returned. How he had come to her, after the deed on the Battersea Bridge, and she had taken the bloodied knife from him and thrown it in the Thames, knowing nothing of what had occurred just moments before.

When the details were revealed in various newspapers, and the family where she worked as a governess let her go, she understood. She was, in fact, relieved. She began using her mother's maiden name and took another job teaching twin girls.

Fatigue enveloped her in the months that followed. Some days she had wanted to sleep and sleep and never wake up. Other days she had walked to Millbank Prison simply to stand in the shadow of its walls, knowing that within was a man she loved, a ghost, a remnant of her father.

Do your dreams live on? she wonders. If you lay them down, if you discard them, can they jump into the pocket of someone else? Do they drift from you at death to find some other mind or heart?

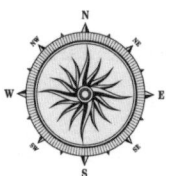

Van Diemen's Land appears out of the sea mist, with soaring cliffs and a shore of tumbled pewter boulders. Waves crash against the coastline, plumes of water shooting high into the air. Captain de Hoog tells Caroline that if the sou'wester continues to blow, the journey's end is within grasp.

Caroline can smell peppermint, earth, forest. The quietude of her cabin, and this creaking, steadfast vessel that has delivered her all this way, must soon be left behind. She braces herself for the world ashore. Observing the dense forest cloaking the hills and the mountains, she considers how it had been here all this time while, elsewhere, empires had risen and fallen. Will it be very primitive? How much could have been achieved in some thirty years by convicts and settlers and soldiers? And what of the native peoples? Were there native peoples? It seemed that there were people everywhere she had travelled.

Her thoughts turn to Quill. Mostly the crew seemed to treat him well. He ran about the ship as if he was born to it, but the sea was hungry and impetuous. How easily such a small person might be washed overboard, crushed in broken rigging, fall ill from a wound or be taken with a fever.

'If you did not act with such recklessness,' she says. 'A little less climbing . . .'

'It's the only place I can be alone,' he says. 'Except when I'm with you.'

She understands. She, too, is weary of being observed whenever she leaves her cabin, of the impossibility of solitude amidst crew and passengers. But what of the boy beyond here? Maybe he would come under the gaze of some brute who would misuse him, or be shipwrecked in a violent storm. Perhaps he would abscond in a harbour where the trees made good climbing, the fruit was plentiful and the street life appealing, becoming a pickpocket or a beggar.

Had his father done the boy a favour in sending him to sea? She has seen children hurrying to the factories of London before dawn with their bruises, burns and wounds, with arms and legs too thin, too small, for the work expected of them. Perhaps Quill has been saved from such a fate.

In her father's apothecary, children and adults were carried in with broken spines or crushed limbs. He never charged a fee when it was a child in need, or it was apparent that a person could not pay, but he charged a little more for those who sent a manservant or a lady's maid for a remedy.

Her father had translated books from French into English, one about the beliefs of the Hindoo. He wrote pamphlets on the benefits of diet, the care of the body and the care of the spirit.

'The great sadness is that the people who need these the most do not read,' he said one day, as they unpacked the latest leaflets from the printer's boxes and arranged them on a shelf in the shop. 'Cannot read.'

'Will it always be so?' Caroline asked.

'Will there be a balancing of good and bad, right and wrong, a future far beyond the comprehension of our lifetimes?' he asked.

'An act of human kindness takes but a moment in any time,' said Caroline. 'Or are you suggesting there is a different way to see the world?'

'I am always asking this of myself, dear daughter. To be curious is to be truly alive.'

Sometimes recipients of her father's generosity returned to show him a healing scar, a rash disappeared, a broken bone mended. They offered him a ginger kitten for his girls, a pale pink seashell said to have come from a relative who had sailed with the East India Company. They knitted him socks. One old man, whose symptoms had been eased with a remedy of *Filipendula*, presented a tiny drawing in ink. It depicted Caroline at work measuring herbs. The artist had made the world in the shop stand still.

'*Ah, vous êtes vraiment un maître,*' Father said. 'A master.'

When the man departed, Caroline said to her father, 'I want to believe there is grace for the good. Or perhaps I mean grace for the poor.'

'But is it not the wealthy who are blessed by God?' He was teasing her now.

'I think it would be harder to be good if one is poor.'

'Unfortunately,' her father said, 'I have witnessed almost the opposite. Here in London and beyond, it seems that poverty itself is a crime, if one believes the priests. Yet consider the man who was just here; if circumstances had been kinder he might have become a great artist. He has not only captured your posture, your expression, the shop itself but, most vitally, he has conveyed something of your nature.'

Caroline nodded. In the picture she looked absorbed in her work, and quietly amused.

'Maybe how we see the world makes the world we see,' her father said.

'It feels as if there is some sort of order,' said Caroline.

'Where?' he asked.

She might have said in the very rhythms of her body through each month, but instead she said, 'In the seasons. In the moon cycles. Apples in autumn and blossom in spring.'

This was how they spent the quiet moments in the shop. He had tutored Caroline and Augusta in French and history, literature and Latin, chemistry, biology and a little astronomy, while their mother had tutored them in English, mathematics and geography. It was only after their arrival in London that any thought had been given to the two girls attending a day school.

'You feel an energy that imbues weather and cycle, the earth and all that grows upon it?' her father enquired, as he held aloft a vial of gentian steeped in wine and decanted it into a stoppered vessel.

'Yes,' she said. 'Yes, I think so.'

'Do you think a force so grand, so ancient and eternal, has an interest in every living thing? In the small notions we might call sin? Any interest in our daily lives at all?'

'I don't know,' Caroline said.

'Your mother would say yes, of course, for faith is her way and I have great regard for the peace it brings her. But I am of Spinoza's view that we are more suited to the laws of nature than to be governed by a God of commands and decrees.'

'How could that work, Father?'

He laughed. 'How indeed! But let me try . . . The God of which the churches speak, at least since the fifth century, when all other Christian faiths were destroyed and many other ancient faiths as well, has been a God of punishment and reward, a God like a king. But Spinoza saw a divine law at work. How could such a force, an energy that made this bountiful world, possibly care for the day of the week we have ascribed to worship, or the name we have given it? The covering of your head or the way you clothe your body? If you are born a man or a woman? Such an entity is unconcerned with the particularity of us. Divine laws cannot be broken, unlike the laws that govern notions of sin and goodness.'

'So there will be no Day of Judgement?' she asked.

He smiled and handed her the final bottle for labelling.

'The Quran says the greatest battle a man ever wages is the conquest of himself. So how will you live, dear daughter? Or—and I offer you this at the start of your long life, in the hope that when it comes you will be ready—what will be in your heart when you die?'

'Ah, Papa, how I have pondered that,' she sighs. She lies down upon the cot and cannot say if her tears are born of regret or longing, or fear of the things that might have grown in his heart while imprisoned. Later, she restores the cabin to anonymity. No more clothes drying or drawings pegged to a string. No tea, herbs and spices vying with playing cards and books for space on the shelves. All that has accompanied her on the voyage is stowed in preparation for a new life, except for a brass compass in a case of blue Morocco leather. A start to negotiations, or perhaps a sweetener at the end.

'Captain de Hoog,' she says, 'what price would you want for the boy?'

'Do you own me now?' Quill asks when she tells him that she has freed him from his debt to Captain de Hoog. They are seated at the small table in her emptied cabin, the table where they had sat so often together, where he had pursued his studies and learned to play chess.

'No, Quill,' she says. 'I do not. You are a free person. You belong to yourself, now and always.'

She wants to explain how she abhors the idea of owning him, she wants to talk of slavery and emancipation, but it would only lead to her talking of her father and mother, of her father's pamphlets and her mother's meetings.

'You can stay here aboard the *Alliance* and continue your voyages with Captain de Hoog, but you will no longer belong to him. You will receive wages like the other men.'

What a negotiation it had been—worse than with any glass merchant for the apothecary.

'Or perhaps,' Caroline continues tentatively, 'you would like to stay with me, here in Van Diemen's Land.'

Quill stares at her, his eyes wide. 'Stay with you? As your servant?'

'You would not be my servant, Quill. We would live together, and I would care for you, until you are grown and can make other choices. But you must think about it. There is time while the ship is in harbour to make up your mind.'

'But what will I do?' he asks.

'Be a boy, I guess.'

•

In the late morning, they enter Storm Bay, which is well named, for despite it being summer there is a persistent horizontal rain, the seas broken, the air chilled. Between rain squalls Caroline glimpses doleful forested hills.

She imagines crocuses lifting their heads in London, the apricot, pear and apple trees that will soon be in bloom. Jonquils awakening with the early daffodils, lilies and irises, their new leaves pushing up from the earth, roses soon beginning to bud. The seasons are turned upside down, and with them the fruiting or flowering of all that is familiar to her.

Then the storm passes as if a celestial composer has begun a second act. The clouds disappear revealing a bonny day. Dolphins race the ship.

The Quaker widow comes to stand at the railing beside her. She is pale and thin. Caroline thinks to take her hand but instead, to her surprise, the other woman takes hers.

'God placed us on this ship,' the woman says. 'My husband's death would have been far worse without you.'

'I was powerless to save him,' says Caroline.

'You eased his way, which is all we can ever hope for I think.' She releases Caroline's hand. 'My brother lives here. He and his wife are building a community of Quakers. I will stay with them until the ship departs. I will be sure to tell them of your kindness. If you need anything, I know my brother will be willing to assist you.'

'Thank you,' says Caroline.

'It will not be easy to establish yourself here without family. But I suppose there are many doing the same.'

'Yes,' says Caroline, unsure how to respond. 'And you must go on to Sydney?'

'I have a daughter there. It is eight years since I have seen her, and she has three children now.'

'I am pleased for you, and sad that she has lost her father.'

'It will be hard to arrive with such news. But children have a way of healing us.'

A mountain comes into view, more a giant shoulder than a peak—not like the soaring sentinels she had seen in Rio or the volcanos of Otaheite. They pass a lighthouse on a small flat island of rock. Upriver, a broad harbour offers sanctuary to a flotilla of vessels large and small, some underway, others anchored at rest. Buildings and roads are evident along the foreshore and into the lower foothills of the mountain. A British flag is flying. For a place of penury, it is dramatically beautiful.

Perhaps he is her son. But surely she is too young to have a child that age? There is speculation on every passenger arriving. Fame travels on a name, infamy, too.

'He is her ward,' the clerk tells a friend that night in a tavern at Sullivan's Cove. His work was to keep the ledger for the colonial government, recording the arrival of every ship in a neat, unembellished hand. In his previous life he was a banker found guilty of forging a bill of sale. He had a ticket of leave now, and was the first official encountered by those who arrived in the colony.

The young widow had a most pleasant face and spoke with a clear voice, though she looked properly sombre in black from head to foot. He remembered their names.

A Mistress Caroline Douglas and a Master Quill Douglas from New York.

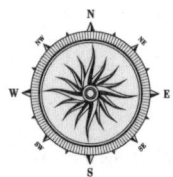

The shingle outside says: *Room to rent*. It is one of several stone cottages above the foreshore, this one the furthest from the odour of whales being flensed and close to the military barracks. There is a large ship's bell in the front yard.

'This one?' asks Quill.

'Shall we knock on the door and see?' Caroline replies.

The bedrooms they are shown are clean and pleasantly appointed. Mrs Roper, the landlady, invites them to descend the stairs to the sitting room, where a fire burns. The window looks out towards the harbour which is bristling in a late afternoon breeze. They also have a view of the warehouse where Caroline and Quill have overseen the storage of her trunks until they find somewhere permanent to live.

Mrs Roper is a small woman, her hair white beneath her cap, her whole complexion giving the look of someone in need of sunshine, or comfort. Yet her blue eyes twinkle. She serves them rabbit stew accompanied by warm bread and butter. This is followed by two generous portions of pound cake with custard and strawberries. She says to Quill, 'You're a lad who's had a big adventure.'

Quill retreats into the bowl before him.

Mrs Roper takes a cloth from her shoulder and wipes away a few crumbs left by the bread board. 'Just the two of you, then?'

'I am recently widowed,' said Caroline. 'Quill is my ward, so here we are.'

Mrs Roper nods, as if this is an adequate answer.

When Quill is gone up to bed, Caroline moves to a chair near the fireplace and warms her hands. The world is still swaying, her body still preparing to brace for the next wave, but it does not come and she breathes and feels her feet upon a steady floor. Mrs Roper returns with a hand-drawn map. She shows Caroline the streets of Hobart, pointing out key landmarks and the shops she might be needing.

'We are looking for a cottage of some sort,' Caroline says. 'Somewhere a little distant from the town, but not too far—near the sea perhaps, with enough land for a garden.'

'Well,' says Mrs Roper, indicating a road leading out of the township, 'it might be worth looking over the hill in New Town. People there are raising sheep and such. There's a few vineyards and orchards out that way, too. Could be a cottage for renting.'

'There are vineyards?' Caroline asks.

'Yes. There was a place that produced quite a famous wine. Must be ten years ago now.'

'What happened?'

'It got caught up in a legal matter, as I heard it. A lot of work, of course, something like that.'

•

Caroline and Quill walk out along the main road leading north. Wagons and horses, single riders, carriages and gigs pass by. As soon as they can, they find a path leading away from the road until they are skirting the fringe of the forest beneath the mountain's slopes, above cleared fields where sheep and cows graze, the stumps of immense trees evident. Homes are scattered across the valley.

They walk until they come upon a rundown cottage. The place looks uninhabited. To one side of the dwelling is a eucalyptus, so enormous it might take six or eight people to surround it with their arms outstretched. Its trunk is sienna and umber, palest grey and linen. Long lengths of cinnamon-coloured bark are hanging between its limbs and piled at its feet.

'It is a giant,' says Caroline, walking towards it and laying her hand upon its trunk.

'A king,' says Quill.

'Or a queen of the ancient world,' says Caroline.

At the front of the cottage there is a young oak tree. A tree that might grow wide and green, providing a place to lay a blanket for a picnic or a branch to hold a swing for a child when its boughs grow strong.

She takes in a high stone wall behind the cottage—a kitchen garden, she assumes. There is also a drystone wall surrounding an overgrown field set away from the cottage. Then she realises that she is looking at grapevines tangled with wild grasses. She notices, beyond the eucalyptus, a wooden bridge leading to a stone barn, where a plume of smoke escapes the chimney.

A house of grand proportions has been built further down the creek, where the land flattens out before a wide bay on the shores of the river. A row of young pine trees flanks the road leading to the large house, and she can see workers in the gardens and the nearby fields.

A man emerges from the barn and sees them. He raises his hand in a friendly gesture and walks towards them. As he comes near, Caroline sees that he is a black man dressed in a long leather apron. He takes off his cap. Caroline can see his hair is close-cropped and greying, the lines on his face sunk as deep as furrows in soil after ploughing. His back is a little stooped, but he is still a man of powerful size. Perhaps he is a convict. His shirt, trousers and boots are all ingrained with soot.

'Good morning,' he says, bowing to Caroline and Quill. 'I am Cornelius, the blacksmith. I live there.' He indicates the barn. 'Can I help you, mistress?'

The man's accent is similar to those of the black sailors on the *Alliance*.

'Hello, Cornelius,' she says. 'I am Mrs Douglas and this is my ward, Quill. We were just walking the path above and saw the cottage. Does no one live in it?'

'It hasn't been occupied in some time, Mrs Douglas. It is used to house feed for livestock and such.'

'We are newly arrived and are seeking a place to live. I have heard there may be places to rent here in the valley.'

'You should speak with Captain Swanston, who owns all this land. He lives in the big house down there. He has been thinking for some time of selling the cottage, and the vineyard there with it.' Cornelius indicates the vines behind the stone wall.

'Do you know what sort of wine was made there?' Caroline asks.

'Champagne and red wine,' the blacksmith replies.

Champagne? Caroline is incredulous. Surely not. She could tell Cornelius that her father's family provided champagne to Louis XIV, Louis XV and Louis XVI. That were it not for the Revolution, her father might be making wine still. But she does not.

That evening after their meal, and with Quill in bed, Caroline invites Mrs Roper to sit and presents the landlady with a bottle of port she has acquired that day. Once drinks are poured and they are settled by the fire, Caroline asks Mrs Roper about the large house.

'Ah, that will be the Swanstons'. They call it New Town Park. I believe it is very fancy. They say the wife comes from a British merchant family in India. Quite the beauty, though I have seen her only from a distance.'

'And her husband?'

'Well, Captain Swanston is the director of the Derwent Bank, one of the two big banks in town. A finger in every pie, they say. Nothing he doesn't know that's worth knowing. Not very happy with the current Governor by all accounts. He has a clever wife who has all sorts of notions that do upset people.'

'You mean Mrs Swanston?'

'Oh, likely she is very clever, too, but I was talking about the Governor's wife.'

'And you approve of her?'

'Not my business to approve or disapprove. The men of this town seem to grumble about her a lot, but I think a lady willing to brave the wilds of this island is worthy of a little admiration . . .' She pauses. 'Captain Swanston's wife might be very glad to meet a person of your standing, Mrs Douglas.'

'Are they in need of a governess, by any chance?' Caroline asks.

'Well, they have eight children in all, I think, but only a few are left at home now. The older boys are gone, and the daughters are both married to men here.

'I never heard a bad word about him as a master, Captain Swanston,' she continues. 'Convicts used to be assigned to the likes of him. Now you'll see them making roads and bridges. Chained, poor devils. Breaking rock and such. Government work. Every day more of them arriving and put to work with not a thought to how such work can break a man down. And a woman, too, for they get little better at the women's prison—the female factory they call it, for that's what it is. A grim, cold factory. Now the murderers and rapists who've done their time on Norfolk Island are being sent here.' Mrs Roper shakes her head.

Norfolk Island. It feels dangerous to hear the words spoken aloud. Dangerous to speak them. Caroline refills their glasses while Mrs Roper settles another log onto the fire.

'You'd not know it was summer these past weeks,' she says. 'This rain and such a chill wind today. Last week we had snow on the mountain, and at Christmas, would you believe. You never know which way the weather is going to turn. It takes some getting accustomed to.'

'May I ask why you are here, Mrs Roper?' Caroline asks.

'Oh, Mrs Douglas, we don't talk of that kind of thing in this town.'

'I do apologise,' says Caroline. 'I did not mean to give offence . . .'

'And no offence taken. Everyone is doing their best to forget exactly what brought them here, and what stops them going home, as you'll soon discover. Once their sentence is done the job is to make something of themselves. It's what sets me in my place and you there in yours. You'll be like honey to the ants in this town, Mrs Douglas, when word gets about.'

'Word?' asks Caroline.

'Plenty will already be asking who you are. There'll be those who saw you come off the ship and took your luggage. People wanting to know why you are here and what you intend to do. And when you intend to pack away those widow's weeds and find yourself a new husband. There's a shortage of eligible women and not many who are young and pretty like you.'

'My husband is not dead a year, Mrs Roper,' Caroline says, her eyes downcast.

'I am only giving you fair warning, lass. But perhaps I'll leave you now to have a little quiet.'

'Mrs Roper,' says Caroline, 'you have made us most welcome and comfortable. Thank you so much. I do appreciate it.'

'You and the boy are welcome to stay with me as long as you need, Mrs Douglas. No point rushing into anything. Take some time to get a sense of the place.' She moves to the door. 'Can I bring you another pot of tea?'

'Thank you, Mrs Roper,' says Caroline. 'That would be perfect. It is quite strange to be somewhere that is not rocking.'

Mrs Roper nods. 'Well I remember it,' she says. ''Tis a mighty long way you've come, and no doubt a relief to find yourselves on land again.'

'It is all a little unreal,' says Caroline.

'And it may be for a while yet,' says Mrs Roper. Then, almost as an afterthought, she says quietly, 'I stole a horse, Mrs Douglas. I was just a slip of a girl, barely fourteen. It was outside Manchester. Truth be known, I'm still a little proud of it. Those few hours were the greatest night of my life.'

'Was there some urgent matter that required a horse?' Caroline asks.

Mrs Roper gives her a keen look and says, 'There was, not that the judge ever asked me. Running away from a man, of course.'

Caroline blushes and hopes the lamplight has disguised it. Perhaps she was also running away from a man, or towards him. And having stolen so much more than Mrs Roper.

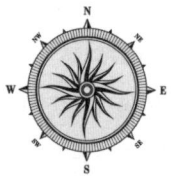

'I said no more,' her father said.

Caroline overheard the conversation while weighing camomile flowers. They were to be steeped for sleeping draughts. For a stronger remedy there were red poppies for opium tincture that came, her father had told her, from a place where women are veiled and, if you steal, they will cut off your hand.

Caroline observed the two bolts of cloth Tante Henriette had laid in front of her father. '*C'est magnifique, non?*' her aunt said, running her hand across the fabric. One was cream with a pattern of silver that glowed and shimmered; the other was a pale green silk.

'*Bien sûr,*' her father said. 'But I cannot.'

'It is a lovely shop you have, *petit frère,*' Tante Henriette said. 'So many good clients who trust you. I have seen how they speak with you. You sense the nature of illness. It is your skill. To listen. To care for these people who come to you. This is what makes you a good chemist. Even doctors seek your counsel. You have done very well for an *émigré*. And what is my skill?'

There was a pause. 'Henriette . . .' Jacques-Louis began.

'To watch. To see. To find opportunities in what I see. Opportunities to reward us both. Are we not reclaiming our dreams?'

'You could make other choices . . .'

'Marry an Englishman? It would be the greatest offence.'

'I am not suggesting that.'

'Some Frenchman, then? Some sorry creature who escaped the Revolution, who survived the delusions of Bonaparte? His lands gone, no doubt his money, too. What could he offer me? His wardrobe of outmoded fashion? Or perhaps the dream of a plantation in South America where he might grow rich again. Some sticky place where I will spend my days fanning away flies and making conversation with savages.'

'I think you'd quite enjoy conversing with savages,' Jacques-Louis said, and Caroline smiled.

'You do know your daughter is listening to us,' said Tante Henriette.

Her father turned towards Caroline, seated on the stool across the shop.

'*C'est vrai*, Caroline?' he asked.

'*Oui*, Papa,' she replied, without looking up from her work.

'And what do you make of it?' her father asked.

'The fabric is very beautiful and I can see the wife of Doctor Arnold thinking the cream and silver perfect for her renovations. The green will make several perfect gowns for the coming season. Perhaps one for Tante Henriette's ladies?'

The bolts of fabric were included in their inventory. When Doctor Arnold came to the apothecary for the cocaine powder he replenished each month, it was Caroline who showed him the fabric, just arrived from Paris, she said. Perhaps Mrs Arnold might like it, and if not, there were other ladies . . . A measure of green silk was quickly purchased, too.

When Tante Henriette heard of this, and the price achieved, she was amused. 'You will go a long way in this world, dear niece,' she said. 'I am watching you.'

As a child Caroline had wanted to go every day to the apothecary to weigh the lemon drops and humbugs and licorice crunch—her favourite. She liked to visit the leeches kept at the rear of the store in a large jar and given out only to the servants of doctors. The leeches were fed on rats her father purchased from street boys who presented them to him in boxes, or sometimes from their pockets.

'One thing feeds upon another, Caroline,' her father said. 'If you look, you will see it everywhere.'

Jacques-Louis had never intended to become an apothecary. He had grown up in a chateau amidst acres of vineyards. When he tended the vine that grew their table grapes, he spoke with a special affection.

'We cannot know how it has arrived here in England, and yet here it is. This vine is a descendant of other peoples and other times. We grow where we can, dear Caroline, just as plants do.'

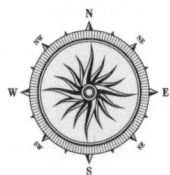

Caroline yawns discreetly behind her black-gloved hand as she awaits the arrival of Captain Swanston. She has slept fitfully this past week, unable to stop her mind from dwelling on all that has happened, and all that might yet happen. Dawn arrives quickly at this latitude, and then she finds she cannot return to sleep but must rise and walk.

Since disembarking the ship, she has discovered Hobart to be a colourful, bustling town with occupants of every provenance, yet the architecture and bureaucracy is all England. There are formal sandstone houses and government buildings as well as small cottages of turf, wattle and daub, some with picket fences. There are churches and chapels of various denominations, shops, guesthouses, hotels and all manner of drinking establishments from which much singing emanates. There is a gaol, a hospital, a court-house, a barracks and a bond store. Hunter Island sits to the far side of the harbour with its stone warehouses of government supplies kept under guard. Government House is a rather shambling assortment of low buildings in the centre of the town.

Swanston's clerk assures Caroline that he can be of assistance, if she would care to explain her business. He is a narrow man, hardly older than her, with wet, pale eyes and an overbite. Perhaps you are descended from a tasteless fish, she thinks. She rises and smooths her gown. 'If Captain Swanston is incapable of keeping the appointments made for him, then perhaps I will be better served by the Van Diemen's Bank.'

The clerk insists she resume her seat. He himself will go in search of the captain.

When he arrives, Captain Swanston has the smell of horse about him. He is well built, sharp-eyed and fair-haired, with a high forehead and a long aquiline nose—a far cry from the aged, round-bellied, bespectacled creature she had expected. There is something of the seasoned hero in his comportment. She assumes he rides a white horse, and is amused to discover later that he does.

'My sincere apologies, Mrs Douglas,' he says, ushering her into his office. 'I had an inspection at . . . well, I do apologise for keeping you waiting.'

She hears Tante Henriette saying, 'You can never know a man until you see him with other men. That is the true measure. Who does he become? What a woman hopes for is a statesman, but too often we are persuaded by a visionary, or charmed by a poet or seduced by a goat. I myself prefer the company of women, and in time you may find this is true for you, too.'

Caroline does not see a poet. Captain Swanston is a man of energy and purpose. Whether he is a man of vision or a goat is yet to be known. What does he see when he looks at her? she wonders.

Summoning Tante Henriette, she lifts her chin, settles easily into the chair and assumes a relaxed air. She has nothing to prove. Quite the opposite. It is Captain Swanston who must prove his worth.

'You are here with family?' he asks. His manner is a little brusque.

'I am not, Captain Swanston. My husband and I had intended to come together, but that . . . well, it was not to be.' Her black silk dress and bonnet, her demeanour as she says these words, makes further explanation unnecessary.

'I am very sorry to hear that, Mrs Douglas.'

'It is a trial with which God has appointed me. But Hope smiles on Effort. My husband always said that. I have heard from several sources that you are a man of merit. Someone with whom I might entrust my affairs.'

Caroline can see him assessing the quality of her gown. The rings on her fingers now she has removed her lace gloves. The pearl brooch at her neck. She lays two documents before him: a marriage certificate and a death certificate.

Swanston adopts the sober air of a banker, accustomed to taking charge of other people's money much like an undertaker assumes charge of the deceased. She must be wise. Her investment in the cargo of the *Alliance* has proved as rewarding as Captain de Hoog had promised; coffee, tobacco, sugar, salt and rum were exactly what this colony needed. But she knows that money is easily lost. Lost in dreams and speculation, lost in madness, and in revolutions.

'Captain Swanston,' she says, 'I am sure you are a confessor to many people, when you take their money into your hands. I hope that I do not need to explain to you the precariousness of my situation. I am a widow alone in this strange place. We do not know one another, and I understand that for a woman to have control of her financial affairs is highly unusual. As such, I wish any arrangement to be a matter of complete confidentiality. If I were to place this trust in you, I would be entirely reliant on your discretion. But I believe I can make it worth your while.'

She places before him a bank cheque from London. If he is startled at the document, and the sum, he does his best to disguise it. Still, she notices a glint appear in his eyes. He presses his palms onto his desk. Then, as if he has come to an agreement with himself, he nods and says, 'I assure you that nothing of your affairs will leave these walls, Mrs Douglas. I am not simply managing director here; I am also a member of the Legislative Council. My own company trades in goods in Canton, Madras, Calcutta, Manila, Mauritius and the Netherlands Indies. I have investors abroad and also here who rely on me to safeguard their interests. I will personally see to your deposit and you may rely on my assistance for any future needs.' He adds, 'We are also a mortgage bank, and thus are able to offer capital should you require it; land is not cheap in this colony.'

'Thank you, Captain Swanston,' she replies.

'However,' he continues, 'I must warn you that you will be the subject of conversation, Mrs Douglas. This is a place sorely deprived of young women of your standing.'

'So I have heard, Captain Swanston, but I am only recently a widow and I loved my husband dearly,' she replies.

He nods, and she sees his surprise at her fierceness.

'A more pressing concern,' Caroline goes on, 'is a home. I seek somewhere with a view of the river. I do not want anything that might draw attention to me. A simple cottage will suffice. Somewhere in proximity to the town with sufficient acreage for a garden and possibly further cultivation. If you can assist me to find such a property—again, discreetly . . .'

'Let me give your situation some thought, Mrs Douglas,' he says.

He bows when he takes her hand in farewell. Only then does it occur to her that Captain Swanston is grateful for her money. This unsettles her a little, and then it pleases her.

The following day, he is awaiting her arrival. Again he ushers her into his office, and tells her of a cottage on his own land that is part of the estate he purchased in New Town ten years ago. He has been meaning to sell it, along with seven acres. It is just over the hill from the harbour and has been unoccupied for some years, used for storage. It is in need of new shingles, a whitewash and some other maintenance, but all that can be easily accomplished if the house is of interest to her.

'I will look at this property you suggest, Captain Swanston. And perhaps you know of others that may be suitable?'

'Of course, Mrs Douglas.' His voice is clipped, as if he has practised it as a necessity of his position. She suspects it could lean to irritation. His long nose in profile reminds her of a deer, although she is sure he would prefer her to think of him as a stag.

'I intend to take work as a governess, Captain Swanston,' she says. 'I have letters of introduction from my previous employers. I speak French fluently. I know Latin, mathematics and a little science. I am more than capable of preparing boys for their continued education back in England.'

'Mrs Douglas,' he says, and Caroline sees a small smile at his lips, 'you must meet my wife; we have three young sons in need of instruction. May I take you to see her?'

'Thank you, Captain Swanston,' says Caroline. 'That is most kind of you. But first let me look at your unpainted cottage with its roof in need of repair.'

'Tomorrow?'

'Yes, but please arrange for an employee to accompany me. I would not like to be seen with you and cause idle speculation.'

Unexpectedly, he laughs. 'I think you are going to do very well in this unlikely place, Mrs Douglas,' he says.

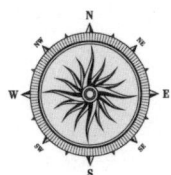

S wanston's clerk is driving the gig. Quill sits beside him wearing a navy cap, white pants and a white shirt under a jacket of green wool, all made for him in the township. He is still thin, despite the food he is consuming morning, noon and night. Caroline watches him turning this way and that as he takes in this new world. What would Quill's father make of his son now? What would his mother?

Quill has never spoken of his mother, and Caroline has not pursued the subject. It is easier this way, she decides. She had asked Captain de Hoog if he knew the exact age of the boy. He did not. Nor did Quill.

'Ten, or thereabouts,' de Hoog had said.

'Then let us say you are ten,' she had said to Quill on their final day aboard the *Alliance*. 'It's a good age. And you will need a birthday. It makes you official. Is there a month you prefer? Or a date?'

Quill shook his head.

Caroline suggested the first day of May. 'It was my sister Augusta's birthday. I'm sure she would be happy to share it with you. May Day. A day of ancient rituals for the return of spring, which seems opportune if you really are sure that you wish to accompany me. It cannot be easily undone, such a decision.'

'I am sure,' said Quill.

The gig takes them up over the hill. Caroline turns and surveys the river, sparkling and calm. She can see the warehouses where the whale boats come ashore. Walking from Mrs Roper's into town one morning, they had stopped to observe a leviathan laid out upon the cobblestones and the workers climbing it with pick and rope. The smell had been ferocious.

'The oil goes all the way to London, where it lights street lanterns all over the city,' she had told Quill.

The boy had been quiet as they walked away. When he spoke at last, he said, 'Why does something so big have to die for something as small as a lamp?'

'This road leads north to the town of Launceston,' the clerk calls back to Caroline in the gig. 'But we turn off here.'

The wagon track is taking them towards the slopes of Mount Wellington. The sky is blue with high white clouds dappled and combed.

'The large stone house over there to the right, beyond the pines, is Captain Swanston's,' says the clerk, indicating New Town Park across the valley. Then, nodding to where the track carries on up an incline, he adds, 'There is the cottage.'

The dwelling Caroline and Quill had seen on their walk looks larger from this approach. The front verandah is broad and the attic windows catch the light. A tingling ripples across Caroline's skin.

'It is your Scottish blood,' her mother would say to her daughters, when they felt something they couldn't explain. 'From the old folk, the wee people. Listen to it if you want to be wise.'

As they bump up the narrow track, Caroline takes in the view to the north and the east. Blue hills roll away from the wide river, softening into greys. There is hardly a breath of wind. The grasses are lit with butterflies. The mountain above them is richly forested and mysterious. She imagines secluded waterfalls and dappled glades upon those steep slopes. The majestic gum tree near the house observes them as they approach.

Captain Swanston steps from the cottage. He is better suited to the outdoors than the confinement of the bank, his military bearing more apparent, the vitality in his stance. Caroline imagines him bearing down on her with sword in hand and cutting the legs off her horse. She has heard that he was wounded in India after a bloody battle where he and two other officers, on the brink of disaster, rallied and slaughtered every Arab mercenary. She wonders if such memories are behind him.

Caroline has treated the unhealed wounds of those returned from battle: common soldiers and sailors as well as those of rank. She has seen the tremble in their hands and heard them speak of the dreams that did not fade as the battle receded. Captain Swanston is a man who has killed, she thinks, as she takes the hand he extends to help her down from the gig.

He is a little surprised at Quill, whom Caroline introduces as her ward, but after greeting the boy he says nothing more. Caroline has instructed Quill to make no mention of their having visited the cottage previously.

'I am playing a small game,' she had said to him.

'Another game,' he had replied.

'Yes. There may have to be a few, Quill, if we are to establish ourselves here with any success.'

'I don't mind,' he had said. '*Aunt* Caroline.'

To the clerk, Swanston says, 'Go down to the house. There is a box of paperwork I wish collected, and Mrs Swanston may have a list for you. Be back in half an hour.'

The young man nods and takes the gig.

'I hope you don't mind me sending him away, Mrs Douglas. I thought it best you peruse the house unobserved,' says Swanston. 'No need for the clerk to imagine you are anything but a potential tenant.'

'Thank you,' she replies. 'That is thoughtful, Captain Swanston.'

'The parcel is from the fence line there to the stand of eucalypts where the creek divides the property. In our years here there has always been water. There is also a well at the rear, and a pond further back. The vineyard is a relic planted by a man called Broughton, the previous owner; I had intended to turn it back into pasture.'

'You have no interest in vines?'

'Wine is not a lucrative venture here, Mrs Douglas. This colony runs on rum, beer and sheep. It would be wheat, too, if the government would allow us a meaningful export trade to New South Wales.'

'Will such things change?' she asks.

Captain Swanston scrutinises her. 'The free settlers who have invested in land and property here want nothing but to see this place prosper. Yet the government insists on misusing the convict labour for works that do little to support free enterprise. It was not always so. They were assigned to us and many learned skills that saw them able to take on a trade, and even own their own land in time. No more, Mrs Douglas. We hope for better when we free ourselves of this governor.'

'I know nothing of farming, Captain Swanston, nor of commerce,' Caroline says. 'But I saw a gang at work this morning as I was out walking. They all appeared to be very young.'

'It is a sight you will become accustomed to, if you remain here,' says Swanston. 'And I do not recommend you walk about unaccompanied.'

She wants to tell him that Quill accompanied her, but that may appear ridiculous to a man who does not know the boy as she knows him. She looks around for Quill now, and realises he is standing a little to one side, out of Swanston's direct gaze but close to her.

She is still adjusting to life with Quill. Sometimes she quite forgets him, only to realise that he has been downstairs at Mrs Roper's organising her a pot of tea, or retrieving their washing.

'You are not my servant, Quill,' she reminds him.

'No, I am your ward, and I like to help,' he replies with a fleeting smile.

At dusk the evening before, they had walked in the nearby park and Quill had almost instantly climbed high into the branches of a tree. There were other people out for an evening stroll and she had looked about to see if he had attracted their notice. Apparently not. So she had taken a seat on a bench up the hill where a rose garden was in late bloom. She waited. The park emptied. At length, Caroline observed Quill sliding back down the tree and running towards her.

When he sank onto the bench beside her, she said, 'We do not live on a ship anymore, Quill. Do you remember in Buenos Ayres, when I said to take note of the people who had wealth? To watch how they conducted themselves? And in Otaheite, when I asked you to observe the native peoples and how they carried themselves with such an esteem for this world?'

'Yes,' said Quill, kicking his legs back and forth.

'We will find a home here together where you might run and climb enough to your heart's content, I promise. And I am also committed to helping you become a young man of no small reputation for your poise, your manners and your education. Is that still agreeable to you?'

'Why do you wish it?' Quill asked.

Caroline paused and considered the question, gazing into Quill's amber eyes. Because she yearned for family? Because since he had come into her life, she had not felt so alone? No she decided; it was because she had seen his quick mind and his dear soul and she wanted a good life for him. Aloud she said, 'Because I can help you to make something of yourself—if you are willing.'

The boy nodded.

'It will not be easy, dear Quill. There will be many temptations. Many trees you wish to climb when to do so is inappropriate. And, as you know, we cannot talk of meeting on a ship, nor that you were a cabin boy. All these things must become secret in you, if we are to be what we must be here, guardian and ward. You are the orphaned son of a relative of my father. Even with the friends you will make, you must maintain this fiction.'

Quill said nothing, but he nodded again.

'If you pay close attention to the way that I speak, to the way people of influence speak, and mimic their manners, you will soon sound as if you are one of them.'

'All right,' he said.

'Good,' she replied. 'It is a pretence no different from that most people you meet will be engaged in, Quill. They have mastered their speech, their handwriting and reading, their etiquette at the table, the way to dress and to hold a conversation. If you use that young mind of yours for astute observation, then you will master these conventions, too. In time you will grasp history, literature, philosophy and poetry, arithmetic and science—and, I hope, one or two other languages. If you grow inquisitive about the great minds through the centuries, observe nature and the stars, you will broaden your understanding of character and the many interests that can fill a human life. If you find in yourself reasons to laugh and delight, and you have manners and education, then the world will perceive you as being of great value.'

'And you?' asked Quill.

'I will be proud of you,' she said.

'How do you know I will be able to do all these things?' he asked.

'Because you are a boy who has chosen his destiny, and you have availed yourself of a companion. A patron, no less. I will not fail you, Quill. And I do not think that you will fail me.'

'So no climbing trees,' he said.

'I want you to climb as many trees as you wish; I only ask that you save such exploits for when we are unobserved. Or if we are being pursued by a wild dog, or a boar or a tiger. In that case, you must help me up, too.'

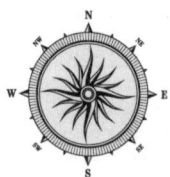

Caroline steps through the front door into the chill air of a home long unoccupied, an aroma of hay and grain and, underneath it, the musty smell of mice. Swanston has left the back door open, too, to air the house, illuminating the cobwebs that cling to the corners of the hallway. Caroline realises the house has been emptied and swept in haste.

The front rooms have broad stone tiles, the walls are plastered, the doors panelled. Each of the formal rooms and the two bedrooms has a fireplace. Each casement window has four glass panes. Above one there is a swallow's nest and bird lime on the walls and floor. A hallway of wide timber floorboards leads to a kitchen with a wood stove. A large black kettle hangs from a hook above a fireplace. There are more bird droppings and the roof has leaked, leaving the dank scent of mildew. Before a long window facing a rear courtyard sits a stone sink. The other rear room has no window and many empty shelves. On one wall there is a heavy sideboard with twelve large metal drawers.

'Protects against mice,' says Swanston.

'We must get a cat,' Caroline says to Quill.

He gives her a brief conspiratorial smile.

A washhouse with a bath besmirched by dust, dirt and droppings, and a fireplace, is at the rear of the courtyard.

'Broughton was a man of comfort, as you can see,' says Swanston. 'Even with this, his first house. Some said he was the nephew of a lord.'

'He was from London?'

'A recipient of free passage, thanks to a little burglary and larceny. Of course, in those days there was no prison as such. This island was the prison and every man was put to work according to his skills. Broughton was assigned as treasurer to both the naval office and the police fund. Within a few years, with his ticket of leave granted, he paid five thousand pounds for much of this valley. An extraordinary sum for the time. He built first this cottage and then he began work on New Town Park, where we now reside.'

'And this did not attract any suspicion, a convict so quickly amassing such a sum given his prior achievements?'

Captain Swanston smiles. 'It did, Mrs Douglas. There was a great kerfuffle. But no records had been kept by the officer in charge, nor by Broughton. And neither would testify against the other, so the charges were dropped.'

'And it was Broughton who planted the vineyard?'

'He did, with convict labour. Landowners, especially those with resources, had the first pick, back then. Clearing land, tending sheep, building houses, any task an owner saw fit. And women, too; maids for the house, cooks and the like.'

'But after he passed away, was there no other winemaker who took an interest in the place?'

'There was a rather protracted dispute between Broughton's sister in England and the wife he had taken here. I had to wait until the matter was settled before I was able to make the purchase, which took some years. By then the vines were mostly as they are now. Many vineyards have failed here, Mrs Douglas. The weather is too cold, the rainfall irregular. Hail blights the summer fruit. The grapes moulder and rot or simply fail to thrive. I have men raising sheep in the midlands, and I have more men taking sheep across Bass Strait, to the pastures of Port Phillip Bay. But a vineyard? The rewards are merely speculation.'

'And without labour . . .' she said.

'Indeed. Few that are enterprising want to stay here once they receive their ticket of leave. And those who must stay have been hardened and broken down by this new system of earning probation through government works. I must realise the expectations of my investors, as I am sure you appreciate, Mrs Douglas, so there can be no romantic speculations.'

I am an investor, Caroline thinks. I have invested funds in this Derwent Bank. Has she made a wise choice, entrusting her affairs to this man? The disrepair of both this cottage and the vineyard unsettle her a little. Is Captain Swanston wise with his assets? Or is he so successful that this small corner of his estate has been of no consequence? He holds a position on the Legislative Council. People in Hobart speak of him with cautious respect and a measure of admiration. Not someone who wasted time with fools, they said, by which they usually meant the Governor.

Caroline looks into the large walled kitchen garden, her fingers folding about a tall gate of wrought iron forged to look like ivy, twined and leafy. She thinks of the blacksmith, wondering if it is his work. What was his name? Ah, yes: Cornelius. Not only a black-smith, an artisan.

In the garden, she spies a rosemary bush protecting what appears to be a lemon tree, and there is a fruitless peach or nectarine. Perhaps the fruit had already passed, or been plundered by birds. Certainly the tree is in need of pruning. The stone walls around the garden are topped with a strange arrangement of sticks pointing up and out, like the stone walls about the vineyard.

'Opossums,' says Swanston, noting her gaze. 'We have applied the same and found them to be very successful at keeping the varmints out. But do not leave the gate open or you will wake to a devastation that will surprise you. Dogs will keep the trespassers at bay, and howl if anyone comes within range of the house.'

'Trespassers, Captain Swanston?'

'Oh, I mean the wallabies and the opossums, Mrs Douglas. They will eat anything we leave unguarded.' Then he adds, 'In truth, there is very little real crime here, Mrs Douglas. Once freed from their sentence, the convicts generally avoid the law. Drunkenness is their major fault. There were a few bushrangers years back, but the more remote farms were their target. They are done with now, as are the blacks. And there is a conspicuous police force that must be paid for by settlers, despite England contributing all the criminals.'

Caroline nods. 'There is much to take in, Captain Swanston.'

'Indeed there is, Mrs Douglas,' he says. 'My wife and I would be happy to introduce you to people whose company you may welcome, when you are ready.'

He is a salesman, she thinks.

'Take the time you need to consider the property,' says Swanston. 'I shall remain outside.'

Back inside the cottage, Caroline climbs the staircase, wiping away a layer of dust to reveal the lustre of mahogany. She remembers the great stands of mahogany trees in the gardens of Rio de Janeiro, wreathed in dark leaves and festooned with butterflies as large as her hand. And the wharves filled with timber cut and stacked for export. You and I have both come a long way, she thinks.

Upstairs is not the loft she had imagined, but three small bedrooms, each with a slanting ceiling and dormer window. The two rooms at the front of the house look to the river while the one at the rear has a vista of the mountain. This house could be hers. A place where nobody passes her door. Where horses and carts will not rattle through the night. Where there are no cobblestones, or streets crowded with people and cabs, horse dung, putrilage and slops, laneways strung with washing. Fights, fracas and factory whistles.

The silence enfolds her. As if someone had breathed in and was yet to breathe out. Maybe that was her. Maybe she has been holding her breath since fleeing London, since crossing the Atlantic, since biding her time in New York and then boarding the *Alliance* to travel to this isolated southern latitude.

Her heart swells with regret, loneliness and anticipation. It is as if she had this wish tucked deep inside herself. A cottage amidst fields that fall down to the sea. A mountain at her back. A place of seasons. A place where the light had a sparkling quality to it.

Her mother had talked of how, as a child, she had stayed at her grandmother's cottage surrounded by moors of purple heather, with a brook where they had caught trout with their bare hands. But that had not been Caroline's life. She had only a few memories of Scotland before they moved to London. London, with so many people, with friends and her father's clients living in the streets all about. Tante Henriette returning from the Continent with gifts from France and Italy, everyone speaking French around the table.

Caroline blinks and swallows. 'Is it where we should live, Quill?' she asks, as they look out the attic window across the old vineyard. 'Here, in this cottage?'

'A home,' he says, as if he is trying out the word for the first time.

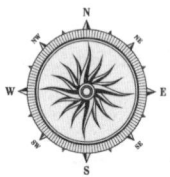

Swanston's clerk delivers her to four other properties for her inspection through the coming week. Despite their various attractions, Caroline knows her decision is made. But it does no harm for Swanston to believe he must negotiate with her if she is to buy his cottage.

She returns early one morning to walk the boundary of the land and to take in the view. She visits the pond and the overgrown kitchen garden. She sits on the stairs to the verandah and imagines waking and looking out at this great river. Today it is mercury in the new light.

She thinks of her father saying that a state of quiescence is not a state devoid of senses. The apparition of a rainbow, the immensity of a cloudless sky, the light of a candle dancing on a wall, all these things can vivify the experience of concord.

'When we rest in the whirls and eddies, when we float and dream,' she can hear him say, 'we can feel we are of this. And this. And this.'

She listens to the birds calling. She watches Quill embrace the trunk of the enormous eucalyptus, laying his head against it. She strolls over to join him.

'Do you remember in Rio de Janeiro, when we saw the butterflies all hanging upside down on the bark?' she asks.

He nods and then says, 'The tree told me it can talk to trees all over the world.'

'Did you ask it to send a message?'

'Not yet,' he says.

Caroline settles herself into the leather chair in Swanston's office. Tea has been delivered on a tray and poured. Their conversation—of the weather and the latest ships in harbour—is at a pause.

'You have made a decision, Mrs Douglas?' Swanston asks. His manner is contained, a man required to be at the beck and call of many.

'I have,' she says. 'It requires the most work, and is the least convenient to the township, however I believe your little cottage is my pick.'

'Mrs Douglas,' Swanston says, returning his cup carefully to its saucer, 'we both know the property, while in a state of some mild disrepair, is nevertheless in a most favourable position.'

Did he know that she'd made a visit to his competitor at the Van Diemen's Bank a week ago and made a deposit there, too? She had banked a portion of her proceeds from the *Alliance*'s cargo, just enough for her to appear as she wished to be perceived: a young widow of some means seeking work as a governess.

She takes a metal box from a bag at her feet and places it upon his desk. She does not unlock it. He tells her what he had hoped to get for the land and cottage. It is a wishful sum and he cannot prevent his eyes returning to the metal box.

Caroline offers him a third less. As he knows there is growing concern for land values in the colony. Property prices have been slipping. The house is in a state of advanced dilapidation. The walls must be replastered. The roof reshingled. The floors repaired and the whole place painted inside and out. The gardens and outbuildings had been sorely neglected. The property had, after all, been deemed worthy only of hay and grain storage. 'But still, I find it charming, for the right price,' she concludes.

She senses a ruthlessness in him as he replies. 'I spoke previously, Mrs Douglas, about ensuring the shingles are replaced, the exterior restored, and the plaster made good. I stand by my word on that, but the sum you offer, for the parcel of land and the cottage, it is hardly reflective . . .'

He finds her a mystery, she sees. He does not want mysteries. He wants money. He wants to sell it to her, and she knows that she must be resolute.

'It will not be inexpensive to return the property to a liveable condition, even with the efforts you propose, as you yourself know or you might have undertaken it already. This is my best offer.'

He smiles. 'I have spoken to my wife about the role of governess for our three youngest sons. She will make an appointment for the two of you to meet. Perhaps she might also let you have one of our maids to help you settle in, should we come to an arrangement.'

'That is most kind, Captain Swanston,' says Caroline.

'There is a government school nearby,' he continues, 'of which you may already be aware. Our youngest go there. It offers a piece-meal education but school is not all about lessons. I propose they take private lessons from you in the afternoons. I am not averse to your ward being included in those lessons if there is no interruption to my sons' studies. I shall be strict about that.'

Caroline unlocks the box and places before Captain Swanston a stack of pristine British pounds, never circulated, carried from London. She knows such currency carries with it an esteem beyond its face value.

Spanish coin, lumps of silver, brass and lead, florins and farthings, pennies and rupees are all currency here in the colony. Wherever ships travel, money travels. But the British pounds have a purity about them. They represent class, and Caroline has determined in the short time she has been in the colony that class matters here perhaps even more than in England, for so few people have it. As Mrs Roper had remarked the night before, 'Most of these free settlers, they are military men or third sons at best, seeking the fortune and position their older brothers will never have to work for.'

Some said the island needed men with vision and Swanston was such a man, as Caroline had learned. Self-made and deliberate, moving with precision towards a future he intended to command. But visions are expensive. He had extensive investments. Some said he was stretched too far. Surely he would see these crisp new pounds for a rundown cottage on a far corner of one of his vast estates as an easy win.

'You will find it is the exact sum I have offered, Captain Swanston. No one need know of our transaction. To all beyond this room, I shall be your tenant as we agreed. This is the most important condition of my purchase. My previous deposit will remain intact.'

Captain Swanston regards her, and the virginal currency before him. 'I believe you and my wife have several things in common, Mrs Douglas, not least your cleverness.'

Caroline is not sure if this is flattery or something else.

'You shall have your bargain and my discretion. I will have the transfer of land drawn up. I hope you will be very happy there.'

Is there a catch? Caroline wonders. Has it really happened? She can hear Tante Henriette saying, 'Money makes its way. It is not only a means of acquiring beautiful and necessary things. In the accumulation of your own wealth, you will find a luxurious and almost dangerous sense of liberation.'

Swanston is one of the colony's most esteemed men. As they both stand and he shakes her hand, she realises she has bought, along with his discretion, an alliance of sorts. Perhaps her new life begins here. Perhaps she can begin to worry less about looking back over her shoulder.

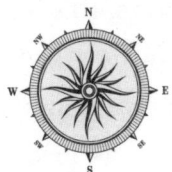

Dear Papa, she begins, at the desk in her room at Mrs Roper's. Her father knows nothing of her departure from London. She cannot be certain he is even alive. Still, how to proceed?

Who is she writing to? The father of her childhood? The father who bounded down the stairs each morning excited to begin the day? The man who turned their garden and their glasshouse into a world of healing herbs and flowers? He had said to her, 'I want you to take these seeds and germinate them. Observe what makes them grow and what makes them fail.'

He had given her a journal in which to record her observations. She drew fruit and leaf, bud and seed. She had been perhaps nine or ten when the growing of things became a sort of music in her.

Her father remembered the need of everyone who sought his counsel. And yet he was the most discreet of men who never proffered a greeting to a client in the street unless he was greeted first and invited to converse. He would give back a penny if he thought a person had miscalculated his change in a shop. He would take the arm of an elderly woman to shield her from the mud of a passing carriage. Those who could not afford to summon a doctor would send a messenger to him at midnight or two a.m. A rap of the knocker waking the house, and he would always go.

'To give them my attention, this is not such a big thing, is it?' he would say to her, when she asked him about his nocturnal excursions. 'Sometimes simply listening will help to heal a person more than any medicine. But we give the medicine, too, for who can say that the two are not reliant one upon the other.'

Often it was a child he was called to attend, and usually too late for anything but death, yet Jacques-Louis went. Afterwards he would grieve. 'So many little souls too fragile for this world,' he said.

Is she writing to that man, or is she writing to the man he became after the terrible fall, after his head was cracked open? The man Tante Henriette felt they should never think of again. But how is she to do that? How to stop her heart singing across a darksome lake?

Dearest Papa,

I hope this letter finds you well. I have sailed from New York around Cape Horn where we survived waves ninety feet high. I saw great fields of whales, for a flock or a school are insufficient to explain the quilted world the sea becomes when they and their young are all at rest together in a bay. There is a language they speak that is haunting and strange.

I have a child in my care. His name is Quill. He was a cabin boy on the ship, indentured to the captain, who was a good man, in truth, but being my parent's daughter, I could not bear to think of the child in this unchosen servitude. He appeared well treated, but what would I know? I found I was incapable of not knowing what would become of him. He is ten years old, we think—we cannot be sure of his age exactly. He has learned to read and write and is proving an excellent student.

I have purchased a cottage in walking distance of the township . . .

But here she can go no further. There is an abyss of unsaid words she does not know how to traverse. He is not who he had been. Perhaps he did not know who he had been, not always. But he knew what he had done, she was sure of that.

She takes the sheet of paper and burns it in the candlelight, words she would never send now as smoke, as hope and as yearning.

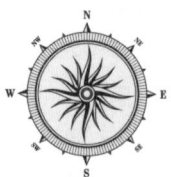

'Come,' says Mrs Swanston. 'Let us go look together. Are your shoes sensible? Oh, good.'

She takes a well-worn path towards the stone barn, an animated woman, tall, slender, with a long, loping stride. Caroline is struck by her willingness to take off across the fields in search of furniture that might suit Caroline's needs at the cottage. She had imagined Captain Swanston to have a wife worn down from birthing and raising eight children. Yet here is this handsome woman with rich chestnut hair and large, serene eyes. It says something about their marriage, Caroline is sure, and wonders what it is.

She can hear the ringing of struck metal.

'It is Cornelius,' Mrs Swanston says. 'I shall introduce you. Do not be alarmed by him. He is our tenant, too. He is from the Americas and has an apartment within the barn. He has been here since before the British arrived, long before we arrived. He was employed by the previous owner. He will prove a valuable neighbour if you wish for tools and repairs. And he keeps a sharp eye on the place for us. I suspect he has many secrets, Cornelius. Oh! I should not have said that. Please, pretend I did not. You will find that he is a dear soul and is clever at anything he turns his hand to.'

Caroline nods.

Mrs Swanston says. 'I am so sorry for your loss, Mrs Douglas. Will you tell me about your husband?'

'There is not really very much to say,' says Caroline. 'He died in an accident.'

'I did not mean to be insensitive. Please forgive me.'

'I am not offended,' says Caroline. 'One can grieve and pine, but it does not bring them back.'

'Still, I am very sorry. Although perhaps husbands are overrated,' says Mrs Swanston, 'though I do not speak of my own.' She colours.

'You are the first person to make me smile about it,' Caroline offers, warmed by the erratic candour of the woman who is to be her new employer.

'I am afraid that I have a penchant for frankness, Mrs Douglas. I have tried, as you can imagine, to curb the impulse. My mother assured me it was fortunate I did not grow up in England where it would have been beaten out of me at a boarding school. Ungovernable was the way she characterised it. I see myself in our Robert. Thankfully in India I was allowed a great deal of independence.'

'And that is where you met Captain Swanston?'

'Yes. My family has lived in Madras for three generations. I was born there. If you haven't seen India it is almost impossible to describe it. But surely you stopped there on your way here?'

'I did not,' says Caroline. 'We made the passage via South America.'

'Oh! Why on earth did you do that? Was it not a most arduous and dangerous way to go?'

Caroline laughs. 'It was at times, but I did not expect to ever have the opportunity again. It took some time to find a suitable ship. Now I am able to look at my map and say I have rounded Cape Horn.'

'I understand that, I do,' says Mrs Swanston. 'My father insisted we were all schooled in geography. It was my favourite subject. Without it, I might never have agreed to live here, at such a remove from the rest of the world.'

'They are Hindoos, yes?' says Caroline. 'The Indians?'

'Yes, mostly. The English lament that they do not embrace Christianity. Yet their faith touches every part of their day. My father has many Indian colleagues. Hindoostani was my first language, learned from my ayah. English my second.'

'You miss it.'

'I do,' she says. 'My mother is still there, and two of my sisters. My father trades in dried goods: tea, rice, spices. Cotton and opium, too. There are always guests on their way to China, or arriving from the Cape of Good Hope or New South Wales. People who have seen the Incan temples, or been to Boston and California. Captain Swanston was the most handsome of all these visitors.' She smiles. 'I was seventeen when we married. Once my own girls reached that age, I found it hard to believe I had been so determined to leave my family to wed a soldier who had captured my heart. Now here I am with all these children . . . though only our youngest are at home now.'

'You and Captain Swanston have made a singular life here,' says Caroline.

'Oh, it is Charles's doing. He is the one with the grand ideas. His determination is irrepressible. He believes there is such promise here and he is enormously frustrated by the colonial government that will not give this island a chance to grow out of its convict roots.'

'Does it trouble you, to live amongst . . .'

'Oh, I think if one was fearful of such things, this would be a very worrying place. But as you will see, there is little indication that those who were transported here are England's worst criminals. They go to Norfolk Island.'

Each time Caroline hears its name, her heart thuds. Norfolk Island. The most infamous prison in the British Empire.

They find the blacksmith working the forge, hammering a shaft of hot metal on a large anvil. He moves slowly and deliberately, habituated to the rhythm of his work. Caroline takes in the bellows, the tools carefully aligned, the barrel of water. When he sees the two women, he ceases his work and wipes his hands on a cloth.

'Good afternoon, Mrs Swanston,' he says, bowing his head.

'Hello, Cornelius. This is Mrs Douglas, who has leased the cottage. You are about to see much work being undertaken before she can move in. And she is to be a tutor for the boys. She has newly arrived from New York with her ward.'

'Good afternoon, Mrs Douglas,' says Cornelius. There is a brief moment of recognition as he bows his head to her in turn, but he makes no reference to their earlier meeting, and nor does she. 'I hope you will be very happy here.'

'Thank you, Cornelius,' she says. 'May I ask, were you here when the vineyard was making wine?'

'Indeed I was, Mrs Douglas.'

'Do you have an interest in the vineyard?' Mrs Swanston asks.

'I have little knowledge of such things,' says Caroline. 'And I am hardly arrived.'

'Well, let us look at furniture you may need, so that your settling in goes easier,' says Mrs Swanston. 'Perhaps, Cornelius, you will organise the wagon to deliver any pieces that Mrs Douglas chooses?'

'Of course, Mrs Swanston,' he says.

'I am pleased to have made your acquaintance, Cornelius,' says Caroline.

'I am always here if you are in need of assistance, Mrs Douglas,' he replies.

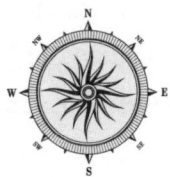

The maid Mrs Swanston sends from the house is easily startled. Every time Caroline enters the room, the girl seems close to tears. Mrs Swanston has told her that Bessie was a girl of fifteen when she was dispatched from England for poaching. It earned her a sentence of fourteen years. Bessie had been aboard a convict ship that had taken some eleven months to reach the colony. Apparently there had been severe storms and diversions to make the necessary repairs. Mrs Swanston had said no more, but the story had hung in the air between them. Eleven months for a voyage that would normally have taken six, seven at most, even with storms.

Caroline wondered if men talked of it over rum and whisky, that voyage. Perhaps they reminisced, boasted, laughed and joked about what befell the one hundred and seventy-three women and children aboard. None of the women wrote an account, but there were, of course, rumours. It was too long. Bessie herself barely spoke a word. At nineteen she was so small as to be easily mistaken for someone much younger.

Mrs Roper had told Caroline that the female convicts used to be paraded on deck before disembarkation. There they were perused by soldiers, settlers and ex-convicts who had earned the Governor's favour. If a woman or girl was chosen, she was assigned a master and expected to work for him as a domestic servant. Some of the properties were remote. If she fell pregnant, or had some disagreement with the master or his wife, she would be returned to the female prison in Hobart, a place of misery and madness. When she was deemed ready—the penury of solitary confinement generally mollifying her and the child placed in the government orphanage—she was once more paraded for selection to more prospective employers. If she was not selected, she laboured with the other women in an endless cycle of boiling wool, sewing convict garb, and laundering and mending the uniforms of government and military officials. Women who received no placements lived out their sentences at the factory.

Bessie had twice been so assigned, Mrs Swanston had told her, and twice returned. But no children, as far as Mrs Swanston understood.

Caroline had tended many sorts of women in the apothecary with her father. Some women found themselves impoverished when a parent fell sick or died. Some were injured in factory work. Plenty were pimped by a man or used for his criminal purpose. If a woman wasn't married she was a concubine, a moll, a whore, a mott, a ewe, a bat, a crack, a flash piece of mutton or, the saddest of all to Caroline, a kinchin mott: a child prostitute.

Caroline had seen women lift their skirts and be taken against a wall for the price of a few coins, returning when it was done to the two children hunkered down at the entrance to the laneway. Without a man to protect and care for her, a woman must do what she could to make her way. Young girls were meant to wait for a prince, but princes were not to be relied upon. Caroline knew that story.

Swanston made good on his promise. Workers come to repair the cottage walls and windows. They also replace the thatching and whitewash the exterior.

Inside, Caroline, Bessie and Quill sweep away the cobwebs and mouse droppings. They scrub off the silt that dusted the walls and windowpanes. Caroline discovers nests of straw and some long-disintegrated woollen coat or trousers in the large metal-drawered kitchen cabinet. There is a lingering musk of furred bodies and blind hairless young. How many mice had inhabited the cottage, and had they, too, come all the way from England, or America, or their ancestors perhaps? Did they have stories? Had this chest of drawers once been a great apartment, each drawer a different family, or a different political party? Had the mice on the top floor been Church of England and the drawer below the Papists? And the bottom drawers? Well, that would be the atheists, she supposes.

One morning she comes across a creature that looks like a large brown mouse wedged into a space beside the washhouse, quivering from some encounter. When she picks it up, it bites her—but not hard—with its long curved teeth, and she wraps it in a handker-chief until she can feel its racing heart settle. Upon examination, its face is longer than that of an ordinary mouse. Its hands and feet are ready tools for digging, or climbing. And then she realises it is like the wallabies here. Native to this place. She shows it to Quill and Bessie, then takes it to the edge of the forest and sets it down.

'Goodbye,' she says. 'Go well. Stay out of the way of crows. And snakes.'

For a moment the creature is frozen with uncertainty. Then it twitches and scampers away, disappearing into the leaf litter.

Bessie removes with care the nests in the eaves where bird babies had hatched. She lines up these creations of mud, twigs and dried grass on the washhouse sill.

'What shall we do with them?' Quill asks.

'I'm not sure,' Caroline replies.

In London, the great flocks of waterbirds that once inhabited the Thames had removed themselves to other wetlands. The kestrels, falcons and starlings had also learned to live further afield. Here, the wild occupants vastly outnumbered the human. It felt as if the newly cleared lands, the cart tracks and roads, were a temporary incursion which in a few years might be grown over, the bush and its occupants reclaiming all.

Before Caroline and Quill walk back to Mrs Roper's, she sets out a blanket in the garden and offers Bessie and Quill mint tea. Bessie insists on serving them.

Quill looks up at the roof. Within a few moments, he has enrolled Caroline in helping him to place a ladder at the side of the house. 'Let's go up and see,' he says.

Bessie looks uncertain. But, with encouragement, the girl climbs onto the new roof and the three of them sit there, drinking tea and eating Mrs Roper's Banbury slice as the river turns gold and mauve in preparation for the late summer evening.

This is how my father's life changed, Caroline thinks. Falling off a roof. Or had it been the night on the bridge? The two events are inextricable.

•

Once the floorboards are repaired, Caroline, Quill and Bessie lay down sacking from the barn and whitewash the walls. To Caroline's surprise, Bessie with a paintbrush is a thing to behold. Her arms have freed themselves from her narrow body. Caroline watches in silence from the doorway as Bessie moves the paint across the wall with a thoughtful ferocity. She is humming. It might be a dance.

'You must let me know if she doesn't suit,' Mrs Swanston had said. 'I admit she is unsettling. You will think me unkind in offering her to you, but I had not wanted her to be without a place of employment. Our big house with all its comings and goings seems to daunt her . . . But do be strict and watchful.'

I shall keep her, if I can, Caroline thinks.

Cornelius brings a cart loaded with the furniture Caroline has chosen from the unwanted pieces Mrs Swanston has stored in the barn. Another servant of the Swanstons' accompanies him, and over various trips they lift and carry beds, chairs, mattresses and tables into the cottage. Caroline and Quill retrieve the trunks they have had in storage, and pack their belongings from Mrs Roper's.

When they arrive back at the cottage, Caroline finds that Bessie has been busy in their absence, trimming back the weeds and grasses leading to the front and back doors. She has also collected a number of stones, each a little larger than a currant bun, which she has whitewashed to mark the pathway. When Caroline expresses her surprise and pleasure, the girl nods but says nothing.

Once they are settled in, Caroline makes a lunch of coq au vin and offers Bessie another helping, but the girl shakes her head. She tries not to need anything. Caroline considers what Bessie needs so very much to have become that way.

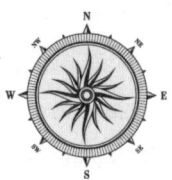

Caroline remembers the first time she saw Tante Henriette's apartment. The walls were covered in a cream-striped wallpaper, the tall windows hung with pale damask curtains. The carpet in the sitting room was turquoise, patterned with flowers and cherubs. There was a glass chandelier and a leadlight lampshade alight with yellow butterflies. The chairs were embroidered fabric, the cushions a fur of some sort. Caroline ran her fingertips across them. A glass-fronted specimen case held a selection of green beetles, some almost as large as her hand, creatures Caroline had never imagined existed.

The books were bound in brown and red vellum, the words printed in gold on each spine, their titles in English, Latin, French, German, Italian—science and medicine, the *philosophes*, mathematics . . . She had opened the door with a little brass key and leaned in and smelled them.

'You have such beautiful things,' Caroline said.

Tante Henriette set down a tray of coffee and touched the walnut table with her fingertips before passing her niece a napkin of starched white linen.

'It is all about the choices we make,' she said.

'Tante Henriette is rich,' Augusta had exclaimed upon receiving a teacup and saucer painted with pale pink roses for her fourteenth birthday. The porcelain was so delicate it was almost translucent.

Their father had said, 'What does it matter what a thing costs, if it is given with love? Money is not at the heart of things.'

Their mother had said nothing.

Caroline loved Tante Henriette. She loved the gifts her aunt gave her, too. The silver bracelet, the volumes of fairy tales with colour plates, a specimen case of *Arachnids of the New World* she had received for her sixteenth birthday. It had shocked them all, how enormous and terrifying such creatures could be.

'I will never travel the world,' Augusta had said, and it would prove to be true.

It wasn't that Caroline and her family did not live well. The apothecary was successful, her mother and father respected. They were a household of two worlds and two languages. The silver serving dishes, the crystal champagne coupes, the special crockery, the coffee cups and silverware, the vases on the sideboard, the embroidered table linens, the two worn velvet rabbits . . . all these things were from her father's family, taken out of France in the dead of night before her father and Tante Henriette became orphans.

Their housekeeper, Esther, had travelled with them from Scotland to London when Caroline was six, Augusta four and baby Isobel still growing within their mother's belly. Their home in Chelsea had two storeys and an attic. Their beds were warm and comfortable, each mattress on a wooden frame, the head and foot of wrought iron painted white. Both Caroline and Augusta had a quilt sewn by their mother and three dresses apiece and a special dress for occasions. Their boots were of good leather and their gloves, too. Each had a Sunday bonnet and a day bonnet.

Yet the carpets in the hallways were growing threadbare along the strip where they walked, and about the edges. The everyday plates and cups were earthenware, the sort that would not easily break or chip. Mama and Esther knitted and sewed their clothes, embroidered linen and worked lace, and taught Caroline and Augusta these skills, but Augusta was always the better student with needle and thread; Caroline preferred to be in the garden.

Father had built a large glasshouse at the rear where he grew plants for the apothecary. Calamint (useful for women's troubles, including preventing conception but also jaundice, leprosy, worms and a persistent cough). Water caltrops (making a poultice for hot inflammation, cankers and sore throats). Rhubarb, both English and Italian (for ulcers, sciatica, gout and cramps). Sage (for the gums) and rosemary (for head, stomach, liver and belly, dim eyes and to quicken the senses). Gooseberries (for expelling stones in the kidneys). Strawberries (whose leaves, when boiled in wine and water, cooled the liver, while the fruit was excellent for inflammation).

Father said his mind was like a compass drawn by the mysteries of nature to the study of plants. If she wished it, she could follow in his footsteps, assisting him in the apothecary, the first woman chemist of London. It would be hard work, but it would be a gift to the world.

At fifteen, she began her apprenticeship, studying in the evenings and helping her father in the apothecary whenever she could. The curious child who had rolled together sprigs of wild mint, lavender and thyme, placing them beneath her pillow so she might breathe them in before she slept, now dried these same herbs and made them into nosegays for sale. The child unperturbed by wound or injury, intent on understanding what lived beneath the skin or festered upon it, assisted clients with an ulcerated mouth, a weeping eye, a boil on the neck, a rot in the foot. She was discreet when a man arrived with a problem only fit to share with her father at the rear of the shop. Women would come also, worrying that she was too young to share the discharges or blisters between their legs, but they learned that she was always heedful and the remedies effective. Sometimes Caroline had to walk to the river before she could return to work, so awful were the things she saw inflicted on a woman's body.

Now here she is in a cottage at the foot of a great mountain. She has purchased rugs, crockery and cookware. Not the beautiful things Tante Henriette might have bought, but good, practical, durable things her mother would have chosen. A few particular treasures had travelled with her from London, but they remained secure in one of the locked trunks upstairs.

On Quill's bed is the quilt her mother made for Augusta. The other quilt, made for Caroline, is lying over her as she reminisces. Her fingers run along the familiar edging and over the pattern of squares that has always soothed her. Mama would be pleased to see the quilts here. But what would she make of her daughter living alone as a widow, guardian to a boy of no family or history, in a cottage purchased through criminal enterprise? Pretending to all the world that she was someone she was not . . .

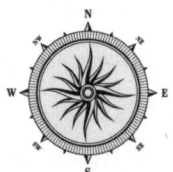

Tante Henriette had promised Caroline a high tea. They meet at her apartment, Caroline wearing a new dress with a green velvet sash her mother had made for her birthday.

'You are eighteen, dear niece,' Tante Henriette says, upon her arrival. 'I think it is time I teach you something.'

She takes Caroline's hand and draws her into the bedroom. It is large, with an Oriental carpet and a four-poster bed. Along one wall are three walnut wardrobes.

Tante Henriette opens the first wardrobe to reveal a collection of dresses in various styles. On the shelves are an array of shoes neatly paired. There is also a drawer that holds necklaces and earrings that twinkle as they catch the light.

Then her aunt opens the second wardrobe to reveal a series of wigmaker's heads. On each head sits a wig of a different colour and style. Within this wardrobe, drawers contain trays of moustaches and beards in various colours and styles.

'Real human hair,' her aunt says, stroking one.

There are cravats and neckties, socks and tie pins. Cufflinks and rings. In the third wardrobe there is a selection of men's trousers, coats and shoes.

Caroline is intrigued. Tante Henriette is a companion. Caroline is unsure which duchess. Arlington. Darlington. Blessington. Poole. There are a few. Tante Henriette accompanies these ladies when they travel abroad. She is often gone for months at a time. Being fluent in four languages is a useful skill. She says the English speak foreign languages with as much flavour as their overcooked vegetables.

'You have a lover?' Caroline asks.

Her aunt laughs at Caroline's puzzlement. *'Regarde et apprends!'* she says.

Tante Henriette chooses a dress of patterned chintz with sleeves edged in white lace. She takes down a wig of long pale curls. She opens one of the boxes stacked to one side of the room and takes out a hat of cream straw with a small adornment of fabric bluebells. Lastly she puts on a pair of women's shoes constructed to discreetly give her several inches in height.

'I would not recognise you,' says Caroline, when her aunt reappears in her new attire. Her face is powdered, her lips are a soft pink and she wears a pair of rose-coloured lunettes. She looks younger, coquettish, English.

'Exactement,' says her aunt. 'Now you. Who would you like to be?'

Caroline considers. 'I would like to be a boy,' she says.

Her aunt selects a suit of grey poplin and a white shirt. Once Caroline is dressed, Tante Henriette chooses a wig of short blond hair and, with some giggling, tucks Caroline's hair underneath. She ties a cravat at Caroline's neck and affixes a tie pin—a pale stone in a gold tulip. Lastly she chooses a pair of men's shoes.

'Helpful that we are the same size,' says Tante Henriette. 'And now, *le chapeau.*'

They stand in front of the full-length mirror.

'How do you feel?' asks her aunt.

'Naughty,' says Caroline, laughing.

'*Très bien. Tu es parfaite. Alors, si tu es prête, on y va?*'

'We are going out?' Caroline asks.

'Why not?' replies Tante Henriette, smiling. 'But you must never breathe a word of this. Not to Augusta. Not to your father. Not a word to your mother. It is our secret.'

'*Alors c'est notre secret,*' Caroline agrees, and out they go.

They attend a production of *Macbeth* at Covent Garden followed by high tea at Brown's. Caroline finds it highly amusing to play the role of a young man, and to witness Tante Henriette as an English lady, her French accent evaporated, her rounded English vowels flawless. But upon their return to Tante Henriette's, having shed their disguises, Tante Henriette sits Caroline down.

'Your mother is dying,' she says, and the fun of the birthday afternoon crashes into silence.

'No,' says Caroline, but she has seen the tremors, the pallor of her mother's skin. She has seen her mother drop a cup on the table as if her fingers could no longer hold it. She has observed the increasing effort of speech.

'We must not pretend it isn't so. It does not help her. I have seen this palsy before. Your father knows it, too. It will waste her away to nothing. We must hope that it is quick. But your father is not well either. You see how his brain is still addled from the fall.'

Caroline stares into her aunt's face. 'What must I do?' she asks.

'Give her every care. It will be difficult, but you have Augusta to assist you. I cannot anticipate how your father will cope without your mother by his side. You must not rely on anything he has promised you.'

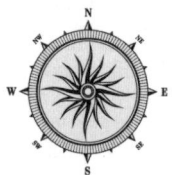

Caroline thinks of a French saying: *Weather, wind, women and fortune change like the moon.* If only her spirits and humours changed with the lunar cycle instead of hourly, tossed about by the unpredictability of the Hobart weather.

Despite the saints days and proverbs being antithetical to the season, there was talk in every shop as if the wind of Ash Wednesday, and the clear day on Palm Sunday, had indicated a bad year. Yet what was to be done when January had been so fierce and cold, and February moist? Last year's late spring might prove to be a blessing, but did the rain on the first Sunday after Easter still predict a good harvest and a fat pasture? Or plenty of grass but little hay? Surely the snowfall at Christmas had been a good omen, not a bad one. Or would there be rain for the entirety of the next summer? Despite the latitude, all these truisms were employed with liberal affection by the residents buying tallow and salt, sugar and garden spades, fabric and buttons, as if they still applied to Cornwall or Dublin or Lancashire.

In the kitchen garden, Caroline begins to feel her way into this upside-down world. If there had once been turnips, carrots and other useful vegetables, it was hard to tell amidst the lush weeds rooted firmly in the earth. Bessie discovers potatoes—purple, tawny and beige—but they lack flavour when cooked, though they eat them anyway.

A climber of some sort has almost jammed the beautiful wrought-iron gate. The rosemary has gone woody. Two espaliered apple trees appear to have died off, tangled with passionfruit vine. Raspberry canes have proliferated but are producing only a few bitter fruits. Caroline prunes back the lemon tree to a manageable size and the other fruit trees, too, taking out the damaged or dead wood and sealing the cuts. Bessie chops back the creeper and the rosemary and together with Quill they prepare for winter crops.

The gardening is tiring but Caroline feels stronger for it. Her body warmed by sunshine and a brilliant sky above, she finds her mind is less likely to wander into dark pools of thought. With her hands in the soil, the uncertain future becomes less compelling than the soft texture of the earth and the food she imagines budding and ripening.

She could place an advertisement for another servant to assist them, but she does not want to announce herself in this way. The *Hobart Town Gazette* is a spyglass into all that concerns the colony. Every advertisement is assessed and interpreted. Between Bessie, Quill and herself, they will make do.

Quill carries the tumble of weeds and cuttings to a pile outside the walled garden which, they discover, is quickly eaten overnight by the opossums and wallabies. A new space is given to compost within the walled garden. Mrs Swanston gives them cuttings of geraniums, nasturtiums and daisies and seeds for marigolds and calendula from her gardens. Caroline places the cuttings on the outdoor table ready for planting, but by morning these too have been consumed.

Caroline hears Quill saying to Bessie, 'Damn and tarnation on those opossums and wallabies for they will eat anything and everything!' She is so in agreement she does not remonstrate with him about his cursing. Instead she shows him how to plant out a seed tray. He is to ensure each morning that the soil is moistened and that he talk to the seedlings in French. *'Grandissez, les petits, grandissez!'*

He and Bessie ferry cow manure from the nearby paddocks, finding the task both repellent and highly amusing. He makes a game of throwing the dried pats to Caroline, rather like spinning disintegrating dinner plates, and it makes them laugh.

Caroline thinks of all the plants grown for the apothecary. The lavender oil she diffused. The rosemary steeped and rose petals dried. The draughts of violets in wine, the decoctions of comfrey, the ointment of shepherd's purse. A salve made from winter green, a syrup from onions and honey. But she'd always had her father and her mother to guide the garden through the seasons, knowing when to plant, when to harvest, and when to cut back and start again or leave to reseed. Having her own garden, in a new climate with quixotic patterns of weather, required patience and persistence, adaptation and continual attention.

Mrs Julia Walker, a Quaker from across the valley, visits and says to Caroline, 'My sister-in-law has written from Sydney. She remembers you fondly from the voyage out, and your assistance during the terrible loss of her husband. She has reminded us to ensure that you have all you need to get established . . .'

Bessie suggests chickens. There is an old henhouse and, in the coming days, Caroline is surprised to find Bessie more capable with timber, hammer and nail than the kneading of bread dough. Hay is carried from the barn and nests are made ready. Bessie visits the Walkers and returns with five small brown Quaker hens. She holds their feathered bodies as if they are old friends.

Caroline can hear rain falling, a light, persistent shower. She draws the bedcovers close to her chin. There is a weariness in her back and neck, an ache in her arms and legs after the work in the garden. She feels the solitariness of the cottage perched beneath the mountain slopes.

'Oh, Mama,' she whispers, 'if you knew the things that have happened since you died.'

'Mousie, you are not alone,' she hears her mother say. 'The best-laid schemes of mice and men go oft astray.'

The overwhelming weight of the past sweeps her up, the fearsome twists and turns she has taken. The rain falls harder, drumming on path and sill, window and door, and tears fall, spilling out of her, running down her cheeks. She has had to be strong. To lie and disguise, to plan and deceive. She has invented a self to lay over the girl she is inside.

But the other Caroline, the Caroline Colbert of her youth, she is still young and vulnerable and lonely. She would like to rest. She wants to be true to that Caroline who tended a glasshouse of medicinal plants, who was tutored in healing, who lived in a house with French silver and threadbare carpets, and lost everyone she loved. But Caroline Douglas does not cling to ideals. She knows that only disappointment lies that way. She is waiting for opportunities, biding her time. But will this new Caroline keep the old Caroline safe? Will she be able to care for Quill and Bessie?

Her breathing quietens. She senses that the two Carolines are allies of sorts. They need one another. And she needs to hold fast to both of them, lest she break apart. Lest she lose some part of herself that might yet find the courage to repair the past.

She wants her mother to hold her. She wants Augusta asleep nearby, not laid in a grave. She wants her father to whisper in French that he believes in her, but he frightens her now. He is not the man she once loved. He will never be that man again. Even if he were here, how could she ever trust him? Yet he had been her dearest friend.

When the grief settles at last, she turns on her side and falls asleep. Outside the rain continues. The waxing autumn moon is hidden by clouds. Night animals with their pouches and bounding legs, their brown and golden fur, hide in burrows and shelter beneath ferns and trees. Birds sit mute upon branches observing the night world. Spiders rest within curled leaves and insects seek the protection of bark. The mountain is alive with water slipping between rocks, splashing on fronds, sliding down the stems of grasses, sinking into soil, peat and moss. Harder and harder comes the rain. The flagstones in the courtyard are washed clean. The rainwater barrels fill and overflow. The chickens roost deep in their straw. The house sleeps. Strange dreams chase Caroline until morning.

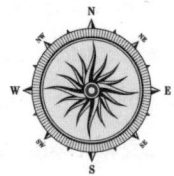

Chère Tante Henriette,

*Our neighbours across the hill, the Walkers, came to visit.
He is Mr Washington Walker and is strikingly handsome,
although most earnest. He is the brother of a woman I met on
the ship whose husband died on the journey. His wife, Mrs
Julia Walker, is warm-hearted and has made us most welcome.
Last night, they visited on the dark moon, and Mrs Swanston
brought her three youngest sons who are my new pupils. We all
sat in the garden well wrapped in blankets, for the evening was
cool. Mr Walker gave us a lesson on the stars of the Southern
Hemisphere which we all found most engaging.*

*I find it strange to imagine that you do not see these same stars
but look into another sky, with other constellations. Or at least I
hope you do. We have no North Star but neither is there a South
Star. The Milky Way is no small tail as it is above London, but
a river of stars midstream, rising from behind the mountain all
the way across the river to the horizon. But such a description is*

insufficient to capture the immensity of the skies here. I am trying to familiarise myself with this multitude of celestial dimensions, of dark portals and illuminated passages that suggest unimaginable distances. I find myself in those moments feeling utterly inconsequential, grateful to be salvaged by this good earth.

Mr Walker talked of the ancient occultists and their belief that all of life was about becoming. Tiny grains of rock and the particles of earth, they are all in the process of becoming human, while we humans, almost in reverse, are in the process of becoming planets. When one considers the time that these stars may have been shining on their infinite stage, perhaps it may yet be true. The dust I will become after my death may yet become stardust, and the earth that grows cabbages and potatoes will, in a way, become human, for do we not eat what transforms from seed into plant? How much he reminded me of Papa in that moment.

Like Papa, Mr Walker is fond of the Greek mystics and explained to the boys the words of Aristotle: 'Yonder, therefore above the stellar virtues, stand other heavens to be attained.'

Julia Walker spoke of how such men also believed the Milky Way contained the seeds of our souls and every human soul descended through one of the twelve doorways of the zodiac. This caused much animation in the boys, who wanted to claim the ram, the lion or the bull, but I reminded them that if they were to look to the ancients for power, it was the female figure of Isis who was said to transmit intelligence. It recalled for me an evening in London, with you and Mama and Papa wrestling over some notion, and it pressed upon me, the absence of you all.

The Walkers speak of establishing a Quaker school where children might benefit from a gentler, more expansive education. At the government school nearby, an education is considered the

ability to recite a Psalm, construct a short sentence or calculate
three numbers. I worry what will become of children offered such
rough knowledge.

The Swanston boys are the twins Nowell and Robert, who are
twelve, and their younger brother George, aged ten. They attend
school each morning because their parents insist they must learn
to engage as young gentlemen with all manner of people. In the
afternoons, along with my ward, Quill, they are under my care
and endure my curriculum. When they see no point in speaking
French I sing to them. Later I hear them in their garden as I walk
home across the paddock . . .

'Et le cou, et le cou,

Et la tête, et la tête

Et les yeux, et les yeux,

Et le bec, et le bec,

Alouette, Alouette!

Ah! ah! ah! ah!'

Do you remember teaching it to me? They also like to hear
me tell stories from the Revolution. I have taught them 'La
Marseillaise'. I know it may be considered scandalous in this
British outpost, but I am expanding their minds. Liberty, equality,
fraternity remain noble sentiments when not accompanied by
violence, I remind them. Of course, I say nothing of our family.

Quill and I are reading Robinson Crusoe *and he is excited by*
it. He is also learning vocabulary. A sailing ship is un voilier,
and butterflies fluttering around the verandah are les papillons.
Birds in the trees are les oiseaux. *Darting across the wall are* les
petits lézards.

The other morning he presented me with a clutch of late lilies
and in a near perfect accent said, 'Regarde, Tante Caroline,

des fleurs du jardin pour toi.' *I was so excited we breakfasted in French.*

Last week, although it is only autumn, there was a snowfall on the mountain. A bitter wind growled down the slopes behind the house worrying every door and window. Within a day of the snowfall, it was all blue sky and sunshine again, and snow melt filled the creek by the cottage. Today flurries of rain rattle against the windows. The fields and paths are wet and muddied and the river has disappeared behind a gauze of mist. I cannot see even the other side of the valley, and still it rains. But there is a warm fire burning and I can smell the bread Bessie is baking. She is no natural cook but is willing to learn. She is also unlettered so we are beginning with recipes.

We have been gifted a kitten from the Walkers. A completely black one that is settled on my lap as I write. Quill has named her Malachy and she is to become our resident mouser, although at the moment she gives no indication of any skill but affection.

What I have not mentioned until this moment, for I can hear you cautioning me against garnishing the past, is that a vineyard lies in disrepair beyond the cottage. It once produced a very good champagne, or so I have been told on excellent authority by several who remember it. Perhaps some things, like stars and rain, have an ability to stir things ancient within us. Forgive my wistful soul.

I hope you are well, dear aunt. With great affection and fervent wishes for the day when we will see one another again.

Your niece,

Caroline

She does not dare to send this letter either.

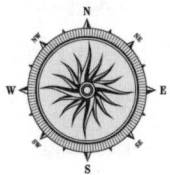

Caroline's early walk becomes a ritual. Often the dawns are calm, the river breathless and silken, so wide it might easily be mistaken for the sea. Beginning in the distant highlands, it is now saltwater, the ocean close. Along the river's edge, she sees trees bent in the wind, their trunks twisted, yet still their branches grow. She sees clouds reflected in rockpools. Crabs nestle and periwinkles cling to crevices as the water laps. Great banks of brown and green sea grasses wash ashore after rough weather. At low tide, she levers oysters as big as her hand off the rocks, taking them home in her basket to shuck them with Quill and Bessie. They eat them raw for breakfast or cooked in a simple cream sauce with a bread topping for supper.

She discovers a grove of rough-barked oak. Instead of leaves, long fine needles hang from the branches, each encircled with pale amber rings, the ground covered in a thick carpet where they have fallen. When the wind passes through the grove, it sighs.

At the heart of the copse she finds a single enormous tree. Its lower branches are barren and grey, and it would be easy to assume the tree is dead but, looking up, Caroline sees a profusion of hard brown geometric nuts on every twig and branch. All the trees about this one have formed a grand circle. They are her descendants, this tree a great-grandmother with her children and grandchildren living close. A matriarch wizened by time, stiff in her branches, slow in her movements, protected from wind and still living in their midst, her life's work about her.

Caroline takes Quill to show him.

'Look,' he says, and lies down in a hollow of soft needles. It is the perfect size for his body.

Now Caroline observes other hollows and sees the impressions other bodies have made. She finds a fire circle almost covered over. She lies down in the hollow beside Quill, feeling the shape of the body that had lain here before her. A hip, a shoulder, a person of her size. Quill passes her one of the dark shards of stone scattered on the ground. It fits into her palm and she curves her fingers around it, her thumb fitting a groove for purchase.

'Look,' she says. 'I think it is a knife. See the edge? It is a blade for cutting away furred skin or carving meat from the bone. Levering an oyster from its shell.'

'Who made it?' asks Quill.

'The people who were here before us.'

'Why didn't they use knives?' Quill asks.

'Because they lived in another time,' she says. 'If we had come forty years ago, even ten years ago, we might have seen them.'

Quill is thoughtful, looking up into the trees. 'Where are they now?'

'Gone. Killed.'

'But why?'

'For this island. For their land. They might have welcomed you,' she says, 'for you are yet to be formed. But not the rest of us. We are strange people come to a place that is not our home.'

'Except it is,' he whispers. 'This is our home now. We do not have another.'

Caroline recalls London with its fog and mist, rain and mildew, its crowded streets and the pervasive smells of seepage, garbage and sewage. An old city mouldering beneath a downcast sky. Here was a radiant new world with high blue skies and fresh winds, momentous clouds and sunshine. This is where I will live out my days, she thinks. It feels a remarkable declaration.

'Forgive us,' she says, as she places the flint back on the oak needles.

'Who must forgive us?' Quill asks.

'The past,' she says. 'And the future.'

Some mornings she follows paths and wallaby tracks up onto the mountain and finds creeks and waterfalls, pools of sunlight and boulders covered in lichen, trees with their roots wrapped around rocks and others balancing on the edges of cliffs. She sees a golden echidna bury its head in an embankment when it senses her nearby.

On a ridge, she looks down into a quarry where convicts are at work in yellow suits marked with arrows. Their legs are chained and their bodies are bowed by the weight of rocks they push in carts. The overseer applies a whip to an older man he believes is working too slowly. The other prisoners continue on, disregarding the punishment for the ordinariness of it.

In the schoolroom at the Swanstons' Quill rarely volunteers an answer to her questions, but when Caroline passes behind him at his desk he is steadily reflecting on a myth, pursuing a mathematical solution or drawing a picture with a minimalism of line that reveals something of life. They have a new ritual as they sit by the fire after supper.

'The sun was a stripe across the bed when I awoke,' she says, by way of a beginning.

'There were two flies on the door of the outhouse. Black with inner wings of something paler,' he says.

'I saw two blue dragonflies doing loops, round and round over the pond,' says Caroline.

'There are so many different ones,' says Quill, giving her a brief smile and stretching out his toes, which do not quite touch the floor when he sits in the leather armchair. 'Four came up on the dice more than three, when George and I were playing. But with Robert it was a day of sixes.'

'On my morning walk,' says Caroline, 'I saw a pine cone rolling in the pull and give of the tide. And there were ladybirds resting on a line of foam.'

'The sky was the colour of a bruise this afternoon,' he says.

'Yes,' she says. 'I think rain is coming.'

'I visited the big tree,' says Quill.

'And how was it today?'

'Friendly,' says Quill.

'I visited it, too,' says Caroline. 'It does feel friendly. My father would say there is one life that pulsates in all things. He would talk about a man called Spinoza, a philosopher, who thought that our minds were nodes of infinite thought and this allowed us to rise above the senses in a sort of God state. But my father thought that our minds were at their finest when they were in tune with our senses. For him, life was about the sense of connection with all things—plants in particular. And if that were true, then we would all be familiar to one another, I guess.'

'Friends everywhere,' says Quill.

Caroline notes the colour in Quill's cheeks and realises the boy is filling out. He is still lean but he appears more substantial. His hair is now over his ears, the chestnut shine a pleasing contrast with his striking amber eyes. He is taller, too, and she resolves to place a ruler on his head and mark the wall with a pencil, to keep track of all this growing.

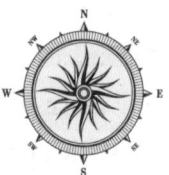

The Swanstons' front door opens onto a spacious vestibule hung with Chinese paintings. The morning room looks out upon a fountain fed from the creek. There are low sculptured hedges and circular rose gardens, trellises of jasmine and beds of geraniums. All the downstairs living rooms have French doors that open onto the surrounding sandstone patios. Cedar lines the walls and the shelves of the library which adjoins Captain Swanston's office. Every room has a marble fireplace and several rooms have carved doors of lacquered rosewood. Alcoves hold bronze statues of dancing Indian deities, and there are tapestries of Indian myths.

At the western end of the house, a conservatory has been created to catch the afternoon sun. Wicker furniture with soft, plump cushions and a glass-topped table make a sitting room amidst citrus trees heavy with fruit. There are several types of lemon, a cumquat and a lime, and the air is sweet with zest. Mrs Swanston is keen to point out the pots of pink and white orchids from China and tomatoes from South America ripe with red and yellow fruit climbing towards the glass roof.

Caroline, too, could build a glass room on the western side of her cottage in which to grow seedlings and frost-intolerant plants. But then she reminds herself that she is, to anyone with an interest, a tenant and nothing more. She must go slowly, quietly, as is proper for a widow, and wait to gain a better measure of the place.

She presents Mrs Swanston with a gift of a cordial she has made from lemons she had been gifted by the Walkers.

'How delightful,' says Mrs Swanston. 'I love lemon in everything. If you need more, please have one of the maids pick them here for you. Now tell me, are you settling in? It did take me a while.'

'Yes,' says Caroline. 'Thank you. We are settled, and very grateful for the furniture you so generously offered.'

'I am pleased it is being used,' Mrs Swanston says. 'My husband threatens to hold an auction whenever I fall in love with something new.'

As the tea is being poured, Caroline asks about the smoke signal she had seen on her early walk.

'Across the river?' Mrs Swanston asks. 'That will be a communiqué with Port Arthur. Perhaps there is an escaped convict or some request for supplies. More rum for the soldiers, perhaps.' She gives a slight roll of her eyes.

'You have visited the prison?' Caroline asks.

'I have not, but my husband has made the excursion on two occasions. He tells me that men work as beasts and are treated little better. Perhaps worse, for no horses or bullocks are allowed onto the peninsula. In fact, there is a railway where the convicts are forced to pull the carriages for visitors. I try not to imagine it. I know none of us would be here if it were not for England's felons, so I must be grateful, but I doubt anyone there feels the same.'

Caroline nods.

'I have read that some of the prisoners have only intractable opinions. Chartists, for one. And there are Canadians who revolted. Some of the Irish leaders, too.' Mrs Swanston colours and stops. 'But of course it is not my place to judge the law. Still, how will the world ever move forward if it is a criminal offence to have an opinion?'

She looks so young, Caroline thinks, and yet she must be in her forties, with all these children: two sons establishing a sheep farm at Port Phillip Bay, the eldest in London studying, and her two daughters now both married.

Caroline's attention is diverted by the sight of Nowell and Robert, the Swanston twins, fleeing down a ladder from an elaborate treehouse in the garden. They are being pursued by their younger brother, George, uttering a bloodcurdling cry, while Quill jumps from branch to branch until he lands perfectly on the ground, rolling, then rounding on the larger boys with a sword in the form of a stick, pinning them to the tree while George attempts to tie them to the trunk.

'Your Quill is remarkably agile,' says Mrs Swanston.

'The months we were at sea,' says Caroline. 'I could barely keep him out of the rigging. The crew did encourage him.'

'Perhaps he has a career ahead in the navy.'

George is marching back and forth giving the prisoners some kind of instruction, while Quill has climbed back up the tree to hoist a large piece of sacking marked with a skull and crossbones.

'Or as a pirate,' Caroline says.

They both smile, then Mrs Swanston says, 'Mrs Douglas, I hope you will understand me when I say that I want my boys to seek out their own opinions. I would be happy for you to join me in that quest, if you are willing. Perhaps that is too much to ask until we know one another better. But when you are the fourth, fifth and sixth son, I believe it is essential.'

She pauses for a moment. 'It matters a great deal to my husband and myself that when our boys arrive in London to further their education, they are equipped with the skills to forge their own way, and to hold their own in any company.'

Caroline had seen Mrs Swanston at St David's Church each Sunday, her boys accompanying her. Caroline had chosen the Anglican church for just this reason. Perhaps, unlike Caroline, Mrs Swanston went because she was devout. Or she might be fond of the teachings with which Caroline largely agreed. To love one another. To do unto others as one would have them do unto you. These seemed useful tenets for a peaceful society. It was not evident that the British government instilled such morality, but the Church was intrinsic to Her Majesty's reign and, in this outpost, not to appear each Sunday in the Church of England was to set oneself apart from a certain section of society, and to lose touch with one's neighbours.

In Mrs Swanston's case, it also gave her an opportunity to speak with clients and colleagues of her husband. Captain Swanston was a much less frequent observer of the Sabbath, being often away on business, as she had heard Mrs Swanston say to other parishioners on several occasions.

'I have a confession, Mrs Douglas,' Mrs Swanston says, 'and I hope you will not be offended. I have listened, from time to time, as you have given your lessons—with my ear at the door like a regular eavesdropper. I do hope you will forgive me. This colony is a colourful place. Few people are entirely as they seem, but please know that what I have heard has reassured me.'

'You are always welcome to join us in the classroom, Mrs Swanston.'

'Thank you, but that is not my point. The boys heed you. Even dear Robert, who has been in trouble again at school for failing.'

'I would not say Robert is not keen to learn,' Caroline says. 'As you know, he finds reading difficult and fears to make a mistake.'

'I think his small hands have been the subject of harsh punishment at the school, a discipline I would never administer,' says Mrs Swanston. 'Although I do love the way that he writes. Nothing spelled correctly, but he writes the way a thing sounds.'

'And what he is expressing is often quite wonderful,' says Caroline.

'Perhaps Robert *is* born to be a shepherd,' says Mrs Swanston. 'It's almost impossible to get him to school on a clear morning, or a wet one. It makes no difference.'

'He benefits from the outdoor lessons. Thank you for agreeing to those. His study of birds is coming along with an accuracy he cannot bring to arithmetic.'

'Boys do seem to need to move,' Mrs Swanston says. Her face has relaxed and her eyebrows are dancing. 'And the autumn weather has been lovely. The light is so beautiful.' And then she sighs and adds, 'We are far from the industries of England here, but the industrialists will come. My sons cannot all be the gentlemen farmers of Melbourne that my husband imagines.'

'Well, I assure you they will have all I can impart, Mrs Swanston,' says Caroline.

'I guess this is the luck of the youngest,' Mrs Swanston replies. 'I tried all the rules and strictures on the older ones, but they grow into themselves regardless. Now, is there anything you need? How is the cottage? Do you have a piano?'

'No, but I have loved hearing you play,' says Caroline. 'Mozart and Bach drifting through the house while I am with the boys.'

'Yes,' says Mrs Swanston. 'They are great favourites of mine. Do you play yourself?'

'We both had lessons, my sister and I, but she had the affinity for it.'

'You must play here.'

'I think it might be best for everyone that I did not,' Caroline says.

Mrs Swanston laughs. 'I heard you have been most industrious in your kitchen garden . . .'

Caroline observes her.

'Oh, I do apologise. I spoke with Bessie, but only to assure myself that she is well, and it is clear to me that she is.'

'I understand,' says Caroline. Bessie returned to her room at the Swanstons' at the end of each day, as part of convict regulations, a report on life at the cottage might well be requested. Perhaps in time, when her sentence was done, that arrangement can be changed.

'Please know that I consider it the worst of life here, the gossip,' Mrs Swanston continues. 'I assure you I admonish it in my servants, my children and my friends. The girl has been of concern to me, as you know. And of course we do live in this small valley, in this very small township. And people do love to find something to say about one another.'

'Mrs Swanston,' Caroline says, 'my father taught me that discretion was one of the noble sentiments. You may be confident that I will exercise it here with your boys in my role as tutor. And with anything else you care to share with me.'

'Thank you, Mrs Douglas. And I extend to you the same assurance. But may I call you Caroline? It is the name of both my sister and one of my daughters, and these formalities feel onerous when we must live in such daily proximity, don't you feel? In return, I insist on you calling me Georgiana.'

Caroline is surprised by this kindness. 'Oh, thank you, Mrs Swanston. Georgiana. And please, yes, call me Caroline,' she says.

'Well, then,' says Georgiana, 'that was all a little awkward, wasn't it? But here we are. No damage done. Now tell me, how is it you are fluent in French?'

'Well . . .' says Caroline, and pauses. 'My grandparents were French. We always spoke both French and English at home.'

'And your father, what were his interests?' asks Georgiana.

'He was a man who loved science, history and philosophy, and he taught me to love such things, too.'

'And he is no longer . . . ?'

'No. Nor my mother or sister. Each from an illness within the space of two years.'

'I am so very sorry,' says Georgiana.

'As am I,' says Caroline.

'And Quill's parents?'

'He is the son of my father's cousin. Orphaned.' And she is grateful when, at that moment, two maids arrive bearing trays of cake and lemon cordial followed by a pirate gang called in from the garden.

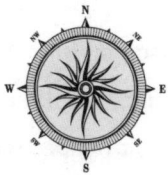

In London Caroline had lived with the death of all that had previously been hers. Truthfulness had been whipped out of her like a tooth pulled by string and a sharply shut door.

She had taken her mother's maiden name. 'I had not expected to become a governess, of course,' she had told her prospective employer. 'But with both my parents now gone, and our affairs not as they had seemed, I find I am in need of employment. Perhaps at least my education will prove useful.'

She became a governess to ten-year-old twin sisters seemingly born to lives of vanity and indifference. They required little of her intellect but much of her patience. She had a small bedroom below stairs with a wooden dresser, a narrow bed and a window that looked onto a basement wall. She wore dresses of grey wool or poplin. She wanted to be as invisible as light when fog swallowed it whole. This was what her dreams had come to. This was what her father had done.

She missed the apothecary acutely. The quiet satisfaction she had found amongst the glass cabinets with their tins and jars, ointments and salves, herbs and tinctures. She missed their housekeeper, Esther, at home in the kitchen with pea and ham soup at the ready. It was all gone.

She could hear her mother saying, 'You are young, but one day you will want a family of your own. It could cause more harm than good, all this learning. Do not expect men to like it. Not everyone has the temperament of your father, Caroline. Far from it.'

And yet it was not the education her father insisted on that had caused her predicament.

The brother of her employer had arrived from Amsterdam to stay a few days in the house. He was young and handsome with his hair worn long and his frock coats embroidered.

'I came to visit my nieces,' he said, entering the schoolroom, 'but I hardly expected to find such a vision of loveliness.'

Caroline had blushed. She had not been without admirers over the years, but none had quite awakened her in the way this young man did with his confidence and wit. He sat with her and the girls on several mornings, enquiring into their lessons, wishing to see their work and to know Caroline's plans for their ongoing education. He had spoken to her in French and said that her accent was perfectly Parisian. How lucky his nieces were to have such an accomplished governess!

One morning, after she had set the girls to work on their compositions, he asked her to walk him to the door. She did, and was startled to feel him push her ahead of him. He drew her across the hallway and into an empty guest room. She had thought it a game. Then, with his mouth pressed on hers, he began pulling at her skirts. She had tried to push him away but he was much too strong. He pinned her hands above her. She wanted to scream, but she couldn't pull away. His lips, his tongue, his body were all forcing her against the wall.

Still she resisted, but he was lifting her skirts, reaching between her legs, pushing his hand into her most private parts. Hurting her. When he pulled back to undo the buttons of his fly, she swung away from him, biting the arm fixing her to the wall. She felt his flesh give and he wrenched away, slapping her face hard. The force knocked her to the floor. But it gave her a moment and somehow she got away from him, desperately flinging open the door.

She ran down the hallway, descending to her room and locking it behind her. She had cried. Perhaps this behaviour was normal for girls in service. Had she encouraged him? She didn't know. She had thought him wonderful. Now she was embarrassed and appalled by her naivety.

After some minutes, she washed her face, the slap still smarting on her cheek. She smoothed her clothes and hair. After composing herself, she returned to the schoolroom, her heart galloping, but he was nowhere to be seen. That night she hardly slept for fear of him.

The following day, she and the girls were breakfasting in the morning room when he arrived to farewell them. He rolled their curls in his fingers and kissed their cheeks until they giggled. Caroline's skin crawled. Then, as he was taking his leave, he came to her.

'I do look forward to the next time, Mademoiselle Caroline. Meanwhile I have this to remember you by.'

He indicated a bandage beneath the lace of his sleeve.

'J'espère que cela laissera une cicatrice,' she said.

He bowed and was gone.

'I think he likes you,' said one of the girls, and her sister giggled.

Had this happened to Augusta? Or Tante Henriette? Surely Tante Henriette would never have let such a thing happen. But Augusta had been so young and would have been easily overpowered. Caroline wanted to rage then at her father for stealing their lives. She missed her mother acutely. She mourned Augusta. Tante Henriette was in Europe for the summer. She had no one to confide in. The cook in the house was irritable and the housekeeper was certain to report any story to the mistress, which would no doubt result in Caroline's employment being terminated. It had taken more than a little artifice to secure this work. She could not give notice and expect a reference without some plausible excuse. How had she let this happen? How had her life come to this? She mentioned the incident to no one.

And then Tante Henriette came home.

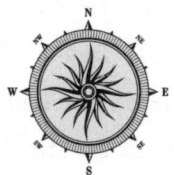

'We are leaving for the tropics,' Caroline said to the saleswoman with a large bust and pince-nez. Caroline was looking and sounding like a young man in a winter frock coat and lace cravat. Did she know, when she engaged the woman at her aunt's suggestion, what she was making possible?

'Tell me, what is your recommendation to offset the perils of damp on a long voyage?' she asked. 'My uncle and I know little of such things and of course the servants will make good. But to line the trunks? Do you recommend straw or wool?'

Meanwhile, Tante Henriette, in the attire of a French gentleman, perused the cutlery, the little silver salt cellars. She picked up a cigar box then touched a silver napkin ring, set in a box with eleven companions patterned with shamrock. Was Caroline surprised when the French gentleman arrived at the counter with a list of items he wanted boxed up? The standing lamp, that Persian carpet there, and the silver pitcher and bowl because he could not take one and not the other. And those whisky glasses. Yes. *Parfait.*

Then the French gentleman placed a card on the counter and the woman regarded it, and then she regarded him. 'Of course, your lordship.'

A negotiation began which Caroline observed with interest. Tante Henriette was skilled and ruthless but the woman was wily. A price was at last agreed.

'I will send a manservant to complete the purchases on Friday. I trust it will all be readied.'

'Of course, sir, I will see to it myself,' said the woman.

They laughed as they made their way along Broad Street. Manly laughter, but Caroline felt the delicious rush of duplicity.

'You are a natural at this,' said her aunt.

'This?' Caroline asked.

Tante Henriette laughed again, a rich deep laugh.

Tante Henriette guided them to a laneway behind her apartment and stopped at a weathered stable door. She produced a large key. The room they entered had riding tack hanging on the wall and two stalls filled with hay, but there were no horses nor a carriage. Instead, there were several trunks and wooden boxes stacked neatly to one side. Tante Henriette unlocked an interior door. Inside, she lit a lamp to reveal a room lined with empty shelves still bearing the prices from a haberdashery: *1 shilling, 2 shillings, £1, £2, buttons 3 for a 1p.* The front door and windows were obscured by heavy drapes. In the centre of the room stood a long table once used for the rolling out and cutting of fabric. Now, a long length of white muslin was draped over it.

When Tante Henriette drew back the muslin, she revealed silver teapots, silver ink pots and toothpick boxes, embossed cutlery, carving ware and beautiful silver cigar boxes. There were also gold snuffboxes, a gold pocket watch and several gold rings. Necklaces set with pearls and precious stones lay in velvet boxes. There were two Wedgwood tea sets. There were rolls of fabric.

Tante Henriette smiled. She made a handsome man. She opened her leather satchel to reveal two silver salt cellars that Caroline had seen on display earlier that afternoon at the first shop they had visited. She also produced a gold brooch fashioned into a ladybird, its body studded with rubies. These new items were nestled within the display.

'It is always something to let them go, to pass them on for a good price,' she sighed. 'But tonight all this will be gone.'

Her aunt had stolen all this? Caroline felt a flutter in her chest. The wigs and disguises—this was what dressing up was about? A subterfuge for theft? How had she not suspected?

'Are you not frightened?' she asked.

'What I fear, dear niece, is poverty.'

Caroline remembered her mother's face when another gift arrived from Tante Henriette for Augusta or herself. She thought of the specimen case of spiders for her sixteenth birthday. The bolts of fabric brought to her father's shop. She had thought her aunt an opportunist, a woman with a clever eye for beauty and style, eager to benefit from a bargain. She had not imagined this.

'If my father, your grandfather, had not been such an altruist,' said Tante Henriette, 'how different our lives might have been. But revolutions change destinies, dear Caroline. I have found a way to make some small restoration. If you wish to join me, I will teach you. Have I been correct? Does it excite you?'

Caroline felt a chill travel across her skin.

'One must have people who can procure, fetch, carry and disperse,' says Henriette. 'People who can make documents, cards, and forge currency. It is an enterprise I have been building for many years, and it has been very successful.'

Caroline contemplated. 'How does it work?'

'A most unassuming manservant will collect the items I put aside today,' her aunt said. 'He will present the same card I left with the assistant and the requisite payment. Counterfeit, you understand. But almost indiscernible, even to the most well-trained eye. He will disperse those items, and most of what you see here, to colleagues in Liverpool, Manchester and Edinburgh. Some of it will go to Paris and further afield to other merchants. It is a web and I am the little spider at its centre.

'And of course my employment as a lady's companion continues to afford me entry into many homes,' Henriette continued. 'That was how it all began. There is an art to looking like a merry, wandering guest. My position has allowed me time to map the rooms of a house, observe servants, to learn the names one might utter at just the right moment if one is discovered. In such homes there are always things of beauty and extravagance. Of course it cannot happen then. I made that mistake early and I have never repeated it. There must be a later incursion, planned and orchestrated. I have people who keep watch and observe patterns, the comings and goings of a house's occupants, the habits of servants, the schedule for regular deliveries. Such information becomes very valuable.'

Her aunt regarded her. 'Dear Caroline, all you had, and all you had hoped for, has been lost. Your dear mother is gone and your father has committed an unspeakable crime. He is as good as dead, though I know you do not want to believe it. But I will not desert you. True independence is hard won for a woman, but this is how I am achieving it.'

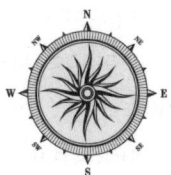

Tante Henriette moved away from the trestle table and pulled back a curtain to reveal a hidden doorway. Beyond it a narrow stairway led upwards to another door that opened into her apartment.

'I searched for some time to find such a situation, the shop and stables below, the apartment above,' Tante Henriette says. 'One must plan ahead. There must be more than one avenue of escape.'

Caroline considered anew the contents of the apartment with its furnishings, books and ornaments.

Tante Henriette went to a drawer and withdrew a pocketbook to show Caroline. The balance was a spectacular sum.

'A woman cannot open a bank account,' she said, 'but as you know, being a man is not unpleasant. If you prove a good partner, we will open one for you.

'But you must think about it,' her aunt counselled, as she undid the pin of the cravat at her throat. 'You must be able to sleep at night. You must be able to laugh. If you decide it is not for you, then you must say so. Do not feel obligated. If the idea intrigues you, even thrills you, then you will become my apprentice. Your dear mother, of course, would be gravely disappointed. You may have to wrestle with that.'

'Do you not feel guilty?'

Her aunt, who was now peeling off the beard and moustache she had been wearing, smiled.

'I will offer you twenty per cent of the profits while I am training you,' said Tante Henriette. 'After that, we shall see. Of course, you must keep your role of governess, as I keep my role of companion. A necessary artifice to remain invisible. But ensure you leave your current employment. You are looking far too thin. It clearly does not suit you. Find a family that needs you only for morning or afternoon lessons so that, should you choose, you are free to pursue your other interests.'

Caroline stood on the wall of the Thames, staring into its opaque depths, and weighed Tante Henriette's words. She thought of the faraway places her father had spoken about. How two hundred sparrows had eaten from his hand on a balcony in Venice. He had seen shrines set into the cliffs of the Amalfi Coast and striped dolphins filling the Gulf of Corinth.

If she remained a governess, she would have her meagre wages and a small trunk with a few possessions. She would move from house to house as children grew and flew, while she remained a winged but stunted thing, encumbered with failed promises, wary of the world. Or she could become something entirely unexpected. It was too dangerous, surely. Yet Tante Henriette was obviously very successful. She had amassed enough to relocate to America, to France, to anywhere in the world.

'Thirty per cent,' Caroline countered, when her aunt opened the door to her apartment. She had not worked for years in the apothecary and learned nothing.

'I see,' said her aunt, ushering her inside. 'Let us settle on twenty-five.'

And so it began.

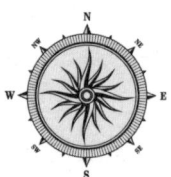

It is first light and the birds of the forest are beginning to rouse. Caroline throws back the covers and is out of the cottage in nightgown and cloak. She breathes in forest and salt air. She thinks of her father holding the bark of cinnamon verum to her nose and telling her it was the scent of Ceylon. But this is the scent of here. The mint tang of eucalypts and the freshness of mountain air.

She wonders if there is more to birdsong than simply to herald the day. Are there announcements when certain delicious beetles emerge from months of underground slumber on the mountain slopes, or flies muster over a pond? She suspects there are stories in those calls, if only she knew the language. She has begun to identify the different species by their pattern of flight and their particular calls. Currawong, wattlebird, cockatoo, magpie, rosella, robin, parrot, honeyeater, the large forest raven and the oystercatchers that walk the shore.

She treads softly between the bushes that surround the pond behind the cottage and peers through the reeds. The frogs have abandoned their nocturnal melodies and she can see no evidence of them. No small wet bodies, bright eyes or throats moving. She removes her cloak, slips off her clogs and steps into the water. Mud pushes up between her toes. The water is so cold it almost stings.

She imagines Captain Swanston raising an eyebrow. For all his industry, his charming wife and elegant home, he is a reminder, the bank manager, that she must fit in, observe and comply. There must be no stories that reflect anything other than her modesty and propriety. He is someone she must not surprise. He has the ear of the Governor. Not that he wasn't doing his best to oust the man and his wife.

The previous governor, Georgiana had informed her, distrusted and disliked self-made men. 'This new governor is similarly deter-mined to ensure the island retains its fearsome reputation. My husband has worked hard to avail himself of the many opportunities Van Diemen's Land offers, but his initiatives are often met with obtuseness and invidiousness from Government House down . . .'

The water is up to Caroline's knees now. The chill of it grips her and she almost panics. The morning is so still it is as if breeze has yet to be invented. The trees wait. A few stars remain. When they had lived in Edinburgh, she had yearned to be outdoors, even on the wildest days, loath to wear shoes, loath to submit to the tedium of the Sunday service. Her mother had been exasperated each time she threw off a clean pinafore or loosened the rags in her hair.

'You're a wild thing,' she'd say. 'You've got the Highlands in your bones.'

Caroline drags the nightdress over her head, tossing it back onto the bank, where it hangs awkwardly across reeds. She moves deeper into the pond, feeling the soft sediment between her toes. She gasps, pauses, and then lowers herself in, the water over her belly, rising up under her breasts, over her breasts, now up to her neck. She submerges then surfaces quickly, brushing the water from her face. It has been years since she was a girl swimming in a Scottish loch. The water tastes sweet in her mouth.

How would it be to sleep in the forest? Not the cock crow to start a day, but a wild bird call. Eating wallaby, bird and fish trapped and caught by her. To cook not on a kitchen fire, but in a forest clearing. Her bare feet running on the soft litter of leaves, standing under a waterfall on the mountain slopes, wrapping herself in furs.

She kicks and then she is paddling, arms and legs moving, her body deliciously weightless. She rolls over and floats on her back. Perhaps the gods of earth, sea and sky, the old gods of Troy and Atlantis, Babylonia and Egypt, had been sent here to continue their existence, to go on undisturbed by the presence of the new churches with their saints, seers, prophets, martyrs and zealots that followed through the centuries.

Was this place at the end of the world the very birthplace of deities? The genesis of the original angels of earth and sky before they were dressed in robes and adorned with haloes, snakes, crowns or swords? Perhaps here I could make my own god, she thinks. For what can Homer's gods or Shakespeare's woodland sprites or Milton's angels offer her amidst this unintimidated wild?

Maybe a goddess would be more fitting. But if she chose a goddess, what goddess might it be? An Athena of sorts, a huntress mother. A goddess for the forests, the grasses and wetlands. An Aphrodite? But what does she know of sensual love? Only that imparted in poetic myths and grand ballads. The tender way her father held her mother, his hands resting on her hips as he kissed her full on the lips. Yet Aphrodite is not only sensuality; she is a carrier of prayers, a bestower of gifts, the goddess of sea, earth and sky, of the morning and evening star.

Was there some goddess of the lonely, the broken-hearted? A goddess for the mistakes of the past? A goddess who listened to all remorse and sin and rage, and held all these as tenderly as a mother might hold a dying child? A goddess who forgave, though not in the Catholic way where sin came with life; no Catholic Mary in all her elusive goodness and purity. Not a goddess who encouraged the faithful to judge, to subjugate, to punish and blame, to curse and torture one another. People who might once have put Caroline to the stake and burned her alive, just for being her own kind of woman.

Caroline wanted a goddess who knew there was, at heart, an innocence that yearned to be reclaimed by all who had walked into their own being, and found there a dark and uncontainable power. Maybe she needed a bronze-skinned goddess tattooed with intricate patterns. Like the noblewomen who undressed within the private rooms of the apothecary, removing their finery to reveal the pale skin of their bodies adorned with flowers, birds, faces, animals, poems, symbols, religious icons and biblical images.

'Is it not painful?' she had asked one such lady, whose liveried coachman waited outside with a carriage and six black horses. 'To have such things done to the skin?' For the woman was a living painting from her shoulders to her toes.

'This is how I claim myself,' the woman had replied.

If one needed coins to cross the Styx, what was required for passage beyond the land of the dead to a place of reinvention? A service of some kind? What might be enough for a goddess? Was it the care of Quill until he was grown to a man? Tante Henriette had offered her an occupation. Was this new life so different? Was it a sort of restitution, whatever it was she was striving for here?

Caroline had been reckless taking on the boy, and now she and he were cast into a life neither had imagined. He had told her that his favourite place to sleep on the ship was in the manger where the goats lived, where the cows were tethered and the chooks roosted.

She remembered her father telling her how the Hindoos accepted that life was enormous and perplexing. If a person could be at peace with that, then one need not be consumed with the confusion that comes with trying to understand the workings of it. One simply chose a moral code to live by, that brought each day its rituals and rewards; that was enough for anyone. She smiles. I am beginning to understand now, Papa, she thinks.

And then a dog barks and she knows someone is up. Soon there will be people about, a kettle to fill, her nightdress to dry on the line, the walk with Quill to school, the garden to tend, a lesson to prepare. Then the afternoon will be upon her and the Swanston boys and Quill will be frowning over verb conjugations and ancient history. Knowledge on paper, words and language, it would all burn and blow away in time. But this world, this place of mountain, hills, water, reflections, this will abide.

Her feet slide in the mud as she pulls herself onto the pond's edge. She dries herself quickly with her nightdress and wraps the cloak about her. The sky is magenta now, with a stripe of gold, an ecclesiastical sky in this pagan world. She walks to the old vineyard on her way back to the cottage and pushes against the wooden gate, squeezing through to confront the craze of vines clothed in the last of their gold and russet leaves woven through with weeds.

She squats and searches in the grasses for the gnarled trunk of a vine, finding its rough texture, feeling its sure footing in the soil, and remembering a poem she spoke to the plants in the glasshouse in London.

. . . *celestial Light,*
Shine inward, and the mind through all her powers
Irradiate, there plant eyes, all mist from thence
Purge and disperse, that I may see and tell
Of things invisible to mortal sight.

Oh, Papa, she thinks. Is it madness to contemplate such a dream?

· 2 ·

Jacques-Louis

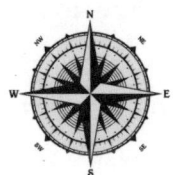

Jacques-Louis is at the Observatoire in Paris with his father, the only boy amongst the scientists, writers and *philosophes* gathered together to watch the moon through an enormous glass. He smells cigar smoke and touches the lace at the edges of his sleeves. He watches the moon consumed by the earth's shadow. But instead of the utter blackness he has anticipated, the moon begins to glow the dusky red of a Tuscan lamp, colouring walls and seeping into faces and furniture.

How is such a thing possible? How can colour disappear as if it were a contrivance? The green of trees and plants, the blue of his new frock coat, the white lace, were they all disdained by the moon? He had taken the moon entirely for granted, a fruit that was constantly ripening, blooming and then diminishing. The poem his father had him learn only a week ago . . .

But for my fate on the turning wheel of heaven
Forever whirls, forever changes shape
Even as the face of the inconstant moon
That never keeps her form two nights the same . . .

His father turns and smiles at him, his skin and teeth reddened and spectral, as if he is in the grip of death. He encloses Jacques-Louis' hand in his, a large strong hand that warms the boy's own.

'A perfect alignment of sun, earth and moon, Jacques-Louis,' his father says. 'There is nothing to fear. Soon enough, the moon will be free.'

Jacques-Louis waits for things to be right again. The men around him are arguing some point and his father is suddenly keen to walk home on this mild evening. They make their farewells and dismiss the waiting carriage. The red suffusion is dissolving and his father is returning from the undead.

But the sense of desolation does not quite leave Jacques-Louis. Colour, it seems, is in contention. Or had it been his eyes? Perhaps there will be more of this, a certain unreliability to all that appeared solid. He is perplexed.

The limbs of oak trees meet above them. His father says this boulevard was planted in the reign of Louis XIV, *le Roi Soleil*. Yet it is shards of moonlight that draw Jacques-Louis' attention. Tiny scimitars are rippling and glimmering in every direction, scattered and shivering across the cobblestones.

'See, Jacques-Louis?' his father says. 'The leaves of the oak trees are projecting the moon above as it emerges from the shadow of the world, casting and multiplying these images onto the path. It is a camera obscura!'

His father laughs and Jacques-Louis laughs, too. They hold hands, father and son, and whirl within a forest of moons, a kaleidoscope of lunar crescents. Jacques-Louis feels himself bound to forces unknown.

'These are important times,' his father says as they resume their walk, both a little breathless from their spinning. 'There are ideas in the new America that are awakening France, Jacques-Louis. That might awaken all of Europe. What you have witnessed this very evening is that all men, even boys who are yet to become men, are inconsequential. The darkness is no bubble or sphere of blown glass but leaks out in every direction, an infinity, and what are we? Pffft. Just a puff of dust and time. It dwindles a man's sense of himself, and so he must attend to his inner world. That, Jacques-Louis, is at the heart of enlightenment.'

'And Henriette?' Jacques-Louis asks. 'Must she also attend to these thoughts?' He cannot imagine his sister's life as inconsequential. Nor his mother's.

'Ah, a woman is a different creature altogether,' his father replies. 'It is a mystery what a woman is and, as such, we have no chance to understand them. But if we love them well, delight in their sweet and powerful mysteries, protect them, celebrate them, then we are better men. That is a truth, my love, that you will discover in good time.'

Henriette, his only sibling, is four years older than Jacques-Louis. She and his mother are at the chateau in Reims while he is in Paris with his father. Jacques-Louis has never before come to Paris alone with his father, but his father says it is time to begin the larger education of his mind. Soon he will be sent to an eminent school and, in preparation, he must become fluent in Latin. Meanwhile, a German physician has been employed to tutor him. Jacques-Louis must read Diderot and Descartes, his father insists. Spinoza and Locke.

'We are preparing the soil and planting the crops that will fruit into the young man I see in you,' his father says. 'I know you love the industry of agriculture, but you must balance this with the cultivation of the mind, the intellect, Jacques-Louis.'

Henriette is passionate about the writings of John Locke who talks of equal rights for women. Henriette has declared she will not marry—or if she does, and she is unhappy with her prince or duke, she will divorce him immediately. There is a new parliament in France and now women can divorce, they can own property, they can vote. Henriette says it is all bubbling into a soup that will spill across Europe, and their mother says, 'But wait until you fall in love and taste those pleasures, my daughter. Perhaps then you will be less inclined towards soup and wish to sup instead from the entire menu of a woman's life.'

Jacques-Louis' family are the *noblesse d'épée*, the most honourable of nobles in all of France. His father is a duke and his mother a duchess. His father's father was a general in the King's army. He was wounded in battle against the Prussians and died before Jacques-Louis was born.

'Kings take death lightly,' his father had said, for he too had led troops into battle, 'but still it is a great honour to fight for the King.'

The ten-year-old Jacques-Louis is missing bud break at the chateau. The mist hanging low in the valleys and dew beading on the leaves. The tiny bursts of green erupting along the vines. The tightly folded leaves beginning to unfurl, every variety of grape into its own unique shape.

Later in summer, plumped by rain, warmed by sun, those same leaves will hide grapes hanging heavy and full, and he and Philippe, their vigneron, will walk between the vines, lifting away the foliage. Philippe's father was the vigneron before Philippe. Mathilde, his wife, is their cook and knows all Jacques-Louis' favourite foods.

Sometimes Philippe offered Jacques-Louis grapes to taste and invited him to consider the tart brightness. 'This is why we pick champagne grapes earlier than grapes for table wines: to preserve that vibrant piquancy before the grapes become too sweet. But will it be a good year? Or has the late rain diluted the flavour? Has the storm that damaged much of the hillside caused a more intense flavour to emerge in the grapes that survived the battering? All these things must be considered. Many can grow grapes, but very few can make a great wine. It is your destiny, as it was your father's and his before him . . . a great legacy.'

Jacques-Louis has been lowered into the barrels to press the grapes with his feet, toes deep in skin and juice. He has walked the caves with his father, inspecting the rows of bottles in the flickering light, listening to the muffled hush of their feet in the dust of white chalk.

'Observe the pale yellow of this one, Jacques-Louis,' his father said. 'Watch how the bubbles float up in the glass as if they are in no hurry at all. Smell the bouquet. A scent of caramel and toasted brioche, yes? Taste a little. What do you find?'

'It tastes of summer,' Jacques-Louis said.

'Can you tell me more?' his father asked.

Jacques-Louis took another sip and held the wine in his mouth as he had seen his father do. He swallowed and said, 'The bees are buzzing in the sunshine, and there is honey and lemon tart and soft cheese.'

'*Alors*,' his father said, 'you have the palate of a winemaker indeed.'

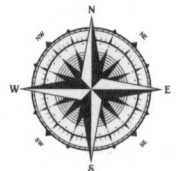

'Dangerous words travel fast,' Jacques-Louis' father says to the friends gathered in their library. It is a room that contains two thousand volumes on shelves that reach all the way to the ceiling. Books with golden words on their spines and covers of red leather and brown Japanese vellum. Some of the pages are soft and almost transparent, the print tiny. The words are in Greek and Latin, Italian and French, English and German. Some are so old they are kept in drawers and must be opened with the greatest care. Within them are circles inside circles, seven-pointed stars, the chemical syllables of cosmic law, and illustrations of beasts of cave and water.

'They all await you, Jacques-Louis,' his father has told him. 'Here is a feast prepared for your mind that you can dine upon at will, at any hour of the day and night.'

There is no room in the chateau where Jacques-Louis is not welcome. Even when he has guests, his father always gestures for his son to enter, ordering a cushion to be brought by a servant so that the young marquis might sit beside his father's chair.

Gatherings have been more frequent at the chateau of late. Often they take place after Jacques-Louis is asleep, but he smells the residue of eau de cologne, wine and tobacco the next morning. Friends and family arrive in carriages that are no longer gilded or fanciful, their house arms painted over to obscure their identity. They come after sunset, cloaked and hooded against the cold. Snow falls, the trees are bare. The King and Queen are both captive. His mother says this winter is perhaps the darkest France has ever known.

Visitors no longer wear feathers or fur, diamonds and silks. The house has slowly secreted its silver and crystal, its porcelain and paintings. Henriette is piqued. 'But where has it gone, Maman?' she asks. 'Where is the silver cup and tray for my *chocolat chaud*?'

Maman reminds Jacques-Louis and Henriette that all men and women are born free and equal in rights. The family must be seen to embrace these new circumstances. They are not to worry. Certain items, treasured items, have been sent away. All will be restored in due course. But there are heated words and fierce debates in the library.

'We are the citizenry and this is our music,' says de Dolomieu.

'*All men are created equal,*' says Oncle du Pont, who is visiting from America. He is holding a large tract of paper, a copy given to him in Philadelphia by his friend Benjamin Franklin. 'This is where it started. Let us not forget it.' And he reads: '*They are endowed by their Creator with certain unalienable Rights. Among these are Life, Liberty, and the pursuit of Happiness . . . Furthermore, whenever any Form of Government becomes destructive to these ends, it is the Right of the People to alter or so abolish it . . . to instigate a new Government, laying its foundation on such principles and organising powers . . . most likely to affect their Safety and Happiness.'*

'Liberty and equality will conquer despotism,' Papa says. 'The Americans have proven it.'

'But on the borders other nobles conspire to undo every step we might make for reform, agitating for war and tumult,' replies du Pont. 'No good will come of it. Especially for the King.'

'We must not pretend that a new government will be formed as if it is all a game of chess being played by a skilful hand,' says Condorcet.

'We wait for progress from above, but all that is happening is reaction from below,' says Madame Dalmas.

'The King needs reminding that, while unpleasant, songs of sedition cannot limit royal expenditure, nor will the proliferation of books and bulletins, pamphlets and opinions feed the hungry,' says Desmoulins. 'And the people are hungry.'

'Where does the law begin and end when unrest rumbles within every institution? Magistrates arrested in their homes, the clergy, too. It is only a matter of time before we must side with or against . . .' replies Maman.

'Perhaps a time will yet come when the sun will shine only upon free men who know no other master than Reason,' says Condorcet.

'Rubbish,' responds Madame Dalmas.

'Paris,' says Papa, 'our city of lights and theatres, cafes and chestnut trees, our magnificent nation, will never give way to something uncivilised.'

'It has already given way to something uncivilised,' says Madame Calonne. 'They will have all our heads before they are done.'

'Privilege and hierarchy do not assure us of good leadership. As Wollstonecraft and Paine have written, a nation must have the right to abolish a government unsuited to its interests,' says Maman.

'The notion of an hereditary government is as ludicrous and dangerous as hereditary judges,' says Oncle du Pont.

'But not hereditary nobility?' asks his father.

There is an awkward silence.

'France will never embrace a republic,' says another man, whose name Jacques-Louis does not know.

'We are fools if we think it will not come to that for all of us,' retorts Madame Calonne. 'The King is as good as dead. His children, too.'

Christmas comes quietly and departs. Then it is January and still there are gatherings. Men and women debate in the library night after night, and Jacques-Louis listens until he falls asleep beside his father.

'France is a republic. Why do we need a King?'

'The monarchy is all but dismissed. There will be no right of veto.'

'You know Pitt will never acquiesce to our annexation of the Austrian Netherlands.'

'So you would stir the British to war?'

'We must build government, not anarchy.'

'And rebuild our army to give us victory all the way to the Rhine.'

'Surely the nation exists before everything. Its will is always legal; it is the law itself.'

'There are no laws above the laws of man,' Jacques-Louis hears his father say.

'Only the laws of nature,' says Jacques-Louis' mother. 'And no one will ever tell me what God I might pray to.'

The King is executed. Spring arrives with no respite from the turbulence of ideas, the shortage of food in Paris and the general disorder. Further afield French soldiers conquer the Belgians and the Austrians. Holland is invaded and a royalist uprising is quashed in Lyon. Young men die or return home wounded and broken. More young men are sent to fight.

Their house in Paris is being used by the army for the manufacture of guns, and on their trips to the capital Jacques-Louis and his father stay in another family apartment on the rue Saint-Honoré. All the while his father impresses upon Jacques-Louis the importance of this moment. He must watch and listen, and in all things he must remember moderation.

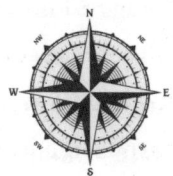

Jacques-Louis' father goes to Paris again as the unrest increases. He is distracted and unusually short-tempered. Jacques-Louis hears wagons leave in the night. His father dresses as a craftsman. The carriage is never used. Friends have already departed for America. Others have moved to England. Jacques-Louis' German tutor returns to his homeland.

Henriette is full of stories she has heard from the servants. Stories of Monsieur Guillotin's invention employed to eliminate arguments and dispatch unwelcome adversaries. Stories of heads being severed and corpses carried away.

The press is printing words that foment discontent in London and Paris. Treatises are being read in taverns, workshops and coffeehouses. Pamphlets, newspapers, magazines and plays inflame arguments of despotism, entitlement and liberty. Jacques-Louis' father tells him that a conversation on the nature of society has begun that cannot be ignored.

Across the Channel, the English lords are rumbling their concern. They do not want the French unrest to infect England. English gaols are spilling over with the poor and unlucky who have run afoul of justice. Dissenters, opponents and ruminators, unable to hold their tongues, are sent to join them. Disease, hunger and discontent spreads.

Government men infiltrate meetings across London, Birmingham and Manchester. Spies operate amongst the French sympathisers. The instigators are charged and sentenced. There is to be no discussion of the removal of the privileges of nobility anywhere in His Majesty's empire.

In France the summer is benevolent and warm. Philippe tells Jacques-Louis that there is a promise of a good harvest and a fine vintage, but there are not enough workers. His father tells him that too many young men are dead in foreign fields, and too many have returned home broken in body and mind, unable to work the farms that feed the rich and the poor alike. The grapes rot upon the vine for want of picking. Wheat moulds. Grain prices continue to rise. Cows give milk but the cost of transport has risen.

In Paris the new prisons built within the abandoned convents and monasteries reek of sullage and bloom with disease. A maximum price is set for bread but this enrages the market women. Faction fights faction. Women's political organisations are forced to disband, which infuriates Maman and Henriette. A new Law of Suspects defines those who *by their conduct, relations, utterances or writing had shown themselves partisans of tyranny, of federalism and enemies of liberty.* Henriette tells Jacques-Louis that those people are relieved of their heads.

The Queen is dispatched by the efficient guillotine only a few months after her husband. A tyranny of bloodiness unfurls. Unholy alliances are created between rival factions and organisations. Many reach for control of government. Desmoulins and his friend Danton are both beheaded on the same day.

'This is the nature of revolution,' Jacques-Louis' father says. 'The extraordinary becomes ordinary. The extreme becomes commonplace. Violence becomes the instrument of moral transformation. Who knows when it will end, or how? Who will be victors and who will be victims? The prudent attempt to plan for an uncertain future.'

He is called to Paris again. Maman does not want him to go, but nor does she wish her husband to be silenced, to cease his public arguments for an end to the Terror. It must stop. Someone must reason with Robespierre. She insists on accompanying him.

They depart on a beautiful afternoon. The pond in front of the chateau is blooming with pink lilies. There, in that reflected world, no premonition or concern exists.

'They will return,' Henriette says, as they watch their parents ride down the long avenue of sycamores and poplars.

It is the last time Jacques-Louis and Henriette will ever see them.

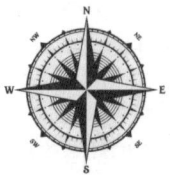

Jacques-Louis is concealed within a trunk for he cannot be trusted to play his part. Henriette has insisted upon this, and Philippe and Mathilde have concurred. At great personal risk, they are posing as Henriette and Jacques-Louis' parents.

'Will they come for us?' Jacques-Louis asks Henriette.

She looks momentarily bewildered. 'They are dead. They will never come.'

Then she realises her brother means the people who imprisoned their parents and judged them guilty.

'If we are not here, they cannot find us,' says Henriette. 'If we are stopped on the road between Reims and Calais, you must not make a sound or they will cut our throats.'

'Did Papa do something wrong?' he asks.

'It is not what he did or did not do,' Henriette says. 'Now you are the *duc* and you will never be safe.'

'Because of who I am?'

'Because of what you are,' she says.

•

The wagon is stopped on the outskirts of Paris and the passengers are interrogated by men and women with knives and pitchforks. Henriette is already the actress and has no trouble convincing them she is indeed the daughter of this hard-working couple. Mathilde becomes a *sans-culottes* who knows all the right things to say and sing; she tells these arbitrary revolutionaries that she is going home to care for her father. One of the interrogators is also from the region and knows of her family.

Jacques-Louis waits in trepidation, rolled inside bedcoverings and squeezed into the impenetrable darkness of the wooden trunk. He cannot stop imagining the guillotine slicing off the head of first his mother and then his father. Where are their bodies? Where has death taken them? Where have their thoughts gone?

He had heard Henriette ask Philippe, 'Where are my parents' bodies?'

'They are in the Picpus Cemetery, Mademoiselle Henriette,' Philippe had replied.

Jacques-Louis understands his parents are with others who have died. He closes his eyes and sees heads cut away from bodies, heads tossed into wheelbarrows, bodies jolted away over cobblestones slick with blood.

Jacques-Louis screams silently into the blankets.

Only when the wagon stops, and the trunk that bears him is stowed in some desultory inn where the rooms smell of onions and dogs, can he be released to unfold his numbed limbs. As he attempts to sleep, squeezed into a lumpy bed beside Henriette, he thinks of his mother walking with her chin up—not walking to her death, but as if she is on her way to pick peonies from the garden. She kneels to pull a weed, then rests her head upon the wooden block. And the blade falls.

•

Crossing from France to Scotland, he knows only that he is sick and the sea is unforgiving. In Leith, Philippe and Mathilde deliver their charges into the care of Doctor and Mrs Douglas; Mrs Douglas is their mother's cousin. There had been a plan in place, Jacques-Louis learns: he and Henriette, their mother and their father, would all travel to Edinburgh together and stay there until the turbulence in France had abated. Mathilde and Philippe were to care for the estate until they could return. Household items, favourite books and a few treasured heirlooms had been sent ahead in anticipation of their new home. Financial arrangements had been made. But only Jacques-Louis and Henriette arrive.

The doctor and his wife welcome the siblings into their small family. They have a daughter, Hannah, who is four years old.

'It is lucky he was so young,' Jacques-Louis hears Mrs Douglas say to her husband one evening. 'In time he will barely remember. But Henriette . . . well, I do not think it will be so simple with that one.'

Jacques-Louis dreams of ravens screeching in the trees. They spread their wings and, gliding down, alight on a mosaic of death to pick at eyes that gaze up at the mottled sky, eyes surprised by death, or the terrible loneliness of an angel. He wakes to find that he has left the bed and curled into a corner of the room, concealed beneath a blanket.

Four-year-old Hannah, with her dimples and shining dark hair, seeks first the attention of her new cousin, Henriette. When Henriette responds with utter disregard, Hannah turns her attention to Jacques-Louis, whose hand she must hold whenever she goes up or down the stairs with him, and when they take a walk between rain showers. Sometimes they walk in the rain under a black umbrella with Mrs Douglas beside them, or with the maid Esther on an errand for the housekeeper.

Hannah likes to sit on Jacques-Louis' lap as he reads to her from a picture book in his accented English, and she corrects him in her Scots, and his tutor corrects him with his Oxford English. Jacques-Louis is unmoored in the wet grey city, with its narrow stone streets and low ceilings. He feels the careful observation of the Doctor and Mrs Douglas, as if he is a frail thing that might break at any moment.

He was born to be a duke. He had been schooled in astronomy, philosophy, mathematics and Latin. He had walked the vineyards his ancestors had first planted on the banks of the Marne in the province of Champagne. He had picked the grapes and seen an eclipse of the moon. They had lived in a chateau with countless servants and attended the opera and the theatre in Paris. He had visited the palace at Versailles, where they had walked the halls and gardens and been entertained by jugglers and fools. Who was he now? He was no longer the marquis. He was a duke of nothing. He had no future.

Under his pillow he keeps a soft white kid glove he had found amongst the books and clothes packed for him in the months when the world had grown restless and covered wagons had left in the night. He can smell his mother's scent upon it. When he wakes from nightmares, he holds it under his nose, breathing it in, wishing fervently that Maman would soon be walking into the breakfast room, bringing music for his lesson.

When he turns fourteen, Doctor Douglas suggests that, beyond his normal studies, Jacques-Louis might wish to learn the work of an apothecary. If he finds it to his liking, perhaps in time he can become the doctor's apprentice. And it is here Jacques-Louis finds at last a modicum of rest from his fractured thoughts.

At the university there is a friend of Doctor Douglas who begins to tutor him in biology and chemistry. There is an extensive garden at the university and Jacques-Louis learns about the propagation and care of medicinal plants from across the British Isles, the Americas and the lands that encircle the Mediterranean Sea, the Indies, the Orient and even the Himalayan mountains. In this way, he visits landscapes and climates which, in his mind, are filled with the vibrations of insects, the songs of strange birds and people who wish him no harm.

At home, he and Henriette study under careful and patient tutors. They navigate the strange Scottish tongue—a mangled kind of English, Henriette declares. The lack of couture, the soft taste-less food, the low pious skies and the humourless people: Henriette despises it all.

'They are little more than Highland savages,' she says to Jacques-Louis. 'I cannot stay here.'

'You will not leave me?' he replies anxiously.

'Of course I will,' she says. 'As soon as I am able. I cannot wait here for you to grow up so that you might be of some use to me. But when you are ready, you will come and find me and we will make our way back to France. You will have a vineyard and I will have a chateau and all of this will be forgotten.'

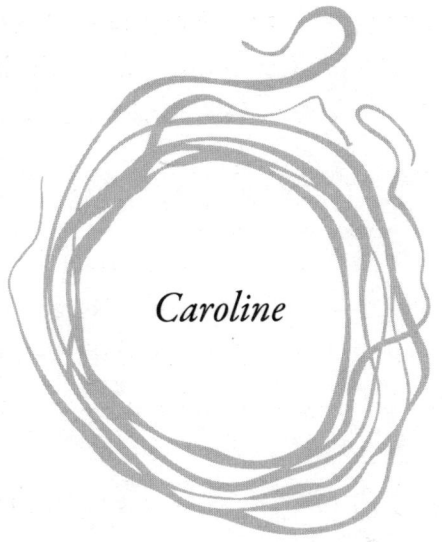

· *3* ·

Caroline

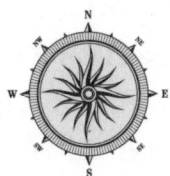

'Mrs Douglas has expressed an interest in the vineyard, Charles,' says Georgiana to her husband. 'And I suggested that it is a task she might begin with the boys.'

'Strange work for a lady,' Captain Swanston replies.

He has joined them for tea in the conservatory. It is the twins' birthday, and a table is arrayed with scones, sandwiches, a leg of smoked ham, fresh bread and preserves, and for each boy his favourite cake—a fruitcake for Nowell and a gingerbread for Robert.

'Surely such a task requires a phalanx of workers, Mrs Douglas?' Swanston says. 'These rogues are almost certain to be insufficient for the task.' He tousles the head of the nearest son.

'Father!' says Robert. 'We want to help!'

'We do!' say George and Nowell.

'And you will continue to learn your sums?' Swanston asks his boys.

They nod enthusiastically.

'I shall see to it they do, Captain Swanston,' says Caroline. 'It will just be a little pruning to see what might be revealed.'

'I cannot imagine anything more healthful, after their mornings at the school,' adds Georgiana.

'You know my thoughts about winemaking here, Mrs Douglas,' says Captain Swanston, 'but Dalrymple was saying to me only yesterday, at the council meeting, that good wine is hard to come by. You might speak with the Walkers. They have a vineyard and some knowledge of the process though, being great advocates of temperance, they make only vinegar and a rough medicinal wine for the hospital. Still, if, after your explorations, you find small boys inadequate to the task, perhaps I can be of assistance in securing more effective labour.'

Caroline inspects the Walkers' vineyard with Julia Walker, who points out some of their older vines and where there are early indications of rot and insect incursions. These will be replaced with new plants. She speaks of mildew and mould. She shows Caroline how to cut back all but three or four strands of the healthy vines to just a few feet long.

'It looks straightforward here,' says Caroline, 'but the whole vineyard is tangled with weeds. It takes minutes to free even one of the plants before I have any chance to observe the plant and cut it back.'

'Have you any experience in grape growing?' Julia asks.

'I do not. We grew table grapes in our glasshouse in London, but we did not make wine. And . . .' But there Caroline halted. There must be no mention of her father. 'Perhaps it is the potential that calls me. I do not like to see such an opportunity gone to waste.'

'And you have an understanding with Captain Swanston, should you entice the vineyard to become productive once more?'

'Yes, of a sort.'

'Well, do not let your hard work go unrewarded.'

'The Swanstons have both been nothing but kindness,' Caroline says.

'Yes, Georgiana is a delightful woman, but Captain Swanston . . .'

Here she pauses and Caroline waits.

'I want only the best for you as you settle in here,' Julia continues at last. 'Captain Swanston is a shrewd and capable man of business and politics. I do not wish to speak out of turn, but only to ensure that you are well protected in any commercial arrangement you might make with him.'

'Do you think investing here is imprudent?' Caroline asks.

'I think all of it is a great risk in this colony, for there is no certainty we will ever be without the strictures the colonial government insists on imposing. My husband and I prefer to keep our savings close and to live modestly until we can secure a suitable building for the school. We go slowly, ensuring we are not reliant on the decisions and ambitions of others. But perhaps you are keen to be underway.'

'Thank you, Julia,' Caroline says. 'I do appreciate your counsel.'

'I think you are wise to seek the allegiance of Swanston, but he is a man who will always put his own interests first. Now, shall we go in for dinner? My sister and her husband will be joining us. She is expecting her third child.'

It is the second time the Walkers have made Caroline welcome at their dinner table. Caroline finds she likes the Quaker silence before the meal. It gives her a moment to settle and breathe, to find repose beyond all her racing thoughts.

As they are finishing the roast lamb, Caroline says, 'I find it very strange to think that there was an entirely different people here such a short time ago.'

'You refer to the natives?' asks the husband of Julia's sister. 'They were removed.'

'It would be more accurate to say murdered and kidnapped, Mrs Douglas,' says Washington Walker.

"He that loveth not his brother whom he hath seen, how can he love God whom he has not seen?" quotes Julia.

'It is very grim, by all accounts, the place to which the last of them have been sent,' says Julia's sister.

'But we have heard that there is a church and a school,' says her husband.

'We are the beneficiaries of their stewardship,' says Washington. 'When I first came here, it appeared to me as a sort of garden. There were many great trees and wide grasslands along the river and far up into the hills, but now it is given to sheep.'

'Or has become overgrown,' adds Julia.

'You may have seen a few of their children about, Caroline,' Washington says. 'Half-castes and such. I cannot understand why they have not been sent to be with their own people.'

'The Queen's Orphan School has quite a few, too,' adds Julia. 'Did you know there are more than seven hundred children residing there?'

Caroline did not.

'I am told that the slightest offence is met by a flogging,' says Washington.

'Perhaps when we begin our own school,' says Julia, 'we can offer scholarships for such students.'

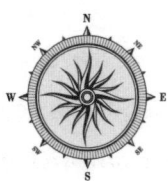

The Swanston boys and Quill are leaping from the loft into the straw below. Caroline stands in the door of the barn and watches a shower fall across the fields leaving behind a double rainbow arcing across the entire valley. She turns and sees an eagle mounting a current. It seems strange to have the boys learn of English kings and queens, ancient Greek and Latin, when it is all so far from here. The histories of London, Constantinople, Athens and Rome. As if those peoples belonged to another world.

How was she to convey to these boys the sense of their part in the continuum of human life, when the houses, the buildings, the boats, the wagons, the gardens, even this vineyard planted barely more than fifteen years ago, all of it was new, a replica under construction, paying homage to a country the boys had never seen.

She could take the boys to the grove of she-oaks and show them the flints that she and Quill had discovered. A people now gone as the Phoenicians were gone, the Spartans, the Lydians, Thracians and Parthians. Perhaps Marco Polo had felt the same when he visited the Orient. Did he find evidence of peoples who lived there before and now dwelled only in story and myth? What became of stories when no buildings or statues, carvings or crypts remained to recall the people of such times? What could she convey of her own ancestors? What did she really know of their daily lives, their curiosity, their habits and peculiarities?

She thinks of the blacksmith, Cornelius. She can often hear him at work in the barn. The various notes of his tools striking metal. What brought him here? Who were his people? Did he feel, perhaps, as she felt? The reassuring distance of Van Diemen's Land from all that had come before?

The conqueror Alexander might have done it differently if he, and not the English, had arrived and sought to enfold the peoples of this place into his kingdom as he had the Orientals. But spiritual tolerance was not the way of the English. Nor the French. Nor the Spanish.

She felt doubt dampening her spirits. She must look upon Europe as the future destination of the Swanston boys. That was where they would go within a few years to complete their education and find their professions. Possibly Quill, too.

But is it wise or right to think in that direction? Would the society here ever rival that of Europe? Was here the new future? She might be living at the birth of an empire, but how would one know? How would one prepare?

When Caroline had asked Mrs Roper, on a recent visit, what she made of the young Queen Victoria, Mrs Roper had said, 'Treasonous words I know . . . but I have been pondering what I owe her? I am sure I would like her well enough if we were to sit down and have a cup of tea. I expect she is very polite. But being sent off with not a thought to how I might fare, a girl of fourteen, and never allowed back. Gone so long from that place it hardly seems real. What a lot of fuss it is, really. The soldiers in their uniforms. The Governor with his plans for some new Government House, a great thing to be built out there on the riverfront.'

'To what or whom do you feel a sense of loyalty, Mrs Roper?' Caroline asked.

Mrs Roper turned her head and stared out the window. 'I'm getting old. I know when snow is coming because my hands ache something terrible. I'll be buried, and that will be the last of me. And I don't mind that; I've had an interesting life. But it makes me think that maybe what I am really the subject of is that there river, and the mountain. Am I crazy to have such thoughts?'

'Not at all,' Caroline said. 'Should we bow? I do sometimes feel like bowing to the mountain.'

And they chuckled at this, and Mrs Roper poured them both another sherry.

The clouds clear, the rainbows have dissipated. A brilliant blue sky returns and, with it, the welcome warmth of winter sunshine. Caroline calls the boys to her. They come with straw in their hair and clothes twisted and pulled from their antics in the hay. She instructs them to tidy themselves.

Nowell jostles George, who stumbles against Robert. Robert pushes him back. Quill looks on, amused.

'I remind you that a classroom can be many things,' Caroline says sternly. 'You could have your knees under a desk and a teacher with a switch to settle your fidgeting fingers. Or you can be here, on this special occasion, learning about grapes. You are expected to work with all the diligence you give to your indoor studies. Am I understood?'

They look at her with a sort of fear attended by regard. It is almost a recipe, she thinks. She wonders what Captain de Hoog would make of her young crew.

Georgiana has provided a pair of gloves for each of them, and as she pulls them on Caroline observes the *S* stamped carefully into the thumb. 'Who makes such things for your family?' she asks.

'Cornelius,' says Nowell. 'He makes our shoes, too.'

He sticks out his foot and Caroline observes the sturdy leather boots.

She gives each boy a pair of shears and asks them to gather about as she kneels and begins to chop back the grasses. The ground is damp and Caroline is grateful for the mats Bessie had sent with Quill. Feeling around the first vine, Caroline hopes it is true that there are no snakes at this time of year.

'They are extremely venomous,' Georgiana had said. 'Both the black snake and the copperhead. Several men have died from the bite, and last year a child in the midlands was bitten and suffered a horrid death.'

Robert had shown her a picture he had drawn of his father with a dead snake. Captain Swanston had his arm outstretched and the snake hung from his shoulder to the ground.

Caroline remembers sarsaparilla. *Grown in Italy, Spain and other warm countries. Both leaves and berries drunk before or after any deadly poison are an excellent antidote. It helps the aches of sinews and joints, running sores in the legs, all foulness of the skin and cures the pustules of venereal disea*se.

Her father's friend, the herbalist Dr Culpeper, would have to begin afresh. A world of plants that would take a lifetime to study and document. Had any of the early settlers learned from the natives the medicines of this land? How foolhardy it seemed to her that all the ancient knowledge of this place might have been lost.

She had spent many days walking the banks of waterways and traversing fields with her father looking for comfrey, hedge mustard, the roots of elecampane for ridding the stomach of worms. Flaxweed or toadflax for weals, pimples, spots and leprosy. Cowslip to strengthen the brain and nerves. There were mosses and fungi from ground and tree, many useful for women and each with its own properties. Plant knowledge that had been gleaned, passed on, shared and refined. People living alongside plants, tending and harvesting them for both food and medicine.

'It was my boyhood,' her father had said. 'Amongst the grapes with Philippe and the other workers, learning the way of grapes.'

'Do you wish for a vineyard, Papa?' she had asked him.

'Henriette and I talk of it. She is very keen to live there again one day.'

'In France?'

'In Champagne,' he had said, and his face took on a look she rarely glimpsed.

'Does it make you sad, Papa?'

'A little,' he had replied.

At last the trunk of the vine is revealed, low, gnarled and grey beneath the weeds. She shows the boys how to trim away most of the outer growth, choosing two or three canes and cutting these back to a foot or so in length.

'Do not chop your fingers off,' she says. 'Nor anyone else's.'

'This is going to take a long time,' says Nowell, sighing.

'It is lucky then that we have until spring,' says Caroline, but as she regards the overgrown acres, she sees that he is right. Progress will indeed be slow. And lessons must continue. As they set about their labours, she calls out to the boys, 'What mineral sits on the table every night?'

After a pause, Robert says, 'Salt.'

'Yes, Robert,' Caroline replies, 'and what is meant by minerals?'

'Rocks,' he says. 'Everything beneath our feet. It's all made of minerals.'

'Nowell, can you add to this?' Caroline asks.

'Coal is a mineral,' he says. 'And limestone. Clay. Sandstone?'

'Yes,' says Caroline. 'It is composed of minerals. And do you remember what makes coal special?'

'It burns,' he says. 'It keeps us warm.'

'And where does coal come from?'

'Mines,' says George. 'Convicts dig it up.'

'Not always convicts,' Caroline says. 'But here, yes. And somewhere close by there is a very large mineral.'

Quill looks up at her, and then his eyes widen. 'The mountain,' he says, staring beyond her to the slopes beguiled by cloud.

'Yes,' she says. 'I understand it is dolerite, and some say it was once a volcano. Who remembers where the word "volcano" comes from?'

'He was a god,' says Nowell. 'Vulcan.'

'He threw thunderbolts that he made for Jupiter,' adds Robert. 'I drew that.'

Soon Caroline's back is aching from the bending, and her arms are weary from the tugging of grasses and the wrangling of vines. She wonders if letting in the chooks might be helpful in breaking up the weeds and soil. She will discuss it with Bessie. The scale of the endeavour seems overwhelming.

'*Ne sois pas découragé,*' she can hear her father saying—a phrase he employed when snails or slugs had eaten the greens in the glasshouse, or a rat had been at the lemons.

All right, Papa, she replies. I will not be discouraged yet.

She spies a large wombat hole disappearing back under the stone wall. She and the boys gather around it, observing the curious square droppings at the perimeter of the burrow.

'Do you think this is the only way out?' she asks the boys.

Robert says, 'I have seen them run down a burrow like this, but come up later over there.'

Caroline and the boys stuff the hole with weeds and cuttings. She trusts that the wombat, if he is still within, will find another exit from the vineyard.

She looks about at their small patch of effort. A tiny section of the vineyard has been cleared of weeds and pruned, the passage between the plants tamped down by feet and knees.

'You have done a wonderful job, all of you,' she says. 'But it is growing chilly. I think that is enough for today. We have made a beginning.'

'Huzzah!' says Nowell, wielding his shears.

'Be careful!' she admonishes, but the other boys are joining in the cry. 'Huzzah, huzzah!'

Caroline cannot help but raise her own shears and join the boys in their salute.

Back at the barn they stow mats, tools and gloves. Caroline can hear Cornelius at work in the forge.

'Robert,' she says, revealing a cake tin hidden in her basket, 'you cut, the others choose.'

Robert dances for a moment with delight, then dives towards the tin.

'I'm so glad to have girls,' she hears her father say. 'A boy is easily motivated by food, but a girl needs curiosity.'

'And Quill,' she says, 'will you please take a piece of cake to Cornelius? Tell him he is most welcome to join us.'

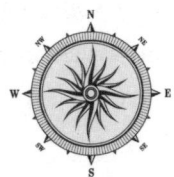

ornelius brings Caroline a stool to sit on. He places a slate on
the bench and invites her to put her hand upon it. She is made
slightly uncomfortable by the ease with which he has arranged her,
his proximity to her, and yet he is gentle and deferential.

Jefferson, the manservant of the family where she had been a
governess in New York, the friend who had posed as her servant
when she secured her passage on the *Alliance*, had been born a free
man, the son of a Southern slave who had fled north. The sailors
on the *Alliance* had all borne evidence of accident and brutality,
but the black men's scars were by far the more serious.

'I do not ask about their past,' de Hoog had told her. 'If they
prefer the sea to the land, that is enough.'

Cornelius produces a length of chalk and begins to trace the
outline of Caroline's hands. She sees the way his nails are almost
as black as his hands, a blacksmith's hands, and she looks down at
her own and finds new affection for the remnants of earth evident
under the nails.

'I have set myself a task, Cornelius,' she says.

'No small task, Mrs Douglas, if it's the vineyard you have in mind. And with a small tribe of boys.'

'They grow weary of it even after two afternoons. But if we can retrieve something from beneath all that . . .'

Caroline realises that from his forge, the whole valley is laid out before Cornelius. There is little he doesn't see of the movement of humans to and from the harbour, and the wagons and carriages going north towards other townships.

'There have been more than a few who have planted a vineyard here,' Cornelius says. 'But few who outlasted the cold, the rain, the birds, the opossums, or simply the years waiting for the vines to mature.'

Caroline observes the lines in Cornelius's face as he captures the boundaries of her hand.

'Have you grown grapes before, Mrs Douglas?' Cornelius asks. His voice is low and soft.

'I have not,' she says. 'And I do not know what is really involved in producing a single bottle of wine.'

'Yet still, you begin.'

'Does it seem ridiculous to attempt such a thing?'

He turns away, placing the slate with her outlined hands on a bench.

'Some might say it is a calling,' he says.

'Do you remember the vineyard when it was flourishing?' she asks.

'I do, Mrs Douglas,' he says. 'I remember it very well.'

'And was the wine good?'

'By all accounts, very good. Mr Broughton sold a great deal of it. It went to England and to Europe. One crate was sent to a famous wine merchant in London. Unfortunately, most of that cargo was lost on the voyage, bottles being easily broken. Little of the wine survived, but in a letter the merchant pronounced it very fine indeed and said he wished to make a sizeable order.'

'And then?'

'Mr Broughton never read that letter. He was gone by then. He died in his sleep a young man. His heart gave out, they said.'

'Oh. I didn't know.'

'Many a day he was there at dawn and still there in the moonlight. He sent plants to people wanting vineyards both here in Van Diemen's Land, outside Sydney and to South Australia. I imagine some of those vines are growing and fruiting still.'

Lineage. Caroline feels it. Something that binds the past irrevocably with the future.

'It's the right time to be cutting back,' Cornelius says. 'Mr Broughton started in May, especially if the snows came early. In July he grafted new vines onto the rootstock. He experimented with many varieties of grape. He had no time for the vines from the Cape colony. He found the grapes that did best were the same as those that did best in the cold parts of northern France. That's why he had the notion to make champagne. And he always racked the wine under a new moon because he said the pressure in the bottles was at its most subdued.'

'What is racking, Cornelius?'

'It's when the wine is separated from the sediment that gathers from the first fermentation, Mrs Douglas. Sometimes it might wait in the bottles for a year and a half, sometimes longer.'

'Did Mr Broughton keep any journals? A library, perhaps?'

Cornelius regards her. A fresh-faced young woman with a dimple in her left cheek, pretty green eyes, small hands, and a formal way of holding herself. She is not who he had imagined might ask him such a question, yet here she is, wanting to know.

'The land will teach a person a lot,' he says. 'Best to watch, let a year go round, Mrs Douglas. It takes time to get a sense of a place.'

'I am foolish, I think, to be contemplating this, Cornelius,' she says.

'Seems to me that we should attend to the things in our hearts, Mrs Douglas, if we can. So no, not foolish.'

· **4** ·

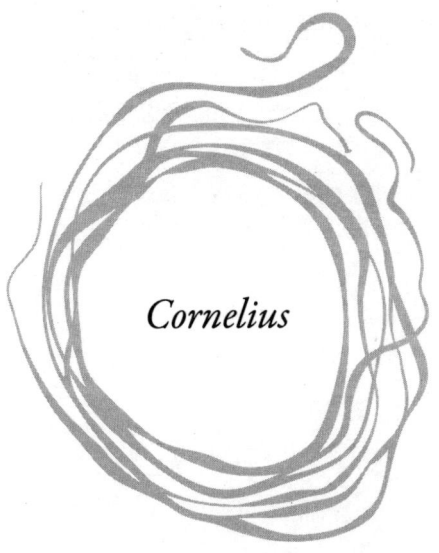

Cornelius

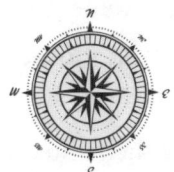

Cornelius has observed Caroline amongst the vines, her black dress catching in the briars. He has seen her out there under the stars, staring at the vineyard. He has seen her take those four young boys into the vines to pull away the weeds. He has come upon her swimming in the pond wholly naked and he has walked away, surprised but not alarmed by her boldness. That kind of freedom must be hard won for a woman, he thinks.

To grow a thing is to grow a little certainty, satisfying a soul that life is worth living. Take a hit when it dies and start anew. Be grateful when the wallabies and opossums haven't got inside the fences, or when birds don't strip the fruit before bottling, or some fool hasn't walked drunkenly through a new crop of squash or corn.

After she departs, he sets aside leather and metal to make a pair of shears and gloves to fit her small hands. A week later, Cornelius presents these items to Caroline. She tries on the gloves, delighting at the fit, and marvels at the lightness and convenience of the shears. Cornelius then draws from beneath his workbench a pair of boots and tells her it must be ten years now that he has been saving the leather. A kangaroo skin from the red deserts far away to the north, won in a card game. He has lined the boots with sheepskin.

'Plenty of cold days ahead yet,' he says, 'even in summer, and likely wet ones, too. Feet like to be warm.'

'How did you know the fit, Cornelius?' Caroline asks, doing up the laces.

'Mrs Douglas, if I know the hands, I know the feet.'

'They are perfect,' she says. 'I do not know what to say . . . but thank you. Thank you, Cornelius. I am . . .'

He smiles.

'What shall I pay you for them?' she asks.

'No, Mrs Douglas, the gloves are as we agreed, but the shears and the boots are a gift. Mr Broughton would be well pleased that you have intentions for his vineyard. Consider them a gift from him, if you cannot accept them from me.'

She smiles. 'I accept them from both of you gratefully, Cornelius. And if you are speaking with Mr Broughton, there in the after-life . . .'

'Yes,' says Cornelius.

'Then please let him know I have no skills, but I take strength from his encouragement and I will do my best to learn.'

She cannot know the pleasure Cornelius has taken in the crafting of his gifts. He wants to remember the goodness of the world. Caroline must be about the same age as his youngest daughter, if she lives. He doubts it. In some ways he hopes not. He hopes she has been dead for years and no longer endures what must be endured at the hands of men. Her mother, too.

He will never see any of his children again.

He walks to the back of the forge and takes down a hoop of rusted metal.

'Mrs Douglas, do you know what this is?'

Her gaze is thoughtful. 'It is from a cask.'

'Yes, it is.'

'You made the casks for Mr Broughton?'

'I repaired a good many. All French oak. Some had stored brandy, others rum. He did things properly, Mr Broughton.'

In the coming years, Cornelius and Caroline will watch the seasons transform the valley. They will admire golden afternoons and night skies. Caroline will share stories with Cornelius that she will share with no one else. Cornelius will do the same, when he has the courage to remember. It is a slow unfolding.

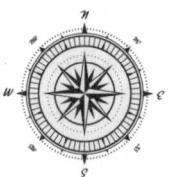

A white woman could be the most dangerous thing in the world, Cornelius knew. Don't look at them, don't talk to them, watch out for them. They feared you. They would make you suffer for that fear, especially if they liked you a little bit.

The brands on his arms were old now, worn down over the years to smooth. His fingers still travelled over them some nights when he lay awake, proof of things he had survived. A boy dragged from his village like a fish on a line.

He was not put to work in the fields but apprenticed to the blacksmith. When he was barely grown, he was given a wife. Her first husband had died running. Running away with her, shooting at their pursuers with a pistol he had stolen. When they caught him, they cut off his manhood in front of her, cut out his tongue and dragged him behind four horses. They shackled her and brought her back, whipped her though she was pregnant. When she gave birth a few months later, the child was light-skinned. She took it to the big house and gave it to one of the slave women there.

'I will kill it otherwise,' she said, and the woman understood.

For four years, she and Cornelius were man and wife. Her skin smelled of the wind, of the baking she did for the master and his family. She did not resist him, but nor did she surrender. She behaved as if their bodies were separate from them, her eyes almost always closed. Sometimes she took him, surprising him with her passion, but it faded afterwards into an aberration of the night.

'Don't you go loving,' she said. 'Don't let that in the door. It will bite you like a wasp and then you will stop breathing. Don't be a fool. Love is for people with hope, and we don't have that.'

He tried to give her a place to rest with the things he could make, the work that he did, waiting for a softening in her that he thought might be possible in time. At the forge, he made nails, horseshoes, hooks, wheel rims, hammers, pitchforks and shovels, the fire taking his lust and his anger and burning it all into metal and dust. Thinking he might yet make her smile, really smile.

'I saw his arms torn out of his shoulders,' she told him. 'The skin scraped from his body, and still he lived and they dragged him until he was a rag of flesh. I'm not going to feel anything if that happens to you.'

She birthed two children, a boy and a girl, and they were dark-skinned and bright-eyed and he thought he had never seen anything more beautiful. He held them, sang to them, tried to remember stories from his childhood to tell them, and wished for a different world. She tended them, too, ensured they had what they needed, but she was not an easy mother.

'They are going to be living all their days with fear in their bellies. The fear of life itself. And if they forget, I will remind them. Nothing to trust here. Nothing to rely upon.'

She was fierce in her unloving, and he came to love her for that more than anything.

Word came of a dispute, some legal matter the master was implicated in. All the women and children were to be sold.

'Will they keep them together?' Cornelius asked.

'They fetch a better price sold one by one,' was the overseer's reply.

The day they were taken away, the men who had lost their wives and children were chained in irons, and they worked in irons for the next two weeks. Six of them were given one hundred lashes each and left overnight on the triangles for refusing orders. A week later, two of them were lashed again, and every slave was called to watch.

The man who had taught Cornelius all he knew of fire and metal, coal and wood, was dead from a hacking cough. A cough that had him spitting blood until he collapsed on the path and was buried in the back field where they were all buried, their graves unmarked.

Cornelius was the master blacksmith now. The mistress of the estate came to see him, bringing with her a fragrant pink rose that she laid upon the bench. She was accompanied by a house servant who waited beyond the forge.

'I wish to give my daughter a wedding gift, Cornelius,' she said. 'Could you fashion one just like this, wrought in iron?'

She had a small body that had grown soft with fancy living. 'Why are you called Cornelius?' she asked.

He didn't know why he had been given the name, only that a man with an eye as white as an egg had assigned it to him, written it on a board and hung it about his neck. That was the first auction, just off the ship, their soiled bodies washed down with buckets of salt water. Then they were given oil to rub on themselves and paraded naked. From then on he was Cornelius.

There was another auction, and another voyage, until he arrived at the plantation with its long fields of sugar cane. At first he shared a room with a dozen other children. When he was given his wife, they got a hut of their own and they made a little garden to grow corn and beans and squash. Now he lived in the hut alone and the rains had washed away the footprints of his wife and children that had lingered by the door and between the garden beds.

'Would you like to hear a poem, Cornelius?' the mistress asked.

He didn't like her asking this. He didn't like one of the house slaves waiting beyond. She had perched herself on a bench and was turning the mistress's parasol in her hands, making eyes at him.

Unaware, the mistress began in her low voice:
'Dim as the borrowed beams of moon and stars,
to lonely, weary, wandering travellers
is Reason to the Soul; and as on high
Those rolling fires discover but the sky,
not light us here, so Reason's glimmering ray
was lent, not to assure our doubtful way,
but guide us upward to a better day . . .'

She had him repeat the words, returning on several days to hear it, until he could recite it himself.

Perhaps it was unintended, but he felt an invitation. They seemed like words to light the place where his hatred lay. The hate he felt being unable to save his wife and his children from whatever had befallen them. He knew what had befallen them. He imagined it over and over, and it took all his focus to keep it from eating him alive.

•

He made her the rose and, before he could stop himself, he said, 'I could make a gate. A gate of roses. A wedding gift.'

The gate was the finest thing he had ever made, a thing he lit the lantern for at night just to go visit it, amazed that he could make such a thing. She came often to see its progress. When it was finished, he packed it in straw, piece by piece, and took three other men with him to fit it together.

The mistress and her daughter came to inspect it. They clapped their hands.

The mistress invited Cornelius to the verandah of the big house. There was someone she wanted him to meet, she said, a guest at the house.

On the verandah, he was offered lemonade by a maid. He did not accept it. He was observed by a young man on the verandah with a waxed moustache and wet black eyes, wearing a white suit, white shoes and a straw hat.

'I have recommended you, Cornelius,' the wife said, as if she were granting him a favour. 'You are to go to Panama.'

There was no saying goodbye to the people he had lived with all those years, nor the forge where he had breathed fire and metal. No farewell to the hut hollow with the past.

Keep breathing, he told himself, on the journey to the harbour. His legs and arms were shackled alongside four other men. The road took him away and he knew he would never find her again, nor his children. A scream curled tight within him, a burning howl he could never let loose.

In the hold of the ship were many others, gathered from the markets. Scars on their bodies, ridged, scored, singular and many. The days and nights were all the same below decks, an eternity of sickness and torment. Upon arrival in Portobelo, he was branded again, each man marked on his shoulder with a crescent moon.

Cornelius worked a forge in a warehouse on the waterfront. No making things of beauty now. Wagon wheels and axles and every metal thing it might take to move a cargo of tobacco, coffee and sugar from the Caribbean to the Pacific Ocean. To travel across Panama was to avoid thousands of sea miles and the risk of losing the cargo in the mighty oceans off Cape Horn. Some said the real cargo was gold and silver. The man in the white suit, Cornelius learned, had made this journey over the mountains to Veracruz before. He was a Spaniard, and to the men he was known as El Diablo.

A caravan of wagons drawn by bullocks, along with slaves loaded with packs, departed the town. The weight of the cargo on their backs was formidable. The mud of the jungle was red, the air close and thick with mosquitoes. The hills were steeper than any Cornelius had ever seen. Men dropped in the heat. They dropped from fever. Alive at night and then dead in the morning, their faces haunted with the yellow agony of death.

'What does it matter?' El Diablo said, smiling his youthful smile as he turned to the men gathered before him, the dead laid out in the mud. 'You are here because you are strong,' he said. 'Strong as bullocks. There are always more bullocks.'

The word whispered amongst them as they lay shackled at night was that only half of them might survive the crossing.

It was his smile Cornelius would come to despise. El Diablo smiled when the day was wet, when it was unbearably hot. He smiled when he had his overseers flog a man for lagging, even if the man was sweating from fever. He smiled at the young girl he'd taken from a village to wash his clothes and make him meals. In the afternoon, when the rains came and they rested, he took her into his tent and they could all hear him with her, and her cries. One day he stripped her naked and had Cornelius tie her thumbs and her ankles to a board, a strap of leather tied across her waist. Then he lashed her with a short, plaited whip. Three cords, each tipped with silver.

The overseers watched indifferently as they played cards, laughing and smoking. The slaves continued cooking and mending, chatting, making themselves busy, resisting the horror.

By the time Cornelius was instructed to untie her, her back looked as if she had been attacked by a jaguar. This is how we forget to be men, Cornelius thought.

He hated poetry then. He hated the roses he'd crafted from iron.

The girl found a blade and cut her own throat. When El Diablo discovered her, he had her naked corpse nailed to a tree, her arms flung wide like the foreign god.

The caravan of bullocks and wagons continued across rivers, up mountains and down, the mud and the wet and the heat and the crescendo of the jungle all inescapable. Cornelius dug wagons out of the mire and repaired the things that broke. Dragging a fallen tree from the path, he felt something give low down in his back. He did his best to conceal the pain.

He was so tired. Tired of heat and damp, the smell of men, the smell of himself, the smell of rot and mud and death. The hot iron to sear a wound closed. The salt used for flogged skin. The yellow fever busy sucking away life all around him.

Dim as the borrowed beams of moon and stars,
to lonely, weary, wandering travellers
is Reason to the Soul . . .

He resolved that he was not willing to die for this man. He glimpsed that *Reason* might be another word for *running* . . . and this idea took hold in him. Deep in the journey, he wrested life from two overseers as fast as he might pull a snake from a woodpile and throw it to the ground. Bringing the axe down, cracking open first one skull and then another. Desperation was a fiercer wasp than love, but there was no peace in murder. No peace at all.

He ran all night along the track that led the wagons in the direction of the setting sun. He was hunted by El Diablo's men, but he pushed his body on and on until he knew he was hours ahead of them. A day. He kept on running until he came out on a ridge and looked upon the Pacific Ocean. It took his breath away. It was the biggest thing he had ever seen and there was nothing beyond it.

He slipped down through the jungle into the township. When night fell, he stole clothing and food. He followed a group of men and entered a tavern on the waterfront, looking for those with pitch on their hands. They were not hard to find, the men willing to risk their lives on the sea.

The captain had a temper if he was disobeyed, but he was not an unreasonable man. Aboard were men from all parts of the globe, good men and bad, every one of them hardened. They ensured the arrival of chocolate beans and cotton, artefacts and sugar, tobacco and timber, animals and seeds across the globe. On one voyage, a Catholic priest showed him the dried breast of a woman from the Amazon turned into a pouch for coin. He had seventeen for sale.

'Only one breast is taken,' the priest said. 'The women live but their babies cannot survive. It makes the natives docile.'

From the Americas, the ship made safe passage into warm places, islands where the people reminded him of his own people, gathered on the fringes of white-sand beaches eating fish cooked over a low fire. He hadn't thought of home in a long time. He wondered if anyone there was still alive. He had forgotten all their faces.

He sailed south with whalers to the Bay of Islands in New Zealand and then across an intemperate sea to an island called

Van Diemen's Land. It was a chill and sparkling place of dark green forests, hills, mountains and towering clouds. He sailed up a great river under a flock of birds moving south, obscuring the sun for most of the morning.

The whales in the harbour were so plentiful they could be killed by a harpoon trebuchet launched from the shore. The mountain slopes were abundant with kangaroo. There was a settlement of sorts. A few hundred sealers and whalers, explorers, deserters and truants, men and women from many lands who had taken to the sea for adventure, fortune or survival, and found a place where discovery was unlikely.

There were broad hunting fields where the grasses moved like sunshine and the trees were greater in girth than any he had ever seen. The native people came and went quietly from forest and river in small groups, hunting kangaroo and birds, eating shellfish on the shore. Sometimes there was a little trading and an attempt at a shared language.

It was a place of whale blubber, whale guts, whale stench, seal stench, fur skins, seal oil, whale oil. He learned it was a new century, although the idea of it escaped him.

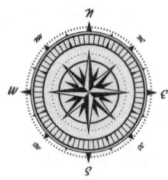

Within a few years, the English sailed in and made an encampment on the other side of the river. They put up a flag. Soon after, word came of a massacre of the native people after the kidnapping of one of their children by a soldier. The new arrivals relocated to the whalers' settlement, where a rivulet ran from the mountain to the bay, a place they began to call Hobart Town.

Their convicts laboured to fell trees, to mill timber, to cart and to carry. The settlement rambled along rutted streets and muddy lanes. Clay was dug and fired for bricks, stone was mined and carved, land was cleared. Rocks were broken and crushed, gravel was exhumed and shells were barrowed from the beaches to be ground into roads. Sheep were loosed onto the open grasslands. The rivulet was sullied with waste. Drinking water had to be collected further upstream. English hunting dogs were sent from New South Wales to bring down the population of kangaroos. More soldiers arrived to bring down the population of the natives.

The New South Wales Corps were the sort of white men Cornelius had seen everywhere, drunk on certainty and rum. A few years passed when no English ships arrived and there was no tea, flour or sugar, and no salted beef for the English garrison, but still there was rum. Soon it became a day's walk and more to bring down game, and the whales came less often into the harbour.

Cornelius had a gold cap on a rear molar and scars of every sort, small and large, inflicted and accidental. He had the height of a warrior, a broad chest, eyes that had seen the worst of people, a hip that had bothered him ever since Panama. The government officials had a long list of tools required for building, taming, baking and breaking. His forge was close to the harbour. The hearth, made of brick, was as deep as it was wide. Smoke drifted up through the shingle roof. There was an order to his tools, and an order to the room in which he slept and cooked. He made allegiances. He dressed carefully to ensure he was not mistaken for another kind of black man. He gained a certain standing for his usefulness.

Buildings arose, wharves overtook the shoreline, railings, walls and fences enclosed property and corralled livestock. Taverns, dwellings and shops proliferated. Prisoners continued to arrive, stumbling from the holds of ships, weary men and women hollow with hunger and weakened by captivity, quickly put to work. Soldiers strutted the streets and the flogging yard was always busy. Seeing white men enslaved brought Cornelius no balm. Cruelty was a boundless cycle of suffering that deserved no allegiance.

One afternoon, on a walk on the mountain where he liked to sit awhile and look down upon the town, a woman stepped out of the shadows. She wore a necklace of small green shells. A wallaby skin across her shoulders was her only clothing. Her hair was cropped close. They had no shared language, but he knew what she asked. *You, with skin the same colour as mine, do you wish to visit with my people?*

Cornelius spent nights in the secluded valleys of the mountain with fire, songs and stories, babies sleeping in their mothers' arms. He made love with the woman under the clouded stars. Theirs were different ways. There was nothing of owning, just belonging. Her people moved between mountain and sea, gone for seasons then returning. She laughed when she saw him again and welcomed him back to the fire and the dance. A child was born and he looked into her bright eyes and felt as if he had been given the moon for safekeeping.

More and more ships arrived. Shepherds and settlers were found dead in the hills, speared, their servants, too. He heard stories of raids and massacres. The woman's people were hanged on the waterfront for theft and murder. Roving parties of soldiers and convicts set out and returned, sometimes bringing with them a woman shackled, or children tied by a rope, pulled through the township behind dogs and horses. Every time, he feared it was her or his daughter. He did not know what he would do if it were them.

One day he saw a soldier pull a man's head out of his pack, the hair ochred, the jaw slack, the colourless eyes rolled back. A great cheer went up at the waterfront gin. He stopped going about after dusk.

She was taken from the shore by whalers heading north, along with two other women. And his daughter. The loss was almost enough to split his heart. He was mad with grief, enraged beyond reason. He sharpened knives, sought out a boat and acquired a map to go after them. But looking at the miles of coastline, the countless islands north and south, he realised the futility of the task. They were gone and he could not save them. He knew this demon. It had been with him a long time.

The keeping of hunting grounds and forest gardens, the smoking, stitching and skinning, the making of clothes and the threading of necklaces, the carving of ornaments, the welcoming of bird and fish, the harvesting from shore and sea, the gathering of clans, the ceremonies and seasons, it went away. Stories on bark were burned, markings on rocks disfigured and grown over. Dances went undanced, tales untold, songs unsung.

Wood, water, fire and air. These were the elements that governed and gave. There was a burgeoning population with wants and needs. Men came with orders and took away his handiwork. In the forge he fed the fire, watched the shape and colour of the flames to determine the heat, judging the flow of air, waiting for red, yellow and pale blue flames. He made axe heads and the rims for cartwheels. He fashioned hinges, bolts, locks and keys, and he kept to himself. He worked the coke, cleaned out the clinker and removed the ash and dust. He was reliable and trade was steady.

One early winter day, a young man of good bearing visited Cornelius and offered him a barn where he might have a bigger forge. 'It is over the hill, away from the town with its moods and habits. I have a cottage there. If you think you might like it, I will install an apartment within the barn where you might live.'

Bartholomew Broughton had high spirits and big dreams which he shared with Cornelius. They walked the land and Broughton invited him to dine.

'I have been in this town long enough to observe the people who can be relied on. You are such a man, Cornelius. No doubt you have heard rumours of me, as I have heard them of you. I know that my family in England would appreciate from me a veneer of respectability. If you will help me achieve mine, I will help you achieve yours. A win for both of us. What say you?'

The barn became his new forge, scented with oak barrels still smelling of rum and brandy, but it was a home. Cornelius made the scythes and shears that kept the grasses in the vineyard at bay. He made the spades that dug out the cellar and the shears that cut the grapes when they ripened. He stitched gloves and boots. Convicts dug and built, harvested, carried and cleared. Broughton spoke to Cornelius about his wine, but Cornelius refused to taste it, disliking anything that might dull his instincts or summon his memories.

By the sixth year, there were not enough buckets nor barrels for the bounty. There were not enough bottles. Broughton had made a champagne from earth, sunshine, vine and rain. The township was surprised by this unexpected boon, a wine far superior to anything that arrived by sea. *Here is a future never imagined for this place,* the newspapers proclaimed.

Broughton read the news to Cornelius, laughing as they prepared bottles for transport to New South Wales and to Port Phillip. They sent wine to London, Paris and Copenhagen. Broughton gave cuttings to new settlers. Tastings were offered to prospective buyers. Winemakers from New South Wales toured the farm. When the next vintage was ready, cases were loaded onto wagons and stacked onto the backs of gigs. Customers returned, pleading for another order.

Broughton planned a grand house to be built on the other side of the creek. Convicts cleared the land and established pine trees to line the way from the road to the residence. Sandstone was cut and footings laid. Fences were established. Gardens were planted. The house rose from the land as if it had always belonged there. And then Broughton was dead. Perhaps it was why the young winemaker had been in a hurry with his dreams; he may have had some sense that his time was short.

He was mourned by many, especially the young woman who had left her husband in the township to live with him, she from a wealthy family, too, a great scandal. Cornelius liked them well together. Like two matching bowls. Broughton's sister sailed from England at the news of her brother's death and attempted to claim the farm for herself, despite Broughton having willed it to the woman he loved. A legal duel ensued.

The years passed. Blackberries encroached. Grasses tangled with vines. Birds and opossums feasted as the crop ripened. Fruit dropped to the ground. Last year's growth was overwhelmed by the next.

Cornelius stayed on in the barn, both blacksmith and caretaker. He had money saved, and briefly considered leaving. There were always ships willing to take a passenger. Always places in need of a blacksmith. But he was no longer a young man. His hip still troubled him and his elbows ached in the evenings, and the mornings, too. He needed an eyeglass in poor light to thread twine for leather goods.

It had claimed him, this place. The seasons, the water of the mountain creeks, and the endlessly changing light upon the river. The mavericks, dreamers, scoundrels and survivors who made a life here. It was all in his bones now.

When the estate was finally settled and sold, Captain Swanston arrived with his wife and children. Swanston's interests were in banking, land, stock and politics. He proceeded with Broughton's plans for the new house but dismissed the vineyard already gone wild. There was no future in it, he told Cornelius. Other vineyards had failed. Only fools would invest in such a folly. He employed Cornelius to make all the tools required to equip his convict labourers. Trees were felled, the land given to sheep and planted with wheat.

A decade after Broughton's death, a young woman appeared with a boy at her side, asking about the cottage, the vineyard. She appeared again with Mrs Swanston and was introduced to Cornelius as the new tenant of Broughton's cottage. Soon he was moving furniture for her from the barn.

He saw her pushing her way into the wild scramble of the vineyard, turning about and taking it in, as if she knew something of its past or could see something of its future. On the morning he discovered her afloat in the pond when he went to take his wash, her eyes were open and she was staring into the morning sky as if she were having a vision.

As he watches her walk back across the field in her new boots of kangaroo skin, he wonders if she is yet accustomed to the sensation of the world having flung her adrift. Mostly what he'd seen of people was a yearning to take away the dread of uncertainty. To be content in a smallness. But some people seemed to harbour greater thoughts. Mrs Douglas, he thinks, is doing all she can to manage this unfamiliar life, and to make something of it.

· 5 ·

Jacques-Louis

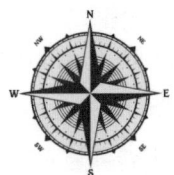

At the age of twenty, Jacques-Louis completes his apprenticeship in the apothecary under the judicious Doctor Douglas. But when it might have been assumed that he would don the apron and continue his work in the shop, the doctor reminds Jacques-Louis that an apothecary well versed in human nature makes a wiser practitioner. Perhaps it is time to go abroad, to expand his mind, to make peace with the past.

From Edinburgh, Jacques-Louis goes to Paris to visit the Picpus Cemetery. There he sits beneath a young tree and reminisces with his parents. He does not even know under which expanse of grass their faces and limbs moulder. He resolves to make enquiries and have a plaque placed. He leaves the shaded pathways emptied by the encounter.

In Reims their vineyards had been broken up and allocated to others in the devisal of modern France. The chateau that had been his childhood home had been destroyed in a fire. There is no way to reclaim the estate under the laws of the republic. But in the village, he is delighted to find Philippe and Mathilde, who had risked their lives to ensure he and Henriette escaped. They are so moved to see him that Mathilde falls at his feet.

Mathilde and Philippe's sons have been conscripted into the navy of Napoleon, whose reign has become a series of battles and blockades waged at sea and on land against the English, the Austrians, the Germans, the Russians, the Prussians, the Spanish and Napoleon's fellow Italians. It is a dangerous time for one such as Jacques-Louis, a member of the *Ancien Régime*.

Mathilde worries that Napoleon's declaration of an amnesty for returning *émigrés* is not enough to protect Jacques-Louis and that he might suffer a similar fate to the Duc d'Enghien—the last descendant of the house of Condé—who had been suspected of a plot to overthrow the new emperor. Kidnapped in Baden, he was brought across the border to be shot, despite Napoleon being assured of his innocence.

What if Jacques-Louis is discovered and called upon to fight. To fight for France? It seems as ridiculous to Jacques-Louis as asking him to fight for England. He knows not where his loyalties lie, other than with some notion of a past he does not know how to recapture.

But Napoleon has a particular love of champagne and farm labour is in short supply. He keeps his armies and his allies well supplied. The fields that made the Colbert wines now supply the house of Jean-Rémy Moët, maker of Napoleon's favourite champagne. Philippe has found work in the Moët cellars. He obtains a position for Jacques-Louis as a labourer in the caves, pretending he is a nephew, and Jacques-Louis quietly resumes the education that had been cut short.

A government minister and chemist, Chaptal, has written a book which Jacques-Louis acquires and reads aloud to Philippe, who has long been certain that the flavours of a particular wine, the very texture of it, derive from the place where it is grown. Certain vineyards produce grapes whose wine evokes truffles or raspberries, while others nearby produce flavours of honeysuckle and citrus. The addition of sugar is nothing new, but sugar is in short supply, wars and blockades having halted shipments from the Caribbean Sea. Fields of sugar beets have been planted at Napoleon's instruction to avoid a champagne crisis, spreading a new green mantle across the soil.

There is much to learn from Chaptal, and from Philippe and his colleagues when they inspect the vineyards before harvest. Vine spacing, pruning, the care of the soil. The pitfalls of interplanting or harvesting varieties together, which results in a wine of no particular character.

In the cellars Jacques-Louis, with the eyes of a chemist, observes experiments of fermentation. He notes the effects of lessening or increasing the time the grapes and skins are in contact, the time the grapes remain in the first fermentation, then the moment of union when the blending begins, and the perilous balance of sweetening. The smallest variables are consequential.

There is an optimal time to pick the grapes, when they are neither too ripe nor too green. Rotten grapes must be discarded. No stems are to be crushed with the grapes, nor too many grapes crushed together. He is reminded that the wine must not be stirred too often, and that vats must be washed with lime and water, barrels regularly replaced, the *vins clairs* covered. Philippe encourages him to learn the nuances of flavour within the wines, and what might be blended, what must wait, and what would blossom yet.

Every year brings its challenges. A wet summer, a particularly bitter spring. Results are unpredictable and the flavours in the wines from riverfront or hillside, north- or south-facing, vary. Jacques-Louis discusses all this with Philippe, and he shares it in his correspondence with young Hannah at home in Edinburgh. She cheers him with her reflections on her teachers, the neighbours, the books she is reading, the seasons passing through Edinburgh and her interactions with fellow students.

Jacques-Louis has been in France for four years when Philippe and Mathilde receive word that both their sons have been lost in a sea battle. Philippe ages overnight. Within a matter of weeks, he is laid in his grave, as if the lives of his children had been the animation of his soul.

Mathilde, blighted by grief, counsels Jacques-Louis to leave.

'Do not linger here from some sense of duty or obligation. Do not risk the madness of Napoleon. Of all I have cherished, you alone survive.'

He goes south and east to the Italian states, considering he might expand his knowledge there, but he finds wine of an inferior nature. The vines are allowed too much vigour, and grain and vegetables are planted in their midst making pruning and harvest particularly arduous. In the cellars the grapes are not sorted, and new grapes are added to the old from the day's harvest. He writes to Hannah:

> *The vines give of their bounty in a dance between man and fruit,*
> *season and patience, but only in Sicily and Tuscany have I found*
> *anything of merit. Elsewhere it is in abundance, but it is wine*
> *fit only for poets and their friends, as I heard it described. There*
> *is little consistency and much petty squabbling between various*
> *sovereignties, so industry is sorely limited. Napoleon is celebrated*

as founder, restorer and conqueror, having declared a new
Kingdom of Italy and himself Emperor.

He proposes to a merry, curvaceous girl and has his heart wounded when she decides to marry someone of greater means and lesser wit. He thinks to work passage from Sicily to Greece and on to Constantinople where he might find a ship to America and see the vineyards he has heard of in California. But when he reaches Athens a letter arrives from Hannah, much delayed, telling him that her mother has died of a haemorrhage during a late and unexpected pregnancy. The baby had died, too. Jacques-Louis feels the loss keenly, the woman who had taken Henriette and him into her family. He knows he must return to Edinburgh.

When Hannah descends the stairs to greet him, he sees that the years he has been away have transformed the girl of his memories, with her chestnut braids and plaid dresses, into a beautiful woman.

'You are not as I remembered you,' he says.

'You are exactly as I remember you, Jacques-Louis Colbert,' she replies.

Had Doctor Douglas foreseen that the daughter he treasured and the boy once destined to be a *duc* might share a destiny?

'It seemed prudent to see what a little time might do,' the doctor says with a twinkle in his eye.

When Jacques-Louis expresses his delight at finding himself in love with her, and his desire to marry her, Hannah laughs and says, 'Did you not always know that you adored me?'

Returned to the apothecary on High Street, with its familiar contents, and with Hannah nearby to welcome him home, a sense of tranquillity descends upon Jacques-Louis.

'Perhaps in time,' Doctor Douglas suggests, 'with wisdom, you will be sufficiently successful to grow the vineyard you imagine. Napoleon will not live forever, and France may yet find its way to more peaceful times.'

Jacques-Louis and Hannah are married, and when they return from their honeymoon in London, Jacques-Louis discovers that Doctor Douglas has altered the words on the glass door of the apothecary. It now reads:

Apothecary & Chemist
J.M. Douglas and J.L. Colbert

A year later, Hannah gives birth to Caroline, and two years later Augusta is born. Esther, the maid who has known Hannah since she was born and who had cared for the orphans arrived from Revolutionary France, is now their inestimable housekeeper.

Doctor Douglas dies of a stroke on a beautiful summer day. Jacques-Louis reads a verse of Robbie Burns at the funeral service, which is well attended by the physicians, surgeons and patients of Edinburgh who have relied upon him.

The chanting linnet, or the mellow thrush,
Hailing the setting sun, sweet, in the green thorn bush;
The soaring lark, the perching red-breast shrill,
Or deep-toned plovers, grey, wild whistling o'er the hill . . .

Henriette returns from London to attend the service. She urges Jacques-Louis and Hannah to bring their young family to London. His skills are needed. They are not bound to Edinburgh and the apothecary would sell for a good price. London offers so many opportunities for his practice, and for their daughters. There is a future there waiting for them all.

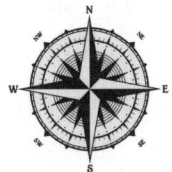

In Edinburgh, patients had visited him on the High Street with their aches, rashes and agues, but in London he finds himself administering salves and ointments to the displaced, the destitute, the dissolute and the abandoned.

Before dawn each day, the factory bells sound and, soon after, Jacques-Louis hears the footsteps of children, women and men passing by in the darkness, returning only as night closes in, and later. He hears of a white moth, well known in the midlands, which had become easy prey to owls and other birds for its newfound conspicuousness on the coal-blacked walls of the factories and houses. Over a few decades, it has begun emerging from its chrysalis with black wings and body, thus demonstrating, he supposes, the thinking of the time. Adapt; comply; survive, if you can.

The new century had been filled with promise, as new centuries tended to be. But he had not perceived the importance of James Watt inventing a separate condenser for the steam engine, empowering the machinery of mining and manufacturing. It was a scale of production never imagined. He had never seen the spinning jenny that multiplied the power of the weaver eight-fold. He had not reckoned on African slavery ever ceasing, but the British seem set on outlawing it. The new slaves are in the factories of London. He sees the chronic throat infections, eye infections, the incessant coughing and lung disease of the workers and those who lived close to the factories. The girl with the missing arm caught in a machine, who tells him that she rarely left the factory for it was warmer there and, if she was late for her shift, the foreman beat her with a whip. Without an arm, her future is the poorhouse or the brothel. He sees the split fingers and crushed feet. He tends to people with broken spines and ruptured organs. He closes the eyes of those who come too late. The woman who had sought to rid herself of the baby she was carrying, for she could not afford another child, and bleeds out in the back room of the shop. Nothing to be done, by that late stage, but to hold her in his arms and watch her light fade.

It isn't only London. It is evident in Derbyshire and Leicestershire, the guilds and their apprenticeships lost, the skills of artisans, men and women, livelihoods extinguished by machines impervious to the cycles of daylight, weather, seasons and community, a legacy of craftspeople gone in a generation. Ned Lud saw it in Nottinghamshire. Workers in the woollen mills sought a regulation of wages and hours. Public letters were written and affixed to every door and published in the papers, all signed with Lud's name, or sometimes signed King Lud, which made a lot of people laugh, though not the real King, of course. The adamant refusal of factory owners caused riots.

The government busied itself stamping out Ned Lud and his Luddites. How dare a common man, easily replaceable, rail against the ingenuity, the sheer brilliance of invention and efficiency, this juggernaut born of steel, steam and coal? A worker might as well rail against an ocean he hoped to calm with a ballad. How dare he protest against men who had staked their capital on distant lands, and whose wealth built factories and machines? Such men were the landlords of the world. Justice had no time for dissent, insurgence or radicalism.

Of the one million people living in London, one hundred thousand of them were criminals. The captured ships from England's wars were rotting in fog-filled estuaries and swamps, until one British lord conceived of them as places to house the flow of thieves, forgers, embezzlers, fornicators, schemers and opportunists, the detritus of the new industrial age. Someone calculated that it cost a great deal less to transport such vermin than to maintain them in England. There they could also provide a useful workforce. And was it not prudent for a parliament of aristocrats to rid themselves of the poor and disenchanted before they rose up against their masters, as they had done in France? Hereditary power, the privilege of position, must remain as fixed and enduring as the sun in the sky.

England had sent more than fifty thousand convicts to Maryland, Georgia and Virginia over the past two hundred years. When America won her independence, she ceased to accept such cargo. Over the coming century, the English government would send more than one hundred and sixty thousand convicts, to a place of waterfowl and wildlife, of estuaries, forests and mountains that would become Sydney. It was as far from England as it was almost possible to sail, a land the maps referred to as Terra Australis. South of Terra Australis, there was a group of islands, one quite large. The Dutch had named this archipelago Van Diemen's Land. The French explored it, but the English claimed it.

· 6 ·

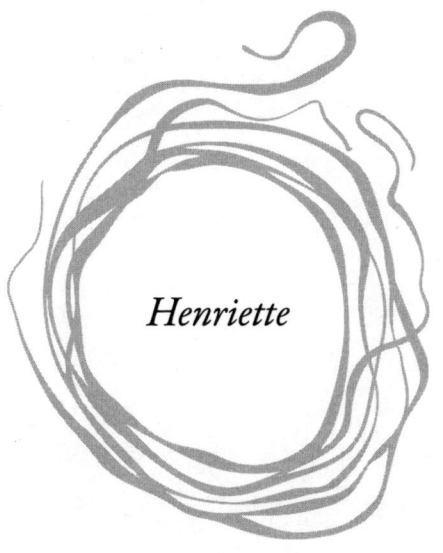

Henriette

Henriette is nineteen when she answers an advertisement for a lady's maid in London. She has delightful English and her French, of course, is impeccable. She is modest and shy, for Henriette has observed that this is how the British like their young women, especially those in service. She is a treasure, she is told, by a potential employer and, but for the imprudent French, she might have been a lady herself. This observation said with such indifference rankles Henriette but it is decided that, instead of a lady's maid, she will make the perfect companion for a granddaughter who is soon to enter society. Within the week, Henriette is living in a home of twelve bedrooms, with a barouche-landau to travel in and an entire retinue of staff at her beck and call. She is not housed in the servants' quarters but in a pretty bedroom close to where her mistress sleeps, so that she might be on hand as required.

She is expected to be practical and attentive, offering assistance, conversation and, from time to time, sisterly advice. She tempers herself so that neither her beauty nor her wit detract in any way from her rather plain, indifferently educated and very rich mistress, who is three years younger than Henriette. The father, recently made a knight of the realm, has made his fortune in cotton, although mills are never mentioned for fear of the stain of trade.

When her mistress visits the homes of her friends, Henriette accompanies her. The first thing she steals is a tiny ivory elephant. The third is a sapphire necklace.

The party is an afternoon affair, and she has been invited to entertain the ladies with stories of France. She recounts riding the fields at dawn with her brother. There is mist lingering on the River Marne. She speaks of the tiny tendrils of grapevines that cling and curl and are as pretty as earrings. She tells a graphic story of the guillotine. The ladies gasp and coo and wave their fans and blush. It is too horrible, but do tell us more . . .

Henriette's eyes fill with tears at their kindness.

Cake and champagne are served, and the ladies are laughing now. It is not their revolution, after all, nor their parents at the guillotine. Henriette, fatigued by the recollection of things past, begs a brief reprieve while the heiresses stroll in the garden. She observes them as they disappear along an arbour of lilac in bloom, the flagstones sprinkled with mauve petals. She asks the maid taking away the tea things where she might find the water closet.

It is an elaborate invention of embossed porcelain with a robust ceramic chain. She knows that a home with such a water closet will have small things that will not be missed immediately. She enters a bedroom, and then another, feeling her way by smell and instinct. This one a man's, this one a lady's.

Henriette lifts garments of satin and silk from a drawer, each pressed and folded. Peach, lemon and cream lingerie as beautiful as any she had once owned. She lifts a chemise to her cheek and sees a key nestled on a brown velvet ribbon. It opens an inlaid cabinet that reveals boxes with soft interiors of blue satin, white satin and dark velvet. She discovers a bracelet, a set of earrings, a sapphire necklace and a pearl tiara. She slips the necklace into her pocket.

In her room that evening, she lights the candles beside her mirror and becomes the duchess she was born to be. The stones twinkle at her throat. The past is softened. She imagines a lover downstairs awaiting her arrival for a late supper. At dawn she will go to the stables where her horse is saddled, and she will ride across the green fields in the light of a new day.

By the time the theft of the necklace is discovered, many people have come and gone from the house. It might have been missing for weeks. No one could say. Everyone is questioned.

The man who comes to interview Henriette has a moustache and sharp eyes. He is a Bow Street Runner, an investigator for those who believe themselves robbed or otherwise mistreated. Bow Street Runners are paid for their services according to the value of the item, and a sapphire necklace is a very valuable thing.

'I can hardly recall the house at all,' she says. She had visited so many, she tells him, and they all overwhelmed her with their beauty. They may have wandered the gardens.

'Are you sure you walked in the garden and did not stay behind to rest?' he asks.

'A companion is easily overlooked,' she says, and does not sigh, determining that the theatre of the moment requires seriousness without melancholy. 'I am sure you understand.'

'Of course,' he says.

She can tell that he has made his way in a world where one's accent immediately reveals one's place of birth and likely relations.

'It is an appalling thing to have someone steal a family treasure,' she says, intimating some reference to her past. She asks that he convey her sympathy to the viscountess.

The theft creates a stir in various homes of London. She hears that a manservant has been arrested and charged, having been found with a sum of cash, though not the necklace. He is sent to the colonies. After this she becomes more thoughtful and calculating in her methods.

When her young mistress goes abroad with her grandmother on a tour of Europe, Henriette accompanies them. She sells the necklace to a jeweller in Paris who declares himself willing to accept any further pieces she wishes to move along. Henriette is delighted by her newfound wealth, but makes no purchases nor any changes that might convey her situation.

Returning to London, she finds a merchant who receives the Austrian lace, Venetian bibelots and other baubles she has acquired on the European tour.

Her mistress is to be married. She insists on introducing Henriette to a certain duchess who is leaving for a winter in Rome and is in need of a companion and translator. Henriette is employed in another grand house. She and the duchess return from their Italian sojourn via Paris, at Henriette's suggestion. She again visits the jeweller, who greets her warmly.

One day in Knightsbridge, on an errand for her employer, she comes across a fabric shop where she runs her fingers over Indian cotton, silk and muslin, Irish linen trimmed with lace in black and cream, fit for a funeral, fit for a wedding. All the great ladies of London run accounts. In the name of her mistress, she purchases a length of white muslin with spangles that catch the firelight, and when it is delivered she fails to inform her mistress and hides the fabric away in a chest in her room. A bolt of deep red silk is delivered in the same way, along with several pairs of kid gloves her mistress has requested. The gloves delight her mistress, the husband pays the bills, and the fabric is never mentioned.

Henriette loves the touch of each item, to feel them against her skin. She has to resist availing herself of small things wherever she goes. But the thrill of it: to find a bauble in her hand and steal away with it. She knows it is shameful and she should stop, but she cannot. The fascination is compelling, as is her success. She has found a medicine to assuage the unrest she has felt since her parents' death. It cannot be wrong to care for herself in this way. She refuses to believe it. She even likes the risk of being caught. The hammering of her heart, the tingle on her lips and in other places on her body. The guile it requires to avoid all suspicion.

She makes the acquaintance of Gulliver Wendover, recognising him as an astute man, a man willing to move on pieces she might wish to sell without asking questions nor expecting more than his share. He has excellent connections.

She thinks to perfect a disguise. Perhaps a wig and spectacles. Or to dress as a man. She sees the future. But to succeed, she needs somewhere of her own. A place where no one may observe her movements. It takes some time before she finds a suitable premises to rent near Mayfair. Formerly a shop, it has an apartment above it and a discrete rear entrance.

'If you can establish yourselves in London,' she says to Hannah and Jacques-Louis, 'you might have a shop of diverse wares. Medicines, yes, all that is needed for tonics and such, but perhaps also a store for oil and tallow, string and rope, tea and chocolate, needles and ribbon. Even fabric to sell. Imagine the opportunities such a life might afford you all.'

Jacques-Louis finds a location to establish his apothecary in Chelsea and Henriette offers him a down payment of a year's rent.

'I have generous employers and I live very simply,' she says.

Her summer tours of Europe with this viscountess or duchess or lady allow her occasion to acquire what she needs. Fabric is shipped, jewellery and silverware, some of it accompanied by genuine receipts and some not. Herbs, medicines and spices are purchased for her brother, too.

When Jacques-Louis discovers Henriette's subterfuge he is appalled at the risks she is taking, at the danger she has brought to his door. She offers him a larger share of the profit. If they work together, she tells him, there is a chance that they might yet reclaim something of their old lives. She knows he still dreams of planting his own vineyard in France. Is that not a worthy cause?

'Perhaps,' he says. 'But Hannah cannot know.'

'Your wife is very astute,' she replies.

'I will keep a separate ledger.'

'*Ce serait prudent*,' she says.

Onward they go, although she is never reliant on him. She and Wendover have assembled a select troupe to lift and pilfer, lie and deceive. Profits flow and treasures accumulate, but they have to be moved along no matter how much Henriette loves the feel of them in her hands and the sight of them on her person. Those she cannot bear to part with make their way upstairs to her apartment.

In the years that follow, she is unsurprised to find an accomplice in her niece, Caroline. She has always been a little untamed, despite her mother's best efforts. There is something burning in the girl's soul. Something that refuses to bow down. Caroline, Henriette observes, feels when other people think. She laughs when she is startled. She remains unperturbed when others might be fearful. Henriette understands this perfectly. Jacques-Louis is promising the girl things that might never be hers. Henriette knows this story from her own youth.

In time, she sees she has been right all along. Her brother has failed them all. Caroline will never have the future planned for her. But perhaps she can have a future Henriette imagines for her. A future that might suit them both.

· 7 ·

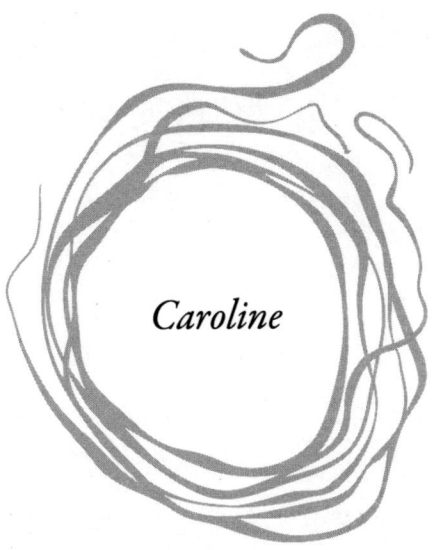

Caroline

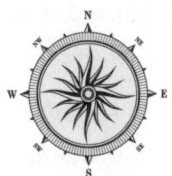

Her father did not remember falling from old Mrs Toomey's roof, which he and Jimmy Dunlop had been repairing for winter.

'One moment he had hammer in hand, and then I was looking down to see him upon the cobblestones,' Jimmy recounted. 'So much blood that you'd have thought someone had cut the throat of a goat.'

Insensible, but a pulse, so not dead, Caroline ascertained, but perhaps soon. Mama sent for Doctor Arnold, the surgeon, who made fair work of stitching up the wound. The skull itself was broken, the brain likely bruised. He set the arm where the wrist was fractured, and removed two teeth shattered in the fall. 'It will be a marvel if he survives,' he said. Caroline and Mama strapped his ribs with comfrey leaves. Complete rest and quiet were prescribed.

Caroline measured a tincture of opium, mixing it with honey, placing it on her father's tongue when he began to twitch and rouse. Sometimes he wailed in pain and other times in anguish, railing against some inner force of dream or memory. They strapped his arms to the bedsides to prevent him further injuring himself. That had been May.

By September, he was still in bed, the shining braid of scar across his brow giving him the look of a brigand. His clear, brown-eyed gaze was clouded, his vision blurred so that he mistook them one for another. They laid iced washcloths over his eyes to ease the vicious sparkles, as he called them. The drapes were kept drawn. They trod softly and whispered in the hallway so as not to disturb him.

When he could venture from the bedroom, he did so with a cane, his other hand stretched out before him, for all things appeared in duplicate. Sometimes he fell down in a fit and Mama had to place a wooden spoon between his teeth to prevent him from biting his tongue. Afterwards he had no recollection of the event. The man who had been the source of so much merriment had become a restless, irascible, unpredictable creature.

They tried to soften his world with love and kindness. Esther made hot wine with herbs at night and, in the morning, warm bread which they served him with butter and the citrus marmalade he loved. Every day Caroline offered to read to him. Sometimes they made their way through a poem or a few pages before he sighed. '*C'est suffisant. Merci, ma chérie.* There comes a lightning storm in my head.'

When the fits receded and he was able to cross the garden to the greenhouse, navigating the pathways tired and frustrated him. The smallest inconvenience could provoke rage. After one event, which their mother refused to discuss, all knives and razors were removed from his reach and kept in a locked cabinet.

Caroline's and Augusta's schooling was interrupted, but Caroline was relieved to be free of the classroom and Miss Pinkerton's lectures on catechism and morality, the singing of hymns, the mastering of piano scales and the painting of flowers. Singing and piano and painting were Augusta's talents. She had friends amongst her fellow students, while Caroline preferred the seclusion of a book to the incessant conversations of girls. She would have liked to discuss literature and plants, astronomy and animals, but her fellow students had no interest, laughing at her passion for such things.

It had quickly become evident to Miss Pinkerton that Caroline would be most useful teaching French. But beyond basic vocabulary and a few useful phrases, the girls, whose fathers were in banking and trade, were mostly indifferent. Caroline embarked on a translation of *Les Liaisons dangereuses*, in an effort to revive their seemingly numbed imaginations, and found the girls enraptured. Miss Pinkerton, learning of this, was scandalised and reprimanded Caroline severely.

Once Papa could be left in the capable care of Esther, Hannah began opening the shop each morning. Having assisted her own father in Edinburgh and Jacques-Louis in the establishment and running of the London apothecary, the work was familiar and the money necessary. At night, she showed Caroline the ledgers, teaching her the accounting of the various streams of income and expenditure. It interested Caroline, this work with numbers.

Caroline kept the inventory, ordered supplies, ran errands, ground herbs, made the salves and tinctures her father had taught her, and also listened attentively to those who came seeking her mother's assistance. She wrote labels in Latin: *Isobeliae sulpatis, Tincturae jalaep.*

Midwives, herbalists and healers continued to make their purchases despite Papa's absence, but the flow of men, including medical men who comprised a great deal of their business, dwindled.

•

Enquiries were made as to Papa's health, and the answer Caroline and Mama gave was always the same.

'He is improving, thank you. We trust he will be returned to his work before long.'

Caroline had four years of her father's training, but she was young and a woman. She knew it was easy for clients to doubt her knowledge. The year before, a pharmacist nearby had poisoned twenty-five people when he dispatched arsenic rather than daft, the powdered limestone cheaper establishments used to extend the mixture for boiled sweets. Papa had been furious when he heard of it.

'*L'idiot! L'idiot!*' he had declared. 'How will people trust us?' He had reminded Caroline of the responsibilities of correct labelling and the checking and rechecking of ingredients.

'*Oui*, Papa, poisonous powders in green glass bottles, liquids in pink. *Ne t'inquiète pas. Tu m'as bien appris ça.*'

The balances on the ledgers declined. Caroline heard her mother discussing their household expenses with Esther. Casseroles became soups; soups became broth. Tea-leaves were reused again and again.

Tante Henriette arrived with four plump chickens to add to the henhouse in the garden. A hamper of tea and Scottish short-bread arrived, along with a box of oranges and another of pears, two pounds of butter, almonds, dried dates and figs. Esther and Augusta baked a tart with the butter and pears. Augusta made several loaves with the dates and bottled the figs in syrup. Chickens reluctant to lay made their way into the pot or roasting tray and afterwards the bones were used for soup.

Jacques-Louis' black curls turned grey at the temples. There was grey in his whiskers, and shadows beneath his eyes. Then his walking began.

At first it was only in the afternoons that he longed to be free of the house. Caroline accompanied him. But once he could walk without the cane, he preferred to go alone, wearing his wide-brimmed black hat to disguise the wound across his brow. Then he began to walk out in the evenings and he did not always return. Mama went in search of him, hearing from this person or that in what direction the Frenchman, the apothecary, had gone. He was well known in that part of London. She alerted neighbours and friends, and sometimes they were able to find him wandering the streets and guide him back to the house.

Then he began staying away for days, returning lean and hungry, the soles on his boots worn down, his coat and hat wet from rain, unable to say where he had been. When he saw their faces, he seized each of them and wept, declaring how pleased he was to have found them.

Some nights he burst in on Caroline and Augusta as they slept, pleading with them to turn down the moon for it was singing too loudly. Another time he urged them to come now, in their bedclothes, to see the tide turn on the Thames, for the waters flowing in were from the very centre of the globe.

Mama led him away, saying, 'Back to bed now, my love, and you too my darling girls, and don't mind your father. He is not well.'

He had known the things that intrigued Caroline's mind and soothed her soul. He knew which book would engage her, what fact would pique her interest, what story would make her laugh. He understood her love of polished boots and had always taken particular care to ensure they awaited her each morning, long after she was old enough to polish them herself. He had taught her to see and smell and taste the world, to look with kindness upon beauty and hardship in all its manifestations, to respect its rhythms and be patient with its particularities.

'You are at the heart of all you create,' he had said to her. 'Which means you are immense, but also very small, if we can allow those two notions to live side by side.'

Where was that man now? Was he still inside this person who resembled her father? Or had he departed, leaving this other man in his place?

It was almost a year before Jacques-Louis stood at the counter again, consulting on an ulcer, a fever, the cleaning of rust from a lock, a tincture for sleeplessness. The man sitting on a stool measuring powders or sweets was a shade, a brittle semblance of the ebullient Jacques-Louis. Caroline discreetly corrected remedies he had assigned to certain disorders, remeasured quantities and amended entries in the notes and accounts. The ring of the bell above the door, the breaking of a bottle, a crying child, horses on the cobblestones, all these things might agitate, disorientate and sometimes enrage her father. Despair brought him low for days at a time.

At home he could not find the things he needed. He left books and clothes about the house. Sometimes he was excitable and energetic, other times he wept with frustration.

And then Caroline noticed the tremor in her mother's hand. The stumble in her foot.

'Mother, is something wrong?' she asked.

'Nothing to worry about, my love,' her mother replied. 'It will pass.'

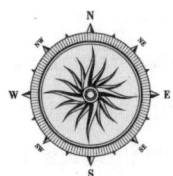

Jacques-Louis was convinced he could find a cure. He searched through volume after volume upon his shelves and sought the opinions of numerous doctors and colleagues on Mama's decline, but nothing—no tonic, potion, powder, not even the despised leeches—restored her.

Within half a year, it was Mama who must walk with a stick. Who could not rise from a chair without assistance. Who tired if she attempted the simplest task. Whose hands could no longer hold a spoon.

Caroline held her mother's limbs and moved them for her, a strange involuntary dance that seemed to soothe. She rubbed her mother's feet with lavender oil. They smiled at the strangeness of the child who must care for the parent as the parent once cared for the child.

'I wish you could be well again, Mama,' Caroline said to her.

'See the blackbird on the branch out the window there?' her mother asked. 'I grow jealous that it can feel the sunshine. That it can fly.' She insisted the curtains were never drawn so she might see clouds, the sky, and the moon and stars at night.

'We will try to move you outside on the next warm day,' Caroline said.

Jacques-Louis resumed disappearing into the night and returning days later. Such episodes frightened Caroline so much that she begged him to do all he could to remain in the house. Her mother suggested adding a sleeping powder to his evening tea. Caroline did so and was relieved to find her father at home the following morning.

'I would have loved to see you full grown and married, Mousie, and your sister, too,' Mama said. 'But the good Lord knows what's best.'

It had seemed so natural to find her mother preparing a meal in the kitchen with Esther, mending and sewing, working late into the night when there was a surfeit of berries to preserve, or vegetables to prepare for bottling. Always ready to teach Caroline or Augusta a new skill, or note their achievements. Keen for them to carry themselves as young ladies and make their parents proud. Her mother loved fresh flowers for the vases and candles lit for the dinner table. She wanted to listen to the news of the day, to upsets and irritations, offering reassurance, sagacity or a mischievous dose of humour. Caroline saw that her father had urged her to grow wings, but her mother had reminded her that there was a soft place to fall.

'How will I settle Papa when he gets into his moods, Mama?' she asked. 'What will I do if he wanders and I cannot find him? What will happen to the shop?'

'At heart you're Scots, Mousie, and don't forget it,' her mother replied. 'You have your father's mind, but you have a fair streak of your mother's determination, too. You're tough, my love, tougher than you know. Hold on to that.'

'I can't do without you,' Caroline said.

Mama patted her hand. Her eyes were closed, her body so small in the bed. 'There will be an end to earthly cares for us all,' she said softly. 'But first you must live your life, my Caroline.'

Some years before, Caroline had concluded that she could bear her mother's Presbyterian church, with its hard pews and resolute liturgy, no longer. She knew it was a grave disappointment to her mother, but Papa said it was a choice Caroline had the intelligence to make for herself.

Papa was an atheist, he had told Caroline, when she had shared her misgivings. 'I have ruminated often on the nature of the soul,' he said, 'for I have seen too much of death not to.' He thought that humans were no different from the celestial bodies in the sky. The sun breathed, the stars, too. Air was the source of all life. Life was breath. When the time came for degeneration, the illumination of the body faded and the breath ceased.

'If there is a soul that carries us beyond death,' Papa said, 'I do not need a religion to attest to it. It is the mystery of life, and being a mystery it is, by its very nature, inexplicable and unknowable.'

After she stopped attending her mother's church, Tante Henriette had invited Caroline to a discreet private chapel in Piccadilly where other French Catholics worshipped. Mama had encouraged her, saying it was better to be a papist than to have no faith at all. Caroline liked the incense and chanting. Her eyes lingered on the rich carpets, the shimmering gold and green embroidery on the vestments of the priest. She observed the altar arrayed with a gold chalice, the elaborate candlesticks and tall slender candles. She stared at the blood dripping from the wounds of Jesus on the cross behind the altar. In a painting, she saw him healing the sick.

During the long months of her mother's illness, Caroline went daily to the chapel to light candles. On Sunday mornings she accompanied Augusta to the Presbyterian church out of sisterly companionship, but on Sunday evenings she attended Catholic evening prayer and went to confession. She had words to say to the Lord. Each night, before they blew out the candles, Augusta read aloud a Psalm and insisted that she and Caroline pray.

Their mother's words became harder to understand. Her face became less mobile. No more the quick smile, the twinkling eyes. She could not bathe, dress or toilet herself. The shapely woman with her shining smile and generous nature became a frail, wilted thing, barely able to tolerate the removal of the bedpan. Frustration and limitations seeped into the dust motes.

'Read to me,' she said, and Caroline read aloud the poems her mother loved.

'Happiness is but a name,
Make content and ease thy aim.
Ambition is a meteor-gleam,
Fame a restless airy dream;
Pleasures, insects on the wing.
Round Peace the tenderest flower of spring;
Those that sip the dew alone,
Make the butterflies thy own;

Those that would the bloom devour,
Crush the locusts, save the flower.
For the future be prepared,
Guard wherever thou can'st not shun;
But thy utmost duly done,
Welcome what thou can'st not shun . . .'

The new curate, tall and vital with red hair and pale grey eyes, visited each week. He recited his words with a gentle passion.

'Dearly beloved, know this, that Almighty God is the Lord of life and death. Know your sickness is God's visitation. Whether it be to try your patience for the example of others, or else it be sent to correct or amend in you whatsoever doth offend the eyes of your Heavenly Father, know that if you truly repent of your sins . . .'

What did the Lord know of her generous, affectionate mother? Caroline wanted to argue. How could she have offended in the eyes of the Lord? Her mother was kind to everyone she met and seldom found fault. She had nursed their father day and night after his fall and had borne patiently the nights when he did not come home. She had walked the midnight streets in search of him. She had borne the loss of dear baby Isobel at two years old.

Caroline saw that her mother had submitted to her life, and for what profit? This harrowing disease? How dare this be God's idea of her mother's passage into everlasting life.

Caroline ceased her church visits. She said to Augusta, 'It is up to us, here in the world, to make what we can of all that is too big for us. Prayer may bring solace, but it is not initiative.'

•

Caroline held her mother's hand. She could feel her mother's pulse beating on, stronger than her frail body, a determined animal with its own habits. Breath, a pause, a pause, a pause, and then at last another rattling breath.

When her life departed at last, all that remained of the woman she had been was a withered chalice, her cheeks and eyes and mouth having lost all her essence, becoming within minutes an aged yellow mask. Outside the city was solemn after the wind and rain that had harried the streets for days. Caroline and Augusta wept. Esther, inconsolable, showed the priest to the door. The house settled into a void.

'Mama is not Mama anymore,' said Augusta.

'No,' said Caroline. 'But she will always be with us.'

'Not when we choose our husbands or birth our babies. What is to become of us then?' asked Augusta. 'What if Papa is never well again and we must close the shop? How will we live?'

Caroline took Augusta in her arms and held her close. She had no answers. Death was incontestable. Papa had fallen asleep with his head on the counterpane, still holding Mama's hand. When he woke he regarded Caroline and Augusta sitting on the other side of the bed. He said, 'We will go to Paris. It's the most beautiful city in the world. Jacques-Louis will go home.' Then he laid his cheek again beside his wife's dead hand and slept once more.

Oh, heart, you are a fickle friend, Caroline thought. She wanted to write it down, to find some poem to hold this moment, but she was so tired.

They washed Mama's body, Caroline, Esther and Augusta, rubbing her skin with bergamot and rose oil. Caroline and Augusta chose a gown for her. They arranged her hair. They managed to pull on stockings and shoes, although the undertaking was not easy and they began to giggle.

'She would want you to laugh,' Papa said. 'Perhaps in this very room, she is watching on and laughing, too.'

At the funeral, Caroline found it hard to remember people's names.

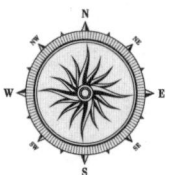

The night after the funeral, Caroline woke and tiptoed to the room where her mother had lain. The curtains were still open. Esther had stripped and remade the bed so that Papa might sleep there again.

She went in search of her father, expecting to find him sitting late in his study, but he was not there. In the hallway she saw that his hat was missing, along with his brass-topped cane that held a vial of whisky. He had gone walking.

He was gone for a week.

'I have made arrangements,' he said when he returned at last, a beard darkening his face, his clothes dishevelled. His mood was strangely placid. 'Your mother has counselled me, and the solution is clear.'

'Arrangements, Papa?' Caroline asked. 'Arrangements with Mama?'

'Yes, yes. It is all agreed. You and your sister are to live with Madame Murray. She has agreed to offer you both lodgings. It is for the best.'

•

Mrs Murray had the guesthouse next door with a little Baptist chapel in the rear courtyard where once there had been a stable. People visiting London went there to pray. Her only child was a son the same age as Caroline, a boy who took pleasure in practical jokes as they were growing up. Mrs Murray found such antics amusing, telling the girls that it was just the way boys were, and if they had a brother they would know all about it. Caroline and Augusta had learned to be wary of him.

Late in Mama's illness, Mrs Murray had offered to sit beside her so Caroline or Augusta might sleep after a long night of watchfulness. In the shops about, Caroline began to hear how good it was of Mrs Murray to be caring for their mother, what a help she must be to Caroline and Augusta and their poor afflicted father, hardly out of the sickbed himself.

Mrs Murray had begun entering their house by the back laneway they shared, surprising Esther in the kitchen. Esther had harrumphed to Caroline about people taking liberties. Such incursions happened when Augusta or Caroline had departed on an errand. When running an errand was still possible. Caroline had wondered if Mrs Murray watched to see who was arriving and leaving the house.

'I know she wishes to be kind,' Mama had said, 'but she pure exhausts me.'

'Papa,' Caroline had protested, 'we do not need to live with Mrs Murray. Esther can keep house, and Augusta and I will assist you in the shop.'

'I have advised an agent,' he said. 'I am selling the house. I will use the funds to make investments. We will make enough to go back to France. Yes. Yes! We will return to Champagne and I will make wine. I have been away too long. We have all been away too long.'

'Papa, no!' Caroline said. 'Please don't do this. We will manage somehow. Mama would not have wanted this.'

'Dear Caroline, do you not think she is with me every moment? Mrs Murray has offered to find you both employment. I am assured that you and your sister will be cared for.'

'But, Papa, what of the apothecary? Our life is here. Do you mean to abandon us? What is to become of Esther?'

'Esther . . .' he said, looking about as if he had misplaced her. 'Yes. Esther must go back to Scotland.'

'Papa, please—you are going too fast,' she said.

'Time is unknowable. Too fast, too slow. You do realise, do you not, that nothing is real? If I do not leave London my mind will unpeel.' He laughed and clapped his hands. 'It's a rhyme. Ha! We must pack, Caroline. Pack up! All these bowls and plates. Come, let us make a start. My books. I must pack my books.'

Caroline took his hand and guided him to a chair. 'Sit, Papa,' she said. 'You are very tired, are you not?'

She wet a cloth and placed it upon his brow, stroking his head the way Mama used to, her heart a rock in her chest.

'The lightning in my head . . .' he said. 'You must pack every-thing away, Caroline.'

'Yes, Papa,' she said. 'But first, rest. Hush now, hush now . . .'

The next morning he was gone.

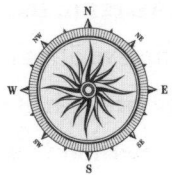

In the garden where she had grown up, she had sensed that plants were not living only to be harvested. Something more animated them, a communion of knowledge. She didn't understand it, but she had observed it. The sun shone from behind a cloud and the lavender released its fragrant oil. When she watered the peppermint, it emanated perfume in delicious waves. It was as if the plants were paying attention, trying to tell her, through their language, that they were aware of everything about them. She was sure they grew and flowered and offered more fruit when she paid close attention. She had sat and read poetry to them and was certain they were listening.

'Goodbye mint,' Caroline said, as she farewelled them all. 'Goodbye French lavender. Goodbye strawberries, raspberries and currants. Goodbye brassicas, fennel, spinach, lettuce, radishes, celeriac. Goodbye potatoes. Goodbye jasmine growing on the back wall.' She had loved its night scent wafting into her bedroom window. 'Goodbye venerable borage. Goodbye red rose, pink rose, yellow roses, too.'

She put her face into the grapevine, smelling its soft green scent, remembering her father's voice as he talked, passionate but also gentle.

'I was seven for my first harvest,' her father had said. 'There were many vineyards and winemakers in the village, so the picking was the work of everyone. Of course, it was different when I returned as a young man. The Moët family had many workers in the fields and in the caves. Still, the method is much the same for growing table grapes or wine grapes. The same pruning and weeding and the mulching of the soil—but carefully, for the roots of the grape are close to the ground.

'As the fruit ripens, you must watch for powdery mildew, black spot and mealy bugs. Depending on the variety, some grapes will remain green, or even turn golden when ripe, while others become red and purple and almost black. Each variety ripens at a slightly different time. You must wait for the moment of optimal sweetness.

'All the vines of France and England date back to the Greeks and Romans. Back to vines that grew when there were kings in Egypt, to the time of Pan and Ishtar, the Babylonians and the Assyrians. When wine was first made, we do not know. But it seems to have come to Europe with the assistance of the Etruscans, who imported both wine and vines from the Phoenicians. They stored them in clay vessels, the colour of the clay denoting a particular region. The people knew where the wine had been made by those colours. Thousands of these amphorae were shipped across the Mediterranean in ancient times.

'The making of wine,' he had said, 'is a particular skill. But the making of champagne requires energy and alchemy, and something more. A type of magic.'

She remembered him asking if, in her estimation, the plants preferred one poet over another.

'Marlowe and Marvell, Papa!' she had said.

And he had replied, 'Ah yes,' and recited:

'*What wondrous life is this I lead!*
Ripe apples drop about my head . . .'

She had joined in:

'*The luscious clusters of the vine,*
Upon my mouth do crush their wine.'

And they had laughed.

She farewelled it all, and could not believe this was really the end. Surely they would resume their work in the apothecary? It was only a temporary interruption while her father recovered. But how would they ever create such a garden again? Did he really mean for them to move to France? Tante Henriette was on a tour of the East, companion to a dowager who had wanted to see the Great Pyramids. Caroline was unsure when her aunt would return.

Linens and bedding were packed away, the silverware and crockery, pots and pans, their father's clothes, their many books, all the stuff of family life. It was to be housed in Mrs Murray's attic, on Papa's instructions. But when they said goodbye to Esther, there was a sorrowful finality in their hearts. Each understood that the severing was not of the moment, but of something deeper—irrevocable and absolute.

'You know where to find me in Dundee,' Esther said to Caroline and Augusta. 'Mind,' she added, 'that a sailor is not surprised when the wind blows against him. Nor a doctor surprised when a patient becomes unwell. There will be better days, you dear wee girls. There will be better days.'

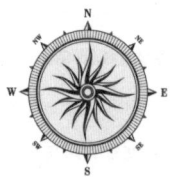

They were given a bedroom downstairs at the rear of Mrs Murray's house from which they could see, above the fence line, the trees in their own back garden. But it was no longer their home. New occupants had arrived. Mrs Murray had organised the sale of their furniture to help with the expense of keeping them. She put them both to work in her guesthouse. Augusta was to help in the kitchen, preparing the lodgers' meals and cleaning their rooms. Caroline was to change the guest beds and wash the linens.

Mrs Murray said, 'Not the lives you imagined, I am sure, but you're both capable of work and more than old enough. I am not a charity.'

When Papa had been gone for three months, Mrs Murray secured both girls positions in service. 'Too well educated for the work you can get,' she said. 'People like to think it causes trouble, a girl being as educated as a boy, but it gives a woman opportunity.'

Caroline was to be a governess nearby and Augusta was to train as a cook in Blackfriars. Both positions required them to live in. Each girl took a trunk of their possessions to their new place of employ.

Father had made no arrangements for the apothecary. Each Sunday, which was her day off, Caroline dusted and cleaned, imagining a time when the paper was taken down from the windows, the sign on the door turned to *Open*, the bell ringing as another customer entered.

Deliveries continued to arrive and Caroline did what she could to return them to their suppliers and to cancel orders. There were silverfish in the calico, weevils in the wheat, moths in the silk. She contacted customers awaiting orders but she was rarely met with sympathy. She knew people believed her family had been cursed by ill fortune.

She used money Papa had secreted in a metal box at the rear of the shop to continue to pay the landlord his rent. She packed a trunk with jars and bottles containing the herbs and remedies that seemed most important. It was an impossible task, the choosing of one medicine over another, like plucking a handful of daisies from a field in full bloom and expecting to brighten the world. But she felt a sense of reassurance, too. She had the trunks removed to her place of employment, where they filled the little space between her bed and the door. When she looked at them, she knew she was waiting for her real life to resume.

A family friend sent word to Caroline that they had seen her father in a state of agitation and dishevelment on Worthing Pier in West Sussex, and that he had not recognised them. When they suggested he return to London with them, he had fled.

Each time Caroline locked the door of the apothecary, it was an effort to keep her despondency at bay.

And then one Sunday her father was standing by the shop window as if he were waiting for someone. His black hat was badly weathered. He was no longer carrying his brass-topped cane but a carved stick of questionable provenance. His frock coat was in need of repair, his beautiful boots worn down and unpolished, his hair long and lank. He had been gone for one hundred and twenty-three days.

Caroline wanted to run into his arms. She wanted to turn and walk the other way. She wanted to rage at him, to hurt him, and yet she could not. She could not help smiling. Relief washed through her. He was back. Everything would be all right.

She unlocked the door and they went inside, the dust and mustiness now of no concern to her. She turned and embraced him, resting her head against his chest, smelling his smoky unwashed self.

'Where are you staying?' she asked him.

'I have taken lodgings,' he said. 'I must tell you that the inventory is to be sold. I believe Digby in Leicester Square will take it for a fair price. I have advised the landlord of my departure.'

Caroline felt as if she had been stung by a wasp. 'Sold?'

'Madame Murray thinks it is too much for me,' her father said. 'It *is* too much. Your mother knew this. You know this.'

'Please, Papa. I will assist you as I have always done. We can find a new home and reopen the shop.' But she could feel him trembling beside her.

'*Je suis malade du cœur et de l'esprit,*' he said. '*Je suis désolé, chère fille. Il est précieux, le calme bonheur.*'

'Let me and Augusta take care of you, Papa. Let us find that calm happiness together.'

'I cannot allow it. What life is there for either of you in that?' Rubbing at the scar on his forehead, he continued, 'I have made investments. One or two might yet prove their merit, but there was a shipwreck off the coast of Africa. And,' he added, rubbing his unkempt beard, 'some rogues convinced me that a certain publication would turn a profit. Perhaps I was hasty. Mrs Murray is taking care of it all now.'

'Papa, did you not think to discuss this with me? To entrust me with this responsibility? Did Mama not teach me to account for every pound, shilling and pence here in this shop? And to keep the ledgers for the expenses of our family, too?'

'You carry too many cares, sweet daughter,' said her father. 'It is for the best. I will only disappoint you. Mrs Murray has been a friend in this time of need, a friend to all of us. I hear you both have excellent placements.'

'Am I to remain a governess, Papa? Am I not to become an apothecary?'

He took her in his arms and repeated over and over, *'Je suis désolé. Je suis désolé.'*

Had it all been for nothing, all the schooling he had given her? She wanted to rail at the unfairness of it, at the stupidity of their situation.

Jacques-Louis came and went. He wrote Caroline and Augusta letters. Sometimes they extended to many pages, the writing erratic and the sentences incoherent. Sometimes when he returned he was his old self, gregarious and joyful, taking them to tea, ordering cake and champagne, showering them with gifts—for each a new shawl, a pair of silk stockings. He took them riding in a carriage along the river. He hired a punt to row Caroline and Augusta up the Thames to the fields where they had often searched for chanterelles and pennyroyal, water pimpernel and cress from the nearby streams, greater and lesser celandine, dandelions and cowslips. But these lucid times were short-lived.

When Caroline visited Jacques-Louis in the rooms he rented, she found the desk and bed overwhelmed with leaflets and books, writings and letters, as if a storm had rushed through the place. Wine bottles stood empty, remnant powders of cocaine evident on the table, an empty bottle of opium oil by the bed. Food mouldered in the cupboard, clothes and dishes lay about unwashed. Often her father was nowhere to be found.

'Out walking, I expect,' said the landlord. 'It's what he does.'

Some days when she visited, she found he had not moved from his bed in days. Illness was evident in his eyes and the pallor of his cheeks. Sometimes he could barely be roused.

Caroline tried to remember everything he had taught her. The pattern of leaf and flower, growing conditions and the time of the year for flowering, the ripening of fruit, the digging up of roots. The processes of drying and grinding, the distillation in milk, wine or honey, the boiling into syrups. She pretended it was possible she would find an alternative position, somewhere a female apothecary would be welcome.

'You will be the first, Caroline,' Papa had said to her. 'My daughter will be the first. Perhaps you might even qualify as a doctor.'

But that was then. Now, looking into his shattered visage, she recalled what Tante Henriette had said to her when she told Caroline her mother was dying: 'You must not rely on anything he has promised you.' Not now, and maybe never.

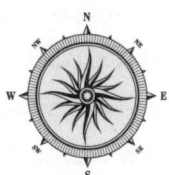

It was a Sunday when her father sent word for Caroline to join him at Mrs Murray's. She had not seen or heard from him in weeks but, when she arrived, she found him wearing a new blue dress coat with lace at the sleeves, a purple cravat, polished shoes and white stockings. He ushered her into the drawing room, where a maid had just laid tea. Mrs Murray rose to welcome Caroline and showed her to a chair.

Papa enquired of Caroline's young charges, and the curriculum she had established for them, while Mrs Murray served them all tea and slices of seed cake. Caroline sensed some revelation, but the conversation lingered on matters of little consequence, until Mrs Murray put down her cup and rose. She glided to a place behind Papa, and settled her hands on his shoulders in the way Mama had once done.

'You see, dear Caroline,' her father said, 'Mrs Murray has made me happy again. Can you be happy for us?'

Caroline did not remember the words that were said, hers or theirs, the food she accepted out of politeness but could not eat. She thought how her mother was not even a year dead. She thought of the soups, custards and jellies Mrs Murray had delivered, things that Mother could swallow, until she could not swallow at all. Mrs Murray counselling Papa to have Caroline and Augusta move into her home, to sell their house. The placements she had found them. It had seemed kind, but had it been that?

Caroline had not seen Mrs Murray show Papa any special attention during Mama's illness, but perhaps she had. Perhaps a friendship had grown between them and Caroline had missed it. Or had Mrs Murray sensed an opportunity? All their household goods, the beautiful things that had come from France during the Revolution, their silverware, ornaments, the brass clock, all their books, the linen and lace her mother had sewn, it was all in Mrs Murray's attic.

There was a strange buzzing in Caroline's head. She had spilled her tea.

'I am sorry,' she said, standing abruptly. 'I feel quite unwell. Please, forgive me.'

'Oh, my dear, let me help you,' said Mrs Murray. 'Do you need more tea? Or a little wine?'

'Please do not go,' Papa entreated.

Caroline was moving towards the door. Jacques-Louis attempted to follow but Mrs Murray told him to stay, and the two women walked together to the front door.

'We are seeing a play at Covent Garden tonight,' said Mrs Murray. 'A carriage has been ordered, and we will dine afterwards at . . .' She mentioned the name of the restaurant, the name of the play. 'Such things restore your father.'

Caroline saw that Mrs Murray had done something for her father that she had not been able to do herself. With Mrs Murray, he seemed to have found a new sense of himself. Perhaps this was a good thing.

'Do you see that he is happy?' Mrs Murray asked.

Caroline wanted to say, *I am not sure he knows his own mind.* Instead she said, 'Forgive me, I am not myself,' and walked away.

The following morning, after a restless night, Caroline wrote to her father and requested that he meet her at a cafe the following Sunday. *Please come alone, Papa.*

Once he had been served coffee and Caroline tea, she said to him, 'Papa, this may be difficult for you to hear, but I am unsettled by this attachment you have to Mrs Murray. I do not believe anything good will come of it.' She could hear the wobble in her own voice as she asked, 'Do you intend to marry her?'

· *8* ·

Jacques-Louis

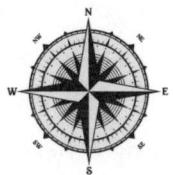

At Millbank Prison on the River Thames it is a long walk from the outer gates to the cells within, through a windowless gloom, and no way to remember which way is out. Or what day is what. There is nothing to ease the ringing silence, the dank unyielding walls that chill him to the bone, no reassurance of warmth or light. The Millbank way is silence, dysentery, cholera, malaria. Take one, take all.

Jacques-Louis is buried within the darkness of white walls and white hallways. He can barely tell the time of day but for the cycle of noises and visitations, so that he might be living the same night and day over and over in some Sisyphean struggle.

There is no book, pen or paper to distract him from the odium of his wrongdoings or the stench of his ruined life. When he leaves the cell for one hour on a Sunday, he is blinkered and hooded, his wrists and ankles chained. He shuffles along in a yard where no words are to be spoken, no sound uttered at all.

Men come and go from his cell. Sometimes it is Socrates, or the ghost of Hamlet. Abraham with his long beard accompanying Columbus returned from his voyage to the Orient and now unable to speak Portuguese with any certainty. Bats appear, their cries strangely soothing, hanging in the corner of the cell, blood dripping from their mouths. Sometimes dogs bark at him, and though he cannot be sure they are not ghost hounds, he returns their baying with his own.

Other men come claiming officialdom. They smell of damp wool, unwashed linen and rotting teeth. He answers their questions in French or Latin. He growls at their attempts to measure his head. He makes suggestions, some of them impolite. He attempts to bite one of them. He is put in a restraint that pins his arms, a leather halter that stops his speech.

They tell him, in the sonorous tones of Roman senators, that he is to be sent to Bethlehem Hospital for assessment. Is he mad? Has he always been mad? The Crown will not hang him if it is so.

At Bethlehem Hospital he is confined in a room alone with a barred window, very high up, offering a frosted patch of grey sky. He is released from restraints. He has never liked porridge, that glue of English life, but when it is delivered warm, with a little milk, it settles the day ahead.

The Bethlehem doctors have more questions for him. They look into his eyes, tap his knees. 'Open your mouth, Colbert, let me look in your ear, let us measure your cranium. This scar, from whence does it come?' They scratch their answers upon page after page.

He is permitted a visit to the garden. There he meets a single tree, a bare winter elm, which from time to time offers him faint wisps of poetry.

The blinding migraines recede. The bats disappear. Socrates no longer visits. Angels and prophets slip back into the walls, leaving only their handprints. He wishes for a blade that he might cut his veins.

Caroline sends him writing materials and a volume of Wordsworth and Coleridge. Augusta sends him a knitted hat smelling faintly of dried rose petals. Spring arrives and seduces summer. The tree in the courtyard murmurs:

'My countenance declares
My inward grief,
And hope almost despairs
To find relief . . .'

There are no flowers. A few blades of grass risk the narrow byways between the paving stones, yet, despite its words, the tree seems to be cautioning him to remember sunflowers. Poppies. Jonquils. Peonies. Marigolds . . . Roses picked and placed in a vase by the bed. Pink roses that smelled of Hannah and the scent of her as she bent to kiss him. It was only ever you, he thinks. It was only ever you.

He reads 'The Rime of the Ancient Mariner' memorising the swell and fall of the words. They had read it aloud to one another, Hannah, Caroline and Augusta, while Esther had knitted and sighed, winter's breath stirring the fire as it reached down the chimney. How little he knew of the absurdity of absolution then.

'There passed a weary time. Each throat
Was parched, and glazed each eye.
A weary time! A weary time!
How glazed each weary eye,
When looking westward, I beheld
A something in the sky.'

A spear of sunshine reaches into his cell from the high window. He begins a letter.

Ma chère Caroline,

I find myself in the barren landscape of shame and regret.
I have taken you into this place with me, my beloved daughter.
I do not ask for your forgiveness. Believe me that I neither seek
it, nor could I accept it, but while my mind is lucid, I feel an
explanation might assist you in understanding that terrible night.
She wore a blue bonnet . . .

When he finishes it, he is so sickened by the words he has written, he tears the letter into small pieces which he deposits in the slops bucket. But he knows he cannot turn away from the brutality of the truth. It is his duty. He begins another letter, containing a complete testimony to his ugliness, so that there can be no doubt of what he is. He addresses one letter to Caroline and one to Augusta.

It is agreed by learned minds, as autumn departs the sky, that he is not mad at all. It is confirmed in writing. Not mad.

'Did you attempt to fool us, Colbert? Did you?' asks a limacine man smelling of camphor and marsh, his collar oily and his fingernails begrimed. 'Pretending madness to avoid the noose,' he says, as he completed the government papers. 'Many have tried and failed. It will not do.'

Jacques-Louis is chained within a panelled wagon that jolts across snow-covered terrain. He glimpses winter trees between the rough boards. His teeth chatter and a dread of life more acute than any he has ever known descends upon him as he enters once more the confines of Millbank Prison.

'Well, Colbert,' says the prison's governor, 'if you have attempted to escape your fate, then your return here is a spectacular failing. But if you are mad, and have been mischaracterised by the good doctors of Bethlehem, as I fear may yet be true, then this is indeed a bitter day for you.'

He is returned to the congress of solitary confinement, the shuffling walk chained and hooded each Sunday, the monotony of the unforgiving darkness, the cold bed and walls. The voices resume their whispering. He will not shout back. Instead he walks the streets from Hyde Park along Oxford Street into Mayfair and through Belgravia towards the marshlands that are becoming Pimlico, then down to the river and along to the bridge. Five steps forward, turn, five steps back, turn. In Green Park squirrels observe him. Several people are carrying umbrellas, but the rain has never worried him.

He finds his father beside him, looking as if he is on his way to the palace. His wig is powdered and he wears a waistcoat embroidered with cornflowers, a violet silk jacket and a white scarf about his neck. The duke says, 'Plato thought he was living in a great age. Diderot insisted that, "If the laws are good, morals are good," but can that ever be true? Rousseau, born on a full moon, enchanted us all with his declaration: "Man is born free, but is everywhere in chains." He conceived of a world where virtue, in his estimation, would make bold the will to do good. But each man is born into the morals, vices and economies of his time and place of birth, Jacques-Louis. Robespierre might have believed he was wielding a virtuous and new morality, alive at the very heart of things, but still he was just moments from his death in the larger calculation.'

Jacques-Louis wonders if the dead meet and mingle to share their stories in some nearby realm unglimpsed. When a child was born, was it cast midstream into a tributary of moment and place, carrying with it memories and hopes? Not so much born new, an innocent, but a renewal of the people from which it sprang, to see what yet might grow? Did death provide answers?

'None, as far as I can see,' his father replies.

Jacques-Louis' days of existence are numbered. Soon it will all be behind him. There will be a yard and a scaffold. He wishes for a guillotine rather than a noose swinging in the breeze. He would have preferred the certainty of that instrument of precision to the possibility of a long strangulation. But who is he to ask favours? He winds the blanket about his head to cover his eyes when the pain comes. Hannah, bearing a candle, beckons him away. A snake moves across the floor, long and black, followed by a hooded figure, but he will not look at her face.

He is taken to the office of the prison governor who informs Jacques-Louis that the Crown, in its infinite wisdom, has offered him leniency. Instead of being hanged for his crime, he is to be sent away for the term of his life. Never to return to England. Never to stain Her Majesty's fair shores again.

'I believe you have daughters, Colbert?' the governor says, as he moves a small brass bell on his desk without allowing it to ring. 'You have a voyage ahead from which you will not return. I think it best you try to forget them, and they you. On Norfolk Island, if the accounts are true, you will find the place governed by a particular kind of man. One who will calculate the anguish of your soul. That seems to be a requirement of the post.'

At this the governor meets Jacques-Louis' gaze. 'A man of your cleverness, Colbert, I wish you well.'

· 9 ·

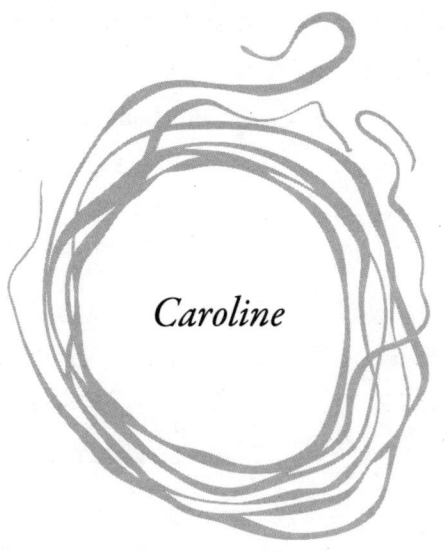

Caroline

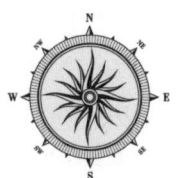

Caroline takes Quill and the Swanston boys along mountain trails to find mosses glowing bright green, light green, soft and spongy like large cushions. They find tender green carpets on the underside of logs. Orange-frilled fungi are growing on the remnants of trees long fallen. There are red-and-white-spotted toadstools, purple toadstools, curling golden fungi and white discs dotted with chocolate, small yellow fungi, soft brown fungi sprinkled with pink tendrils that quiver on embankments and dark steppes of fungi hard to the touch that grow layered upon limbs and trunks.

Back at their desks, the boys learn of battles and discoveries, heroes and villains, kings and queens, gods and empires. Much is discussed and recorded in their workbooks. Mathematics, Astronomy and Geography are slowly absorbed.

Caroline has them memorise a poem each week, and for each boy she makes a list of spelling words to affix by their beds. She makes new lists as they go on, until the boys have mastered many peculiarities of English, Latin and French—except Robert, who cannot get his words organised no matter how hard he tries. His sketches reveal his astute observation of the plants on the farm, and daily life. She has several of his works in pencil pinned up in the hallway of the cottage. There is one of the tall wrought-iron gate at the entrance to the kitchen garden and another of the chickens.

Bessie having received at last a ticket of leave and being free now to live with Caroline and Quill, has moved into one of the attic rooms. The house is newly settled with her there. Beside Quill's bed is one of Robert's illustrations of Malachy, the little black cat who has stolen their hearts and has never caught a mouse.

It is hard for Caroline to believe it will soon be a year since they arrived in Van Diemen's Land. It feels much longer, almost as if she has always been here, and yet still it is new and surprising, too. The garden has flourished and there are gooseberries ready to be picked. She is filling a bowl with fruit when Cornelius arrives.

'You must join us to eat the pie these are to become, Cornelius,' she says.

'Thank you, Mrs Douglas,' he replies.

'Did something happen?' she asks, noting his expression.

'In a way,' he replies. 'But I believe it wouldn't be right to hold it back.'

'Am I to be worried, Cornelius?' she asks, setting down the bowl and wiping her hands on her apron.

'I do not believe so,' he says. 'And it may sound peculiar, but Mr Broughton came to me in a dream and insisted I tell you something of importance.'

'Well,' says Caroline, 'you have me intrigued.'

'There is a cellar, Mrs Douglas,' Cornelius says. 'Under this cottage.'

'A cellar? Here?'

He nods. 'It's been closed up all these years. It was his place of work, but anything might have happened down there since. Rats and such.'

'Should we take sticks?' she asks.

He smiles at that.

Inside the cottage, Cornelius stoops under the beam that divides the front rooms from the kitchen and the storeroom. He indicates a section of timber in the wainscot.

Bending, he slides the timber up to reveal a gap. She hears a bolt slide. A trapdoor drops open in the floorboards, neatly disguised. There is a ladder. Is she really going to descend into that darkness?

'As I recall . . . ah, yes.' He has reached in and brought up a lantern coated in dust. He shakes it. There is still oil. He brushes the glass clean with a cloth from his pocket, then he produces a flint and lights the wick.

'There is a chance the air is poisoned,' Cornelius says, watching the flame lengthen. 'That's why we light the lantern. If it goes out, we leave. Mr Broughton was very careful about that. People die from wine gas.'

He begins the descent down the ladder, then calls up to assure Caroline that the air in the cellar is safe.

At the bottom of the ladder, Caroline finds an earthen floor and long low beams leading away into rows of wooden barrels and racks of bottles. The air is cool, any noise of the world above quite diminished. There is no smell of vermin, only the smell of oak and wine.

'Can any of it be good still?' she asks. 'After all this time?'

'The barrels will almost certainly have soured,' Cornelius says. 'As for the bottles, we won't know unless they are tasted.' He indicates chalk marks on the barrels as they walk the rows. 'One number is the year, and the other is the grape. The bottles beyond are all marked the same. These were the ones Mr Broughton put aside, to see what time did to the flavour.'

Caroline retrieves two glasses from the kitchen. When she returns, Cornelius is holding a bottle. He unwinds the string and nudges out the cork, filling one glass with a measure of honey-coloured wine. There are no bubbles, but the colour and clarity are good.

'You will not try it?' she asks.

He shrugs. 'It's what you think that matters, Mrs Douglas.'

'Caroline,' she says. 'My name is Caroline, Cornelius, if you could become comfortable with that.'

'Mrs Caroline,' he says, and his smile illuminates his eyes.

She lets the flavours settle on her tongue, and senses within the texture of the wine some memory of the bubbles from its earlier life softened to vanilla, moonlight and a remembrance of raspberries.

'It is a mixture of varieties,' says Cornelius. 'Chardonnay, meunier and a grape called black cluster which Mr Broughton brought in from a Mr Gunning, who had a vineyard over the hills in Richmond. It was a sad story, that, but the grapes, he said, were very good.'

'How did he manage access? Those barrels did not come up and down the ladder.'

'There's a passage back there, and a trapdoor at the far end that opens into the barn, with a slope for rolling the barrels down. You'll also find two presses.'

'Mr Broughton dug all this out?' Caroline asks.

'Convicts. That was in the years of assignment. Mr Broughton knew how to secure good labour as soon as it arrived on the wharf. A lot of men worked here.'

Caroline takes another sip. Already the flavour of the wine is changing as it meets the air. Becoming softer with a hint of raisins.

'Has Captain Swanston seen all this?'

'He had no interest in the vineyard,' says Cornelius.

'He does not know it is here at all?'

'I do not believe so, Mrs Caroline.'

'Did he not inspect the house?'

'He did,' says Cornelius. 'It was filled with hay back then.'

'And you did not mention it . . .'

'Captain Swanston had made his disregard for the vineyard very clear to me. But I have seen a lot of people come and go over the years. I thought there might yet be someone . . .'

'Will you tell me about your dream last night, Cornelius?'

'Well, Mrs Caroline, I saw Mr Broughton there in the vineyard. He walked towards me, full of life in the way he always was, and he said, "You will have to show her, Cornelius. You will have to show her."'

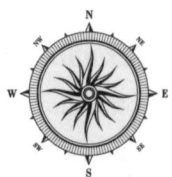

'The scale of the endeavour overwhelms me,' she says to Georgiana Swanston. 'Though the cake and biscuits always meet with the boys' approval.'

'If only all workers could be inspired so easily.'

The two women survey the vineyard from beneath the large gum tree where they have spread a blanket and cushions. The boys are at school and Bessie has delivered a tray bearing a pot of mint tea, two glasses and a plate of shortbread, which Caroline has taught her to make.

'Will you continue with it?' asks Georgiana.

'Quill and Robert remain enthusiastic, but there is no hurry. Without a person experienced in winemaking, the Walkers tell me that medicinal wine and vinegar is all that can be anticipated. They are willing to assist in that.'

'Can you not advertise for workers?'

'I am reluctant to make my interest in the vineyard a matter of public notice. I know my reclusive ways have already caused consternation. The business of calling on one another and being expected to return such visits, it does irk me. The time that is required for such distractions!'

Georgiana laughs and nods.

'Am I strange to be so uninterested in the habits of our society?' Caroline asks. 'Last week I was in the vineyard—weeds are growing at an astonishing rate after all the rain—when the Sweet sisters, who are anything but, came by. In order to greet them I was forced to scrub my face, tidy my hair and don a suitable gown. Then I had to endure an hour and a half of mindless and often offensive observations on this person or that. It was exhausting.'

'Dear Caroline, I have known few women with your industriousness of spirit. Most consider it highly improper to place their hands in the earth. But here we are, a long way from the strictures imposed on us by our mothers. At least, I like to think so.'

'It eases my heart to be outside.'

'And mine,' says Georgiana. 'It's a sweet relief, unlike the Sweet sisters. I will do my best to set those wagging tongues at ease by telling all I meet that you are kept very busy with our boys. I shall say you are a person of retiring disposition bruised by your widowhood. Any attempts to hurry you from your time of healing are repugnant and unchristian.'

Their eyes meet and Caroline feels that they understand one another perfectly.

'You do realise that the women visit to assess you for their sons, grandsons and nephews?' says Georgiana.

'Because the only possible fulfilment is as a wife?' Caroline asks.

Georgiana laughs. 'My dear, do not judge all by your early experience. I have found great contentment in matrimony. But here you are an object of curiosity and no small amount of envy, I expect. This colony defines women by only two standards: married or concubine. It is shocking, I know, but widowhood is not sufficient to curtail the suspicions of those men who believe a modest woman is one who is either chaperoned by a parent or constrained by domestic life. It seems you are not to be left alone, dear Caroline. As soon as you lay aside your black frocks, I fear a scene about your home as if you were a Penelope. Every invitation will be forthcoming. Every eligible man—those barely with whiskers and those with whiskers that have long been grey—will be gathering in your courtyard.'

'Alas, there is no Odysseus to return to me,' Caroline says, 'and make short work of them all.'

'Still, I am sure it cannot be easy to be here alone,' Georgiana says. 'You had not planned to be so, and you keep your husband's absence locked within yourself. Will you tell me something of him?'

Caroline understands that her employer and friend has been patient in resisting this conversation. She folds her napkin, pauses and sighs.

'We were married in New York and took our honeymoon at Niagara Falls. An expedition more than a romantic escape, to be truthful, but he was much taken with the idea of adventure and I was eager to see the famed waterfall. It is the most extraordinary expanse of water in all the world, I think. The sound is deafening. My husband took an early morning walk along one of the rivers that flows into the falls while I was still asleep. Another walker saw him out on a rocky promontory. Apparently he slipped from a rock and was carried over. His body was found floating near the shore three days later.'

'Oh, my poor darling friend, I am so sorry,' says Georgiana, taking Caroline's hand. 'What a shocking thing.'

'It is a hard thing to confess, and I have never said this before'—Caroline hesitates before proceeding—'but I say it to you by way of relieving myself of a burden I have carried since it happened . . . I knew by then, and perhaps he knew it, too, that we had made an unwise choice. It is this that has perhaps unsettled me more than anything. That he might have chosen . . .'

There is an extended version of this story. Names and occupations. A family history. It is a story that could expand should more ever be required, but Caroline knows that brevity assists deceit.

In years to come, she will tell versions of this story to her children and they will pass it on to their children, and so it will be woven into myth, generation after generation.

Her first husband died falling into Niagara Falls while they were on their honeymoon. She arrived here as a young widow. They had planned to come together.

Caroline never mentioned her aunt Henriette, nor that she had been both her apprentice and accomplice. That story was never revealed in all her long life.

· *10* ·

Jacques-Louis

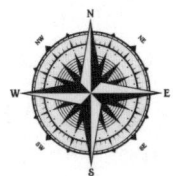

Jacques-Louis rides the outgoing tide, a recipient of the leniency of transportation departing England for the term of his life. He is on a ship—the *Rochester*. Whoever Rochester was. He who lifted his head above the common tide of humanity such that a ship bore his name. Rochester the ferryman, and every man aboard dreaded the destination, anticipating the voyage only as reprieve from the years of incarceration within Millbank Prison.

Jacques-Louis listens to the creaking timber and the groaning of men. He hears some talk of a time beyond their sentence when they might at last be free. There are stories of good land for farming. Some pretend it is all a great adventure and are the quickest to lose spirit as sickness and stench prevails.

His hammock sways. He is lucky to have a hammock, not like those squeezed together four men to a bunk, sixteen inches of berth per man, lice and fleas and count yourself lucky. But they fare better than the poor sops too ill to do anything but lie upon the floor in vomit and faeces as the sea begins to heave. All of them chained at the ankles.

Storms assail the *Rochester* down the coast of Africa. The hatches are closed and covered with tarpaulins so that no glimmer of light can penetrate the hold, nor ventilation relieve the fetid air. The menu is salt beef and gruel, the meat quickly rancid, the bread moulded and tough as old leather. The crew are reviled by their cargo and afraid of them, too. The scant water rations, lowered down in barrels, slop and spill. The sailors above laugh.

When the weather clears, they are beset by a calm that continues for days and weeks as the vessel limps with flaccid sails towards the Cape of Good Hope. Grim men and soft sob for their mothers, for wives and children and the fate that has befallen them.

'Calm water makes for turbulent souls,' declares the captain, and refuses to open the hatches. The airless putrescence below decks intensifies. Men who are not normally godly pray fervently. They pray regardless of guilt or innocence, family, church, village, language or station in life.

When the hatches are at last opened, buckets of salt water are poured onto them. The men below scrabble for the chance to clean themselves, to see sky and daylight, to breathe sweet untainted air. Afterwards they lie wet, half-naked, starved, many raving mad. Some have long forgotten all kindness and expect only misery. This is what a rash moment, a folly, a misconceived plan, an act of violence or the sheer bad luck of the wrongfully convicted has brought them.

The surgeon superintendent makes a game of giving some of them lime juice and others not—to test his theories on scurvy, he says, though the treatment is well known. Once a week he descends into the prisoners' quarters with a kerchief wrapped around his nose and mouth, his watery eyes glistening in the light of the lamp he carries. He inspects the bleeding gums of the afflicted, the red and blue marks that splatter their skin. 'Most interesting,' he says. The rum emanates from him as if he has long laid with the bottle.

They are young, mostly, and Jacques-Louis an old man in comparison. They have been hungry in their villages and towns. There are a few from Scotland, but nothing like the numbers from Ireland and England. Many, it seems to him, bear the guilt of being without any gainful purpose but to survive. Few of them are able to read.

But they are alert to one another. Alert to the risk and the reward of choosing any bond of companionship. A surfeit of power lying dormant in rage and nonchalance. Finding a patron with greater strength, greater violence, could bring reward, but there is always a cost to such alliances. Some simply choose helplessness. But many give thought to how they might turn the canker of imprisonment into something of use.

Jacques-Louis had gone willingly into prison. He had asked for death and been sentenced to death. He had lived for months in anticipation of the steps and the noose. Yet here he is, sailing to another destiny.

He had been gifted a life of privilege and education. He had learned the voyages of conquest and exploration that had changed the world. He was a boy orphaned by a sharpened blade, only to come back, after all, to a blade he had asked a boy to sharpen.

Rounding the Cape of Good Hope at last, they are allowed on deck to see the endless ocean. Jacques-Louis' body uncoils painfully from the stoop of confinement. They are assembled to watch the flogging of five members of the crew for a suspected mutiny, and another flogging for a theft of some possession of the captain's that has not been recovered.

Seeing each other in the sunlight, Jacques-Louis finds it hard to have any dislike for his fellow convicts. They are simply men, regardless of crime or social standing. None unmoved as they watch their persecutors stripped and scored.

At the Cape they are kept below decks for three weeks while rations and supplies are replenished. The noises of harbour and township are tantalisingly close. Hatches are kept closed for fear of some revolt. One hundred and seventy-seven men wait, unable to stand to full height or lie to full length, unable to move without touching another man.

In his fleeting dreams, Jacques-Louis finds himself a boy again on his way to Calais in a trunk. His mother lies beside him, her severed head in the crook of her arm. His father insists on a conversation but Jacques-Louis cannot make out the language he speaks. The men lying close by curse him.

'Save your ravings for the pleasures that await you, you fool,' hisses one man whose front teeth are missing.

Jacques-Louis thinks to do something with his mind, to recite a verse or two. Something to allay the torpor of time. He can feel himself becoming unhinged, splitting into another self, and there is nowhere he might walk to wrench himself back or away. He hears a poem and remembers the habit of the words.

Where had it gone, the book Caroline had sent to him? Where had all his books gone from his study? The way of all his possessions. Everything he and Hannah had created had been lost to his madness. He had squandered it all on one plan or another, believing he might yet create some windfall whereupon he and Henriette, Caroline and Augusta might go back to France. But he had been deluded. He had taken advice from those who were nothing but scoundrels, liars and blackguards.

The past was dispersed, engulfed. In his mind he hears Caroline's voice alongside his own. She is there with him, reassurance in a place no woman would dare enter, and as he speaks, the men nearby grow quiet and listen.

'And a good south wind sprung up behind;
The Albatross did follow,
And every day, for food or play,
Came to the mariner's hollo!

In mist or cloud, on mast or shroud,
It perched for vespers nine;
Whiles all the night, through fog-smoke white,
Glimmered the white Moon-shine.

"God save thee, ancient Mariner!
From the fiends that plague thee thus!
Why lookest thou so?"—With my cross bow
I shot the albatross.'

'Louder,' one says. 'Anything to speed this intolerable delay.'

'What says the Frenchman?' someone calls from the deeper darkness. 'Go back. Once more.'

They lie in their squalor overlooked by Table Mountain, though they know it not, and Jacques-Louis begins.

'It is an Ancient Mariner,
And he stoppeth one of three . . .'

Word travels through the hold that the Frenchman is speaking a rhyme. A poesy. Coleridge's poem is too long for perfect recollection, but it soothes Jacques-Louis to recite the story of a rash act born of delusion, the mariner's complicity unforgiven, his damnation unexpiated. A ballad recounted as prophecy and confession.

The men about him repeat the lines, as if the poem holds some spell to keep at bay their own dread shadow. Even the ship, subdued and constrained by two great anchors resting on the sea floor, seems to listen to the mariner's tale.

'I looked to heaven and tried to pray
But or ever a prayer had gushed,
A wished whisper came and made
My heart as dry as dust.

I closed my lids and kept them close,
And the balls like pulses beat,
For the sky and the sea, and the sea and the sky
Lay like a load on my weary eye,
And the dead were at my feet.'

Jacques-Louis' voice reaches another prisoner, John Bird, formerly a solicitor and amateur thespian in Bath convicted of highway robbery, though he was drunk and persuaded by friends, he says to the nodding men. Bird is a man with a large soft face and a broad body that would certainly have been larger if it had not lived on the rations of a hulk for more than three years. Such men fared less well in their allocated sleeping space, but the poem rouses him. He knows much of the verse and fills in the gaps when Jacques-Louis' memory falters. Together the two men lull their listening companions, alleviating their thoughts from thirst, heat and madness.

Some begin to learn the verse, it being a way to pass the time. They are each the mariner. Repentant or unrepentant, returned to society, none will be unburdened of the past.

'And the bay was white with silent light,
Till rising from the same,
Full many shapes, that shadows were,
In crimson colours came.

A little distance from the prow
Those crimson shadows were:
I turned my eyes upon the deck—
Oh, Christ! What saw I there!

Each corse lay flat, lifeless and flat,
And by the holy rood!
A man all light, a seraph-man,
On every corse there stood.

This seraph-band, each waved his hand,
No voice did they impart—
No voice; but oh! The silence sank
Like music on my heart.'

The sense of something happening below disconcerts those above. Perhaps it is the precursor to some kind of uprising. The captain descends and asks what mischief is afoot. He will put them all on quarter rations, desist from sending down water at all, until someone owns the subterfuge that he believes is brewing here. There is a long silence. The captain declares that he will have his way, and begins to return up the ladder. No water until a confession is forthcoming.

Jacques-Louis speaks. He says it is but a poem, and no harm is meant, just a way to pass the time. Bird begins to speak, but Jacques-Louis silences him, saying there is none to blame but him.

The captain has him hauled up onto the deck. Jacques-Louis repeats that he speaks only a poem. The captain demands to know which one. Jacques-Louis tells him and the captain pales. He will not have that doomed verse on his ship. He orders seventy-five lashes. Jacques-Louis is a Frenchman, after all, and everyone knows sedition and revolt are in their blood. Many an Englishman has died at their hands.

Jacques-Louis is stripped of the putrid shirt he wears and tied to a mast. His arms are bound tight and he has no power to cringe or stir. He knows the code. A prisoner is to utter no word or sound when the lash strikes, no cry, for it will grieve the oppressor if they cannot find satisfaction in the harm. But he fails.

He grapples with a new kind of pain. Not merely the ripping of his flesh and the humiliation of his screams, but the betrayal of all self-possession that has ever been his, witnessed by the captain, the crew and all his fellow prisoners.

'He did more to his victim,' he hears one sailor say.

And there is a chorus of 'ayes' from the other sailors, and the lash spits its fury again and again, as if he will be forever on this deck, against this mast, his heart like the mariner's, dry as dust.

He is washed down with salt water stinging as if a thousand bees have swarmed upon him. His head is shaved and he is returned to the hold and locked within a solitary box where he must crouch for days. The men whisper snatches of verse to console him, but he begs them to cease. He can feel his wounds festering. Maggots writhe in his flesh. He cannot bear the stench of his own rot. He catches his piss in his pannikin and attempts to pour it onto his wounds.

He is a boy in a trunk, without light or solace, voyaging into the unknown, impotent and haunted. He knows his predicament is sharp. His heart pounds, racing, slowing, racing. He tries to move and perceives that he is as light as a moth. Are there people gathered about him? He can hear the voices of an assembly. It sounds like the choir in the cathedral at Reims where his family name is carved into a pew.

He sees his mother in her veil, a yellow dress and small silken shoes. Her hair hides beneath her bonnet. Henriette is bending towards her and putting a wafer into their mother's mouth, as if today Henriette is the faithful administrator of the word of God. When she sees Jacques-Louis there, writing her name in the incense, she crosses herself and smiles.

'*Bonjour, mon frère.*'

'*Bonjour, ma sœur,*' he replies.

She rustles in her purple cassock. 'Have you been well?' she asks.

'Not really,' he says. '*Et toi?*'

'I am as I have always been. I am the harbinger of my own majesty and the raven call of my own doom. Do you know I have transformed your daughter from the fate you offered her tending the sick and the wounded? I have given her a life in which she can acquire the fruits of those born to privilege. She is so good at it. A mistress of guile and ploy who never loses her nerve.'

'Am I dead?' he asks.

'No,' she says. 'You always spent too much time thinking on such things. Believing your one mind could solve the mysteries of the universe. Yet what did you really do? Did you ever stop to think what it is to be a woman? If a man decides that you must die, he will almost certainly be successful. I know your brain was injured. I know Hannah was dead. But you found out that a woman you believed loved you was also earning her living discreetly and quietly with other men. London gives women very few options, in case you didn't notice, brother. When did such things become so very important? Pride. Reputation? We lost all that a long time ago.'

Leaning forward, she places a wafer on his tongue and says, 'I cannot forgive you. In that moment on the bridge, I will never believe you did not know that you could be someone else.'

When he is released from the box at last, he can barely hold his bread ration. For the rest of the voyage, he makes no sound. He will not speak another word of Coleridge, nor any poem, for many years to come.

There is a quicker movement in the ship, the sound of orders being given, shorter waves that denote landfall. When they are allowed up from the hold, the sunlight is so bright it burns their eyes, and for minutes the world is devoid of colour. They cannot move for the tightness in their limbs. Many crawl to the edge of the deck to be lowered into the longboats that will row them ashore. Jacques-Louis is one of these.

Nine of them have been wrapped in cloth and given to the sea, including John Bird, who was pissing blood and languished in a fever, dying two days before they disembarked.

Pine trees edge a small settlement of low white buildings. Sloping fields run into hills yellowed by summer. The sea crashes along the rugged coast. Jacques-Louis can see gardens, a flogging triangle and a yard he will come to know. Yet was there ever such a sky at dusk in England? The beauty of the place is undeniable, and Jacques-Louis feels some vestige of himself return that he thought was ever lost, but it is quickly subdued.

He is chained from dawn to dusk to the long line of men who carry rock, break rock, drag rock from the shore at high tide and low. Most days the wind is ceaseless, the wet and heat, too. When the day is done, they make their meagre meals upon cookstoves in the yard, before they are locked into the barracks. Eight hundred men close in the warm pitch black until the morning bell. And so do the days become years.

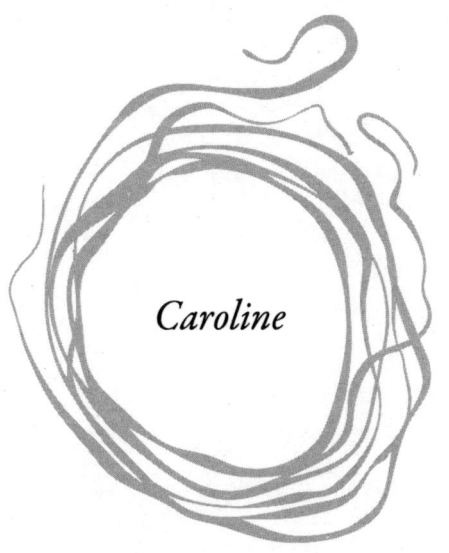

· 11 ·

Caroline

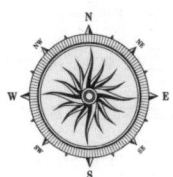

'Are we to celebrate?' asks Georgiana. 'Do you have news?'

A wine bottle in a bucket of iced water and two glasses have been delivered by a servant to the front verandah, where she and Caroline are seated while the boys are off catching tadpoles.

'Yes, there is news,' says Caroline. 'This is one of the last of Mr Broughton's wines. Cornelius unearthed it. I have been studying his journals of the vineyard, too. He believed that the weather in Van Diemen's Land, being very similar to the north of France, offered a unique opportunity. The grapes that comprise champagne like the cold and damp.'

'Have you tasted it? Is it any good?' asks Georgiana.

'Shall we see?' Caroline smiles. She unwinds the string and pulls the cork from the bottle.

'It will be too old now to have any effervescence,' she says, 'but let us try it anyway.'

She pours a small measure into each glass. It is the same pale golden colour as that from the bottle Cornelius had opened for Caroline.

The two women drink and an expression of surprise appears on Georgiana's face. 'It is delicious,' she says. 'So perfect for a warm afternoon. This must enthuse you, Caroline!'

'It does, but if the vineyard is to be restored, the labour required is but one step. Then there is the making of the wine. The barrels and bottling, the knowledge of fermentation.'

'And Cornelius cannot do this?'

'He knows about the care of the grapes, but not about the making of wine. Mr Broughton was the expert in that.'

'I do think the colony would be improved by an allocation of wine instead of rum to the soldiers—and to the prisoners, too, for that matter,' says Georgiana. 'Rum seems only to damage men.'

'A little more?' asks Caroline.

'Please,' says Georgiana. 'I think, if you do not mind, that I will tell Captain Swanston this evening that you have something of great interest to share with him.'

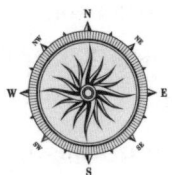

Captain Swanston sits behind his desk and peruses the numbers Caroline has placed in front of him. 'You are telling me, Mrs Douglas, that this vineyard you are attempting to reclaim may prove valuable. That three hundred gallons were made in one year and that you anticipate, on those figures, that the vineyard might make twenty hogsheads of wine next year and thirty the following year?'

She nods.

'In five years,' he continues, 'these figures suggest the yield could be one hundred hogshead. The current price being ten pounds per hogshead?'

'Yes,' says Caroline. 'But if the wine is very good, it could be worth more than twice that sum, I am told by the Walkers.'

'I hear you happened upon a bottle or two,' says Captain Swanston. 'Relics, as I understand?'

Caroline draws a bottle from her satchel and presents it to him.

'My wife reports that it is very pleasant,' says Captain Swanston. He stands and takes two glasses from the sideboard where he keeps a bottle of brandy. He unwinds the string around the cork and releases it. He pours the wine and passes a glass to Caroline. He inspects the contents of his own glass and nods.

'To your good health, Mrs Douglas.'

'And to yours, Captain Swanston.'

He sips, and cocks his head. 'Surprisingly good. No bubbles, though.'

'I fear it is too old for those. But still good, as you say.'

'And I thought to plough up those vines,' he says.

She lays two of Broughton's leather-bound volumes on Swanston's desk. 'The figures you see before you are drawn from Broughton's journals and ledgers.'

'You found these?'

'They were given to Cornelius after Broughton died.'

'Indeed.' Captain Swanston sips the wine and considers. 'Yet you wish to make a request, if I am not mistaken. What is it you would have me do, Mrs Douglas?'

'I am in need of a partner in this endeavour, Captain Swanston, and I would like that person to be my closest neighbour. A man highly regarded in this colony in all matters of enterprise.'

'Mrs Douglas, customs duties are the bulk of this government's revenue, along with our taxes. That is what runs this colony. Perhaps you are not aware that rum and brandy account for sixty per cent of the imports here. Fortified wine is another twenty per cent, malt liquor the rest. The Governor, as you know, has banned the local distillation of spirits, putting an end to six whisky distilleries in Hobart that were producing a product of variable merit. Breweries remain and they proliferate. I think there are close to fifty across the island. There would be a rebellion before they were forced to shutter their doors. I simply do not see a demand for wine, let alone champagne.'

'I was thinking beyond the local market, Captain Swanston.'

'New South Wales?'

'Perhaps. And Europe.'

He shakes his head. 'We cannot even gain an export certificate for our wheat. The price at which we are forced to sell to New South Wales makes a mockery of us. We are stymied at every turn.'

'You are right,' says Caroline, 'I know nothing of these complexities.'

Swanston rubs his cheek, perusing again the figures before him. 'I have disheartened you. But the current Governor will not be here forever, and a man of greater vision may yet follow him. So let us surmise a little. If your calculations prove correct and the wine is good . . . If you can find buyers and it fetches a good price in New South Wales . . . If an export certificate is granted and, by some miracle, it can be shipped to Europe and it sells well there . . . How much are you looking to invest?'

'You know well the state of the vineyard, Captain Swanston. It will be an investment in both labour and goods. Workers are needed to finish the task of clearing the vineyard, repairing the fencing, and to tend the vines throughout the course of the seasons. There is also the investment in casks, for I understand from Broughton's journals that French oak is superior and we must import those from Europe. New plants are needed to replace those that have died or succumbed to disease, and they will take time to mature. Then sufficient bottles must be purchased. England makes the superior version: a thicker glass that will not explode as the French bottles do. These must also be shipped. It is evident from the records that the breakages on the voyage here can be significant, as can the loss of wine when it is shipped.'

'None of that is reassuring, Mrs Douglas.'

'Forgive me, I am doing this badly. May I speak plainly, Captain Swanston?'

'I feel certain that you will.'

'The Governor's wife makes herself unpopular by dabbling in the world of men. I want no such attention. My fervent wish is to ally myself with a partner with the knowledge to make it a success, and who would allow my involvement to remain confidential. I would naturally invest both my capital and my energy, but I would prefer to remain unseen.'

Swanston rubs his top lip and stares out the window for a few moments. It is a windy afternoon and a passing wagon is shedding hay as it navigates the busy street.

'Mrs Douglas,' he says finally, 'I have significant investments both here and abroad, and many are yet to reward my investors in a manner that would subdue my concerns. I fear I would be able to add little to this venture. And beyond these journals and ledgers, you also know little of wine or business. Does it not occur to you as foolhardy?'

'Sometimes it does, Captain Swanston. But Cornelius learned from Broughton how to care for a vineyard. He is willing to train workers in the skills of pruning and harvesting.'

'I did not know that. A great curiosity, that man. And why does it have to be champagne in particular?'

'Broughton's vineyard was planted for that purpose. He chose the grape varieties grown in northern France, in the Champagne region, where the climate is very similar to here. And the wine he made is still good even more than ten years after his death. You are tasting it right now. There is also a small amount of red wine. It is possible we might proceed in that direction, too. But there are records of significant sales and letters declaring the champagne well received by wine sellers and critics in London and Paris.'

Swanston nods and interlaces his fingers. 'My wife is very fond of you, Mrs Douglas, and I am appreciative of the education you are giving my sons, which far outshines that of any other children in this colony. I see that this venture captivates you. Let me review Broughton's figures and we will meet soon. But do not be disappointed if I decline.'

'Of course, Captain Swanston. And should you decide such a venture is not right for you at this time, perhaps you might recommend some other investor. I rely on your wisdom and, as always, your discretion, Captain Swanston.'

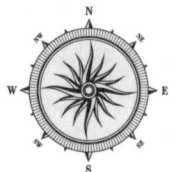

D ays go by, and then a week, and Caroline does not hear from Captain Swanston. Georgiana advises her that he has been called away to Melbourne. When he returns for Christmas, he will be bringing home their two sons who are building their sheep and cattle interests there.

'The boys are in charge of nine and a half thousand acres my husband purchased near a hamlet called Geelong,' Georgiana tells her. 'A great number of sheep were lost in the first crossing of Bass Strait when the weather blew up and swamped their boats near the entrance to the bay. One servant drowned. But my husband was resolute in his vision and sent another cargo with Oliver and Kinnear, our second and third sons, to ensure all arrived safely. They have with them now twelve servants, all convicts once, husbands and wives and their children, too. I understand the convicts are especially glad to be free of this colony.'

'It is a significant undertaking for your family,' says Caroline.

'Charles fought hard for John Batman's treaty with the Melbourne natives to be recognised, but the Sydney government denied it. We could make no claim, despite having contributed to the whole scheme. Finally, the government offered the land acquired through the treaty for auction. He was a strange man, Batman,' Georgiana added. 'I think Charles thought him a scoundrel, but a clever scoundrel.'

'He is no longer?'

'A prolonged illness. I did not like him, although I met him only briefly. His wife left him almost as soon as he became bedridden, which says a great deal, I am sure.'

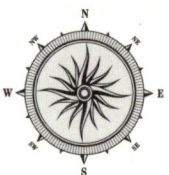

Caroline is making a wreath for the door with long stems of gum leaves and yellow banksia. As she weaves the sturdy foliage, she recalls the smell of Esther's roasted pheasant and cloves in the baked apples. The soft pleasure of crema catalana, a dessert that suited both her Scottish mother and her French father. Bowls of dried fruits and nuts, marzipan leaves on a festive cake, squares of nougat and candied citron, cumin and fennel seed biscuits arrayed on the festive table. The Yuletide log on the fire. Mama, Papa, Augusta, Tante Henriette and Esther, all of them gathered together.

It had been Yuletide when she had first tried champagne, though she was too young to remember it. Mama had woven a rosemary wreath and fixed it above the doorway into the dining room. Each time Papa and Mama met beneath it, they had kissed. During one of these embraces, Jacques-Louis put down the glass he had been carrying and Caroline, at three years old, had picked it up. She had taken a sip and then consumed the entire contents before holding out the empty glass and saying, '*Plus, cher papa, s'il te plaît?*'

'*Non, mon petit bouton, c'est pas pour toi,*' her father had said, laughing as he picked her up.

She had thrown her arms around his neck and kissed him fervently. She kissed her mother and Esther fervently, and Tante Henriette, and her baby sister Augusta, expressing love and affection until she fell asleep. Her parents had loved to recount this story when champagne was opened.

Now Christmas is no longer in winter. Instead, it follows the daffodils and irises. Apple trees are budding green fruit. The roses have bloomed in her garden, large pink and red blossoms that scent her bedroom.

Caroline and Quill have this morning delivered preserves and cordials they have made for neighbours across the valley. In the evening, Quill, Bessie and Caroline walk from the cottage across the field to the Swanstons', where they have been invited to join the household for the service at St David's, followed by supper.

Bessie will dine with the servants, while Caroline and Quill will join the family. Five of the Swanstons' sons will be present, along with their two daughters and sons-in-law. The one child missing is travelling from England, where he is completing his education. He is destined to be a diplomat, Georgiana has told Caroline. He is bringing a friend with him, and they are expected two days hence, having been becalmed south of Madras.

Caroline has decided to wear a dress of grey muslin. Her state of mourning will not protect her forever. She likes the sober greys of the Quakers, and so has chosen this occasion to indicate that while she may no longer be in mourning, in the plainness of her dress, the lack of bauble or lace, she is still, and may always have, a preference for retreat.

Bessie has made a careful arrangement of her hair. 'If your mother could see you, Mrs Douglas,' she says, as she assesses her handiwork, 'she would say you are a very handsome woman.'

At the house, the two sons from Melbourne appear a little awkward in their formal garb—more used to horses, Caroline thinks, than hors d'oeuvres. One of the daughters has her mother's repose but her father's imperious eye, and the other has her father's height with the expressive mannerisms of Georgiana.

Quill, Robert, Nowell and George jostle one another on the church bench, and suppress, and then fail to suppress, their yawns during the sermon. Robert whispers to Nowell when he believes Caroline and Georgiana are distracted. Quill has a way of belonging, she reflects. Of blending in. He had done it on the *Alliance*, with the men of the crew, and he has done it here with the Swanstons. He has done it with her.

She and Quill had discussed many names for the cottage and vineyard since their arrival, laughing at some and pausing over others. Big Tree Farm. River View. Wind Song. Dragon Mountain. Quillville. But Quill had found a name marked on some of the barrels in the cellar when they had gone to select wine to bring to the Swanstons' this evening, a name Broughton had put on the wine that was destined for England: *Everlea*.

The congregation rises. Voices lift to the heights of the chapel. '*Hallelujah, hallelujah, hallelujah.*'

Caroline recalls the fear that expelled her from London. She had run for fear of capture and imprisonment, but there was also the urge to flee from the weight of it all. Her father, her mother, her sister. And Tante Henriette. She is at the far end of the world, and it is Christmas. A melancholy rises in her, and she blinks and breathes.

Quill slides his hand into hers. She squeezes it gently, but does not gaze down at him.

'What do you think of Everlea?' she had asked Quill. 'Is that the right name for this place?'

'It's like forever and everly,' he had said.

'Forever and everly. Yes,' she had agreed.

By the time the hymn ends and the congregation sits, Caroline has muted her emotions but Quill continues to hold her hand.

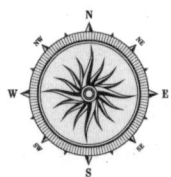

C aroline enters the drawing room and takes in the many Swanston children gathered about. She sees Quill seated on a couch between George and Robert, all of them engaged in a conversation that has them giggling. Two servants are offering glasses of champagne to the adults.

A fanfare sounds and the room stills. Everyone turns to the doors where Captain Swanston is blowing a regimental horn. Behind him come two men. Caroline looks to Georgiana, whose puzzlement is followed by surprise and then delight. She moves across the room in her dress of amethyst silk and holds out her hands to the first young man.

'Charles!' she says, and Caroline sees the resemblance in the large dark eyes, the way they both smile. Charles, the eldest Swanston son, has somehow arrived earlier than anticipated. Captain Swanston is laughing. Suddenly he also looks young, and Caroline thinks this is how he must have looked when he was the military hero of India wooing his wife-to-be.

'And Mr Mercer, welcome,' Georgiana says, offering her hand to the companion of young Charles.

'Mother, this is John. Everyone, this is my dear friend, John Mercer. We have sailed four nights from Sydney to be here, and hope to never have such a cramped passage again, but to see your face, dear Mother, is ample reward.'

'To be all together!' Georgiana says, surveying the family she has grown, all eight of them gathered about. 'My heart is elated. Let us raise a toast. Charles, will you say a few words?'

Captain Swanston gives a convivial toast, adding, at the last, that he wishes to thank Mrs Douglas for the champagne that she has unearthed in the cottage cellar.

'Perhaps in time we will drink Mrs Douglas's own champagne made right here on the land,' he says, as they all raise their glasses.

One of the daughters begins to play the piano and the younger Charles invites his other sister to dance. The two sons from Melbourne make a partnership, too, and there is much merriment. Caroline observes Quill watching all this. Then she finds herself observed in turn by the friend, John Mercer. He is tall with somewhat unruly dark hair. He bows to her.

Georgiana notices this exchange. She takes Mr Mercer's arm and leads him across the room to introduce him.

'This is Mrs Douglas, my dear friend and neighbour, a widow, and governess to our youngest,' Georgiana says. 'I am going to attempt to persuade Captain Swanston to dance while you two become acquainted.' She glides away.

'Would you care to dance, Mrs Douglas?' Mr Mercer asks. 'I know we are only just introduced, but as it is a family occasion . . .'

His soft Edinburgh brogue makes Caroline's heart keen. It is so long since she has heard her mother's accent. It is so long since she has danced. Papa was teaching her the waltz. Augusta was playing Strauss. Tears spring to her eyes.

'I have been presumptuous. I did not mean to cause you anxiety, Mrs Douglas.'

'Yes,' she says. 'But no, perhaps not.'

'Yes but no?'

'I apologise . . .'

'Then you will dance, Mrs Douglas?'

'I will not.'

'Is there a remedy for this state of not dancing?' he asks. His warm eyes are twinkling.

'Lily-of-the-valley,' she says, surprising herself.

'Lily-of-the-valley?' he repeats, puzzled.

'It strengthens the brain and comforts the heart and vital spirits.'

'Your brain does not appear weak, Mrs Douglas,' he says.

She cannot help laughing.

He smiles. 'Is there some assistance I can offer? I am studying to be a doctor . . .'

She would like to look into his playful eyes and say, 'I am sad with the ache of absence of those I have dearly loved, and you have made me laugh. But your proximity finds me unable to gather my thoughts.'

At that moment Quill arrives beside her. 'Aunt Caroline, will you dance with me?'

'I have been usurped by a gallant knight,' Mr Mercer says. 'Did you bring lily-of-the-valley for the lady?'

'I did not,' says Quill. 'I am Quill Douglas.'

'John Mercer,' he replies, offering his hand. 'Take care of your lovely aunt, young Quill,' he says. 'Ensure she does not dance upon another's head.'

'Perhaps I am yet Cleopatra,' she says with a lift of her eyebrow to John Mercer, before letting Quill lead her away.

'What does he mean?' Quill asks.

'It is a poem called 'The Waltz' by Lord Byron. Another time, dear one. We have an engagement with Herr Schubert.'

No expense has been spared to create the Christmas supper. There are oysters, quail, fish, pheasant, goose, duck, beef and vegetables. Caroline is seated between the younger Charles Swanston and Quill.

John Mercer sits opposite Charles and they speak of the shorebirds they saw on the voyage from England. Charles says that one flock, near the islands of Bass Strait, boasted more than one million birds. He speaks of their cleverness in responding to wind and air current, and how varied they are in plumage, wingspan and character of flight.

Caroline thinks to speak of the birds she observed on the passage to Cape Horn—she could tell of Señor Clementi and his collection of dead birds surrounding him in his tomb like some ancient warrior—but she does not. John Mercer has engaged Robert, seated beside him, who begins to speak of the birds he has drawn, and begs to be excused to fetch his drawing book.

John Mercer's profile, as he reviews the sketchbook, has something of the Age of Kings about it. His head is large, his eyes brown, his nose a little hooked, a good strong chin. His complexion, she assumes, is coloured by the months at sea. Caroline wonders if he likes to wander in forests.

Charles, despite his mother's dark eyes and wide smile, is a younger version of his father: fair-skinned, robust and energetic, his voice and manner quick and a little abrupt.

'John is to be a doctor,' he says. 'We met in Cambridge when he came from Edinburgh to meet with a group of scholars. I managed to convince him to spend a summer here, but he will give me only a few weeks before he must return to his books.'

'Perhaps while I am here you will show us your vineyard, Mrs Douglas,' John Mercer says, 'that makes such fine champagne.'

'Of course, yes,' says Caroline. 'But no, I . . .' She pauses. What is wrong with her?

'There we have it again,' Mercer says, amused.

'You are experienced in winemaking?' Charles asks.

'Not at all,' says Caroline. 'The champagne we have drunk tonight was made by the previous owner.'

John Mercer regards her with something she cannot quite define. Warmth? Curiosity? She blushes.

Servants clear the plates. The desserts are carried in. Steaming fruit puddings with jugs of brandied custard. Bowls of fruit jelly and two towers of profiteroles filled with chocolate cream. The children gasp. Mrs Swanston claps.

'We have the best cook in the colony,' she says.

Captain Swanston is reserved, but that is not unusual. Caroline has noticed that he has little time for small talk, although when he is led into a conversation his affection for his family is evident. Perhaps, she thinks, he does not hear very well, and much of the conversation is lost. She had many an ex-soldier enter the apothecary with lost hearing, but that is never what they came for. They came for a salve for the socket where an eye was lost or something to help them sleep when dreams awakened them.

She takes in the lanterns lighting the walls, the beautiful wallpaper, the damask cloth and silverware upon the table. She feels the generosity of having been included in this intimate gathering.

She meets the gaze of John Mercer, but they do not speak above the rising tide of voices as more wine is poured and more stories of family life unfold. She turns to Quill and he smiles at her. On the shirt that she has sewn for him over the past weeks, she has embroidered a sailing ship upon one cuff and the giant gum tree by their cottage on the other.

'Are you having a pleasant evening?' she asks.

'I have not used all the knives and forks in the correct order,' he says.

'But the food is still very good.'

'Yes,' says Quill.

'By the time you are seated at that end of the table,' she says, indicating Captain Swanston and Georgiana, 'all such things will be habit, and will take very little concentration.'

When the meal is done, it is almost midnight. John Mercer walks to her side as farewells ensue. He speaks a few words which she does not recall. What she recalls is the light in his eyes, the sense that he wishes her not to forget him.

Caroline plays the evening over in her mind as she and Quill walk home, a flirtatious moon accompanying them in a firmament bejewelled with precious stones, the sparkle and hush of waves as the sea and the river surrender to one another, entwining current and tide.

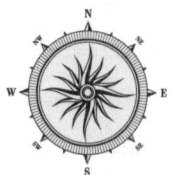

On Christmas morning Caroline wakes to hear church bells in the distance calling all to rise and gather. On her bedside table she sees a letter bearing her name. Inside is a sheet of paper with words carefully copied and crafted . . .

For oft when on your morning walk
In vacant or in pensive mood
It flashes to your wandering mind
How much you like your solitude
But home again, your heart does smile
When through the door a boy does slip
How good it is you did not leave him
Alone, alone on that great ship

Quill. And Wordsworth. It seems a long time since she shaved his head and now she cannot imagine life without him.

At breakfast she presents him with a parcel wrapped in brown paper. It is a book of astronomy with maps of the stars. She had found it in a shop months ago and saved it until now. On a sheet of paper tucked inside, she has written four lines in response to his verse.

'Aloud,' she says.

He reads:

'How good it is I have a boy,
Who fills my heart with so much joy,
How good he is no more at sea,
But here with me at Everlea.'

'And I have another surprise for you,' she says, and takes him outside and across to the giant gum tree where she has had Cornelius hang a swing.

'It can fit us both,' he says, and they sit on the wide seat and gain momentum until they are both adrift in the air and laughing.

Bessie presents Caroline with a bird's nest, whitewashed and transformed into a delicate bowl of sorts, filled with a selection of periwinkles that grow on the rocks by the river, these too painted white.

'I think each of the mantelpieces in this house might benefit from such a nest, or any arrangement, if you care to . . .' Caroline says, and Bessie drops her head to hide her pleasure at these words.

Caroline has crocheted for Bessie a shawl of light cream wool. Quill gives it to her and delights in watching Bessie unwrap it.

'It is too fine a thing for me, Mrs Douglas,' she says, awed.

'There is no such thing, Bessie,' says Caroline.

Bessie insists on draping it about her shoulders, though the day is hot and dry.

Quill and Caroline accompany Bessie to the service at St John's church, a weekly ritual demanded of all convicts and recipients of a ticket of leave. While Quill and Caroline seat themselves towards the front of the church, Bessie joins those at the rear who are in service. In a separate gallery of the church, those still incarcerated stand under guard in their woollen yellow and grey uniforms, the clink of chains evident in the quiet moments. The orphan children are in another gallery, many too small to be seen above the railing. Transportation has brought these people to a community where the future prospects of manumission are evident every day. But what of those men on Norfolk Island? Caroline wonders. What future do they imagine?

She had gone to Woolwich when she heard that her father was to be transferred from Millbank Prison. Other families had gathered, too, held back by a barrier and guards.

When the prisoners emerged from the wagon in which they had spent the night, they stumbled and fell, rising unsteadily to their feet, clearly in a stupor. All were manacled hand and foot, and chained together. From the crowd, a great cry went up. Names and messages flew through the air, final utterances of love given voice, a discordance of desperation and heartsickness. The prisoners flinched at the assault of noise.

So many poured from the wagon Caroline wondered if some had not been crushed to death within. Several prisoners, upon emerging, fell to the ground convulsing. One foamed at the mouth and had to be dragged up the gangplank by the men chained either side of him. Guards cracked whips and shouted orders. The crowd wept and called. Caroline was jostled and pushed by those wanting to meet the eyes of husbands, brothers, sons and lovers one last time.

At the end of the long line of men, she saw him. His hair had turned quite grey. He was a wraith, stooped and gaunt. She called to him in French. *'Père, je suis là, c'est Caroline. Je suis là, Papa.'*

She thought he closed his eyes longer than a blink, almost a whole long breath, but he did not turn to look at her before he stepped onto the gangplank leading to the ship.

If he died, would she be visited by a message? A vision or a dream? What would Georgiana think of Caroline if she spoke of her father? Or Captain Swanston, if he knew?

She imagines saying to them, 'If my father were here, there is little he doesn't know about winemaking and the making of champagne.'

'What a pity he is no longer alive,' Georgiana might say.

'In a way, he still is,' Caroline imagines responding. 'He is a prisoner on Norfolk Island.'

'Norfolk Island, Mrs Douglas?' she can hear Captain Swanston exclaim. 'What on earth did he do to warrant that hell?'

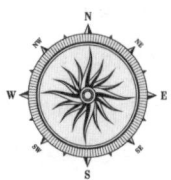

John Mercer and young Charles Swanston visit Caroline on Boxing Day. John Mercer inspects the books upon her shelves and surveys her ornaments and chess set. She wishes she could move her chair further from him, because he unsettles her. She finds herself aware of his long stride beside her as they walk out to survey the vineyard.

'The mark of civilisation,' he says, assessing the vines.

'Things returning to their wild state?' she asks.

He turns to her and smiles wryly. 'Few would think so,' he says. 'Although I have a great fondness for the untamed world.'

'I hear from my brothers there are many vineyards now planted in Port Phillip,' says Charles.

'Does Captain Swanston have an interest in it?' John Mercer asks.

'I am not sure,' says Caroline. 'I suggested a partnership in the venture and hoped it might pique his interest, but he is yet to give me his answer.'

'Father likes the surety of a good return,' says Charles.

•

'The champagne you have unearthed is very good, Mrs Douglas,' Captain Swanston says, when they meet at last to discuss her proposal. 'I have been giving our conversation due reflection but I fear you will be unhappy with my conclusions. There is every indication that the depression will deepen in Van Diemen's Land. The economy is stumbling. Unemployment is high. People cannot afford basics let alone luxuries. Wool prices falter. This colony offers little for the prudent investor. If I am to invest, I will do so on my lands at Port Phillip, where the weather is more agreeable.'

Stubborn. It was a judgement her mother had applied to Augusta, always determined to tie her own bows and polish her own boots, to make her own arrangement of breakfast and set the fire the way she thought best. She also had a particular way of placing her books by her bed, settling her pillow, and practising her piano scales until they were perfect. When she made a *tarte tatin* every slice of apple was perfectly placed.

Sitting on the shore in the late afternoon after her meeting with Swanston, Caroline watches an eagle wheel above her, regarding her as if she were potential prey. As she walks back towards the cottage, she watches it circle above the mountain before it becomes so small she can no longer find it in the enormous blueness. Dear Augusta, she thinks, I have missed you so often. I must muster some of your stubbornness to persist in this venture, for I can hear you telling me that I must not lose heart.

On the day John Mercer sails for England, she finds a parcel wrapped in brown paper on the kitchen table. Bessie gives it a brief flick of her eyes and then continues with the bread she is making.

Caroline walks to the sitting room with it and loosens the string. It is a framed watercolour of lily-of-the-valley. There is a note attached: *May your heart and spirit and lovely brain remain vital. I do hope you will permit me to write to you. J.M.*

A frost comes later in January, and in February, after a day of withering heat, there is a storm. Caroline and Quill stand upon the verandah until well past midnight watching sheets of light and forks of electricity clashing between mountain and distant hills. Hail the size of fat cherries batters every field and roof. Orchards lose their fruit. At least half of the vineyard is crushed.

In March a fungus gets into the pear trees. Black mildew assails the vines and the roses. The hens give less eggs, the goats less milk. Everyone agrees it is a difficult year.

By the time of picking, most of the grape crop is destroyed. What has managed to survive has produced strange bunches, with grapes of varying sizes. Caroline, Bessie, Quill, the Walkers and the Giblins—another Quaker family settled nearby—harvest what they can. And then Caroline, Quill and Bessie assist the Walkers and Giblins in their harvests, and other neighbours further across the hill.

Cornelius puts a little of their harvest into barrels, but the remainder Caroline gives to the Walkers for vinegar. What remains inaccessible beyond the weeds and blackberries, Caroline leaves to be eaten by birds or to spoil and rot into the earth. She despairs at the waste. Her mother's voice speaks to her gently: 'What's for you will not go by you, Mousie.'

Caroline might have employed men to tame the whole vineyard through autumn and winter the year before, and still the crop would have been lost. It was irksome to think that Swanston might be right. Perhaps the weather was too cold. Too damp. Too unpredictable. Who would know? Yet she finds the disappointment of the unseasonal summer spurs her on. Broughton had excelled at this. It cannot be unachievable. She continues her assault upon the wild tangle, stamping her feet and singing songs so the snakes will know she is coming. Her arms are raked with scratches and her face darkens from the sun.

She soothes her skin with calendula at the end of the day and remembers Augusta. When she allows herself time to take up brush and paint, she observes the landscape freshly. She attempts to capture the colours and curves of the giant gum, the oak doing its best to recover from another onslaught of opossums. She paints the cottage, the green parrots that sit on the verandah railing waiting for Bessie and Quill to feed them, and the ducks that are still in residence on the pond. None of her efforts reflect Augusta's skill, nor their mother's, but Caroline finds satisfaction in her efforts.

She and Bessie chop vegetables and prepare fruits for bottling. They make sauces, jams, relish and pickles. Potatoes, turnips and apples are laid down in the cellar with the wine. When John Mercer sends accounts of life in Edinburgh, it is these moments she shares in return.

Through the winter, she employs six women with tickets of leave. She and Cornelius teach them the care and pruning of the vines. Slowly thoroughfares appear between the bushy plants, making for easy tending and weeding, and watering if required. Quill and Cornelius take a cart and collect the fallen needles of the she-oak trees. These are laid along the pathways through the vines to deter new weeds.

Bessie feeds the convict women around the kitchen table and, although she is younger than them, they defer to her. Caroline sees in her a new authority. Bessie is walking taller, her stride is longer, the sound of her humming in the kitchen drifts through the house.

When bud break happens, the growth is quickly luxuriant. Caroline watches a vineyard unfurl in the following days, optimistic in its voluptuous greenness.

'It is the law of nature,' she hears her father say, 'to urge towards the light.' For a moment she is beside him in their garden in London. 'To bud and fruit until the next generation is assured. To provide shelter and habitat. Anaximenes, born a century before Socrates, asserted that air is the universal principle. Everything receives life from it, or is formed by it, and—as everything has originated from it—therefore it must be infinite. The Stoics went further, believing that the soul, being universal and immortal, is a portion of divinity. If nature is the divinity, then perhaps each soul is a part of a natural law that extends to the whole universe. What say you to that, *mon cœur*?'

Papa, she thinks, I miss our conversations.

Caroline regards the store of empty barrels and bottles Broughton left behind. She tallies the corks. No doubt more will be required, but Cornelius assures her they have sufficient, even if there is a good harvest. It is remarkable to imagine that so many bottles might yet be filled with wine.

She employs convict women for the harvest, giving half of it to the Walkers for their medicinal wine, but this time she is willing to accept a small payment. The rest is pressed and stored in barrels under Cornelius's instruction. With the blacksmith's assistance, they identify canes that are dead or mouldering and the convict women dig these up and prune the rest. New root stock takes its place amongst the established vines.

•

Caroline continues to swim in the pond under the early morning sky. The cold that settles into her bones after being held in the water's embrace can take hours to leave her, no matter how warmly she dresses afterwards, or how much she stokes the fire. On the coldest days she arranges for Bessie to have a hot bath waiting for her, and Bessie will say, as Caroline appears in her damp robe, numb with the cold, 'No one is forcing you to do this mad thing, Mrs Douglas.'

Yet Caroline continues to choose a little madness, for she worries that otherwise she might be overcome with responsibilities and forget that when there is mud between her toes in the covert waters of the reed-fringed pond, she sees anew her life as a passing moment of opportunity, and is fortified.

She listens to the world as if perhaps there is a baton that conducts those superb fairy wrens in their vivid blue garb, a pair of red-breasted robins landing upon that branch, the wallaby and her baby who startle and hop away, the love songs of frogs after rain, the black snake sliding under the blackberry bush, the wombats grazing, the currawongs calling, blossom emerging fragrant and alive with bees, an uprush of mushrooms, the arrival of dragonflies, a rainbow appearing in the sky, the departure of shearwaters, an albatross flying towards the river and all of it, all of it, lived beneath an immeasurable artistry of mountain, forest and clouds and the ever-watchful eye of sun and moon.

Another winter nears. Caroline accepts that she is learning patience. Meanwhile she considers her next approach to Swanston. She does not want to hide behind him, but if she is ever to bring her deepest yearning to fruition, his collaboration must be secured.

· 12 ·

The
Commandant

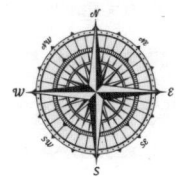

From the desk of Alexander Maconochie
Her Majesty's Prison
Norfolk Island

Dear Washington,

Your last letter was very welcome. I am delighted to hear of
your new arrival and I send you and Julia both my warmest
congratulations.

Much has happened that has kept me from responding to
your welcome letter. I believe I previously related the celebration of
Her Majesty's birthday which caused an outflow of sentiments
amongst this populace of men who believed themselves abandoned
and forgotten on this remote island.

Now that I am better settled, there is much to observe. What I
hadn't expected here is that, along with burglars, pickpockets,
highwaymen, arsonists, murderers and rapists of Britain, there are
Chinamen, Malays, Greeks, Spaniards and the aborigines of

New South Wales. There are slaves recaptured from the West Indies and the Caribbean with their branded skin, and English deserters from the army who bear the ghastly injuries of warfare from some corner of Europe. Each has his own story and I have heard many now. They do not over-elaborate, or if they do, they admit to such with good grace. I am never without compassion, I find, when a man has unburdened himself, and I make no judgement. This appears to ease him more than any other contribution I might convey.

The Commandant before me was a man called Anderson who had the pleasure—and I do not doubt that for him it was a pleasure—of brutalising these men for the past five years. Some of them also survived his predecessor Morisset, a man whose sadism knew few bounds. Anderson learned from him a particular regard for patience.

Under Anderson, men were given one hundred lashes for saying, 'Oh my God,' while on the chain gang. One hundred lashes for singing a song. Three hundred lashes for failing to sow corn properly. Sick men were lashed three hundred times for malingering. Sometimes the first one hundred and fifty lashes were given on one day and the man sent back to work, only to be returned to the yard three days later for the remainder. Some were flogged day after day, in some effort to have them confess to this or that, but no man would. My predecessor also made it an offence to apply any salve to a man after a flogging.

In the summation I received from Anderson, I was told to keep flagellation for the worst or least of them. I was assured that flogging is good for a certain kind of man. That it tempers the clever and vivifies the coward. When he is able to bend again, or lie on his back, there is humility in most. If anything

to the contrary was evident, I was advised to flog him again,
one hundred and twenty lashes being the recommended dose.
I was told to maintain a certain cordiality with others to ensure
that those who might rise up against their rations, or simply
their imprisonment, were kept down. Those more sensible to the
implications of revolt, who had no interest in dying by the noose,
must be given a chance to subdue such conversations in their
fellow prisoners, or sneak their observations into my ears. I was
encouraged to employ espionage between the prisoners preventing
the men from forming alliances.

As you will remember, I know well that for those confined in
solitude and deprived of all light, the days and nights become one,
the lack of any voice or touch becomes interminable. The injured
spirit surrenders slowly. You can imagine how broken the men
were after years of such torment and deprivation. Their limbs
were withered and they looked thrice their years. I saw young men
of twenty with the skin hollowed from their cheeks, their teeth
broken and their sunken eyes devoid of any expression. But I have
already seen evidence of some return of spirit.

I had the hangman's stage and noose taken down. This was
met with silence, there being no trust of authority. I explained
my method, my system, to these men who have lived through so
much—the Old Hands, as they are known—and there was a
small cheer, the first indication that within them still live the souls
of men.

I had the triangle put away. The lash, too.

In my system, new arrivals are put to work breaking rocks for
some weeks so that the notion of punishment is instilled. They are
confined in barracks and given religious instruction before they
may move on to work in the gardens. If they do well there, growing

the food so essential to the island, they will be given a good patch of land to make a garden of their own.

This is how I came across a prisoner who, but for his crime and his own admission of guilt, I would not have expected to find amongst this cohort. He is a Frenchman, apparently of noble birth. He arrived during the time of my predecessor and had been breaking stone ever since. He is not a young man and the labour seemed particularly harsh. At the earliest opportunity, when his tractable character had been established, I placed him in the gardens. When his efforts there proved laudable, I assigned him to the private gardens about the house and he is making it a veritable Eden.

One morning, I found he had restored an apple sapling after a storm. It is now espaliered firm on a wall and is in early bloom. The roses he has pruned grow well. The blooms are pungent. They grace the dining table almost as if we might be in Edinburgh.

I am hopeful there may be a lemon tree arriving on the next ship. And gunpowder. If the men knew how badly equipped is the armoury . . . not that I anticipate revolt. But still, it is wise to be well prepared.

But let me return to my most curious prisoner. He is a man of significant intellect and education. I do not want to guess his thoughts, but he displays no outward sign of restlessness, holding himself with reserve, though I doubt he can know peace. His life under my predecessor records an early flogging, one hundred lashes for 'looking keenly at a guard'. In the yard, amidst the clamour of food preparation, he stands often alone. The other men do not rile him. His reputation precedes him. There are few murderers here, though the newspapers would insist otherwise.

He was, I understand, famous across all England for his crime. Sometimes I have the suspicion he lets me win at chess, but we have spent many a pleasant evening over a game in my study. Perhaps you think me unwise, but this is the work I feel charged to do. To restore these men to their humanity. He alone, perhaps, in all this throng, demonstrates my goals. That a man may be condemned for his actions, may pay as the law deems for his crime, and yet still earn a sense of regard.

I determined that he would be better served by having his own quarters. In return, he was tasked with teaching the men the growing of vegetables and fruits so that, beyond this place, they might have such necessary skills to make their way. Those who do well are able to sell their surplus to the officers.

My prisoner knows he has likely come to the end of his life here on this green rock in the sea. What potential he had is now behind him, although his knowledge of plants and medicines would be of much use in Sydney or even Hobart Town.

Is there madness behind his eyes? I have seen no evidence of it. There's not a man on Norfolk Island that doesn't wish he was somewhere else. Not a man who is undamaged by his incarceration.

Still, there are guards here who feel it their duty to send reports belittling my actions. Even after my own clarifications, written at length to Gipps, my time here is harried by letters of rebuke and remonstrance from my superiors. Gipps, who does his best to support my endeavours, must also look to his own career. In Sydney they fear that making this a place of reform will only cause more criminal activities or, I am told, a slave rebellion. This place must act as a deterrent!

But what is the purpose of a system maintained by extreme severity, that requires constant humiliation? At what cost to the lives of these twelve hundred men? For their sake, I will not relinquish my zeal. All men can be saved. I believe it passionately and fervently and never is it more evident here than in the restored love of Her Majesty, and faith amongst the men.

I await the vines I have ordered from Sydney. The Frenchman says a vineyard might not produce for several years, but he says he has years to wait. I may not see the wine of that fruit for my time here may end sooner than I wish.

My finest regards to you, dear Washington, and to dear Julia and your young family. And to our many mutual friends in the fair town of Hobart. I sign off with this perhaps short-lived title, but one of which I remain proud.

Alexander Maconochie
Commandant, Norfolk Island

· *13* ·

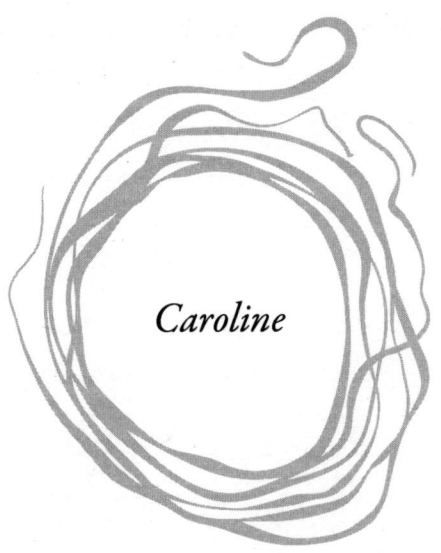

Caroline

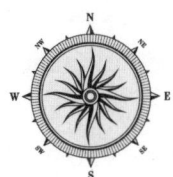

Georgiana measures a length of yellow thread and slides it through the eye of her embroidery needle. Bessie enters the room carrying wood for the fire. Caroline and Georgiana remain silent as she completes her work. After she departs, Georgiana says, 'Our friend Commander Maconochie is to be recalled from Norfolk Island, we hear, though there has been no official word. His ideas do not sufficiently deter those poised to transgress the bounds of legality.'

Caroline looks up from her knitting. 'You are in disagreement?'

'We have had good service from many pickpockets and vagabonds while they completed their sentences. That was the great benefit to assignment. Many learned new skills. There were a few that were lazy or impudent at first, but mostly Charles and I found little reason to fault them.'

'Was yours an unusual home, Georgiana?'

'We were allowed no leniency. We could not invite them to share in the bounty to which their labours had contributed, even at Christmas. It was the law. Mr Meredith, out on the east coast, was threatened with losing all his labour for inviting his convict servants to the family table to share in a meal. Even if a family had emigrated here and was in need of labour, they could not employ a convict who was related to them.'

'Are there families here awaiting the release of their loved ones?' Caroline asks.

'We had a servant, Mary, who confessed to me that she had deliberately been caught for a crime so she would be transported to be near her husband. But he was sent to New South Wales, and she was sent here. As soon as his pardon was given, he came to join her. They have a home in the midlands now, and several hundred sheep.'

Caroline nods.

'We grew very fond of Alexander—Commander Maconochie— while he was here, but he caused the Governor much embarrassment,' adds Georgiana.

Caroline knows Captain Swanston is well pleased with the departure of the previous governor, though his replacement has turned out to be a country squire with seemingly little aptitude for the role.

'What caused this embarrassment?' Caroline asks.

'Alexander was a commander in the Royal Navy. He was taken prisoner by the French, and lived in appalling circumstances for two years. His writings on that subject drew the attention of the Prison Reform Society in London, who were looking for someone who might assess the convict population here. He was welcomed by the Governor, and his report was duly completed after much industry on his part. The Governor signed it off. But when it was publicised in London, it caused quite a stir. The Governor declared he had never read it, and that he had been painted in a deliberately offensive way while he was simply following the orders he had been charged with upholding. It was all most unpleasant. In the London papers, critics of transportation referred to us as petty rulers and slave owners. Alexander was dismissed by the Governor but the authorities in London offered him a posting on Norfolk Island to trial his new methods.'

'And is there evidence of success during his tenure?' Caroline asks.

'Apparently many men who had no hope of ever returning to society have earned sufficient merit to be released back into New South Wales. Only one or two of some hundreds and hundreds released under his authority have reoffended.'

Caroline casts off the final stitches and lays the socks aside. Quill is growing fast. According to the marks she has been keeping on the wall in the hallway, he has grown a full four inches since they came ashore in Van Diemen's Land. His feet in particular seem determined to outgrow his boots and ruin every pair of socks.

'New South Wales,' continues Georgiana, 'would rather import wheat from Valparaíso than accept the goods of Van Diemen's Land tainted by convict labour. England allows our wool to rot on the wharves, making it unsaleable, when the wool that leaves here is of a better quality than Yorkshire can produce. Sydney chooses to forget who made their roads and cleared their lands. Do you know the tide of free settlers coming here has almost entirely dried up? Not a single new arrival in the past twelve months, when previously we have had thousands, but there is no shortage of new convicts. We are left to languish under this burden while Sydney continues to expand and Melbourne promises a glittering future.'

'Perhaps we must offer something new,' says Caroline. 'Something unexpected.'

'Champagne!' says Georgiana, laughing. 'Oh, I am glad that you have not been dissuaded, Caroline! I see the work you are doing, and it stirs me. How I long to join you in your grand emprise, but my dear husband . . .'

'He disapproves?'

'No. He simply finds you unexpected, my dear.' She paused. 'And does it not concern you that you put so much industry into a place that is not your own . . .'

Caroline regards her friend. 'Dear Georgiana, I must seek your forgiveness.'

'Why?'

'Because I have kept a substantial fact from you, and I asked your husband to do the same. I purchased the cottage and the land with the vineyard when I first arrived here. Forgive me for asking your husband to maintain this secret. I did not want the speculation such a purchase would bring. It seemed much wiser to be seen as a tenant.'

Georgiana shakes her head and smiles. 'Caroline Douglas, you are an inspiration! I wish to propose a toast. The men may well be recorded within the papers and books of this colony, but the women . . . where would the world be without our ingenuity?'

'You do not mind my intrigue?'

'How can I mind when it is my husband's work to maintain such discretion? Your secret is safe with me.'

'If only I was a winemaker, or there was one I could learn this art from,' Caroline says.

Georgiana ponders a moment then says, 'It's possible that on Norfolk Island there might be someone amongst all those men improved and restored under Maconochie's care. I am sure it is unlikely, but still . . .'

'I suppose it is possible such a person might exist,' Caroline concedes with measured reluctance. 'A man who knows something of making wine. But as you say, unlikely.'

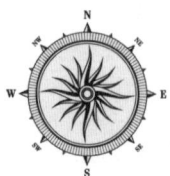

In the work Tante Henriette trained her in, Caroline did not fail to engage the kind-hearted or charm the wary, vanishing after an order was made, a transaction completed, certain items acquired. She appeared as a young man, tall, slender, small and blond, or dark, possibly Spanish, Welsh or European, but surely he was real? This is his signature upon the order. Here the confirmation of delivery. Here, look, this is the very place the item sat within a locked case. It cannot be that there is no such person.

They were returning to Tante Henriette's through Regent's Park one Sunday afternoon dressed as themselves, arm in arm and both a little giddy after champagne and *crème brûlée* at a French shop that Henriette frequented in Drury Lane. They'd had a most successful week.

It was Caroline who noticed, too late, the black carriage by her aunt's front door. The men gathered on the street looking in both directions. She glanced behind her and glimpsed, a little way back, another man who might have been following them. Two men waiting by the apartment appeared to have spotted Tante Henriette and began walking towards them.

'Tante Henriette,' Caroline said, her voice low. 'Police.'

Her aunt slipped her arm, kissing Caroline on both cheeks. 'Walk away,' she said. 'Do not hurry but do not delay or look back. Do not risk yourself for me. Do what you must.'

Caroline stepped between other pedestrians into a lane at her left. She turned right and right again, waiting to see if she was being followed, and then walked quickly to the laneway behind her aunt's apartment. There was no one about. She withdrew a key from her purse and unlocked the stable door, entering the room of treasures. The latest wares lay covered on the central table. Upstairs, she heard footsteps and voices. Caroline took off her shoes and climbed the secret stairs to listen at the door.

'It is a shocking allegation,' she heard Tante Henriette declare. 'I am a companion of Lady Darlington. I have many friends in high places who will advise the Commissioner of your actions. Your egregious suspicions will be dismissed out of hand.'

Caroline waited until she heard the drumbeat of footsteps descending and the apartment door slamming shut. She raced on stockinged feet back downstairs and peered through a gap in the curtains. Tante Henriette was being ushered into the waiting black carriage.

When Caroline was certain there was no one left upstairs, she entered the apartment. From the wardrobe, she quickly took a wig, a suit, shoes, stockings, hat and coat. She folded all these into one of her aunt's suitcases. From a false recess in a drawer, she removed a metal box. She checked its contents and took a second suitcase. On her way out, she saw the inlaid chessboard sitting on the side table. She tucked it under her arm and was gone.

Downstairs she worked quickly, an ear to the street outside. If it was small, she took it, wrapping in linen each precious thing. A dozen silver cake forks and matching teaspoons, two gold snuffboxes, one pair of pearl earrings, one pair of diamond earrings, two pairs of gold-and-diamond cufflinks, a silver bracelet of pearls and sapphires, eight silver napkin rings, eight silver eggcups, several small bowls of filigree silver, a diamond choker and a gold-and-enamel necklace set with diamonds, turquoise and pink tourmaline. She also retrieved the long leather cylinder containing a map of the world.

When both suitcases were unable to hold any more, she squeezed them shut. At the door to the laneway, she checked for any activity. There was none. The light had faded and the lane remained deserted. She went in search of a hackney coach to assist her.

At Gulliver Wendover's door she knocked and was admitted. He sent a boy to enquire at Bow Street police station. The boy returned to tell them that Tante Henriette was still detained.

Caroline called upon the forger, the widow Beck, whose services were not cheap but they were reliable. The papers, she assured Caroline, would be ready in the morning. Only when the hackney coach had returned Caroline to the house where she was governess, and the suitcases were beneath the bed, did her heart stop racing.

Just after dawn, Caroline entered the kitchen. The cook was blowing coals in the oven, and bread was rising on the hearth.

'Miss Caroline,' she said, 'you are up with the sparrows.'

'I have had awful news last night, Mrs Hollis. My grandmother in Paris is dying and has requested that I come in haste. I have spent a sleepless night, but I must go.'

'Aye, of course, lass,' said Mrs Hollis. 'You must. And good luck to you. Take care that you don't let any of those Frenchmen get the better of you.'

'I shall keep my wits about me, Mrs Hollis,' said Caroline, amused at the cook's concerns. 'I have heard there is a service from Paddington that will take me to Dover, and from there I can cross to Calais.'

She handed the cook an envelope.

'I have drafted a letter. Please make sure the mistress receives it with my apologies to the family, and especially to my pupils. I will send word as soon as I can of my likely return.'

'They will be hard-pressed to do without you, that's what,' says Mrs Hollis, and she was surprised but pleased when Caroline kissed her on the cheek.

Out on the street, Gulliver Wendover awaited with a carriage. He stowed her trunks and suitcases and took Caroline away. Their first stop was the premises of Mrs Beck, where the requested papers were waiting. Next she asked Wendover to approach the street of her aunt's apartment, feeling sure she would have been released by now.

To her dismay, the front door was guarded. In the laneway behind the apartment, men were ferrying goods from the stables and loading them into a police wagon.

She had no way of liberating Henriette now. No way of giving her the new identity Mrs Beck had created for each of them overnight. It was only a matter of time before the police searched for associates. They may already have heard of an accomplice. A young man seen with Henriette when she left a certain house. Who was Tante Henriette's family? If the police discovered Caroline's existence and questioned her, they would discover who her father was. Things would go badly.

She instructed Wendover to continue on. She would leave London today and wait for word of her aunt's release. And then she would be ready to whisk her aunt away to safety.

She availed herself of Wendover's apartment and changed into the garb of a man. The wait until the bank opened felt as if time had conspired to torment her.

'I require a portion in cash and the remainder in a bank cheque,' Caroline said to the clerk. 'And I have a letter from my uncle who is also seeking travel funds.'

He observed the amount and regarded the young man that was Caroline. 'Sir, I will have to pass this on to the manager.'

'Be quick about it,' the young man replied.

'A family emergency in Amsterdam,' she said to the manager, who had met both Caroline and Henriette before in their masculine garb. 'We do not know how long we will be gone.'

'I understand, sir,' said the manager. 'I shall make all the arrangements. Would you care for tea while you wait?'

Caroline forced herself not to jiggle her foot or scratch her bearded chin. She drank tea, read a newspaper she was offered and affected the pose of one who was unperturbed, all the while her attention discreetly fixed on the door to the street.

From Paddington, she did not go south to Dover but took a coach north to Liverpool, permitted to share the seat with the one other man while three women squeezed together on the opposite bench. From a modest but pleasant hotel, returned to her female form, she sent word to Wendover to make enquiries.

When word came back her heart dropped.

Imprisoned in Millbank, awaiting trial. He added a newspaper clipping.

The case is causing considerable fascination because the lady has
letters of recommendation from both Lady A— and Lady D—
for whom she has been a trusted companion . . . It is said that
the police found enough stolen goods to furnish a bazaar. It is
uncertain if she worked alone.

Caroline penned a brief note to Tante Henriette.

*Paris is so beautiful in the spring. I long for you to be here,
beloved. I have everything prepared for your arrival. Do let me
know if there is anything I can do to speed your travels.*

She signed it: *d'Artagnan.*
She enclosed the note in a letter to Wendover, asking him to
find a way to deliver it by hand and secure a reply.
When it came, it was short.

*Cher d'Artagnan,
    Alas, it might be some time before I resume my travels.
Meanwhile, I wish you bon voyage.*

Caroline approached a contact of Henriette's in Liverpool and
sold the gold-and-diamond cufflinks. Her identity as a widow was
already forming as she ordered a black silk dress, veil and gloves,
and a suitable bonnet. She bought passage to New York with a
private cabin. She had been using crime to organise her life for more
than two years. During the month she spent crossing the inclement
waters of the Atlantic, she took out the world map and considered
her options.
'You must invent a new story,' she heard her aunt say.

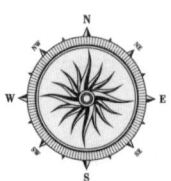

In the reading room in Hobart, Caroline finds an advertisement in an edition of the *Sydney Gazette*: *Henriette Colbert invites young ladies to learn French at her esteemed establishment.*

Tante Henriette is in Sydney! Caroline's heart leaps. Why had she imagined her aunt had remained incarcerated in England when it seemed every other thief was sent to the colonies? Caroline had been sure Henriette's aristocratic friends would have saved her from anything but the most lenient sentence. But no. Henriette was in Sydney. She would never have come to the colonies voluntarily. She must have been transported, and now she had a ticket of leave, or a pardon.

Caroline deliberates for some weeks, but cannot stop considering her aunt's fate. She writes a letter to the address of the school noted on the advertisement. No reply comes. She writes again but several months pass and still there is no word. She goes to the colonial office in Hobart Town seeking information about a family friend whom she believed had been transported. When she returns to the office three weeks later, a letter awaits her. It is on official government stationery. There is Henriette's name and prisoner number. The date and the name of the ship on which she was transported. The date of her arrival in Sydney. The date when a ticket of leave was issued. And then, the date of her death.

It cannot be true, Caroline thinks. She asks the clerk if further information can be ascertained as to the nature of her death. He suggests that a visit to Sydney may be the only way to secure more information. But he assures Caroline that the government records are accurate. For such a note to be in the colonial record, a death certificate must have been issued. He offers his sympathies.

Tante Henriette is no longer alive. She had died four months ago, perhaps on the very day Caroline had seen her aunt's advertisement in the newspaper. She walks up the hill towards Everlea, trying to take in this news. Arriving home, Caroline goes to the big tree and sits upon the swing.

There is nothing she can do. Her beautiful and formidable aunt is gone. Had it been an illness? An assailant? Someone she trusted? Someone she had stolen from? Perhaps Henriette had been caught in an act of theft and killed, or was discovered by an old enemy. Did Tante Henriette have enemies? Caroline did not know, but she supposed there might have been quite a few deprived of their goods content to see an end to her aunt. Such people might feel the same way about her accomplices.

Henriette had apprenticed Caroline into a clever, daring and dangerous life when Caroline had been alone and bereft. It had made Caroline's whole future here in Van Diemen's Land possible. She thought of her aunt's words as the police had stood outside her apartment. 'Walk away. Do not hurry but do not delay or look back. Do not risk yourself for me. Do what you must.'

Caroline had fled from London with treasures and money. She had used it to pay passage to New York and to invest in the cargo on the *Alliance*. She had bought the farm. She had extinguished the debt that had ensnared Quill. And at this she broke down and wept.

She could not tell Henriette of all that had happened. She could not thank her now. She would never see her again. Her aunt would never know the life Caroline was creating, the plans she had for the future.

Caroline had been the only family Henriette might have relied on to help her after she was released. How she must have hated the poverty of her life then, and wondered what had become of her niece. She had been so close that Caroline might have sailed to Sydney in less than a week.

There is a darker truth which Caroline weeps for. She is no longer the ingenue, the orphan, the lost girl with no one to guide her. She'd had far too much to lose if her aunt had reappeared. What would the Swanstons have made of it? An aunt imprisoned for theft on a grand scale? What if Tante Henriette had sought to embroil her anew in criminality?

Caroline did not doubt that she had been a useful partner, someone her aunt could trust implicitly. Someone she had personally trained. A natural at artifice and disguise, light-fingered and good with locks, but also adept at planning and procuring, accounts and ledgers, and sufficiently fluent in French to deal with the merchants in Paris.

Her aunt had been fearless, calculating and determined. Caroline had learned these qualities. And she too had secured an accomplice. A boy called Quill who gave her the illusion of respectability and family. Yes, she had grown fond of him on the ship, offering him the opportunity her aunt had offered her. A different future. A bigger life. But Quill had been useful, too, as Caroline had been useful. She did not like to see this part of herself, yet here she was, in a harsher light.

She remembers asking Tante Henriette how she remained a faithful Catholic in her line of work, and her aunt had replied. '*Sans doute, quand je serai morte, je brûlerai en enfer.*'

No doubt when I am dead I will burn in hell.

She looks up at the contours of the mountain, the lofty, faithless clouds, the swooping swallows, the lucent river, the slumbering vines, the susurrant leaves and the grand graceful branches above her. 'Let me tell you about my extraordinary aunt,' she says.

Afterwards, when she is emptied of every memory she can summon, and so many regrets, she takes a ring from her finger. It is a simple pearl set in silver, stolen early in her apprenticeship, which Tante Henriette had encouraged her to keep. She wraps it in a handkerchief and buries it within the roots of the eucalypt, then she walks back through the golden grass to the cottage.

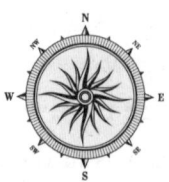

'You are burdened by some matter of gravity, Captain Swanston,' says Caroline. He has asked her to join him while they walk the vineyard.

'I find my labours daily increase, Mrs Douglas. These are times of general distress. When it will end, God only knows. Yesterday a friend, Learmonth, was declared insolvent and, as far as I can judge, his estate will pay nothing. His debts are very large, chiefly absentees, people who have never seen this place, but all expect to be repaid. I have had requests for the extension of credit from some of my best investors, from high-ranking civil servants and pastoralists. All kinds of property, whether stock, land or shares in companies, are unsaleable except at ruinous prices. As yet we have suffered no loss at the Derwent Bank, but we cannot expect to escape. We have reduced our dividends to ten per cent. I had hoped for better with Franklin gone, but the current regime continues its imbecility. I believe the government coffers are empty but none will declare it.'

'I am sorry to hear it,' says Caroline.

'In Port Phillip my sons continue to expand the estate and talk of the vineyards being planted there by neighbours. Perhaps I have been remiss in not giving your endeavour more attention, Mrs Douglas,' he says. 'This colony needs new notions to lift it from its malaise. And it needs them enacted by people of skill and worth. Broughton saw it twenty years ago, and people still speak of the man in the most glowing terms as a winemaker. I have walked this way to observe your efforts on several occasions in the past weeks. I hope you will not think that strange.'

'Of course not, Captain Swanston. And I believe the new season could yet bear a crop that will prove the numbers we have seen in Broughton's journals,' Caroline says. 'But only if we can secure the services of a winemaker well versed in the varietals and climate we have at hand.'

And then Captain Swanston says the words that have almost certainly travelled to him from Caroline's conversation with Georgiana.

'You would think,' he says, 'that in all these tens of thousands of convicts we might find one who is a winemaker. Is such a thing too much to ask? Surely we might find one man here with the necessary ability. What say you, Mrs Douglas?'

'It is an idea, Captain Swanston. Although it would be a risk.'

'I have employed many such men before, and found them pliable and hardworking. If such a person was found and made available, what then, Mrs Douglas?'

'Your partnership, Captain Swanston. As you say, there are people who remember Broughton's success. But your reputation and involvement would make the project successful even before we begin: New Town Park making champagne from the same vineyard that produced such popular wine.'

Captain Swanston nods.

'You know my preference for discretion, Captain Swanston. You must be willing to have it be seen as your affair and receive, in time, the public rewards.'

'If I am to join you in this scheme,' replies Swanston, 'you must understand that I place a powerful trust in you on behalf of my family and my reputation. It cannot fail.'

'You need have no doubt of my willingness to work hard, but it is the winemaker who will make the success.'

'It does concern me that you yourself have no experience in winemaking, Mrs Douglas. And if a man can be found, it is not easy to rely so heavily on the industry of a former criminal. You have no experience in that either. The situation can be intimidating.'

'I employed the convict women who cleared the vineyard and undertook the pruning, and those who picked the harvest.'

'Yes, yes, and I do not doubt they served you well. But this is someone you must align yourself with for some years.'

'If there is a candidate, I do not doubt your ability to intensively interrogate his character, Captain Swanston,' says Caroline. 'And then perhaps we must look beyond his history to our future prosperity.'

'Let us first find a man we believe is capable of the task,' he says. 'I shall enquire this week of the Convict Superintendent.'

'And I shall speak with the Walkers,' says Caroline. 'I know they continue a correspondence with the Commandant on Norfolk Island.'

'Ah, Maconochie,' says Swanston. 'We knew him when he worked for the Governor here. An idealist but a good man. I doubt we will find a suitable man amongst those inmates.'

•

Early the following morning, Caroline visits the Walkers. Washington and Julia and their young son are in their kitchen garden. They invite her to join them for tea.

'I have come to seek a favour,' Caroline tells them. 'Captain Swanston has expressed some interest in assisting with the vineyard.'

'He has overcome his resistance?' asks Julia.

'Almost. He suggests we need the aid of an experienced winemaker. But as you yourselves have learned, it is not possible to attract a suitable person from Europe while our reputation as a place of convict slavery continues.'

'It is indeed the case,' Washington agrees.

'And so it occurs to me, despite all I have heard of that notorious place, that perhaps there is a prisoner with the necessary skills who might have benefited from your friend Maconochie's program of reform.'

Washington looks at her as if he has heard a particular note of music.

'I had a letter some time back in which our dear friend mentioned a prisoner who, as I recall, was planting a vineyard on the island.'

Caroline hopes she does not blush. 'If you would be prepared to write to the Commandant about this, will you ensure that such a request is accompanied by an approach from Captain Swanston?' asks Caroline. 'I believe he referred to Maconochie as fearless.'

'Perhaps a little too fearless,' says Julia. 'Washington, did you not receive word that he is preparing for departure? A letter might not reach him before he is dispatched back to England.'

'I will see Captain Swanston today, if I can,' says Washington. 'Rest assured, Caroline, it is underway.'

As she returns home, Caroline reflects on Julia and Washington's congenial partnership. Her thoughts wander to John Mercer and she wonders what kind of a husband he might make. Were she to become a wife, she would have to surrender many of the liberties she enjoys living with Quill and Bessie, where no one requires her to be anything but herself.

· *14* ·

The
Commandant

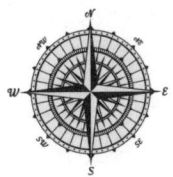

'Prisoner Colbert,' says Maconochie, approaching Jacques-Louis in the garden. 'May I have a word?'

The morning is warm and overcast. Jacques-Louis Colbert lays aside his gardening tools and removes the cap on his head. He stands with his head bowed, wordless.

'I have received a letter from a friend in Van Diemen's Land,' the Commandant says. 'He tells me that an acquaintance of mine, a significant man, a member of the Legislative Council there and the director of one of the two colonial banks, is seeking a winemaker. Swanston is his name and he himself included a note asking me if there is any prisoner with such knowledge within this population. Someone who is of good character and might soon complete their sentence. It is an unusual request but naturally I could not help but think of you.'

Jacques-Louis' head remains bowed and he says nothing.

'I will be gone within the month,' Maconochie continues. 'My replacement is a Joseph Childs. They are determined to return this place to the hellhole it was when I arrived. I fear that, when I leave, you will be returned to the general population.'

'Yes, Commandant.'

'I have been considering requesting a pardon for you. I know you have not expected it, yet . . .'

'I do not ask it, Commandant.'

'Colbert, you could become a winemaker! Not in France, where I fear you will never return, but in Van Diemen's Land. It is an extraordinary opportunity, and I know you have the skills. What say you, man?'

'I do not know, Commandant.'

'What is in my power to give, I have given,' says Maconochie. 'You have seen this in my time here. You have encouraged me in my commitment to bring these men back to their humanity, their sense of worth.'

Jacques-Louis remains unmoving.

'Colbert . . . Jacques-Louis!' says Maconochie, grasping the man's hand, attempting to gaze into the prisoner's downcast eyes. 'I seek to lift you up. Call me not Commandant! Call me Alexander. You and I have sat more evenings in conversation than I have with some of my closest friends. You, Colbert, are my proof of salvation for the convicted man. Look at what you have done with the gardens here. See how the vineyard grows! Van Diemen's Land is a beautiful place and I have seen the property where you will work. It is as fine as any in the colony, as fine as you might find in England. I assure you that this is a moment of renewal for you that neither of us could have imagined. The work of an angelic hand.'

'If angels work to influence a man, then what say you of demons, sir?' Jacques-Louis asks.

'But give a man the chance to live well, to be held in some esteem, and I believe those demons in a man will be subsumed by goodness. I do not doubt it, Colbert. I do not doubt it in you! I will continue to argue that life does not apportion favour equally, and on that we can agree. A man fails through his separation, his alienation, from himself. Arts, education, agriculture and prayer, these inspire the good within us and lead us back to grace. You have seen it amongst the men here. I state only what is obvious to us both.'

'You have more faith in goodness than any man I have ever encountered, sir,' says Jacques-Louis.

'I make no excuses for you,' replies Maconochie. 'But I firmly believe that you are a man who will serve society better doing what you so naturally do with all that grows, not here under the authority of Joseph Childs, who will almost certainly return you to the breaking and carrying of rock, and worse.'

He pauses and waits until Jacques-Louis meets his gaze. 'I have complete faith in the further reclamation of your soul, Colbert. Allow me to recommend you!'

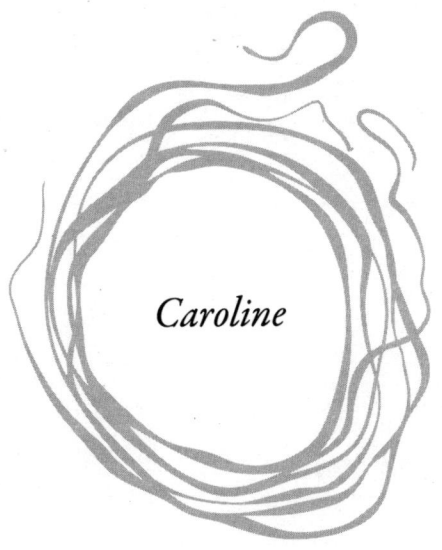

· 15 ·

Caroline

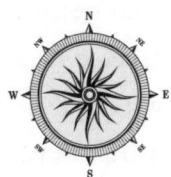

'Why am I worried about just one, when we are outnumbered by them every day?' asks Georgiana. 'To think that, but for the Revolution, he might have been a duke. It is doubtful he will be offended that we are housing him in the barn, after his previous accommodation, don't you think? It was at Cornelius's suggestion that he be close to the vineyard, rather than in our servants' quarters. Cornelius assures me that he wishes it this way. The two of them must learn a partnership if this is to succeed. And I understand that Cornelius has cleared the old entrance from the barn to the cellar beneath the cottage, so that our new arrival might come and go without disturbing you. Still, I imagine he will be often just below you. You are not concerned?'

'We will learn to adapt,' says Caroline.

'You have read Commandant Maconochie's letter?'

'Of course. And I know you have certainty in his recommendation.'

'It seems we must,' says Georgiana. 'We place great store in this winemaker. Perhaps we will surprise ourselves and like him.'

'Some of the most disappointing people I have met have been people I liked,' says Caroline.

Georgiana laughs then urges the horse on. The gig rattles as they continue past a road gang rebuilding the wall by the creek. A few of the workers raise their heads as the women pass. Caroline sees the rough hair and whiskered faces, the mud yellow coats, the leg irons. She wills her thoughts away from prison cells and flogging.

Georgiana says, 'Do you think a man who was willing to murder once, in the heat of passion, is capable of murdering again?'

'I think it best we dwell not upon such considerations but rather on the afternoon tea we are to endure with the Governor.'

'Yes,' says Georgiana. 'A special form of torture. But the man is very fond of champagne, I am told, and he will be well pleased with your gift, I am sure.'

The wooden crate containing six of Broughton's store are packed in straw at Caroline's feet.

'Without his assistance, we would still have no winemaker,' Georgiana notes.

'We shall be duly grateful,' says Caroline.

'And most refined,' says Georgiana.

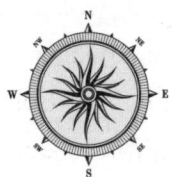

Cornelius is sweeping out the forge. His movements are slow and careful. A wood stack runs along one wall. Caroline sees the red of split she-oak, the caramel of eucalyptus, the pale circles within the drying blackwood. She remembers Cornelius telling her that all timbers burn differently, some hotter, some quicker and some longer. Caroline knows this from the baking oven, but she has never pitted herself against the temperatures that Cornelius has mastered, nor felt the responsiveness of metal and iron wrought, beaten and shaped into form.

'Mrs Caroline,' Cornelius says, turning at her approach, 'I hear a winemaker has been found.'

'Yes,' she says.

He sets aside the broom and invites her to sit. She takes the bench by the barn door and Cornelius eases himself down onto a wooden stool. The day glistens, the air is chilled, the sunshine welcome.

'I believe there is snow coming,' he says. 'My old hip tells me so.'

Caroline draws from her pocket a jar of ointment. 'It has chilli from India for warmth and turmeric and camphor to ease the inflammation, all in the beeswax you procured for me.'

'I thank you,' he says, taking the jar and smiling.

'Old injuries are always the first to complain. I heard it often in London,' Caroline says.

'You could make a business of selling your ointments. They are the only remedies that have ever brought me relief.'

'Has Captain Swanston told you anything of the man we are expecting, his history?' Caroline asks.

'He has, Mrs Caroline.'

'And you are not troubled to have such a man in close proximity to you?'

'If I were, I would never have made my home in a place like this,' says Cornelius. 'But for you I admit I find myself uneasy at the prospect. A crime of such violence, especially against a woman, can be ingrained in a man's nature. I do not doubt he has paid for that on Norfolk Island, but still, if you were my daughter, I believe I would be unwilling to have him close, no matter how excellent his skills in winemaking. Be assured I shall be keeping a watchful eye on all he does.'

'Cornelius,' she says, looking into the face which has become dear to her, 'I must tell you something I have held long inside me.'

'Mrs Caroline, I have shared some terrible secrets with you, and still here we are. I am listening.'

'I fear that in this case it might be too much to ask.'

'I doubt that, but please, go on,' says Cornelius.

'The prisoner, the winemaker, his name is Jacques-Louis Colbert,' she begins. 'He may arrive any day, and I find myself anxious and troubled and uncertain.'

'Because of what he has been or what he might do?'

'No, Cornelius. Because he is my father.'

Cornelius stares at her. He rubs his chin with the back of his hand. They sit in silence, as if time itself needs a moment of contemplation.

At last Cornelius speaks. 'You came to Van Diemen's Land . . .'

'Yes,' says Caroline.

'And you purchased a vineyard . . .'

'Yes.'

'So that one day . . . ?'

'I did not have that plan at first,' says Caroline. 'I had no hope that anything I might effect would bring about his release. On Norfolk Island . . . well, death had more certainty. I believed I would never see him again. But when I looked at the vines, it was as if there was a future. I do not believe the man who comes here will ever harm me. But I am not sure he will be sane.'

'It has all been a great act of love,' says Cornelius.

Yes,' says Caroline. 'Yes.'

Emotion threatens to engulf her. Cornelius yearns to hold her, to remark upon her rare wishful heart. But neither stirs. A raven passes over, calling as it goes. A breeze drifts around their feet.

'And must you keep this from Captain Swanston? From Mrs Swanston? Is she not your friend?' asks Cornelius.

'I could not admit his crime when I entered their employ. I dared not. I needed their trust. They believe, as I first told you, that both my parents are dead. I was, and am, in need of Captain Swanston's partnership. You understand that in this society, it is an impossibility for me, as a woman, to represent the vineyard. He has assured me that he will do all he can to conceal the fact that the new winemaker . . .'

'Is a murderer,' says Cornelius.

'Yes. If that were known, and if I were to be the daughter of that murderer, I fear it would put everything at risk.'

'How do you intend to maintain such a subterfuge once he arrives?'

'Oh, Cornelius, since my father's crime, I do not know if there is subterfuge of which I am incapable.'

Cornelius chuckles. 'Mrs Caroline, I knew from the moment you arrived that you were here for a reason—but I never imagined it might be to show me that I know very little of the world.'

'You know a great deal of the world, Cornelius.'

'That I do. But not of the hearts of women.'

'I am sorry, Cornelius. I have put you in a difficult position.'

'Do not apologise for the things you have done to make your way; we each face our own reckoning. I will make your father welcome. But beyond the two of us, it will be a difficult game. Will Quill not remember him?'

'He will not recognise the man who arrives here because Quill has never met him. I met Quill on the ship that brought me here. He was the cabin boy assigned to me, given to the captain some years before to settle a debt. I found when we were due to arrive in Hobart that I did not want to abandon the boy. All I have done is leave people behind. So I purchased his freedom. And he chose to come with me, to be part of all this.'

Cornelius has observed the boy's skills in climbing and balance, his curious deftness with rope, his willingness to work and his love of order. He has noted Quill's reluctance to speak about the past. But he had not wished to speculate, being one who sought to obscure the past himself. Yet he finds he is unspeakably moved by this admission, by the understanding of what these two are to each other.

'Well,' he says to Caroline, 'we must do all we can to make our new winemaker comfortable. Would you care to tell me about him?'

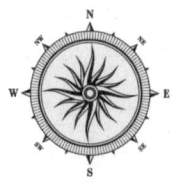

After Caroline had seen her father board the *Rochester* for Norfolk Island, she had written to Augusta, who was at her employer's country home in Berkshire now the London season was over. The sisters had continued to exchange affectionate weekly letters, until a message came from the housekeeper advising Caroline that Augusta was gravely ill and she should come at once. By the time Caroline arrived at the estate, late on a windswept night, Augusta was dead. A cold, she was told. A tight cough, a fever. Perhaps Augusta's heart had been weak, someone suggested. Perhaps it had been broken, Caroline had thought.

There was a brief service, attended by Caroline and Tante Henriette and a few of the household staff. Caroline and Henriette returned by carriage to London with the timber casket. Augusta, her petite sister who had loved music and painting and cooking, barely seventeen, was laid in the earth beside their mother and baby Isobel, in the plot that had been reserved for their father. He would never rest in that avenue of headstones with their loving tributes. His bones would lie far from here, in an unknown world.

Yea, though I walk through the valley of the shadow of death, I will fear no evil: for thou art with me; thy rod and staff comfort me . . . It was Augusta's favourite Psalm, but there was no comfort in the words for Caroline. If she could have exchanged the life of her father for the return of Mama and Augusta, in some devil's bargain, she might have said yes. Yes! Take that murderer. Take the madman and give me back my good mother and my dear, sweet sister.

The rage had come then for all of it. For him offering to fix a roof and falling to the cobblestones. The months following, when he might have died on any day. The care with which they had nursed him back to health. Then the fits, the violent outbursts, the dejection, the nocturnal ramblings that worried their mother sick. And when finally he appeared to be restored to some semblance of himself, to have Mama struck down with the withering paralysis. To have lost their home, their beloved Esther, the apothecary, all the knowledge Caroline had yet to learn, the recipes and remedies in her head useful for naught. She was a governess in the home of strangers and Augusta a kitchen maid.

And then he had killed Mrs Murray.

Caroline had held the knife on that summer night. She had taken it from her father in case he caused further harm, not wanting to know from whence the blood on it came.

He had appeared, in those weeks before the event, to be happy. Caroline had visited her father and Mrs Murray that very day. Mrs Murray had walked with her back to Caroline's place of employment when afternoon tea was done. It had been cloudless, the sky preternaturally blue. London had shrugged off its prudish mood and become young and festive. The women they passed were in pale muslins and silks, the men in light frock coats. There had been horses with floral garlands, and children flying ribbons.

Caroline had asked Mrs Murray if she still intended to marry her father, the proposed wedding having been delayed for some time by then, and Mrs Murray had said, 'In truth, I do not know if I am quite ready to give up the independence I have grown accustomed to as a widow. When you have a husband and children of your own, it consumes every moment of your life. Your waking and your sleeping. I find I might prefer this unorthodox arrangement I have with your father if he is happy for it to continue. Perhaps it is enough.'

'But you do love Papa?' Caroline asked.

'Of course,' said Mrs Murray, 'and we are taught that love will be enough, Caroline, but I assure you it is not. With your mother's death, you have seen how quickly the security you had relied upon can be lost. It has taken me some years to make the life I have for myself and my son here in London . . . so forgive me if I am overly cautious now.'

Caroline had tossed the knife that had killed Mrs Murray into the Thames, never imagining that the woman she had walked home with was already dead.

And then she had lost Augusta. Her father had created a terrible shadow that had descended upon all the women he professed to love. And here she was, years later, still hoping to orchestrate some act of redemption on his behalf.

What was a good woman? She remembered Mrs Murray's comely figure, her carefully curled hair, her high cheekbones and her low laugh. The chic but simple wardrobe of smart dresses, shawls and boas. The food she had made for Mama in her final months. Her offer to take Caroline and Augusta in after their mother's death, when Father was not to be relied upon. The work she had found for them. Had it all been stratagem and duplicity? Had she taken advantage of their situation to acquire their beautiful things, and all father's savings and investments? Had she really been a prostitute?

It seemed that she'd had other lovers of whom their father knew nothing. Was that prostitution? To allow men to give you beautiful things, to buy you dinners, to share your bed, all without the mantle of marriage? Caroline was unsure.

Father had wanted to marry Mrs Murray. He had proposed, and Mrs Murray had accepted. They had arranged the date and Caroline and Augusta were to meet them at the church. But then, Mrs Murray had deferred.

If Mrs Murray had been a prostitute to wealthy men, if it had been well known by neighbours and tradespeople, had her father really been so blind? So much of life, Caroline had learned, was artifice. If Mrs Murray was a prostitute, it had not been the trade of the girls and women who lingered late on the streets. Those women were not taken about in carriages by their lovers. They did not have good teeth or silk bonnets.

'London is no place for a woman alone,' Mama had said. 'Especially when there are bairns that need feeding and no other way than to sell her most private parts.' She had taken soup to some of those women on the coldest nights, and brought the children in to sit by the fire.

Yet if you were a woman alone, with your own money, you were a woman who didn't fit. Unless you were very old and could barely get down the stairs. Caroline knew little of carnal pleasure. She had seen the diseases it could cause. Her own experience of such things amounted to her employer's brother attempting to rape her in London.

She saw the way Mrs Swanston delighted in her husband when he entered a room. How Georgiana leaned towards Captain Swanston, placing her hand on his in conversation. She had seen the affection between her own parents.

She wondered what William Murray was making of his life without his mother. She had written to him, expressing her condolences and requesting an opportunity to retrieve their goods from the attic, so that such a reminder might cause him no further injury. She had received no reply. He had been there every day across the courtroom with Mrs Murray's sister as witnesses gave their accounts of the events on the bridge. She had watched William Murray give evidence. He had hissed at Caroline and Augusta as he had passed. Her father had sat downcast but attentive to it all.

'Never forget he murdered my sister,' Mrs Murray's sister had shouted at the judge. 'He murdered the good woman who was this boy's mother. He must hang.'

After the sentencing, Caroline had called at the house to speak to William but was sent away. She had wanted him to know that she bore the blame. She had failed to understand that her father could be dangerous. That his madness could drive him to violence against another person. She should have secured him in an asylum, but instead Mrs Murray had died. She could not forgive herself. To think she had once believed herself a healer.

She had considered engaging a lawyer to retrieve their possessions and monies her father had left in Mrs Murray's care, but she had decided not to pursue it. Let their possessions, all the precious relics of another life, be a payment of sorts, for harm done. Never a redress.

What would William Murray and Mrs Murray's sister make of Jacques-Louis being released? They would put it down to money, she imagined. Connections. Someone had paid. And they would be right. She had paid. If she had not secured the means to buy the cottage and vineyard, and thus attain the respect of Captain Swanston, Father would not be freed.

Mrs Murray was always, and forever, dead. No amount of remorse or suffering would return her to life. Meanwhile, the man who had taken her life went on living.

· 16 ·

Jacques-Louis

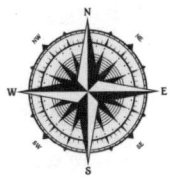

He is transferred by ship from Norfolk Island to Port Arthur and then to a probation station at Saltwater River. There he regards a chartreuse sea brushing against a shore of almond stone and white sand. Oaks and eucalypts fringe the shore. Seabirds soar and cry in a cerulean sky. Such sparkling beauty would once have moved him to tears.

Jacques-Louis and the others awaiting their transition back to society are put to work in the gardens. The soil is fertile and the crops are extensive. Potatoes, turnips, cabbages and beets. Food to feed officers, guards and their families, the leftovers added to the rations of salt pork and hard bread for the prisoners.

At night, in their quarters, he hears of the grim world at the coalmines nearby, where men are locked beneath the earth twelve hours a day, digging, sweating, in an eternity of squalid darkness only to be entombed again in underground cells all night. These accounts are rivalled by the stories of the men who carry the great timbers from the forests at Port Arthur upon their shoulders, sometimes thirty men to a tree, carrying the dread burden three miles and more to the mill, the tallest men worn down until their backs are broken. Jacques-Louis responds only with silence. None of these stories yet compare with the horrors of Norfolk Island during the reign of Morisset or Anderson, but horror has no comparison. All horror is horror.

One afternoon, a few weeks into his stay, he witnesses an overseer beat with a cudgel the boy who ferries the slops in a wheelbarrow from the latrines to the bay. He is barely five feet in height, misshapen and afflicted with a speech impediment. The boy is sixteen and had been at the boys' prison at Point Puer, near Port Arthur, since he was eleven—convicted for theft. The beating of the boy is but a small cruelty amongst countless on the ledger of human suffering, yet Jacques-Louis' hands tremble with the desire to seize the overseer by the throat, to feel the man's pulse weaken beneath his grip, to hurl him to the dirt and pound him down, down, until he is nothing. It burns in him, a rage so fierce he can taste it. But he cannot, he must not.

He turns not to the overseer but to the forest that borders the station, and he screams into the wilderness of trees and into the boundless sky. He screams into some forsaken hollow within himself that light will never reach again. His voice cracks with rage at all that is and all that has been. The cruelty of men. Men who shape this world like a thing of spite and greed, who have fashioned it in their own image and damned it with the same wrath and fear that now howls from deep within him. There is no rest, no peace in living. What survives is but the wreckage of himself, stripped bare by the years and the ruin of it all, tethered to this destruction he once called his life.

When his cry dies, the birds have ceased calling. The men scattered nearby, frozen in the moment, stare blankly into the forest, too. It is as though Jacques-Louis' voice had found something shared by them all; a knowing of a world that feels nothing, that answers only with its indifferent cruelty. In that gaze, they saw their own place, their own smallness, standing always on the edge of a life that was violent, cold, occasionally lit with brief flickers of hope, yet always haunted by the truth. We are alone. There is neither salvation nor absolution.

And then slowly, as if waking, the men stirred, the spell of the moment dissolved. They returned to their tools, their backs bent once more under the familiar yoke of their labours, as though nothing had happened. Everything would carry on as it always had, as it always would. The cry had been no more than the wind.

But the overseer beckons Jacques-Louis with a slow, deliberate hand. 'Does it rouse you, Frenchman, to watch a fool receive his due? It would be dangerous of you to think yourself better than the rest of us, old man. You're on borrowed time. Be very, very careful.' His eyes narrow, his tone is almost amused. 'Maybe we'll set aside a little lesson just to remind you where you stand.'

Jacques-Louis waits through the night, anticipating what will come. But in the morning, he discovers he is not to receive the lash— he is to administer it. If Jacques-Louis refuses to punish the man, he will receive the sentence himself and will lose any chance of receiving his ticket of leave.

He thinks of the flogging he had received on Norfolk Island, beneath Anderson's cold eye, where the lash was crueller and fell harder than anything he had known aboard the *Rochester*. He had bitten his tongue almost in two. The memory sears through him. He cannot endure that again.

His fingers tighten around the leather handle, feeling its weight rough in his palm. The plaited whipcord is stiff as wire, hardened by salt and sun, the tails running through his fingers as sharp as a blade. Nine tails tied with nine knots apiece. Eighty-one ways to cut a man in each stroke. He looks ahead, sees the man's back stretched taut across the triangle. There is no room for mercy here—not in this place, not for him. The past lingers in his grip, and in that moment, the line between victim and persecutor blurs.

There is low laughter from the soldiers watching on. The superintendent says that he will call the number every half-minute, and Jacques-Louis must wait for his instruction, thus ensuring a slow and constant pace for the punishment. 'And do not hold back,' the superintendent adds, 'or I shall make it one hundred.'

'One . . .'

The whip flies and the skin receives. The shock of the contact travels through the tails to the leather handle, through Jacques-Louis' arms and down to his toes. He tries not to look at the grim effect of his work. He steadies the weapon and waits for the superintendent who is scrutinising his pocket watch.

'Two . . .'

The wait.

'Three . . .'

The man on the triangle makes no sound. Jacques-Louis tries to blur his vision, to see not the man, nor the yard, nor the idling guards.

'Twenty-eight . . .'

Wait.

'Twenty-nine . . .'

Jacques-Louis' shoulders ache. His legs ache. He will do this thing. He will not see the web of white sinew and bright blood, the skin on the bones of the rib cage scored away.

'Forty-one . . .'

Wait.

'Forty-two . . .'

When it is done, flies settle on broken and mutilated skin. A three-legged mongrel dog is licking blood off the triangle.

Jacques-Louis awakes to the sound of men in the dormitory moving about him, the morning bell demanding their attention. He is bathed in sweat. He pushes his head back under the blanket but the dream will not leave him. This is what he will know in the years beyond. Memory and dream, the two as alike as if he had lived it all, and the dreams he will have for the rest of his life will be far worse than any of his days.

When he is called to the superintendent's office, he is certain he has prophesied his future and is to be ushered into the yard to administer a punishment. He fears it will be the simpleton he must brutalise, but instead the superintendent advises him that he is to be returned to Port Arthur. A ship is to carry him to Hobart Town, where his ticket of leave awaits him.

· 17 ·

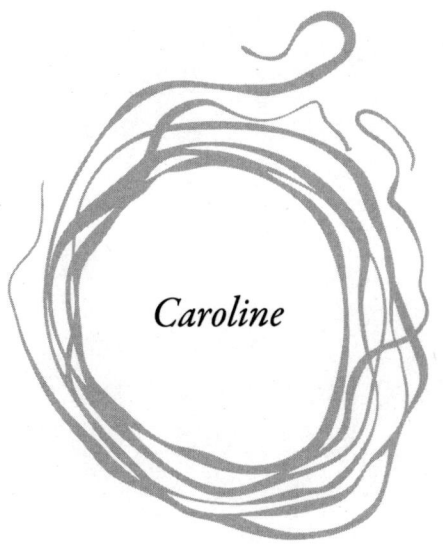

Caroline

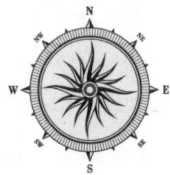

Bessie has prepared the loft at the far end of the barn where the Swanstons' unwanted furniture had once been stored. Now there are new-made curtains at the windows. There is a bed, a chest, a table, a chair, a jug and a washbasin. The floor has been swept and a rug laid down. Caroline sees that Bessie has filled a jar with flowering sage, lavender and rosemary, and placed a cake of soap beside the washbasin. One convict to another, a code of shared understanding. Nothing to be said beyond what has been lived. Fate tallying the cost of folly and frailty with an unyielding indifference, moving through lives with an elegance that belies its harshness, gathering up missteps and weaknesses like fallen leaves.

Caroline sends Bessie and Quill to visit with Mrs Roper, and to collect a list of supplies at various stores, ensuring they will not return for some hours. She sits in one of the wicker chairs on the verandah, a book beside her, a glass of water, too, but she finds her mind unable to settle on the page nor find reassurance in the azure sky, the furrows of high white clouds, a flock of black cockatoos passing overhead.

Who will her father be when he arrives? Will he be a semblance of the man she once knew? Or will he be a stranger, altered entirely by all he has endured? Does the madness still trouble him? Surely it would have been mentioned by Captain Maconochie if it did. She wishes the vineyard was ready for harvest, so that he might see it ripe with possibility. But it is better this way. He can see things as they are.

Perhaps he will not like the way it is laid out, or the way the vines are pruned. More concerning is that he will not like it that she has lured him here as if he is unknown to her. What if he cannot pretend that she is a stranger rather than a once-beloved daughter? What if he refuses to participate in this charade? If Swanston becomes suspicious? What if he is unwell, broken down and unable to be the winemaker that is required, ruined as she has seen other men? What if he is sent away, sent back to Norfolk Island for some misdeed, real or supposed?

'I want you to bring him to the cottage first, Cornelius,' she had said. 'I will walk him to the barn later.'

'Of course, Mrs Caroline.'

'Thank you, Cornelius. Thank you for everything.'

He had looked at her and smiled. 'Don't you worry, my friend. Too late to start doing that now. One step at a time, steady as you go.'

A horse and cart are coming over the hill from the township. She cannot be sure but she thinks she recognises Cornelius, with someone beside him. She hurries inside, smoothing her dress and checking her hair in the mirror. Her eyes look wide and a little startled. She checks the things she has prepared in the kitchen.

By the time she returns to the verandah, the cart is turning into the laneway. She wants to run. She wants to fly down the track past the Swanstons' pine trees, to see his face light up, to have him swing down and hold open his arms so she can fling herself into his embrace. She wants him to hold her so tight that all the years apart collapse into nothing.

But she cannot. Why must Cornelius go so slowly?

Now the gig is past the Swanstons', the cottage and the vineyard ahead. She waits and watches. At last Cornelius stops where the lane splits. His passenger descends with a small sack in his hand. He wears a grey jacket and trousers, a grey cap. Cornelius flicks the horse and the cart moves on and away.

The man is coming towards the cottage, his head down. She steps off the verandah and onto the path. Heedless of the risk, she is out of the gate. He has seen her. She strides towards him. She runs. She is throwing her arms around him, holding him to her, feeling the thinness of his body.

'Papa,' she says. 'Papa.'

'Caroline,' he says. *'Comment est-ce possible?'*

He crumples then. She catches him, feeling the fragile weight of him, holding him fiercely, holding him as if she will never let him go.

'C'est vrai?' he is asking.

'Yes, Papa, it is true,' she says. 'You are home now. You are home. It is not a dream.'

He is like a man off a ship unable to get his footing. She sits him at the table in the sun, behind the cottage. She is bringing a tray of wine and cheese. Two glasses, and a bottle of Broughton's champagne dusted off. She unwinds the wire and pulls the cork. There

387

does not seem to be anything to say. He looks up and she searches for the man she once knew beneath the wearied and weathered visage aged beyond any expectation.

'Champagne, Papa,' she says. 'Because we have made magic happen.'

Mr Culpeper had declared that nothing grows in vain. The earth is a patient teacher and offers no gift without purpose. God and Nature are the unfailing sources from which all cures spring forth, intertwining life and healing in a tapestry both intricate and profound. Each leaf, each root, each bloom holds within it the promise of a restoration, a quiet assurance that in every cycle of decay lies the potential for rebirth, waiting only for the eye to see and the heart to understand.

Once Jacques-Louis has eaten, and the wine has been sipped, she takes him to review the herbs and flowers and vegetables in the walled garden, the chooks and fruit trees. He sees and nods and says almost nothing, yet it is her father. She cannot let go of his hand, until she must. She feels a deep cold in his bones, and wants to wrap him in a blanket, to shelter him from the world until he warms and speaks and smiles, and she wonders will it ever be so.

At the top of the vineyard, she opens the gate and ushers him through. He stops and bends to touch the leaves. She would like to tell him that all is forgiven, that it is time to start anew, to put the past behind them, but that is not true. It will never be true.

'You are here, Papa,' she says instead. 'It is all that matters now.'

He hardly notices the food put in front of him. She watches him spill tea on his shirt. She warms porter with lemon and sugar. Though he is not ill, as such, she thinks the sangaree might benefit him. When she tells him of Augusta's death, and Henriette's, his silence is interminable.

She makes him a new coat, a shirt and woollen pants. Cornelius makes him work gloves and new boots. She sees the scars furrowing his back and the effort it takes to lace those boots and the scars around his ankles. His hands are not the long fine hands she remembers, but gnarled and misshapen from labours she does not want to discuss. He often appears caught in eddies and rapids. For many weeks after he arrives, before she goes to the vineyard to meet with him, she stands and sighs one long deep sigh after another.

Every day he is in the vineyard at dawn. All day he works, bending here to weed about the roots, to untangle a vine, to mulch and water as required. In the mornings, she works near him and is glad of the simple monotony of the work. What must give over, what must succumb to the greater good, what will bear fruit.

Caroline wishes that tending a person was as easy as tending a plant. Where there is damage or disease, excise it with a simple clip from a pair of shears. Where an aspect of the plant is growing in the wrong direction, curving inwards rather than outwards to the light, snip it away to encourage new growth. Where there are dead branches or tendrils, cut them off.

When the day grows late, he likes to sit at the base of the giant gum. Caroline sits beside him, aware that there they cannot be seen by anyone who might look across the valley. She recalls when she first found the speck of land called Norfolk Island and stole away with the map from that beautiful house. She makes in her mind a path of dots of the voyage each of them has taken to be here. Between them they have circled the world, rounded Cape Horn and the Cape of Good Hope, and come at last to this tree and this land together.

Her father regards the vista, but whether it is a vista within or without she cannot know. He is overflowing with silence. Perhaps contrition is a form of survival. She thinks of Mrs Murray at Mama's bedside, and of the night she tossed the bloodied knife into the Thames.

She keeps Quill away from him—just until Papa settles in. But the boy is drawn to the new man in the field.

'Should I speak to him in French?' he asks.

'*Bien sûr.*' She smiles. 'But give him time. There is much he has to adjust to.'

One morning, returning from her walk, she sees them sitting together beneath the gum tree. She realises they are regarding a rainbow at her back, illuminating the morning mist above the river.

Jacques-Louis is explaining the phenomenon to the boy. 'It is a manifestation of hydrogen, oxygen, phosphorus and electrical substances combined in the atmosphere which form that happy accident. The sun is illuminating the colours, just as a lighted candle enclosed in a coloured glass does.'

Quill regards him with interest.

'Did you notice on your voyage here how the wake of a sailing ship often produces similar colours?'

'Yes,' says Quill.

'The prism, the oriental pearl, the mother of pearl . . . all in the ascent of the sun produce these same colours. Atmospheric air is loaded more or less with vapours or gases.

'Have you ever considered,' he continues, 'that everything we observe is through the accomplishment of our eyes? The pupils contract and expand, and the nerves attack and seize the object under observation so that you are capable of distinguishing the familiar, and then other objects, near and far, which are not immediately obvious.'

'Oh,' says Quill, and blinks, and blinks again, as if to see the world anew.

'A curious mind seeks knowledge,' says Jacques-Louis. 'A man called Rousseau believed that each man was a beginning, for within him was all the potential of humanity. Curiosity will help you find your potential, Quill.'

It is the first flow of words she has heard from him since he arrived.

He cannot eat with them in the cottage. It would be inappropriate to invite a felon into the house. Cornelius says he has always managed such things for himself and can do so for both of them, but Caroline insists on contributing meals and provisions. Cornelius tells her that the quality of his fare has improved, and he and Jacques-Louis may have to grow used to it.

'You have given over your solitude to this new guest,' she says to Cornelius.

'My solitude was not a resolution,' says Cornelius. 'It was a necessity. I was a black man in this colony. I still am. Look upon it like this: our winemaker has given me the opportunity to care for someone.'

'You have cared for me since first I came here,' Caroline says.

'It has been a privilege you have allowed me, Mrs Caroline.'

'Caroline,' she says. 'Just Caroline.'

'Caroline,' he replies.

Some evenings, after Quill is in bed, she joins them in the forge, though all the conversation is between Cornelius and Caroline, her father watching the flames of the fire until his head droops. It is then Cornelius wakes him and urges him to bed, handing him a lantern ready to light the way.

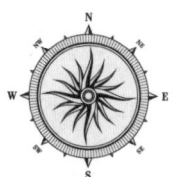

'It is leased, all this?' her father asks, the night scent of the vines lifting on the evening air.

Caroline has been anticipating the question and has thought of many ways she might answer it, but she finds herself saying, 'No, Papa, I purchased the cottage and the vineyard from Captain Swanston when I arrived here in Van Diemen's Land. The story of being a tenant is to protect myself from gossip.'

'Did something happen to make such a thing possible?' he asks.

'Do you really wish to know?' she asks.

'*Oui, bien sûr,*' he replies.

'I apprenticed myself to Tante Henriette.'

'Ah,' he says.

'And I made other investments on my voyage here that were fruitful.'

She waits.

'Perhaps it is time,' he says at last, 'to tell me everything. Shall we begin with Quill?'

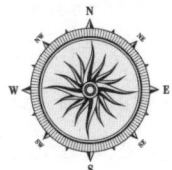

Christmas comes and goes, and the fruit sets. Ripening grapes hang red, pale, magenta, dusty green and golden beneath their distinctive leaves. There is a long stretch of dry weather and they water the vines by hand, buckets being wheelbarrowed to the field.

'Not too much,' Jacques-Louis says. 'Patience and adversity. Nature teaches us that.'

Jacques-Louis and Quill create a series of scarecrows to keep away the birds that come to investigate the crop. But after a week or two, the figures do little to dissuade the feathered scavengers.

Swanston suggests Quill take watch and shoot into the air, lending him a gun. It is effective, and Quill delights in causing a flock to rise into the sky. Caroline does not like the noise of the gun and its reverberations across the valley. Such a method also requires constant vigilance. The summer days are warm and Quill's watch can become distracted by his immersion in a book, and then the easy descent into a snooze. When he startles from the pages to find wattlebirds inspecting the readiness of the banquet, he shoots into the air and fells one of the birds. He is devastated, bringing the wounded creature to Caroline wrapped in his shirt, but the bird dies in his hands.

A few days later, he has the idea that instead of shooting the birds, they could tie cats on leashes throughout the vineyard to leap at the birds.

'Not so they can harm them,' he says. 'Just so it frightens them.'

'The birds or the cats?' asks Caroline, with a raised eyebrow.

It seems an unlikely method, but Quill and Bessie set about acquiring a small company of stray cats from the town. They house them in the woodshed, the howling at first something both terrible and comical, but the meat they are given soon settles them down. Quill, Bessie and Jacques-Louis carry them each morning in boxes to the vines and secure them with rope.

To everyone's amusement, the cats do leap at the marauding magpies, currawongs, parrots, thrushes and cockatoos. They also continue to hiss at one another, and lie in the sun and sleep. At night they are returned to their shelter. This goes on for some weeks, but slowly the cats lose interest and the birds learn to graze at a careful distance. Still, several of the cats become excellent mousers in the cellar, the house and the barn, and find the forge a very pleasant place to reside. Caroline often finds both Cornelius and her father each captive to a slumbering cat when she visits in the evenings. Malachy remains above all this, continuing her decorative life curled by the fire in the cottage, or in any ready pool of sunshine on a windowsill.

It is Bessie who has the idea of turning the ineffective scarecrows into women. She reshapes the figures to make them very tall and dresses them haphazardly in remnants of sackcloth and fabric giving each an embroidered face. She sews together wigs of long lengths of dried ferns, seaweed and strips of cloth that erupt wildly from the crown of the head and move in the breeze. She gives them large splayed hands of sticks, and together Jacques-Louis and Cornelius, Bessie and Quill stretch fishing nets between the wild women, who hold the woven lines in their long fingers above the ripening grapes. It is a field of helpful witches casting spells, Caroline thinks.

At Bessie's instigation, Cornelius creates a kind of instrument of found and discarded objects whose parts move in the wind, knocking together, clacking, chiming, whirring and rattling even in the softest breeze. Cornelius is so surprised at the success of these that he and Bessie create four more. The sculptural instruments are placed throughout the vineyard. Now the witches have accompanying musicians and the new harvest is protected.

The wind becomes the chief antagonist. After a strong westerly, the nets must be mended and stretched anew between the watchful women, and their fingers mended. Sometimes birds must also be freed, and Quill takes great care with this. Neighbours come to look at their inventions and ask Cornelius to make his strange instruments for them. He replies that he is but the manufacturer; it is Bessie who is in charge of design. Several are made and, on a still night in the valley, the gentle clock, knock and whirr is a music Caroline listens for as she is falling asleep.

Jacques-Louis tells Quill that it will be about twenty-five days until harvest for this variety, and a little longer for that one, while the slowest variety will reach peak sweetness a little after that.

They wait for the sugar to intensify in the fruit, for the lurking promise of ripe peaches, golden apples and honey to deepen in the grapes. Every day Jacques-Louis takes Quill to taste the fruit, and urges the boy to record his findings in a journal.

On day twenty-five, Quill and Jacques-Louis return from the vineyard.

'They are ready,' Quill says, eyes shining.

Caroline takes the grape he offers her and sucks it.

'The flavours of this world,' says Jacques-Louis. 'But most of all, your love, Mrs Douglas. And yours, Quill.'

Quill observes him.

'One cannot grow a vineyard like this without love,' Jacques-Louis says.

In preparation for the harvest, Caroline employs two young women from the female prison to assist Bessie in the kitchen. She listens as Bessie schools them in the preparation and clean-up of meals. She is firm but patient as she explains their tasks, and Caroline smiles to hear her admonishing them sternly if they prove idle or truculent.

'Was I such a hapless creature, Mrs Douglas?' she asks.

'A little bit,' Caroline says. 'But look how far you have come. You are mistress of the kitchen.'

The two maids sleep upstairs beside Bessie's room. Quill has long been downstairs, where he can stand upright, which he can no longer do under the sloping ceiling of the attic. He will soon need to duck when he enters any doorway.

The first day of the harvest arrives with a crisp autumnal shine to the air. The musical instruments have been returned to the barn. The nets between the witch women are to be rolled back row by row as the grapes are picked. Caroline has employed ticket-of-leave women who will see the harvest through. They gather early at the cottage for tea, bread, cheese and preserves, and are issued with shears and gloves. Washington and Julia Walker arrive with their little boy.

Also Julia's sister and husband, and the Giblins with their two married daughters and their husbands. The Swanston boys arrive with Georgiana carrying two baskets, each bearing a fruitcake.

When they break for lunch, Captain Swanston joins them. Cornelius and Mrs Roper have arranged trestle tables covered in cloth and decorated with vine leaves by Bessie. Mrs Roper, passing Caroline as they ferry items to the picnic, says, 'The most handsome man in Hobart Town, Cornelius was. Maybe still is.'

'I didn't realise you had known him such a long time.'

'Oh, yes. We both knew this place when the houses didn't go further than the top of Murray Street. Always kept to himself, though. They said he . . . well, 'tis just gossip.' Mrs Roper shakes her head and moves on.

Murray Street. Murray. Caroline considers how it is for her father to hear the name.

The table is arrayed with pies and tarts, cured meats and pickles, tomatoes, salad greens, warm bread and butter. Caroline has brought out the last of Broughton's champagne. It seems fitting to share it at this moment. Jacques-Louis has determined that it may soon pass its peak and should be savoured.

Caroline invites everyone to join in a minute of silence, the Quaker silence she has learned from Julia and Washington before any gathering. A hush settles upon them, punctuated only by buzzing insects and a stirring of leaves above, the distant sound of wood being chopped, a horse and cart on the road going north. When the minute is over, they all sigh, and smile.

Caroline invites Captain Swanston to make a toast, and he does so, declaring it will be a time of hard work but also with the possi-bility of great reward. He thanks them for their labours and urges them to eat well so they might pick every good grape and ensure nothing is wasted. He thanks Caroline for her hospitality. They all lift their glasses and drink.

Jacques-Louis sits with hat removed for the meal, the scar from the fall still vivid and puckered across his brow. Sometimes Caroline feels as if she is a branch in the middle of a river and her father is holding on, clinging to her lest he be washed away. Sometimes he stands on the shore and they watch together, dutiful to memories, respectful in their silence of all the dead. She has not asked him what he has lived through, and he does not offer it up.

She quietly suggests to him that the winemaker might also address those gathered. She is not sure if he will speak and is pleased when she sees him rise. She taps her spoon on her plate to draw the table to attention. 'I have asked our winemaker to say some words also.'

Jacques-Louis says, 'I thank Captain Swanston and Mrs Swanston for entrusting me with the making of this wine, and Mrs Douglas to whom I owe so much. I thank this harvest which is here by the generosity of the earth. I also wish to thank the mountain who tempts the rain, and the clouds who carry it forth. The sun that warms the earth, inspires the buds and ripens the fruit. The moon that watches over the vineyard night after night, season upon season, welcoming the dew that sinks within the roots. This plenitude all about us, and your generosity in bringing your labour to harvest this bounty. It is all generosity.' He indicates the vines about them. 'Before us is a wine we cannot anticipate. Today we are harvesting the future. We will reap what nature and care allow. It will be of this place. And it will be of your good hearts. I thank you all.'

His words leave a small silence and then everyone again raises their glasses and toasts the harvest. Flies are waved away from the food. Dishes are passed. Plates are filled and conversation begins to flow around the table. Caroline looks across at her father, whose eyes are fixed on the plate of chicken pie and salad, bread and new potatoes Bessie has handed him.

'Thank you,' Caroline says to him.

He nods, and then begins his meal. She sees in him, for the first time since he's arrived, the man who might have inherited a great estate. He is in simple clothes amongst his fellow workers, with battered hands and a scarred face, his body ageing, but he is noble nevertheless.

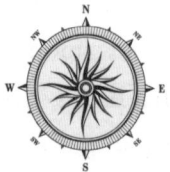

Cornelius has prepared the barrels and kept them filled with water to ensure they do not leak and that the timber does not dry out before they must do their work. The last grapes of the harvest are the meunier.

Jacques-Louis thinks to make a wine using only the meunier, given its vibrant qualities, but he can taste that it may yet be a natural fit with the morillon blanc. To add the black cluster will increase the complexity. Perhaps he will mix only the morillon blanc and the black cluster. Meanwhile the first fermentation of the new harvest begins. After two weeks, Jacques-Louis lets the wine rest in the barrels.

He and Caroline taste the *vins clairs*, the early wines where the varieties are unmixed and the flavour is sharp and acidic. Even this early, Jacques-Louis finds the meunier promises charm. In the morillon blanc there is a litheness. In the black cluster he is delighted by the depth of flavour in the fruit. This is what he has been tasting in the few bottles of red wine in the cellar, aged and grown complex with time. The small amount of wine stored from the previous harvests, too. Jacques-Louis also sets aside some of the wine of this harvest as insurance against a poor harvest in the future. This also gives him the opportunity to see how each grape's flavour matures with the second fermentation.

'Some winemakers mix, they do not blend,' says Jacques-Louis.

'Tell me, Monsieur Chef de Cave,' says Caroline. 'Teach me.'

'Each grape must offer something. It must complement and enhance, harmonise. If I were to blend all three of the varietals we have, we may find that in one glass the morillon blanc may be entree, the black cluster the main meal and the meunier the music in the background. I must find the alignment, so that in one wine the result is vivid and tantalising, yet also complete. But first we must wait.'

As the months go by, they will taste countless times. The morillon blanc becomes expressive. Jacques-Louis says it has opened and may yet become more vivacious. The black cluster is sleeping. 'But,' says Jacques-Louis, 'it will awaken in a few months.' Only the meunier remains constant.

On this north-facing land with its unfamiliar mix of friable and heavy soils, in these foothills looking out across an enormous river, he is learning. It had been a good growing season, the summer was dry and the spring before it cool and wet. In France, when he was in the tasting room with Philippe, it was the interplay of the chablis, a sister to this morillon blanc, and the pinot noir, so similar to the black cluster, that fascinated him. It was a combination of endless complexity and subtlety.

He has tasted the raw wines of the Walkers and considered the land beyond, where Captain Swanston runs sheep. He has investigated. If he were to plant there, nearer the river, within a few years those vines might benefit from the slightly warmer location.

In the fields, he applies different techniques to the pruning, instructing the workers and ensuring they are rigorous with cutting back, and choosing the new canes that will carry fruit into the next year. In the cellar he makes choices, too. He blends new wine with the wine of the previous years. He makes copious notes, assigning scores to each wine. The weeks pass and he tastes and tastes again.

'A wine may be of a pleasing colour even if it comes from mediocre elements,' he says, 'but it is not usual. And it will put the method, and indeed the reputation of the winemaker, at risk. The *cuvée de tirage*, the blended wine, cannot disguise the taste of poor grapes.'

As autumn passes he continues his work in the cellar. The air is chill in its close confines, but not as chill as it is outside. Winter blankets the mountain in snow for weeks and weeks. There is snow in the foothills, and it lays upon the gardens and fields for an hour or two before the sun reaches it. As the first dewdrops poke their heads up to see the world, the bottling begins.

The measuring and dosage to bring about the second fermentation is done with exacting precision. Each bottle is then labelled and racked. The cellar fills with rows and rows of bottles, each with a rudimentary label noting the year and a code. The codes correspond to notes in Jacques-Louis' journal.

The second fermentation begins and, when it is done, the wine that will become their first champagne rests.

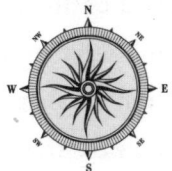

The year circles and returns. There have been ducklings on the pond but they have grown and disappeared. The swallows, too. Geese are moving east. John Mercer's letters continue to arrive every few months. He tells Caroline of his studies and the areas of research he intends to embark on, particularly in the area of infections. When his mother dies, he writes of her with fond affection, sharing his recollections of her and saying how much he will miss her. She can detect no overt romantic sentiment in John Mercer's communications with her, but as the letters amass in her bureau she knows that she is growing more fond of him. In turn she sends him small watercolours of the farm and anecdotes of her days. She likes to move the water across the paper, to trail impetuous colours and create unexpected effects. It is a watercolour world, she thinks. Was this how Augusta saw it, too? A tableau infused by something translucent and transient.

In the reading room in Hobart, she learns of the skull of a quadruped discovered in the mouth of the Mississippi River that indicates the animal had been more than two hundred and fifty feet in length. In Yorkshire the remains of elephants, rhinoceros and hyenas have been found, as well as quantities of petrified palm trees and sugar canes. The formation of the universe could not be a late phenomenon when such infinite discoveries continue to be made. Had there been enormous animals here, too? Had the people before her seen them? Had they hunted them or been hunted by them? A tree discovered in a stream bed in Kent measured four hundred and fifty feet in length. She puts her hands on the giant gum tree by the cottage and wonders what it has seen.

Barrels are made ready for the next harvest. Bottles and corks arrive by ship from suppliers abroad as the new grapes bud, flower, fruit and ripen. Bessie's fishing nets are repaired and replaced, her women with their floating dresses and fern-and-seaweed hair standing sentinel once more. The musical instruments are erected again and continue to distract and startle avian arrivals.

Bessie also takes to making tall, lean figures of bark and sticks in the perimeter of the forest. Some holding the hand of a bark child. Bessie calls them 'the missing'.

Caroline thinks of the letter Columbus wrote to Queen Isabella of his journey to the new world telling her how enchanted he was by the natives and the simple beauty of their lives. Yet he had taken their gold and left behind priests to school them in his foreign faith. Where were those people now? Had they too been lost to a modern world that had no time for their ways of living?

The next vintage results in twenty-six barrels, more than doubling the harvest from the previous year. It is crushed, fermented, bottled and racked. Workers undertake the late autumn pruning, the suppression of the weeds and the insulation of the soil and vines for the coming winter, as well as the maintenance and improvement of fencing. Jacques-Louis is vigilant, fastidious, impatient, genial.

'Some predators are small enough to be seen only with a microscope,' he tells Quill. 'They dust a leaf or blacken it. But of course some bound and climb and fly.'

One day Caroline finds her father lying on the grass in the sun under the giant gum tree.

'Papa,' she asks, for they are alone, 'are you ill?'

'I had a sense of foreboding,' he says. 'As if at any moment my heart might leap from my body.'

'Has it passed?'

'I did not recognise it.'

'What was it?' she asks.

'Happiness,' he says, and he takes her hand and holds it.

The first vintage is good, but Jacques-Louis believes it could be better. He is pleased with some of the blends, but perhaps he will adjust the length of fermentation, both the first and the second. He considers extending the time on the lees, and experiments with reducing the sugar in the dosage.

The blends he has made with the first harvest, using wines laid down before he arrived, are, in his estimation, the more sophisticated. But there is not sufficient stock to replicate it. He is glad for the barrels set aside in reserve.

Cornelius says, 'Replication and consistency, that's what I know from Mr Broughton.'

'There it is,' says Jacques-Louis. 'The greatest challenge—nature being inconsistent, and every harvest bringing its own unique flavours.'

He wants to get a higher yield from the morillon blanc, which does best in the least fertile soil in the vineyard. It is quick to develop the botrytis mould. He appreciates the sweet wines this can create, but it is not good for the wine he desires. He is seeking a sparkling wine filled with fruit and vivacity yet tempered with earth and minerality: a wine of this place. A sparkling wine far from its origins, but from a similar cool climate.

When he retires to his loft, and it is just Cornelius and Caroline by the fire in the forge, Cornelius says, 'He has ambition.'

'He wishes to be a great winemaker,' says Caroline.

Some recompense for all his daughter has done for him, Cornelius thinks, or something more?

Captain Swanston finds an agent for the wine in both Sydney and Melbourne. Caroline meets the costs of an increased workforce. The significant sum she had initially deposited with Swanston has been much depleted but Swanston is winning acclaim for the quality of his product which suits Caroline perfectly. The profits when they come are modest, but still they are profits. When Caroline notes that small income at last, after so much outlay, there is a relief in her. London feels like a long time ago—although whenever she and Quill play chess on the beautiful board, she is always transported back to Tante Henriette's apartment and the treasure room below.

Jacques-Louis will not attend any social occasion beyond the cottage or the forge. In any gathering he is quiet. It would be easy to think he was shy. He walks to the river most evenings at dusk. Sometimes when she and Jacques-Louis walk together, Caroline finds she is still looking about as if the two of them are walking up the river towards Putney. She wishes sometimes for transparency, to know all that is within him. But she fears the past is a riptide that might wrap about their ankles and drag them away, so she does not offer a reminiscence from those times, and nor does he.

With Swanston, Jacques-Louis is at first deferential but, after the second vintage, he becomes more confident.

'That land there, sir,' Jacques-Louis says, 'now given to sheep, it will barely return, as we both know. But give it over to vines and in a few years, *voilà*, we will be making the finest sparkling wine in the world. I have investigated. See how it catches the sunshine all year round? This is what the vines need. The limestone soil, the moist air, the cold days and the summer warmth. The cellar must be expanded in the barn. There is insufficient room beneath the house to rack the quantities we can produce.'

'The man is infuriating,' says Swanston to Caroline. 'Every time I meet with him he has some demand for me. I have no other worker who so completely nettles me and yet there are few for whose labours I have more regard. But do not tell him that. He is Pain by name and a pain by nature. He must cause it in every conversation.'

Mr Pain. It is the name he has given Jacques-Louis publicly, whenever he introduces him. Jacques-Louis Pain, once resident of the Jersey Islands. It is one of the steps he has taken to remove information on Jacques-Louis Colbert from casual investigation. One cannot have such a villain associated with his venture, nor his family. So he shall have a *nom de plume*. Jacques-Louis is quite unoffended and Swanston is amused at his invention. Jacques-Louis is the most stubborn man he has ever encountered, he declares, a typical Frenchman. Jacques-Louis responds that Swanston is a man of vision but lacks imagination, a typical Englishman. But at the end of such exchanges, there is a measure of good wine that Jacques-Louis says is wasted on Swanston's palate, which has been ruined by rum and whisky.

Caroline and Georgiana compare Jacques-Louis' wine with the French champagne that arrives in the colony. They pretend they cannot decide and must drink another glass until they are sure. Jacques-Louis says it is hard to make comparisons with a wine that has travelled six thousand miles by sea, but still the wine they are making at Everlea is far superior.

'Yes, yes,' says Swanston. 'I allow him that.'

One day in the cellar, during the disgorgement, Caroline suggests that perhaps if the champagne bottles might be inclined, the sediment would more easily move towards the cork and settle there so that the final wine might be clearer.

Cornelius creates a tilted rack.

'Let us see,' Jacques-Louis says, 'what gravity will do.'

The bottles twinkle in the lamplight, the wine inside transforms, time elaborating on subtle variations of flavour. Caroline feels the urge to turn the bottles gently as the weeks pass to keep the sediment moving towards the cork. She marks each bottle with chalk. It is a method that makes Jacques-Louis a little uncomfortable, yet he cannot dismiss the ease with which the sediment can then be removed before the final period of rest.

He has Cornelius adapt more racks, and he instructs the workers who assist them to do the same, carefully marking each turn on the glass. There is some loss of wine as the sediment is released but they add wine and sugar to increase the volume. Gradually less wine is lost in the release as everyone becomes more practised. The bottles are given their final corks and tied closed with string. They wait in the cool dim silence for fermentation to summon the enigma of flavour.

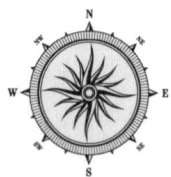

Beer continues to be brewed, rum imported, whisky and gin slyly distilled and distributed. Huon pine from the wet forests of Van Diemen's Land is favoured above all other timbers by boat builders. Celery top pine, too. The Derwent River and the D'Entrecasteaux Channel are plied by dinghies, rowboats, sailing boats, larger ships and steam ferries moving people and produce. Ironware is cast and wrought. New bricks are loaded onto pallets. Ropes, sails and other items of chandlery are crafted. Soap, leather, clothing, barrels and paper, carts, carriages and tools are produced across the island. Wheat and wool remain the colony's most valuable exports, although New South Wales and England continue to pay poorly for it.

Of late, Swanston has become more troubled by the prospects of the colony. The trade in whale oil has almost ceased, coal and gas replacing them. Seal populations have declined. The prison at Port Arthur grows in infamy. Every item exported and sold is tainted with its reputation. Every person born in Van Diemen's Land is stained by it, too.

Caroline worries for the investment she has made in Everlea and the expanding vineyards. Georgiana and Swanston talk of leaving Van Diemen's Land and making their home on their estate near Geelong. Swanston tells Caroline he will not sell New Town Park but would have one of his sons manage it—Charles could return from England, perhaps—until commerce and the colony's reputation improves. Robert and Nowell have already departed to complete their education in England. George will go next year.

Jacques-Louis thinks on the descendants that might succeed him from a place of such disrepute. He talks to Caroline of a different notoriety they might build for the colony. A place that grows wine to rival the great houses of France.

'Can you see it?' he asks her. She observes in him an enthusiasm that she has not seen in many years. A light she had believed was extinguished forever.

'Yes, Papa, I see it,' she says.

Quill becomes an excellent rider, accompanying George and Captain Swanston on trips to various properties in which Swanston has an interest as a banker or a friend—usually both. Quill's face is changing. His nose is bigger, his chin is longer, the planes of his cheeks are becoming more angular. It is a constant fascination to Caroline. Already there is a fine down on his top lip and his cheeks. His amber eyes have darkened into golden toffee. His hair, which he wears long and tied back, has settled into waves. His body is lean and strong and he is almost a head taller than George. She reconsiders, not for the first time, her initial assessment of his age.

At harvest time he lifts countless bales of hay at the Swanstons', the Walkers' and the Giblins'. He carries barrels and casks in the cellar for Cornelius. When his studies are done for the day, he works with Jacques-Louis in the fields. He laughs often and almost every day brings Caroline flowers or some thing of beauty from his walks and rides.

Quill and Cornelius hunt together, bringing back rabbits and ducks, wild geese and wallaby, which become pies and stews. Bessie and Caroline harvest oysters and mussels from the rocks along the shore, and pipis from beneath the sand at low tide. Sometimes there are scallops, abalone and crayfish, scalefish, beef and mutton traded for vegetables, a case of apples or pears, nectarines, buckets of blackberries and bottles of wine.

The cottage now has a glasshouse on its northern side. In the warmth, they are able to grow citrus fruits and some vegetables all year round, just as in the Swanstons' conservatory, and it, too, becomes a favourite place for Caroline and Georgiana to sit.

'I have come to a point in my life where soon my children will no longer need me,' says Georgiana. 'And what will I do with myself then?'

'I am sure there will be much new life in Melbourne to occupy you, if you are to go there,' Caroline says.

'Oh, yes,' says Georgiana, 'but I can't envisage being quite so content as I have been here.'

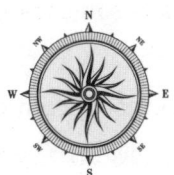

The officially titled Doctor John Mercer sends a letter to tell Caroline that he will soon return to Van Diemen's Land with the young Charles Swanston. At the dinner given by Georgiana to celebrate their arrival, Doctor Mercer sits next to Caroline and surprises her by saying that he intends to settle in Hobart. He has not mentioned this before in his letters.

'I understand there is a need for good doctors,' he says.

'You will have no family here,' she says, knowing he has sisters and a brother still in Scotland.

'I was inspired by the courage of a lady whom I met when I was here on my first visit,' he says. 'Her correspondence has assured me that here is where I wish to be.'

He visits Everlea, walking the vineyard with her, and meets Jacques-Louis. They talk for some minutes about grape growing. Caroline wishes she could introduce Jacques-Louis as her father. She knows he will perceive the doctor's interest in her, and there would be much they might talk about of medicine and Edinburgh.

She invites John Mercer to tea. When he compliments Bessie on her fruitcake, she almost drops a fork. He asks Quill his plans for the future, and if he will be departing, like George, for further education in England. Caroline and Georgiana have discussed sending George and Quill together. Caroline cannot imagine life without Quill. She cannot imagine life without Georgiana.

'If I am to leave,' says Quill, 'I would prefer to go to France, to study under a great chef de cave.'

'How useful that your aunt has encouraged you to be fluent in French,' John Mercer says.

Quill replies, 'Monsieur Pain, as Captain Swanston calls him, insists upon it if I am to become a winemaker.'

Doctor Mercer extends an invitation to Caroline and Quill to accompany him to a play at the Theatre Royal. Caroline agrees, and ensures that Quill is suitably attired for such an event. It is good to see him dressed in a fine suit and striped silk cravat.

'I am so proud of you,' she says.

He smiles. 'I am as you have made me.'

'No, darling Quill, you are as you have made yourself.'

Caroline observes the stylishly attired men and women alighting from their carriages. From their seats in the dress circle, under a regal cupola painted with portraits of the great composers, she looks about at those nearby and those in the stalls below. Some significant portion must have served time for some crime or other. She knows she is little different from them, disguised now in their coats and gowns, tie pins and hat pins, cufflinks and tiaras. Except by some benevolent hand, she had not been caught.

Here was a society created from the doings and misdoings of countless people. All societies must be so. But in London she had taken the weight of history as evidence of stability and perpetuity, while here the future was still a precarious and uncertain harvest.

Her thoughts turn to Tante Henriette and their evenings attending performances in London. Tante Henriette laughed when a woman gave her a coquettish glance, for she made a handsome nobleman. Always they had dressed as they did for their work, never risking recognition by the genteel ladies who had shared travels and confidences with the womanly version of Tante Henriette. Would her aunt have been surprised to see Caroline here, established in this remote destination? No, Caroline thinks. She would understand.

When they emerge onto the street, Doctor Mercer offers Caroline his arm. She takes it, and feels the warmth of him close beside her.

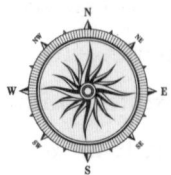

With the latest vintage, orders flow in from Melbourne and New South Wales and across Van Diemen's Land. In the *Hobart Town Gazette*, Mr Pain is noted as *the highly creditable winemaker manufacturing champagne pink and pale, sparkling and delicious, and infinitely superior to the meretricious but insinuating compound imported under this designation . . .*

Jacques-Louis tells Caroline that it is time to set their wine amidst the great wines, to see how Van Diemen's Land's bounty fares in a blind tasting. He wishes to enter their champagne in the Paris Wine Awards and see what great men and women of wine make of it measured against that of the Cape, California, Virginia and the many European countries that vie for such recognition.

'And how would this extraordinary feat be accomplished?' she asks.

'I would go with it, escorting the bottles on the long voyage.'

When they broach it with Captain Swanston, he says, 'Mr Pain, you have one job and one job alone: to make the wine of this vineyard, not to tout your wares in Europe. It is a fantasy of vanity—a most unlikely venture that can surely bring little reward.'

'You are not thinking of the greater good such an acknowledgement might bring, Captain,' Jacques-Louis replies. 'I hold that this vintage is as fine as any in France, and I do not declare this lightly. I do not declare it from vanity. You have seen the response from the buyers. You have tasted it yourself, though we both doubt your expertise in such matters. Which is why you must trust this to me. To win in Paris brings not only the acclaim of the French, it would send a ripple across the world. A colonial wine, a wine from Van Diemen's Land, to garner such acclaim! It will never be forgotten. You wish to remake this place as a pastoral paradise, but nothing you or anyone else has done until now has succeeded. Think how this could declare to the world that we are not all felons and filth.'

'Clearly we are not all felons and filth,' says Swanston, growing more heated. 'But it is a fool's errand and would earn us nothing but derision.'

'None can deride the wine! And it is no fool's errand. Brave men win great accolades, Captain Swanston, as well you know. Come with me, if you doubt me in any way. Come with me to Europe, to Paris, if you cannot overcome this disbelief.'

'You do not have an absolute pardon,' Captain Swanston points out. 'You may not set foot in England.'

'It is unfortunate then that I know no one in the colony who might procure such a pardon,' says Jacques-Louis. 'The English are not who we wish to convince anyway. It is the world. You yourself could go on to England and meet with agents there.'

'Even if I were to secure a pardon for you—and I have no certainty of that—how can I be sure you will not use such an opportunity to abscond with my wine, sell it and establish yourself in some place in southern France, glad to be free of us all?'

At this, Jacques-Louis fixes him with a steely gaze. 'I would never live in southern France. I was once a man of honour, Captain Swanston. You have entrusted me with a great deal, and I have not failed you, but you make a grave error in thinking I will not return here. I give you my word. I do it on the crest of my family, on the lineage of my people. I will return to you with the prize for the finest champagne. You are a man who must think always in profit. Well, there can be no greater flow of profit than if the world knows the fame of your vineyard.'

And on it goes for weeks.

They are two goats butting heads, straining to have their way. The promise of the wine, the dream of acclaim, the possible bounty of success. Caroline wishes that Swanston knew that Jacques-Louis was her father. Then he would understand why Jacques-Louis would never abandon Everlea.

Jacques-Louis perseveres. He speaks with Swanston of orders flowing in from America, England, Russia. 'Wherever champagne is appreciated, there will be connoisseurs keen to taste your wine. This whole estate may yet be filled with vines, and all of it flowing to Europe, the profits flowing back to you.'

Something in Swanston eases. He comes to Caroline one afternoon and declares that he has enquired about an absolute pardon for Jacques-Louis so that he might sail to England. From there, the small voyage across the English Channel to France will be easy. This way he can also more easily keep track of Jacques-Louis. If he departs on a foreign ship and travels through foreign ports, such oversight will not be easy. He cannot risk losing his winemaker and, with pressing concerns in the colony, he cannot make the trip himself.

It is Swanston who suggests that Quill might accompany Jacques-Louis, to be of assistance in managing the wine on the long voyage.

Quill's eyes light up at the suggestion. 'But who will take care of the next vintage while we are gone?' he asks.

Jacques-Louis chuckles. *'Parole de vrai vigneron!'* he says.

Caroline sees the sense in Quill accompanying her father. Jacques-Louis will need Quill's vigour and care. The wine must be moved from shore to ship and ship to shore. It must be tended while they are at sea, no matter the weather. Then it must travel by wagon until they reach Paris. To ensure the wine arrives safely is no simple challenge. And it will all take money.

She fears for the dangers of the voyage and the possibility of failure, but she sees that this is not simply about recognition for their wine, but a reclamation of Jacques-Louis himself, his wish to secure a more certain future for all that they have built here. He can acquire agents for them across Europe. Quill will have an opportunity to see the valleys of Champagne and the grand tradition of which he wishes to be a part. She feels certain he will find a good house that will apprentice him. In a few years, he may return with all manner of skills that will be of value to the vineyard.

Washington and Julia Walker tell Caroline that Swanston's Derwent Bank is facing straitened circumstances that are much discussed in the town. Another bank has failed, leaving a wake of investors without recourse or return on their invested capital. A number of properties have been foreclosed.

Caroline discusses the economic circumstances with Swanston, who declares in a tone lacking neither bravado nor overt concern that such times will pass. They have excellent merchants working for them in Sydney and Melbourne, he reminds her. Are they not optimistic about the returns from this new vintage?

'Captain Swanston, my savings have been consumed by the expenses incurred through the early vintages and the costs of increased production. As you well know, I have invested in the expansion of the vineyards, too. If you will extend to me the capital, I will support this voyage.' She knows it is a risk, but she has risked much before.

'Mrs Douglas,' Swanston says, 'I cannot. The withdrawal of investors from the colony, this infernal depression and the convict stain that continues to cripple this island, makes the lending of money unfeasible, even to one such as you. But Van Diemen's Land will surmount these challenges, I assure you.'

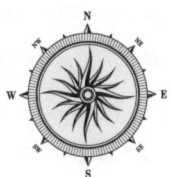

A note arrives from Doctor Mercer inviting Caroline to accompany him to the upcoming celebration for Captain Swanston's birthday. The Governor has been invited to the event, along with Swanston's political allies, visiting dignitaries, scientists and explorers currently in Van Diemen's Land, and the wealthy landed families who have claimed much of the island. Caroline sends back a short note of acceptance.

George is leaving for school in England in two weeks and Georgiana is to accompany him. They are to stop first in Madras to see Georgiana's family. The likelihood of Captain Swanston and Georgiana relocating to Geelong after Georgiana returns appears ever more likely.

The evening of the birthday party is calm and sultry after a warm day. The moon rises almost full across the Derwent River. In two days, the Hobart regatta is to be held and the harbour is filled with all manner of sailing craft in anticipation of the event.

During the afternoon, Caroline receives a delivery. She opens the box to discover a fragrant spray of lily-of-the-valley. Within the box is a note in a familiar hand.

So there can be dancing, it reads.

Caroline wears a dress of emerald watered silk. The floral spray is pinned into her hair with a coronet of pearls, an arrangement Bessie has devised. She also wears the choker of diamonds that she has saved all this time. It is the last of the jewellery stolen in London with Tante Henriette and never before worn. She assures herself that she can explain it away as merely paste, should anyone be too curious.

'You are a most beautiful woman, Mrs Douglas,' John Mercer says, when he arrives to collect her. 'The most beautiful woman I have ever seen.' He is in a plum frock coat with an embroidered emerald waistcoat, and he looks remarkably handsome.

'A happy coincidence,' she says, noting the match of his waistcoat with her dress.

'It is possible that I bribed Bessie,' he says.

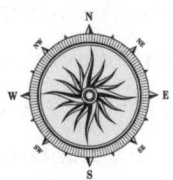

A stream of carriages continues arriving at New Town Park long into the evening, bearing women and men in all their finery. The drawing room has become a ballroom, the French doors open onto the patio where a string quartet plays. The dining room is laid with a sumptuous buffet. The new sparkling wine is being served along with a red wine Jacques-Louis has only now agreed is ready for drinking, and believes will be wasted on the palates of the partygoers. Naturally, Jacques-Louis is not in attendance. Swanston and Jacques-Louis may be equals when arguing over wine and business, but Captain Swanston would never invite him into Hobart society.

They meet with neighbours and friends, and John Mercer introduces Caroline to a number of new acquaintances from the township.

'You are very popular,' she says.

'They have to like me,' he says. 'I know all their rashes and lumps.'

When he asks her to dance, John Mercer does so with a shy expression. Caroline takes his hand and feels the light touch of his fingers through her lace gloves. He leads with ease—reminding her of the savoir faire Jacques-Louis always imparted when he waltzed with Caroline and Augusta. As they dance, Caroline finds she wants to move closer so that there is no distance between them. She wants to breathe in the scent of grass after rain that she catches on his skin. She blushes when he smiles at her.

Later, they stroll through the gardens, which are lit with lanterns. Jugglers move amongst the assembly. Fire twirlers toss batons that spin and circle, and there are gasps of delight and eruptions of applause.

'You have been absent,' she says.

'Have you missed me?' he asks.

'I have,' she says.

'I have been occupied in making a new home,' John Mercer replies. 'I have taken a place in Sandy Bay, and it is at last painted and furnished. I am hoping that you and Quill might come to dine with me as my first guests. I have employed a rather terrifying woman, a Mrs Curtain, who is an adequate cook. But perhaps she will rise to the occasion if she knows I am to entertain the intriguing Mrs Douglas.'

Caroline is about to express her agreement when she notices Captain Swanston in conversation with a lean, older man in a broad-brimmed black hat. They are regarding the new archway into the rose garden. It resembles tiny honeyeaters on a flowering vine. A beautiful piece of wrought iron crafted by Cornelius for the occasion. Something about the scene catches her attention.

'We would be delighted to come,' Caroline says, returning her attention to the doctor. His luminous eyes are watchful, thoughtful. He misses nothing, she thinks. He must be a good doctor.

'Do you know the gentleman with Captain Swanston?' he asks. 'I believe he is a merchant from San Francisco. There is some discussion of the captain and Charles furthering business interests in that city.'

'Ah,' says Caroline. Captain Swanston has made no mention of such an expedition to her. She knows there is a gold rush that is drawing many to California, but surely it cannot be that.

The captain turns and sees them. 'Doctor Mercer, Mrs Douglas, let me introduce you to Señor Clementi from the Americas. He is visiting Hobart briefly seeking opportunities for trade. Señor Clementi, our dear friends Mrs Douglas and Doctor Mercer.'

Señor Clementi and Caroline stare at one another.

'A happy reunion for I have met Mrs Douglas before,' the man says, bowing. 'We travelled together by ship from New York to Rio de Janeiro some years ago. And now I find her here. What a pleasure, Mrs Douglas, and I see that this antipodean hamlet suits you for you are looking more beautiful than ever.'

Caroline's skin crawls. The collector of birds for his own mausoleum. The cockroach. 'Señor Clementi,' she says, 'it is indeed a coincidence.'

'I have learned through my travels that the world is a very small place,' Señor Clementi says with a calculating smile. 'We are appreciating this beautiful archway that Captain Swanston tells me was created by a local blacksmith.'

'He lives here on our property,' Swanston says.

'You are very lucky to have such an artisan in your employ,' Clementi says.

'Oh, he is his own man,' says Swanston. 'And much in demand. But truly, this is quite something that you and Mrs Douglas are already acquainted, is it not?'

'Yes,' says Caroline. 'It is.'

'I fear,' says Doctor Mercer, 'that I have quite worn Mrs Douglas out with dancing, the night being so very warm. I was insisting on taking her inside for refreshments. Will you excuse us?'

As he leads her away he asks, 'Was I right to effect a rescue?'

'You are my saviour,' says Caroline.

'It is unusual,' says John Mercer, 'to see you perturbed.'

She wants to laugh it off, but instead she says, 'Perhaps one day we will discuss it.'

'Will you promise?' he asks.

The sudden appearance of Clementi has indeed unsettled her. How long will he be here? What if he were to recognise Quill? Caroline had not considered how her inventions to settle the past might complicate the future in myriad unanticipated ways. She had thought herself safe, but now she is vulnerable. Her family, too. When should she tell John Mercer that the Swanstons' winemaker is, in fact, her father and, by the way, he is also a murderer? When should she tell him that Quill is a boy she freed from enslavement? When should she speak of the deceit of her widowhood?

Guests are continuing to arrive, and soon there are to be fireworks, but she tells John Mercer that she has wearied of the crowd. Quill is to stay tonight at the Swanstons' with George. Instead of the carriage to return her home, she would much prefer to walk back across the paddock.

She has in mind to stop in and visit her father and tell him of the evening before she rests. She wants to ask him what he makes of Doctor Mercer. She wonders how long the roles she and her father have enacted these past years must continue. Until he receives an absolute pardon? Until the Swanstons depart the island and she must bear no longer the guilt of deceiving them?

And this man who is now accompanying her home. What will this good and dear man make of her artifice and lies? He might never trust her again. He might never forgive her.

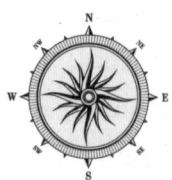

The pathway back to the cottage is easy to follow in the moon-light, and Caroline realises that, with Georgiana and George gone, she will have less reason to walk this way. If Quill does depart with her father, she will be more alone than she has ever been in this town. The coming months loom with uncertainty. It is a weight on her heart.

'Might we sit on your verandah for a while?' John Mercer asks.

'I would like that. There is cold peppermint tea in the kitchen. Let me fetch it.'

They settle and take in the moonlight on the fields, the velvet summer sky pierced with stars. Music from the Swanstons' party drifts through the evening air, accompanied by laughter and chatter.

'Señor Clementi and his son were collecting birds from across the Americas, thousands of them, many species, to line a tomb he was building for himself. His son was employed as sharp shooter and taxidermist. I was very glad when they both departed the ship.'

'So not a cheerful fellow,' says Doctor Mercer.

'I think he supposed I would find him attractive.'

'And he made that apparent?'

'Far too apparent,' she says.

'You are a remarkable woman, Mrs Douglas,' he says. 'You have travelled the world. You pretend a distance from this vineyard of Swanston's, yet I see you are much more involved than you let on. You maintain an allure for all who know you, and there are many who love and admire you. Yet I come to see that none of this is as easy as it looks for you.'

She inhales.

'Thank you for allowing me to be your friend,' he says. 'I see more and more that it is a rare gift you entrust me with.'

He lifts her gloved hand from the arm of her chair and kisses it. He invites her to rise. He takes both her hands in his and looks down at her from his elegant height, his face illuminated by the lantern on the table.

'This may be precipitate, but I find I must speak,' he says. 'I fell in love with you, Caroline Douglas, when I first saw you at the Swanstons' Christmas supper. I could hardly bring myself to leave you behind. There has not been a day I have not thought of you. So many letters I wrote but did not send. I have little to offer you but my heart, dear Caroline. Yet with it, I promise to love you all my days. Do not feel you must speak. I ask only that we might walk your vineyard and share books and speak of all that fills you with joy and concern. And if, in time, you might come to love me, then I will be the most fortunate man in the world.'

She steps into his arms. A single word occurs to her as she feels his chest beneath her cheek. *Home.* She wants to kiss him. She wants with all her heart to say she will spend all her days with him. But she steps back.

'And you would not mind an old widow?'

'I cannot imagine a better proposition.'

'And if I were not a widow?' she dares.

He regards her. 'Not a widow?'

'You may not like what you must hear, dear John.'

'Caroline,' he says, 'I am ready to hear it all. I am not easily frightened. Or dissuaded.'

'Will you come tomorrow?' she asks.

'At dawn?' he replies.

She smiles. 'Early evening. Let us take a long walk.'

'Of course,' he says.

They stare at each other for a moment before his lips meet hers, and she finds his mouth as beautiful and enticing as she had imagined.

When they part, it is as if she has drawn herself back from the edge of bliss. An owl calls *boobook*, *boobook*. The moon is running fast now before a mass of clouds building over the mountain. She must speak to her father. They must discuss how to navigate this new part of life. How will she ever unravel all her secrets?

She sits on the verandah for some time waiting for her heart and her thoughts to settle.

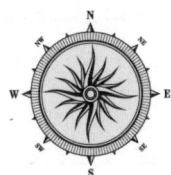

In her bedroom, after removing the evening's finery, she dons a shift and a warm shawl. She slips from the house and walks towards the barn, seeing sparks rising from the chimney. Perhaps they are there together, Cornelius and her father. Perhaps she will seek guidance from both of them. But as she puts her hand upon the door, she hears an unfamiliar voice. She peeks through a gap in the timber to see Señor Clementi. His hat and tailcoat are discarded and he has rolled his shirtsleeves to the elbows. He is tending something in the forge with deliberate focus. The red hue of the fire illuminates the implements hanging on the long arm above him, swinging innocently in the rising heat.

Cornelius is stripped to the waist and bound to a chair. A wound seeps from his head. Blood is running down the side of his face. Clementi's voice is a dark undercurrent in the dim-lit scene.

'Did you think I would ever stop looking?' Clementi says. 'You carry my mark. Right there.' He points to the crescent moon branded long ago on Cornelius's upper arm. 'Need I remind you that your life belongs to me?'

'We are old men,' Cornelius replies, his voice soft and weary, as if he has ebbed away and only a husk remains.

'I searched for you for weeks,' Clementi says.

Cornelius says nothing.

'You were the only one to ever escape me.'

'Not true,' says Cornelius. 'There are the dead.'

'What is death to a slave?' Clementi spits back. 'The dead are merely the weak. Their deaths were at my pleasure.'

Can it be true? Clementi is not simply a ghost from her past, but Cornelius's, too? Can he be El Diablo, the slaver Cornelius had escaped in Panama? Yes, she can believe savagery lives beneath the veneer of Clementi's civility. But how has he found Cornelius? Then she realises. He had recognised his craft in the archway in the Swanstons' garden.

'You have made things of such beauty,' Caroline remembers saying to Cornelius one evening by the forge. 'Your gate at the cottage is one of the things I admired when I first discovered this place.'

'I made that for Mr Broughton,' he said. 'A gift for his thirtieth birthday.'

'You are an artist, Cornelius.'

'Ah, Mrs Caroline,' he said to her. 'A gate like that almost cost me my life.'

And he had told her of the wedding present, the gate of roses he had wrought and all that had ensued until he reached the Pacific Ocean.

•

A blacksmith wielding metal, fire, water and air conjures the tools of farming, seafaring, industry and domesticity. He shapes trivets and toasting forks, kettle pourers and cutlery. He can summon from fragments ornate tongs to lift a single coal to light a gentleman's scrimshaw pipe. He moulds horseshoes, bridle bits and harnesses, chains and iron anchors that demand the patience of hours. Pieces so heavy that wooden cranes are required to lift them to the anvil. He can make axes, files and arrow heads, nails, clips and pins, and all manner of blade, scissors and knives. The knife Clementi has been holding to the fire is now red-hot.

'We are indeed old men, so I will go slowly, gently,' he says to Cornelius.

Caroline's thoughts fly to her father. He will be in his loft but she cannot risk his intervention, his involvement in any scene that might cause him to be sent back to prison. Should she run to the Swanstons' and seek help? But the party deters her. The distant cacophony of merriment is in eerie contrast to the scene within the barn. She inhales deeply, and wrenches back the door. As she steps inside she feels as if she is entering a dream.

'How dare you!' she says. 'You will free him.'

'Señora Douglas,' Clementi says, and crossing the floor with alarming speed, he has her pinned, the blade at her throat, terrifyingly hot.

'Get off me,' she spits.

Clementi laughs. 'Do not scream, Mrs Douglas, or I might be forced to cut out your tongue.'

He is moving her towards the workbench. There she sees a length of chain, a hammer. She struggles. He turns her to face him, then he slams his fist into her stomach with all his might. She gasps and collapses. She cannot breathe. Blackness and pain are overwhelming her. He is stuffing her mouth with cloth. It tastes of ash and grime. She is on her knees, choking. She thinks she will suffocate. He is shackling her arms behind her. There is grit in her mouth. She wills herself to calm, to breathe, to lift her head and face him.

'It is kind of you to join us,' he says casually, hauling her to sit on a wooden crate, resuming his stance at the forge and reheating the knife. 'I have always liked an audience. But if you move, I will remove your tongue. Or perhaps an eye. Do not doubt me. Beauty is fleeting, Mrs Douglas, especially in a woman.'

He approaches Cornelius, pressing the hot tip of the knife into his chest. A hiss erupts from Cornelius's skin. He flinches and trembles, making no sound. Clementi begins to carve. He does it with ease, as if the act of drawing a hot blade through flesh is familiar.

'Such a beautiful flower, the rose,' he says. 'I have travelled the globe and never smelled a more beautiful fragrance. Not in the night scents of the Amazon nor the frangipani in Otaheite.

'You know, don't you,' he goes on, 'that you were ever coming back to me. Who can say that we do not do this dance again and again, life after life, you and me? You the black man, I the white. You the slave and I the master. When we are finished here, we will return to the waterfront where my ship will depart in the morning. It is your destiny, Cornelius. You know it and I know it. You are my property. None here in this little England will dare challenge it.'

The petals curve into an opening bud across the breastbone. Blood is weeping from the wounds. Cornelius's head has dropped back. His breathing is ragged. Caroline sees that a single tear is running from his eye into his hair.

Clementi works the stem of the flower, running it down the centre of Cornelius's rib cage, finishing with a single leaf. Then he takes ash from the firebox and smears it across the wounds, the scourge of the rose now marked with lines of black.

'Yes,' he says, stepping back to admire his handiwork. 'But what shall we do with you, Mrs Douglas?' He takes her face in his hand, his fingers hard. 'What shall we conceive in this world of possibilities?'

She senses movement before she sees it. Jacques-Louis is upon him, a hammer coming down hard upon the side of Clementi's head, knocking him sideways, where he falls at her feet, motionless.

Jacques-Louis removes the cloth from Caroline's mouth and unties her hands. He picks up the knife and slices through the bonds that hold Cornelius, helping him to his feet.

They all turn to Clementi. Jacques-Louis hauls him into the chair where Cornelius had been bound. Clementi's eyes roll open and he struggles, but Jacques-Louis restrains him.

'He is mine,' Clementi's voice rasps.

Jacques-Louis offers Cornelius the knife.

'He is yours,' he says.

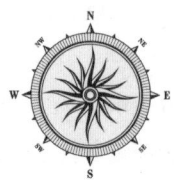

When the Spaniard fails to return to the ship, the captain dispatches a man to investigate Señor Clementi's accommodation at a nearby public house. There the sailor discovers the bed neatly made and all personal possessions removed. It is said he appeared briefly before dawn to gather his belongings, the cook the only witness to his departure.

'He wore his hat,' she said. 'A shade, really, that man, by day or night.'

No words had been exchanged, but he had left money by the bed to settle his bill, with a small surplus. It was assumed he had returned to the ship.

Enquiries are made at the Swanstons'. Interviews yielded few answers. Señor Clementi's departure had gone unremarked amidst the festivities. There had been so many guests. However, a group returning home from New Town Park were passed in their carriage by a lone rider moving at a swift canter long after midnight, a silhouette heading for the harbour wearing a distinctive hat.

Clementi's disappearance leaves behind a trail of intrigue and speculation. Georgiana suggests a reward be offered. The story occupies a few lines in the *Hobart Town Gazette*, but then it evaporates. There has been another drop in the price of wool and more farms are foreclosing. Beyond the colony's economic woes, the annual regatta has been held and the fashions and the sailing races must be reported and reviewed. The weekly list of visitors to Government House is published. A report from the Royal Society is discussed and an extract from a new book by Charles Dickens is attracting interest in literary circles. Mrs Georgiana Swanston and her son George depart for England by way of Madras, while Captain Swanston, it is reported, is travelling to San Francisco with his son Charles to secure investments for the colony.

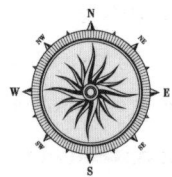

The first snowfall settles on the rugged slopes of Mount Wellington, and Caroline, Jacques-Louis and Quill leave for the harbour. As the moment of departure nears, each finds themselves at a loss for words. They travel in silence, each breath a misty exhalation. A cloudless dawn of fuchsia pink and thistle mauve is seeping into the sky as the phaeton tops New Town hill and they look down upon the river, as calm as silvered silk, the docks filled with vessels at anchor and some already underway.

At the waterfront they navigate workers and wagons. Horses stamp on the bitter cobblestones, and drivers and sailors breathe into their hands for warmth. The briny tang of seaweed meets the mutterings and misgivings of the corralled sheep and cattle mingling with the scent of new-milled timber and steaming dung. Underneath it all, water slaps against the wooden bollards as gangplanks rumble with barrows laden with supplies, workers coming and going as cargo is stowed below decks.

One ship flies a French flag, a barque of some two hundred and ninety tons. It is a research vessel called the *Madeleine.* In its hold lies a cargo of wine bound for France. It had been taken aboard the day before, each bottle placed carefully by Jacques-Louis and Quill into gimballed racks fitted to the ship's interior and lined with felted wool to encase the bottles, reducing movement and vibration.

At the stern of the barque, Jacques-Louis and Quill wave farewell. Jacques-Louis does not have his absolute pardon, for Swanston departed for San Francisco before it was issued. They were assured it would come, but it did not.

Only when Swanston was crossing the Pacific was it discovered that the affairs of the Derwent Bank were in a state of derangement. Captain Swanston, the press declared, was more than one hundred thousand pounds in debt. Almost sixty thousand pounds of this he owed to the Derwent Bank—or, more correctly, its investors.

The *Colonial Times* reported:

> Sufferers had not knowingly, or with their consent, embarked their property in any commercial speculation. Neither had they entrusted the use or care of it to one whom they expected to use it for such a purpose. The man through whom their property is sacrificed employed it for his own benefit and aggrandisement, and that of his relatives, or other associates, in speculation from which, even if successful, investors could have derived no profit.

Countless people, small landholders and large, were plummeted into a world of uncertainty. Creditors demanded their money. Properties were being repossessed.

Caroline discovered that many purchases for the vineyard ordered by Swanston—a number of which she did not recall—had languished unpaid. The sums were significant, and Swanston had ensured all the invoices bore her name.

She reflected on the birthday party, the gardens lit with lanterns, the musicians and fire twirlers, jugglers and actors, food, wine and fireworks. Had it been the act of a man ever certain, despite all indications to the contrary, that the world must right itself in his favour? A last attempt to attract investors? Or a wilfully grandiose farewell? However it had been conceived, the night had been a reckoning.

And then word came that Captain Swanston had died on his return voyage from San Francisco and been buried at sea. There was much speculation about his death, but if it had been a ruse to avoid his debts, it succeeded, for he was never seen again.

Caroline had not wished to trouble Jacques-Louis with her financial predicament, but he knew enough of Swanston to suspect it.

'This voyage is more than a little wine seeking glory, is it not?' he asked.

'You do not need to rescue me, Papa. We will be all right.'

'Do you owe very much?'

She nodded. Then she had given him the jewellery box that contained the diamond choker. 'You must sell this in Paris, Papa. Get the best price you can. It will fund your time abroad and help Quill to establish himself. Whatever remains when you return will assist me with the debts.'

She raises her hand and waves again as the *Madeleine* is towed out into the river, crossing the harbour until the vessel's sails fill in the light breeze and the figures of Quill and her father disappear into the distance. It may be months before news of their voyage reaches her. They have promised to send her letters when they arrive in Batavia, Ceylon and Paris.

The day before, Caroline and Quill had walked amongst the winter bones of the young trees in the Botanical Gardens. There had been frost in the fields, the grass damp and green. They had talked of how it would look in a hundred years, the trees above the entrance way, the ponds stocked with lilies, the slope of pastoral land to the river filled with garden beds and pathways.

They had spoken of his anticipation of being once more aboard a ship. She confessed her worries that he would find himself awoken by new sights, places and peoples, his perspective growing so large that all that was here would be diminished, a strange passage of his life to which he might find it hard to return. That the distance between them would grow too vast and the ties that bound them would fray and fade with the passage of time. She wanted him to know that he was free to do whatever he must, but she was afraid that she might lose him.

He was so much taller than her now, a young man. He had taken her hands and said, 'It is with a heavy heart I leave you, my real mother. My dearest mother. I will never forget you or abandon you. I will always come back to you.'

Mother. A word bestowed after all these years. She held him tight. 'Darling Quill,' she said. 'Yes, I am your mother and you are my beautiful, most precious son.'

If fortune smiled on them, by the time spring returned Quill and Jacques-Louis would be enjoying the late Parisian summer, their precious cargo delivered. A boy who had once dreamed of becoming a winemaker returning to his homeland with a shipment of rare champagne. And a lad who had forsaken the sea now set to pursue a career in the fields of France.

When she returns to Everlea, Cornelius is there to meet her and take the phaeton away. She stands on the verandah looking out across the valley to the river. What will be the consequence of Swanston's fall? There is word that New Town Park is to be sold. She does not know if she can continue the enterprise of the vineyard alone. She does not know how the outstanding bills Swanston has left will be paid. She may be forced to sell, too.

But if the wine does well in Paris, if they secure agents and orders across Europe, if the diamond choker finds a good price, then perhaps it will be sufficient, and she can somehow find credit until the orders are dispatched and paid. Her father must succeed.

John Mercer emerges from within the cottage. He wraps his arms around her waist and holds her close to him and together they regard the view.

'What if he does not come back?' she whispers.

'Your father?'

'Yes.'

'He will come back,' he says.

A storm comes through in the night. John Mercer holds Caroline close. She'd had no idea the pleasures of the skin could be so tender and enlivening. Why had no one told her that this was marriage? They had made love for hours. Now she is waylaid on the tide of dawn, navigated and explored, dissembled and reinvented, cocooned in the contentment of her body.

When she wakes again, light is slipping between the curtains, dazzling her. She closes her eyes and bathes in it. John's breath is soft, his face so dear as he sleeps beside her. How was it possible to love like this? His skin, his mouth, his voice, his laughter, his words and deeds, his kindness. She had never imagined this communion, this confession, this union that is both altar and salvation.

· *18* ·

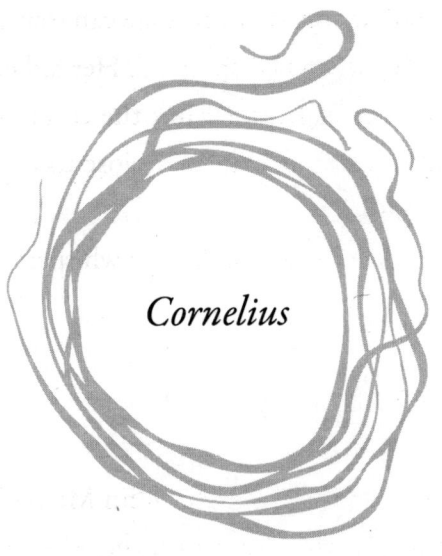

Cornelius

Cornelius had never told Caroline of the nights after Jacques-Louis first arrived at Everlea. The many times he had found him wandering the barn distressed and disorientated. He would call Cornelius 'Maman' and grasp Cornelius's hand and ask him was it true? Did he really live? And he would ask, 'Where is Hannah? Where is Hannah?'

Cornelius had soothed him, shepherded him back to bed, resting his hand upon Jacques-Louis' brow as he pulled up the covers. And he would wait there, calming him, until at last Jacques-Louis dropped into sleep, his breath becoming a light snore.

There were other nights when Cornelius woke to screaming and it was hard to know at first who screamed, for on occasion it was Jacques-Louis in the loft beyond, and sometimes it was his own frenzied voice calling for his children who were being pulled away from him. The man imprisoned night after night by his dreams, Cornelius knew. That was a perpetual sentence. No notice in the weekly gazette declaring your emancipation.

After the events that followed Swanston's party, it was Jacques-Louis who had tended to Cornelius. Made a salve when the burns on his chest became infected. Washed his clothes and made his food. Cared for him as if he were a child.

Cornelius had languished from a fever that took weeks to ease. He saw over and over the light going out of El Diablo's eyes. He remembered the weight of the man's body as he and Jacques-Louis had carried him far into the forest. He remembered Caroline in the moonlight carrying shovels. He remembered the pain of digging, the fervour as they made the hole deeper and deeper, so that no man or woman would ever come across it in years to come. No bones would be washed to the surface after a heavy rain or be unearthed by dogs.

It was Caroline who had thought of the items left in Clementi's room in Hobart. She had suggested Jacques-Louis wear the man's frock coat and hat, and take a horse. How strange his resemblance to El Diablo as he rode away.

When Jacques-Louis reappeared at the forge, all Clementi's things of cloth, leather and paper were added to the fire. The things of metal, including money, buttons and the knife, were melted down until they became brittle. Then Cornelius had pounded them into dust.

· *19* ·

Jacques-Louis

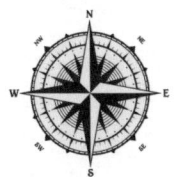

A tempest howls through the western Azores. The *Madeleine* grapples with the onslaught of wind and water but ultimately she succumbs. Her sails catch the weight of the sea and her great masts crack and splinter. After that, there is a roiling torment for the thirty-nine souls aboard, the ship and all her contents becoming flotsam, the bodies of men and beast seeking mercy on sand, rock and the ocean floor.

Jacques-Louis, clutching within his jacket a solitary remnant of the voyage, meets a coral reef which shatters his leg, rends his clothes and much of his skin, and then by some miracle or curse he washes ashore. Dawn breaks and for many hours the sun sears him. Salt encrusts his wounds. With the returning tide, he stirs and is relieved to find the singular talisman still within the remains of his jacket. He hauls himself, in an agony of exquisite proportions, across the beach until he reaches the refuge of trees.

Struggling now to lift his head, he scans the sea behind him and calls Quill's name. His voice is a desperate shred barely recognisable.

The world around him is unresponsive and he passes back into oblivion.

Awakening, he sees a full moon rising over a blackcurrant sea, the ribbon of light travelling across the water appearing to be an invitation to a mighty gathering of the drowned. Come, join the kindred spirits of sailors and sirens, heroes and thieves offering you their lyric thoughts on music and jubilation, miracle and persuasion, remorse and desolation.

He has survived voyages before; perhaps he will yet rally. But he is deluding himself, his wounds remind him. His once-useful right leg is a mass of lacerated flesh. A shattered spear of bone is protruding from his thigh.

He might have met his end some years before with a well-tied noose or from myriad blades and fists beyond. The grim truth, he knows, is that a man co-exists with men more and less violent than his own inclinations; he learns to adapt, or he perishes more quickly than he anticipated.

Caroline would manage it. She may appear gentle and sweet, well schooled by her mother, but he knows her. She would have a sharpened blade to his leg, a hacksaw for the bone, and it would be done.

'Who needs a leg if you will live, Papa?'

He closes his eyes and sees the morning light across the valley. A scythe awaiting its purpose by the barn, dawn's motes hanging in the air. Candlelight flickers in the cellar where root vegetables slumber in beds of soft sand. He imagines walking amidst the dusty bottles. The leaves are blazing golden and red upon the vines. Is it autumn so soon? The mountain is a shade of lavender hung to dry. He envisions uncorking a bottle filled with the sparkling afternoon of the day it was harvested.

Raising it to her mouth, Caroline drinks. 'It is good,' she says, being his daughter, with the natural understanding.

'This dying is not all seriousness,' he says.

'It seems a little serious,' she replies, her eyes twinkling.

Wit is a perilous thing when you are in chains and a hard man wields a lash. Wit is a treacherous thing for a woman, too, especially when she employs it to influence through intrigue. They both have secrets, Jacques-Louis and Caroline, but she will carry them far longer than him.

He could blame the storm, the gods of ocean and sky, the captain, the ship builders, the British government, indeed the presumptuousness of nature and the mysterium of the soul, but he sees it now. Voltaire had been right. Optimism was unfaithful, as insubstantial as any philosophy or doctrine, for what was man but the great inventor of his own justifications, sometimes through the voice of a god, or whatever vessel best served his certainties and eliminated his doubts? Perhaps only those who had done the greatest harm—fools like him—contemplated notions of an abiding goodness, despite all evidence to the contrary.

The vineyard is receding. He wakes to the crash of waves upon the shore, his broken leg swollen now to twice its normal size, the fire of infection running through his veins. There is something he has forgotten, something he does not wish to recall.

And on the pedestal, these words appear:
'My name is Ozymandias, King of Kings;
Look on my Works, ye Mighty, and despair!'
Nothing beside remains. Round the decay
Of that colossal Wreck, boundless and bare
The lone and level sands stretch far away.

His life has come to this, the lone and level sand stretching away, his wreckage complete. He had a mission. But he has failed. Who has he failed? Oh, yes, he feels it anew. He has failed everyone.

A gull is pecking at the maggots burrowing into his leg. His mouth is sorely parched. One eye is closed shut. Has he lived another day? The sun is sinking into the sea. The day is cooler and the uncertain reprieve of night is descending. Where is the bottle he had gripped as if it were life itself? He feels about in the sand. Even this small movement exhausts him. Surely it cannot be lost.

The *Madeleine* had been just beyond the Tropic of Cancer. Europe had felt close. Shepherd, the captain, was discussing the approaching lunar event.

'This is no time for medieval superstition,' he had said. 'We are modern men. The crew will follow my lead. We will stand upon the deck and fashion our viewing implements and take in this great moment that will not come again, so we are told, for another hundred years or more.'

He had a bent for the morbid, Captain Shepherd. He had survived the battle of the Nile and the guns of Copenhagen, serving under Nelson as a cabin boy at seven years of age. He had witnessed Napoleon's defeat at Cape Trafalgar and been imprisoned twice. Back in England he had seventeen grandchildren, all girls. His home, he had told Jacques-Louis, stood upon the cliffs of Dover.

'I was born for the sea,' he said. 'I hope to spend my last day with a wind in the sails and a bright sea beneath.'

Shepherd's wish had been fulfilled. The tempest came after the eclipse. The light was the eerie green that portends a hurricane. Soon came the ferocity of the wind, the magnitude of ocean rising and breaking, the waves that required the ship to climb an impossible wall or be swept aside. It had numbed all senses but terror. The good captain had roped himself to the wheel, insisting Jacques-Louis and Quill get below, shouting to his crew to tie themselves to whatever they could. Quill had insisted on going first to check the wine.

When Jacques-Louis wakes, there is a pounding that feels as if his heart is trying to leave his body. He is shivering cold and raging hot. He had dreamed that he and Henriette were together on the banks of a quiet river, the mirrored surface mesmerising.

His fingers find a vestige of the day's warmth under the leaf matter that spills about. The pain of his injuries is unceasing. The fronds above him make a pretty sound when the wind moves them. The sea exhales. The sky is stabbed with stars. He cannot be sure how long it is since the *Madeleine* sank and he washed ashore. His father is seated beside him, dressed as the *duc* who walks the fields and tends the vines with his workers. He takes in his ill-kempt son, his shredded clothes and fevered skin, his leg a hideous purple. Jacques-Louis feels his father is sure to suggest there will be a late rescue. Some boat that rides in over the reef. Someone who happens along the shore.

But instead of rallying him with hope, his father says gently, 'Nature, Jacques-Louis, is the faithful administrator of a glorious enterprise. She cares nothing for nations that rise and fall or matters of international dispute. She welcomes to the afterlife both king and commoner, babe and mother, the girl and the soldier. All the fallen who decay upon the fields or die in their beds. The good, the bad, the uniforms of blue or red, the woollen hose and pantaloons, the silk, the lace, the canvas, hemp and linen—a hundred years on it is all the same under the ground.'

'Papa,' Jacques-Louis says, feeling the sand running through his fingertips, 'I am seeping into the ground. How long since I was a boy and you and Maman were filled with life?'

He is so thirsty. Where is the bottle? He feels about, but there is nothing to grasp, no promise of relief. He must not be deluded. There will be no rescue from this. There are many days for living that pass as if they are winged, and then just one that comes for the earthly labour of dying.

He closes his eyes. His mind begins to leave his body, seeking better places. Above him, planets wheel overhead. One star is a strange blue, another a fiery green.

His father bends and kisses him upon his brow. 'Jacques-Louis,' he says,

'So live, that when thy summons comes to join
The innumerable caravan, that moves
To that mysterious realm, where each shall take
His chamber in the silent halls of death,
Thou go not, like the quarry-slave at night,
Scourged to his dungeon, but sustained and soothed
By an unfaltering trust, approach thy grave,
Like one who wraps the drapery of his couch
About him, and lies down to pleasant dreams.'

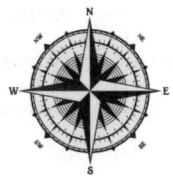

Jacques-Louis' breath is shallow, his body explored by ants, sepsis damaging his lungs, his liver, his kidneys. Mosquitoes bite and buzz.

'Hush,' he tells them. 'Have you no respect for a man's final hours?'

But what wisdom might he impart on the subject of mortality to an insect that dies in a day, while he has witnessed decades?

The gulls know it is only a matter of time, assuring him that death is close enough to kiss his cheek. They will all outlive him. They will feast on the maggots in his leg, the eyes in his head. They will pick clean the cage of his ribs, the bones of his hands. All of him will be washed away by the next full-moon tide.

The sea and the sand will house his last remains but what will house his soul? There it is again, damn the demand of it. The eternal does not fool me, he wants to shout. You gods promise a lot and deliver very little. The earth delivers. The earth has fed me. The earth has given me hope. The trance of life will abate. The rest is foolery. But still he has been known to be wrong, and admitted it.

Ah, Hannah. Will you be there for me? Will you wait for me on the path of dissolution? He wants to see her, he yearns to see her. He whispers, 'I humbly, devotedly, request an audience with my beloved wife.'

Her skin, the smell of her. The laughter on her lips, the music of her voice, the sound of her singing as she tended the garden. No man was luckier than he in loving her. In undressing her. In discovering the softness of her skin. Her breasts, oh, her breasts. Right nipple. Left nipple. Her stomach, her hips, oh, the softness of her thighs. The sweetness of her ankles and tiny feet. If on any day he had glimpsed them beneath the hem of her gown, his thoughts were drawn away to pleasures he wished to enact upon her.

Let me trace the symmetry of your jaw, he thinks, your small straight nose. Let me see once more the lashes that give such shape to your eyes. I want to smell your fragrance as you roll towards me in the bed. I want to smell the scent in the pit of your arm, in your tender terrain of shores and hills and wetland.

I will whisper your name for eternity if it will help me find you again. I was madness without you, and sometimes I was madness with you, and I will never repay the debt of kindness you extended to me. I wanted anything but to feel the emptiness of my soul after your death. I was a man on his knees, begging for reprieve, and when a hand was offered I took it, knowing, knowing it was its own form of madness.

Forgive me. Please forgive me.

He is watching the sun rise across the fields of the world. There is one valley, one vignette of human life, his mind settles on. A cock calls. The cows are lowing. Pigeons murmur in the eaves. Sparrows and finches discuss the day ahead.

Jacques-Louis, the boy, leaps from his bed and, once dressed, runs downstairs to the dining room. Finding it empty, he diverts to the kitchens, where Mathilde awaits with a small warm loaf she fills with butter and cherry jam. She hands it to him with a wedge of cheese and an apple for his pocket. Soon enough he is out the door, running to catch up to his father in his long boots, who swings Jacques-Louis into the saddle before him.

At the vineyard his father gives Jacques-Louis a small sheathed knife, a gift for this vintage.

'Very few people who grow grapes make fine wine,' his father says, 'let alone champagne. But for now, while you are yet young, to learn the art of the growing is all that matters.'

Jacques-Louis fixes the new knife to the belt around his waist. His seven-year-old size is perfect for crawling along the rows and cutting down the fruit the adults have missed.

A luncheon is assembled under the beech trees. Even Jacques-Louis is permitted a little champagne, although he is jostled affectionately by Philippe when he yawns as they return to the harvest.

The last sacks of grapes are loaded onto the wagons. Beneath a thousand-year-old sunset, Jacques-Louis falls asleep against Philippe on the way to the press.

Oh sleep, it is a gentle thing.
Beloved from pole to pole . . .
My lips were wet, my throat was cold,
My garments all were dank;
Sure I had drunken in my dreams,
And still my body drank.

He does not want Coleridge's damned poem, but still it bites. He touches his forehead, running his fingers along the old scar.

He reaches for the wound where the bone in his thigh protrudes. He lifts his head and sees the bloated flesh has turned black. His stomach heaves but there is nothing left in him, not sea water or bile.

Oh, for a cool breeze. His lips are serrated, his tongue large and furred in his mouth. There is nothing to drink. There might never be anything to drink again. He shivers. A breeze blows up, sprinkling his eyelids, showering him with particles of gold, pink and silver, dusting his suppurating wounds. There is a smell that he knows all too well. I am rotting, he thinks.

What is a man? he wonders. An accumulation of acts and memories? A sort of agreement between facts and inclinations? He takes a grape offered by an outstretched hand and presses it to his lips, pushing the fruit in, holding back the skin with his teeth, welcoming the sweet burst of berry followed by a tart note of apple. Aah.

Energy existed everywhere, all theophany, a mystical poetry by which the unknown revealed itself. Why had he never seen that before?

Death is dispersing itself, dissolving men and women, children born and unborn. Every being is encroached upon by tiny creatures as enterprising as any revolutionary or counter-revolutionary, Girondin or Jacobin, Whig or Tory, royalist or republican, pacifist or rebel, all drawn into an underworld of purpose more complex than any bureaucracy. Constellations of tiny creatures are upon him, beneath him and also inside him, scavenging the flesh on his bones, touring his veins, amassing in his lungs. He can hear them, a transcendence at the umbilicus of the spinning world.

In the night a storm reaches into the dreaming sky, a cavalcade of watery battalions drumming on rock and sand, lightning and thunder, the palm trees bracing in the wind and rain dripping, running, pooling. Every splash upon his broken flesh is a knifepoint and every drip upon his face a balm, and every drop that falls into his mouth is as a grain of rice to a starving village.

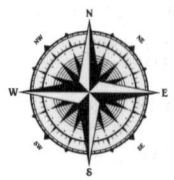

Caroline has brought a fan and the breeze of it is welcome on this ringing evening when cicadas and every other creature that can rub its legs or wings together or use its throat for amplification is making a mockery of peace.

'If you could have heard them, all those other *vignerons* gathered in Paris disparaging the judges' decision,' Jacques-Louis says to her.

'"You cannot call it champagne!" Moët declared. "We will not allow it. What is it? It is Van Diemen something! It cannot be champagne if it does not come from the earth of Champagne."

'"The new world may yet best the old," Madame Clicquot replied.

'I had failed to anticipate her. I bowed deeply, humbled to be in her presence.

'"Madame," I said, you will change the world.

'"I made the world turn in my direction," she said, with a droll lift of her eyes.

'"My daughter did that too," I told her, but she gave me such a look that I dared not elaborate.

'Still, the prize! The Grand Prize in Paris for our colonial vintage, Caroline! It would never have been so if they had not tasted it blind, for their minds cannot conceive of such a thing. Alas that the trophy makes a pretty bauble on the seabed. But still, we won! We won!

'Perhaps,' he says, 'this will go some small way towards expunging the terrible record of my life. I have one bottle from the ship. It was all I could hold onto in the moment when our demise was evident. I took it when I went in search of Quill, who had gone below, determined to do what he could to save our cargo. But the strength of the water was unimaginable, and I was swept out into that terrible churning sea. I held to the bottle as if it was life itself. Do you see it about?

'You, Caroline, and your sisters, your mother, Quill, Cornelius and the wine we made together at Everlea—these have been the greatest parts of my life.'

But Caroline has disappeared. The heat is ferocious without her cooling fan, the pain rattling his brain.

Quill kneels beside Jacques-Louis. He pops the cork, bringing the bottle to Jacques-Louis' lips.

The relief is so intense, Jacques-Louis coughs and gasps, 'I thought I had lost you.'

Quill holds his head and tenderly wipes his cheek and chin. When breath is restored, he brings the bottle to Jacques-Louis' lips once more.

The champagne swells in his mouth. The towering edifice of mountain. The silvered sea. The moss-filled forest. The cries of the black cockatoos as they head north. The scudding rain and howling wind. Currawongs calling in a breathless vermilion dawn and moonless skies where he has looked into nebulae and felt the pull of a grandeur beyond his human life.

Quill has disappeared into the cast gathered about him on the shore. They are conversing, the horde, dressed in finery. There is baby Isobel before the fever took her. She is holding her rabbit with the velvet ears. There is his father ready for the Royal Court in hose and wig. And Maman in a summer gown with a matching parasol. Thank goodness she has her head. And there is Hannah, her eyes sparkling, as beautiful as the day he married her.

'Will you take my hand?' he asks her.

But before Hannah reaches him, a woman in a dress of blood-red silk passes before him with a glittering bauble about her neck. Her hair is carefully coiled and decorated with a butterfly clasp above one ear. As she turns to the company, he sees the wound in her throat. She lifts her arm and points to him.

'J'accuse,' she says.

He watches as every person falls away, disintegrates, disappearing into the etheric one by one. He calls as they go, calls the names of all his dead, and weeps as he loses them all again. Only the one he murdered stands before him. Her expression conveys no malice, only a galling truthfulness.

He hears the rushing blade of the guillotine above him. And finds it a relief to be done with it all at last.

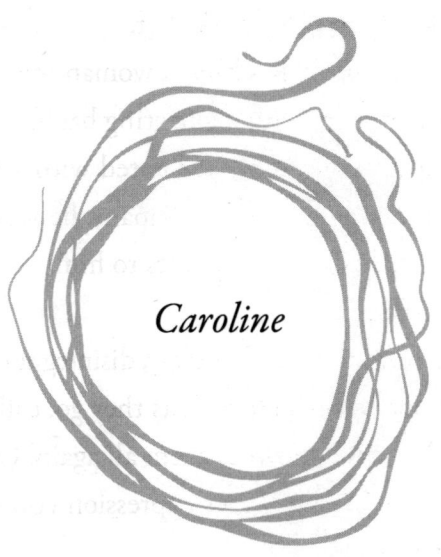

· *20* ·

Caroline

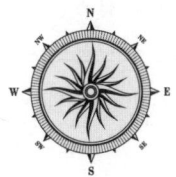

For years Caroline will wonder if her father had made it to some distant shore, lost his mind, and lived some other life. She wants to believe that he would not have abandoned her if he had his mind. If he could write. If he could find a way back.

She takes down the family Bible and regards the name of Jacques-Louis Auguste Henri Colbert. Years later, she adds a year but not a date for his death, because she will never know.

Of Quill she writes nothing in the Bible at all, imagining that he, too, will yet come home, a figure on the pathway, a knock at her door. But he does not, and the ache will remain with her all her life. Thoughts of him come unbidden as she is hanging out the washing, stirring a winter soup, cutting back vines that grow on the wall at the rear of their garden, always a reminder of the vineyard.

You wrote your life, my love, she thinks, when he walked into the fields of her memory. You wrote it upon my heart.

•

Before she departs Everlea, Caroline gives away vine stock to friends. She sends barrels of plants to several farms outside Melbourne and also in New South Wales and South Australia. Vines go to a family on the east coast of Tasmania where the weather is drier and more clement, and another barrel to the north of the island.

Tasmania. It becomes the new name for her island home. A name to silence the past. An attempt to bury the brutal history of Van Diemen's Land.

The major thoroughfare in the city of Melbourne is named after Captain Swanston. The Swanston sons go on to farm an expanding estate near Melbourne and acquire lands in New Zealand. Georgiana never returns from England.

For Caroline there is a new home to tend and medicines to make up for John's patients, ointments to create and powders to grind. It is good to find herself healing people again. There are accounts to manage, and the needs of four daughters who arrive over the ensuing ten years. They lose their baby, Henriette, to scarlet fever when she is five. It is only a few weeks after the death of Cornelius.

For a long time the voices of all the dead call to Caroline, day and night. John is infinitely loving. By the time she emerges from that hollow place of mist and shadows, she feels as if she is getting old. Almost forty.

In time Everlea would be demolished, the vineyard cleared for an orchard, the giant gum cut down. The oak tree would grow and remain for many years, until it too fell to the insistence of progress.

When her hair is white, giving her a fey look, Caroline is given a volume of poems by the American poet Emily Dickinson. She reads the words and is moved.

'Hope' is the thing with feathers –
That perches in the soul –
And sings the tune without the words –
And never stops – at all –

The desire for something more had run through her life. It had all been the fruit of hope. A slow vintage of family, a harvest of souls.

Her father had been the murderer Jacques-Louis Colbert, imprisoned on Norfolk Island, but this was never mentioned. Nor was the story of his disappearance on his way to Europe with a cargo of wine, in the hope of establishing Van Diemen's Land as the new France for champagne. When her children and grandchildren ask her about him, she will tell them that his parents, a duke and duchess, were beheaded in the French Revolution. He escaped to England where he became an apothecary.

She will not mention that he was also a brother, a vigneron, a murderer. If they asked her where he had died, she said falling from a roof in London not long after her mother died. She could find a grain of truth in that. She and John had agreed to this. It was for the best.

Señor Clementi was a ghost who did not visit. She remembered the night in the forge, the tremor in Cornelius as he was handed the knife. She knew he could not do it. Not Cornelius. Nor could it be her father. Yet to let the man live would always risk Cornelius's freedom, and her father's, too. So, she had taken the blade from Cornelius's hand.

She had considered the neck, the ease of severing the carotid artery, but no. Not that way. Laying the point against his chest, she felt the resistance of bone before she twisted the knife and pushed it between the ribs into the muscle of the heart. She observed the light going out of Clementi's eyes, but first the surprise and bewilderment that this was being done to him. And by her.

When she looked at her father, something inscrutable passed between them. I am your daughter, she thought. But it ends here. It ends now.

None of them spoke of it in the days that followed. Nor the years beyond, when there was only Cornelius and Caroline to carry it. The truth must have no feathers to wing it to another time. It must become dust and blow away.

Cornelius became a grandfather to their children, living with them until he died a quiet death while reading in his favourite chair by the fire. Bessie continued to live with them too and never married. She shared with Caroline the grief of losing Quill and Cornelius, and the miracle of every baby that arrived. She contracted measles and died when she was forty-nine.

Caroline's daughters observed patterns in the stars and mused on history, the structure of plants and rocks, and the philosophies and creeds that shaped the world. They kept diaries and sketchbooks, read poetry and wrote some of their own, learned French and painted watercolours. They might have devised mathematical theorems and solved medical riddles to shape the progression of humanity but, despite encouragement, they did not. By the time there was a university in the colonies where a woman might study, marriages had been made and children born. Greatness was neither expected nor sought of women.

Their days were given to the growing and making of food, the healing of wounds. To the love and conversations that hold a community together, and a family. Babies died or survived.

No one avoided the impetuosity of chance, nor the lamentation of loss.

What did endure was a fondness for marmalade on toast. A desire to enquire into the curious. To grow and to harvest. To relish the good. To wonder at the unknowable. To feel the pain of the world and yet not succumb. The square knees of Jacques-Louis appeared in subsequent generations, and his exuberant laugh, along with his and Caroline's love of botany, healing, books and history.

There was Tante Henriette's appreciation for silk, velvet and fine bed linen. Hannah's skill, and Augusta's, too, for painting, quilting, sewing, cooking and embroidering. Tablecloths and napkins, bedspreads and wall hangings were passed down, a watercolour or two, and an exquisite walnut chess set inlaid with a budding vine of gold.

Grandsons started small businesses or took to the land, where they planted fruit trees and tended crops and livestock, pursuits suited to the remote island on which they were born, and vestiges of a grandmother who had been skilled in business and strategy. One great grandson carved a verse of 'The Rime of the Ancient Mariner' into the lid of a chest because he loved the poem.

There was, it must be said, an irritation in the family line with seemingly unnecessary rules and regulations. An urge, in fact, to break them. And a great love of acting. Also a dislike of enclosed spaces. But no one went to gaol. By and large they were kind and generous people. Prudent with money and careful with secrets. After a generation or two, it becomes hard to know who is to blame or applaud for family traits.

The person who takes to drying herbs and planting crops, grinding spices and making cordials or tinctures, performing a sonnet or ruminating on the mysterious fabric of existence gives little thought to an ancestor also drawn to the same. Everything is sensitive to the unreliability of recollection, mould, fire, the whims of a moment. Over the years, journals were abandoned, paintings faded, recipes, letters, poems and photographs were eaten by silverfish and consumed by the great arbiter known as time.

Much of our lives we are feathers, Caroline thinks. Barely touching the earth in the short breath of life. The days, the months, the seasons and years, even the century in which she had lived, they had not been the linear things they pretended to be. She saw that while her life had been particular to her, it had also been a tending to something unfinished. She did not know how far back the threads went; to people who lived long before there was a printing press or the fanciful notion of the earth cycling the sun. And further still to a woman who lived in a stubbled land of date palms and a wilting sun who sent forth, through her womb, stories that would visit the lives of her descendants in whispers and dreams.

Every now and then, she had been a coin dropping down to the sediment. A tidal creature from the great swamp that flows back into molten rock and salt water. A body is a flawed and brilliant container for human life. Hers was almost done and would soon become what it was drawn from. Dust, air, earth. Returned to the great wholeness. A fleeting presence who had seen this sparkling world and then was gone.

'I have trampled out the vintage where the grapes of wrath were stored,' she thinks, varying the poem a little. A battle cry to make sense of a part of her life laid to rest. She knew the desire to be done with the past, and she also knew the desire for the past to contain all the wisdom needed for the future.

She had been a wife and mother, benign names for such ample responsibilities and duties. A daughter and grandmother, too. A great-grandmother. No one would have described her then, at the end of her life, as a diplomat, medico, merchant or vigneron. Nor as a liar, a thief or a murderer.

In this late hour, it is the light that calls her. The quiet fanfare of moonlight, the sunshine as the curtains are drawn back, the light of John looking into her eyes, a new morning cast upon the water. And now, and now, the welcoming light of death. This has been the canto of her life.

HISTORICAL NOTE

The most famous sparkling wine in the world has been made in the Champagne region of France arguably since the 1600s. During the European colonial era, vineyards were established in many parts of the world. One vineyard produced a sparkling wine reported to rival those of France. It was in Van Diemen's Land and was established by Bartholemew Broughton in the early 1820s.

Broughton died suddenly in 1828 and the estate was purchased by Charles Swanston, director of the Derwent Bank and member of the Legislative Council. The vineyard disappeared from history until the 1840s when it again began making exceptional sparkling wine. The winemaker employed by Captain Swanston was noted in newspaper reports as Mr Pain.

QUOTED MATERIAL

Epigraph

'*Thanks to the human heart by which we live*': William Wordsworth, 'Immortality from Recollections of Early Childhood'

1.

'*. . . it was the epoch of belief, it was the epoch of incredulity*': Charles Dickens, *A Tale of Two Cities*

'*With sloping masts and dipping prow*': S.T. Coleridge, 'The Rime of the Ancient Mariner'

'*Continuous as the stars that shine*': William Wordsworth, 'I Wandered Lonely as a Cloud'

'*And now the storm-blast came*': S.T. Coleridge, 'The Rime of the Ancient Mariner'

'*. . . celestial Light, Shine inward*': John Milton, *Paradise Lost: Book 3*

2.

'*But for my fate on the turning wheel of heaven*': From a play attributed to Sophocles – Plutarch – The Age of Alexander – Penguin Classics edition 2011 p. 445

4.

'Dim as the borrowed beams of moon and stars': John Dryden, *Religio Laici, Or a Layman's Faith*

5.

'The chanting linnet, or the mellow thrush': Robert Burns, 'The Brigs of Ayr'

7.

'Happiness is but a name': Robert Burns, 'Written In Friars' Carse Hermitage'
'What wondrous life is this I lead!': Andrew Marvell, 'The Garden'
'My countenance declares': Alexander Montgomerie, *The Solsequium*
'There passed a weary time': S.T. Coleridge, 'The Rime of the Ancient Mariner'

10.

'And a good south wind sprung up behind': S.T. Coleridge, 'The Rime of the Ancient Mariner'

17.

'And on the pedestal, these words appear': Percy Bysshe Shelley, 'Ozymandias'
'So live, that when thy summons comes to join': William Cullen Bryant, 'Thanatopsis'
'Oh sleep, it is a gentle thing': S.T. Coleridge, 'The Rime of the Ancient Mariner'

18.

'"Hope" is the thing with feathers': Emily Dickinson, '"Hope" is the thing with feathers'

WITH GRATITUDE, APPRECIATION
AND LOVE

A Great Act of Love draws from stories shared by Andrew Pirie, winemaker extraordinaire at Apogee, and my sister Melinda, family history super-sleuth, which converged in a strange moment of serendipity to create this novel.

To my Mum, Dawn, for the inspiring family stories. And to our French and Scottish ancestors.

To the Australia Council/Creative Partnerships Australia for financial assistance to write this book.

To Andrew Pirie, Melinda Rose, Kim Seagram, Rod Ascui, Alex Reeve, Rachael Treasure, Gregory Lorenzutti, Nathan Scolaro and John Godfrey, for interviews and correspondence into the art of grape growing and winemaking in eighteenth- and nineteenth-century France, Van Diemen's Land, early California and modern Tasmania, for family history and Old Bailey records, for nineteenth-century sea voyages, Rio de Janeiro gardens and brigantine rigging. All errors are my own.

To Adam Smith, Benjamin Franklin, Charles Darwin, Robert Hughes, Geoffrey Blainey, Lloyd Robson, Walter Isaacson, Michel de Montaigne, Jean-Jacques Rousseau, John Milton, Louisa Anne Meredith, Tony Walker, Cassandra Pybus, Alison Alexander, Charlotte Brontë, Emily Brontë, Maggie O'Farrell, Manning Clark, Hilary Mantel, Charles Dickens, Victor Hugo, Alexander Dumas, Thomas Culpeper, Samuel Taylor Coleridge and some one hundred and sixty additional writers, whose research, poetry, essays, reports, books and letters have been essential to the writing of this novel.

To my publishing team at Allen & Unwin, led by the wise and perceptive Alex Craig, with Robert Gorman, Christine Farmer, Ali Lavau, Christa Munns, Sarah Barrett, Matt Hoy, Sam Ryan, Peri Wilson, Sandy Cull, Pamela Dunne, Sandra Buol, and everyone else on the A&U team who helped to produce this book. Thank you for your professionalism and passion for literature, and your commitment to Australian writers and Australian writing.

To those in the USA, Judy Clain and the entire Summit USA team, and agent Michelle Tessler; and in the UK, publisher Jocasta Hamilton and all at John Murray, and agent Victoria Hobbs. It's a delight and a privilege to work with you all. And to publisher Jane Palfreyman, now at Summit Australia, for early faith in this book.

To my agent of almost thirty years, Gaby Naher, at the Naher Agency. Friend, wise woman, business manager and instigator of so many good things. Thank you for caring for my career.

To Kevin Rose, Dawn Ransley, Belle Rose, Byron Wylder, Alex Reeve, Tania Price, Brett Torossi, Kim Seagram, Katerina Maria Christensen, Davini Malcolm, Delia Nicholls, Genevieve de Couvreur, Caroline Lawrence, Danielle Wood, Katherine Scholes, Caro Flood, Mary Dwyer, Amy Currant, Adrienne Eberhard, Michaye Boulter, Jane Curtis, Jane Bamford, Jane Longhurst, Liz

Caswell, Peter Adams, Helen Rule, Helen Silver, Harrison Young, Indigo Lustig, Carol Penn, my IWF sisters, Jane Zochling, Andrew Black, Stefanie O'Rourke, Virginia Whitwell, Melinda Rose, my students, and so many more dear ones who are my community of fellow writers, artists, inspirers, supporters and creators.

Always to Alex, Brandea, Byron, Belle and Monkey for infinite love, kindness, laughter, patience, wisdom, understanding and guidance.

To all the readers far and wide and especially my fellow islanders across Tasmania.

And to my angel Evan. Thank you for all the love, joy, laughter, curiosity, encouragement, generosity and beauty that helped me bring this book into being. Every day I share with you is an honour.

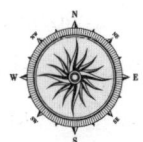

I also want to acknowledge the booksellers and libraries of the twenty-first century. Information has become currency, yet the reading of books is an act of courage, an act of defiance, an act of self-education and a gift of sanctuary. Thank you to all the booksellers sharing their love of books with readers every day, and providing delightful havens in which to read, meet, connect and explore. And thank you to libraries everywhere that provide such essential services to our communities, and without whom I would not be a writer. May we powerfully protect our public libraries, book stores and writers from those who seek to limit our curiosity, hide our history, deny our experiences, destroy our words and dismiss our shared humanity by the banning and burning of literature, and the persecution of artists. Long live hardbacks, paperbacks, audiobooks, e-books and second-hand books. They are repositories of imagin-ation, courage, insight and endeavour. Each of them a rare human achievement. May we continue to gain inspiration from the books we read, share and pass on. Supporting, protecting and promoting the arts is integral to the wellbeing of our minds, our communities, our humanity and our planet.

This book is a work of fiction, drawn from many accounts of history. Jane Palfreyman, an early champion of this work, reminded me that the gaps in history invite the writer of fiction 'to make it up!', and although both a challenge and a precious freedom, I hope you enjoy it as such. There will, no doubt, be many readers far more versed in aspects of the history within this book than I. While much is historically accurate, it is not intended to adhere to precise dates or timelines, but rather to draw from both world and family history, as well as the lives of the colonists, willing and unwilling, of the remote archipelago of islands once named Van Diemen's Land.

The Tasmanian Aboriginal people are the traditional owners and custodians of the lands and waterways of lutruwita/Tasmania. I wish to pay my deepest respect, and acknowledge their sovereignties in land, sea and sky, never ceded. I acknowledge the beauty of this land upon which I live and work, which has shaped my life and those of my ancestors and descendants. Belonging lives at the heart of responsibility and connection.

May every act of courage be a great act of love.

RAISING READERS
Books Build Bright Futures

Dear Reader,

We'd love your attention for one more page to tell you about the crisis in children's reading, and what we can all do.

Studies have shown that reading for fun is the **single biggest predictor of a child's future life chances** – more than family circumstance, parents' educational background or income. It improves academic results, mental health, wealth, communication skills, ambition and happiness.[1]

The number of children reading for fun is in rapid decline. Young people have a lot of competition for their time. In 2024, 1 in 10 children and young people in the UK aged 5 to 18 did not own a single book at home.[2]

Hachette works extensively with schools, libraries and literacy charities, but here are some ways we can all raise more readers:

- Reading to children for just 10 minutes a day makes a difference
- Don't give up if children aren't regular readers – there will be books for them!
- Visit bookshops and libraries to get recommendations
- Encourage them to listen to audiobooks
- Support school libraries
- Give books as gifts

There's a lot more information about how to encourage children to read on our website: **www.RaisingReaders.co.uk**

Thank you for reading.

---

[1] OECD, '21st-Century Readers: Developing Literacy Skills in a Digital World', 2021, https://www.oecd.org/en/publications/21st-century-readers_a83d84cb-en.html

[2] National Literacy Trust, 'Book Ownership in 2024', November 2024, https://literacytrust.org.uk/research-services/research-reports/book-ownership-in-2024